Scott Sadsberry

A DIFFERENCE IN
THE BLOOD

TSV

A novel by

SCOTT SANDSBERRY

ISBN: 1537595180
ISBN 13: 9781537595184

PROLOGUE

Tucker was eight years old and Micah five when Big Frank gave them the falcon stone.

It was shiny and black, like the glistening centers of Tucker's wide eyes as he stared at the mysterious prize in his father's right hand. Flat-faced and circular, half-again as big as a silver dollar, the falcon stone might well have been launched as a perfect skipper across any of the waters of their world. But even had it not been unveiled to them as a treasure of uncommon value, if only to Big Frank, neither boy would ever have considered letting it fly.

For on that hard, flat surface, not quite large enough to span the lifelines crisscrossing the fleshy palm beneath it, was a mark no less indelible.

"It's the footprint of a falcon," Big Frank said. "A prehistoric falcon. See it there?"

Micah nodded, his eagerness to please harnessed by the uncertainty that came with being the lesser son, the younger brother. The younger *half*-brother, as Tucker in that first year of their shared existence was so vigilant to point out. Tucker regarded the stone with his usual intensity, poorly veiled as apathy.

The imprint was inescapable: three lines extending upward and outward from a central point, one line extending down. Tucker and Micah knew nothing of falcons, modern or prehistoric, or what sort of track a bird like that would make. None of that mattered. Each boy instantly accepted its authenticity, for reasons as disparate as the boys themselves.

"I found this when I was about your age," Big Frank said, looking at Tucker. "Dug it out of the dirt halfway up Sauk Mountain. Kept it with me ever since. I guess you might call it my good luck piece. Got me through Nam, anyway. Now I want you to have it." He paused and added with an unmistakable emphasis, "*Both* of you."

He accompanied that postscript with a brief glance of inclusion to Micah, who knew the implicit command was not intended for him. Big Frank then offered the stone to Tucker, who made his father wait several seconds before reaching out to take it. The defiance in that delay was not lost on Micah.

Big Frank dismissed them so he could move on to his nightly routine of beer and whatever was on television. Micah masked his disappointment that there would be no further personal illumination from the father he still barely knew, and who seemed dead set on maintaining that distance. Tucker simply turned away, pocketing the stone with measured nonchalance as he walked away.

Micah took his cue and fell into step behind him.

In the eight months since their separate worlds had been replaced by the painful awkwardness of this mutual reality, certain things had become ritual. Big Frank lays down the law. Micah accepts it like a puppy, wagging and eager to please. Tucker abides in silence, choosing indifference or tacit insurgence over the whipping that would surely follow outright rebellion, then goes for a walk. Always to the same place. And Micah follows.

They marched across the faded, stain-blotched kitchen linoleum, passing Micah's mom, wrist-deep in the dinner dishwashing. Tucker swung the screen door wide open in his mute sedition and Micah, always the conciliatory shadow, rescued its return to prevent a slam.

Their route took them across the lawn, which the Cascades' perpetual spring rainfall had relegated to a patchy mosaic of trampled mud and mower-choking jungle, and under the drooping branches of the western yew that owned one corner of the yard. Tucker blithely barefooted over its spiny blanket of twigs and tiny pollen cones, navigated the thicket of red-osier dogwood along the creek and weaved downstream, pushing through webs of willow branches that swatted Micah when he followed too closely—which, in his timid prudence, he always did.

At the hopscotch course of current-worn rocks that would take them across the creek, Tucker traversed them with his usual daredevil grace, impervious to the deepening menace beneath his feet. Micah was never immune to such peril, real or imagined.

"Slow down," Micah implored. "C'mon. You're going too fast."

"You're just too slow," Tucker said without turning back.

Down dip and around bend Tucker marched. Micah scurried after, feeling the spray of the creek as it was nourished by lesser rivulets of spring snowmelt and fed into Kacheel River, where it grew into a feral, frothing beast. Finally, the trees gave way to sunlight and the boys arrived at a ten-foot-long, waterside expanse of flat rock Tucker considered his own. Micah was allowed to share it only by decree of Big Frank's right hand—but only theoretical decree, as the old man had no idea this was the destination to which the boys so often disappeared. Had he given it much thought, though, Big Frank might have remembered taking his oldest son there once and seeing the sparkle in the boy's eyes. That had been more than two years ago. Before everything changed.

But he wasn't giving it any thought and Connie, Micah's mother, thankfully never asked where the boys went "out to play." The rock upon which Tucker had staked emotional claim and begrudged to Micah visitation rights was barely upstream from the top of Kacheel Falls. In the Salishan tongue of the native tribes that once populated the area, Kacheel had meant dawn—in the most positive way, as a new beginning. For more recent inhabitants, the falls bearing that life-affirming name had occasionally meant the opposite: The 150-foot vertical wall of crashing water had over two decades delivered the guests of honor to a half-dozen funerals.

Tucker plopped onto the rock, draping the callused blackness of his soles into an eddy with a vagabond ease that belied his honest response to the bone-chilling water. Micah sat beside him, dangled his sneakered feet above the water and waited for the older boy to produce their new prize.

Tucker lingered in his deliberate distance, watching the swirling current paint its ephemeral portraits. He kept his feet in the water longer than Micah thought humanly possible before pulling them out, then turned around and leaned on his knees to contemplate the panorama. To one side was the water, legacy of the high-country snow, so close, so powerful, so cold. On the other were the ridges and valleys settling into a textured horizon, each silhouetted tier a different hue. Beyond the falls, a crestline of silver fir basked in the first pre-dusk brushstrokes of April alpenglow.

Micah waited patiently as Tucker lost himself in the layers of his world. Time whispered its passages of water and wind.

Finally, the younger boy could stand it no longer. "Can I see it?"

"What."

"You know. The falcon thing."

"What falcon thing." Spoken not as a question, but—like so many of Tucker's responses to his half-brother—as the reaffirmation of a pecking order.

"You know. The falcon stone."

"What about it."

"Can I see it?"

"You already saw it."

"I wanna see it again."

"So what."

"C'mon. Dad *said.*"

Micah pouted, knowing he couldn't go back and complain to his father. It was a long, scary walk he didn't like to make alone, and besides, Big Frank didn't enjoy playing referee. *Don't be such a wuss,* he'd say. *I don't want to have to fight your battles for you.* He might get angry enough at the interruption—or, more likely, Connie would once again become upset over Frank's bully boy being mean to their sensitive son—to dictate punishment.

Micah didn't want that either. Big Frank would hit Tucker, probably hard enough to bruise. Tucker wouldn't cry. And Micah would.

"Dad *said.*" Micah's voice took on a whining edge.

"Said what."

"He gave it to both of us." He paused, then added apprehensively, "Not just you."

Tucker lashed him with a withering glare. "So?"

"So I wanna see it."

"You'll just lose it. Probably drop it in the water like a dumbass."

"Huh uh."

"Uh huh."

"Will not."

"Will too."

"Will not."

"Will too. Shut up or I'll take it to the Under Look."

Tucker might as well have punched Micah in the stomach. The mere mention of the Under Look made the younger boy's calves tingle in a rush of real and emotional vertigo.

The Under Look was about thirty feet below the lip of Kacheel Falls on the opposite side, traversing a mossy cliff wall that curled to face the waterfall's relentless power. The landing itself was nearly level, perhaps twenty feet long and at no point wider than five feet, the only horizontal relief before the steep face plummeted to the base of the falls. From that vantage point, a person could see and feel Kacheel's inexorable fury. Reaching that outcropping, though, meant negotiating a steep, precarious descent over moisture-slick ground, touching each spruce and fir trunk for precious reassurance along the way and sometimes even grabbing hold, trying not to think about what might result from even the slightest slip.

And even after willing oneself down that heart-pounding, sphincter-clenching path to the brink of the Under Look, there was still the gap to be crossed.

There was no other way onto the Look. The Under Look was furnished with a couple of cracks and boulder crannies—one just deep enough to nestle into—but no alternate route. A guy either had to turn back, tail firmly between legs, or cross the gap. It was barely four feet wide, an easy enough jump, but beneath that span was nothing but air, the rocks on each side were invariably slick from the perpetual mist of the falls, and a slip would be the last mistake anyone would make. Below Kacheel Falls, a body might not be found for days or weeks, perhaps even seasons, as it filtered its way through a chaos of logjams into watery oblivion.

"Nuh uh," Micah protested tentatively.

"Uh huh, I'll do it. I'll take it there and leave it," Tucker said, then added with a hint of dismissive sneer, "where you'll never see it."

"But … what if somebody else finds it?"

That wasn't likely. The way down to the Under Look didn't receive enough foot traffic even to qualify as a trail. For many White Bluff teenagers, a visit to the Under Look was a rite of passage for only the fearless or the foolhardy. Simply having the balls to make it down that winding, double-dare-ya route and across that treacherous gap a single time could elevate a guy to legend status, because its achievement could be witnessed. Anybody on the Under Look could easily be seen from alongside the falls—the vantage point to which most visitors confined themselves.

Nobody went down to the Under Look just to go. A guy went down on a dare or a bet, timing it when people could see or even photograph his audacious arrival, so the word would spread. There might be hell to pay, for sure—from parents, teachers and other grownups who would rant about how "You're old enough to know better." But once a guy had been to the Under Look, he *was* there: He had officially arrived, with a reputation that preceded his arrival in any room and followed his every departure. *That guy's been to the Under Look.* He could no longer be taken lightly. He was not somebody to mess with.

One trip to the Under Look was enough. Almost nobody went twice.

And nobody was supposed to go at all, at least not since the previous summer when a White Bluff teenager named Rodney Hunsucker had slipped over the edge on his way down. His death was not a six-inch news brief buried on an inside page of the Mount Vernon and Everett newspapers. Rodney's father was a county commissioner, elevating the boy's death into both communal calamity and final straw: Public works crews quickly fenced off the route to the Look. But because the fence was too tall and flimsy to climb over, all its construction succeeded in doing was elevating the danger level of the dare. Now anyone beginning that dicey descent first had to grip the edge of the fence and swing around to the other side, an asshole momentarily suspended above a 120-foot dropoff.

The Under Look was a place Micah had never gone, nor could he imagine even trying.

Tucker had been there more than once—or so he had told Micah. Alone. No witnesses. And he hadn't done it for glory or even attention; as far as

Micah knew, Tucker had never told another soul. He had done it in much the same way and seemingly for the same reason he would always have—as some sort of kiss-my-ass to the world that had dealt him unwanted cards: *I wanted to do it, so I did. What're you gonna do about it?*

Micah frowned, trying to pinch off the tears of frustration that always embarrassed him, especially in light of his brother's fierce stoicism.

"C'mon," he implored. "Lemme see the falcon stone."

"I got it now. You gonna try to take it from me?" Tucker didn't say this in a threatening way. They both knew the answer.

"C'mon. You're supposed to share it with me. Dad said."

"So we're sharing it. Now's my turn."

"When's my turn?"

"When you're oldest."

"No fair. When do I get to be oldest?"

Tucker laughed out loud. "When I'm *dead*, you retard!"

ACKNOWLEDGMENTS

This book is dedicated to my wife, Rhonda, who has put up with the bizarre schedule and lifestyle of her husband the crazy writer for 15 years.

COVER DESIGN is by Nicholas Shipley of Design Central Northwest in Yakima, Washington.

AUTHOR PORTRAIT PHOTOGRAPH is by T. J. Mullinax of Selah, Washington.

BOOK EDITORS were Roberto van Eyken of Davis, California, and Lynette Padwa of Los Angeles.

CHAPTER 1

HOMECOMING

It had rained all the way from Everett, or at least what often passes for midsummer rain on the western slopes of the Cascade foothills: an intangible mist that lacks the conviction even of drizzle, sifting through a neutral canopy too indistinct to qualify as clouds.

Such murk felt appropriate to Tucker Dodd, staring out blankly from the back seat. It felt like something long dead.

For more than a minute, the cabbie's radio had been cutting in and out on a catchy pop song by the latest next big thing. Tucker had loved the song the first time he'd heard it—couldn't get enough of it—but in the three months since, it had seemingly taken up residence on all stations at all hours. Now its every note aggravated him more than the intermittent static.

"Hey," he said, "you mind turning that shit off?"

The tone in Tucker's request wasn't aggressive and didn't need to be. Although barely twenty-five years old, Tucker had never carried himself with the callow uncertainty of youth, and men with his aura of animal muscularity and physical confidence rarely have their requests ignored by men of lesser self-assurance. In a bit of false bravado, the driver did a parody of the song's chorus, crooning "This drives him crazy" in time with the music. He glanced into the rear-view mirror at his sullen passenger and, upon receiving no reaction, switched off the radio.

"Comin' or goin'?"

The cab driver's voice stole like an intruder into Tucker's reverie.

"What?" Though he had heard the first time.

"You. Headin' to White Bluff. Goin' to or comin' from?"

Tucker returned his gaze to the window, not caring enough to weigh an answer. There was always a river in the gauzy distance—first the Stillaguamish, then the Sauk and eventually the Suiattle—and each meant more to him than these questions. "Little of both, maybe."

"So what brings you? Business or personal?"

Tucker suppressed an angry retort that would end the inquisition. "Personal business."

The cabbie, a puffy man with a crescent of graying hair that wrapped from ear to ear like half a bagel, nodded as if he understood something. "Not your first time around here, right?"

Tucker fixed his eyes on the cabbie in the rear-view mirror and offered a hard glare: *Why are you asking me these questions?*

"You know," the cabbie went on, oblivious. "You take the airport shuttle into Everett and now you're cabbin' it all this way to White Bluff, scopin' out the scenery and all, takin' a real interest. But not like a tourist. More like maybe you been here before, but it's been a real long time. So: Which is it? You a tourist?"

Tucker considered the ludicrous concept, that any tourist would choose this sodden path. "You a talk show host?" he uttered in a barely veiled warning, and turned again to the window.

"Hey, it's your dime, pal." The cabbie made a production of readjusting the mirror so their eyes would no longer meet.

Tucker stared into the gloom. So much felt different, right down to the overwhelming dampness. He knew these forested foothills the locals referred to as east county had been just as wet when he was a child; but that wasn't his mental photograph of those days. The memories that stood out were the afternoons traipsing through the woods with his mother, Louise, who showed him how to avoid poison oak but not fear the bog birch and salmonberry, how to distinguish the shrill whistle of the marmot from the sharp call of the three-toed woodpecker, who watched in beatific calm, not zealous maternal fear, as he climbed nimbly to the tops of every tree that beckoned. It must have been wet then, too. He just didn't remember that part of it. A boy's vision is always tinted by the glow of discovery.

Even the hillsides had changed. Clearcuts marred ridges where once stood untainted stands of hemlock and alder, leaving exposed stumps like whiskers on a shanty-man's face. He didn't remember those clearcuts, but there had never been any shortage of work for the local loggers in the old days. Perhaps they had simply run out of trees on the lookaway side of those ridgetops and been obliged to plunder closer to home.

Each passing mile buoyed another sunken memory.

There was the bridge across the Suiattle, looking as if he had never left, as if he could step to the edge and throw over a rock or a fishing line and be twelve years old all over again. Tucker took a deep breath when the cabbie turned right after the bridge, onto the road for which there was really only one destination.

He found himself waiting for, then spotting with something like relief, the dirt road leading to the old quarry swimming hole. Legend had it there was an old crane at the bottom—that the quarry workers had come to work one morning to find the pit full of water from an underwater spring that had tunneled its way to freedom. Skelly Radich claimed he swam deep enough once to touch one of the crane's metallic appendages, though Tucker—a much stronger swimmer—had tried countless times and made no such find.

Tucker wondered if the quarry was even still there, or if it had somehow disappeared ... as he had.

Tucker experienced another nostalgic pang as the taxi passed Message Rock, the massive hunk of granite that served as White Bluff's unofficial welcoming signpost. It had been a cultural icon in the remote community for generations, painted over thousands of times with messages to and from almost everybody in town at one time or another. Congratulations to returning sports teams. Proclamations of love, or of class supremacy. Declarations of who was an asshole and why. The occasional threat. Today's most prominent message was two-fold. First, in large, well-defined green letters over a white background:

WBHS CLASS OF '89

Below, scrawled in black by a dissenting artist, no doubt within the past day or two:

SUCKS!
NC rules!

Finally, the cab reached White Bluff and the state road became the town's main street. A sign reminded anyone passing through to decelerate from 50 to 30, but then, there wasn't much reason to pass through. Although the road wound all the way to Marblemount, no one with that destination in mind would go this way: too round-about, the road too serpentine to make good time. Through traffickers were invariably loggers, fishermen, hunters, backpackers, climbers or hermits—people in search of the Cascades' literal or aesthetic bounty. Or a place to hide.

Tucker looked at the many buildings that hadn't changed and the few that had in the six years since he'd left. The library still looked deserted, while the hardware store was still bustling. The gas station's lone concession to time seemed to be a change from Mobil blue to Texaco red. Albert Drug Store, its plate-glass window still adorned with posters and community notices, had not been replaced by some chain store, though he was certain old man Albert would happily sell out to the first one that gave him two nickels to rub together.

Barclay's Drive Inn looked unchanged, and Tucker suspected the town's high schoolers still congregated there for greasy burgers and adolescent melodrama. There had been a time when the Barclay's parking lot had been his own personal fiefdom, one he had readily defended with his fists against anyone foolhardy enough to throw down the gauntlet. But the burger joint now seemed merely small and sad, and it brought upon Tucker no avalanche of memories. It simply tightened the knot in his stomach. He knew he was getting close.

Tucker leaned forward and pointed at a small road, its street sign lost in the unruly wands of an aging birch.

"Turn right up here," he said.

The driver nodded, made the turn and followed the smaller, winding road through what passed in White Bluff for a neighborhood: wooden houses segregated by family crop gardens or conifer clusters, neighbors near enough to shout to yet far enough not to be bothered by. Towns nearer to the I-5 corridor invariably became gentrified, like wild animals transformed by simple proximity into domestic herds. Not here. White Bluff was too far removed. Its every way was its own, right down to the collective chip on its community shoulder.

"Just up ahead," Tucker said even before the house was visible through the trees. He was about to say *the brown house on the right*, but caught himself: After all this time, who knew what color it would be. "Up here on the right."

And there it was. Still brown. Different somehow. Smaller, though at two bedrooms it had never seemed large. There was a car in front—a gray, older-model Toyota Corolla. Nondescript, inexpensive and efficient, an acquisition of rational process, not of heart. Yep. Had to be Micah's car.

The cabbie put the taxi into park and left the motor running. Tucker regarded the chain-link wire fence lining the yard; had there always been a fence? The house, an old rambler, seemed not as tall as he'd remembered, but longer somehow.

The cabbie stretched his arm across the seat as he craned his neck to eyeball his passenger. "So this is where you lived, huh?"

Tucker nodded, not taking his eyes from the house.

"Yeah, I figured," the driver said. "I could tell by the way you were looking at it."

Oh, Tucker thought, *it's the garage.* Once nothing more than a covered carport at the end of the house, the structure beyond the Corolla was now a full-fledged, closed garage. He had forgotten the old man having enclosed the carport after Tucker had stormed out of the house the night of the blow-up. He had always presumed Big Frank did it in his twisted logic to protect something from him—as if he would return some night to damage Connie's car, perhaps, or maybe steal some of Frank's tools. Skelly Radich's suggestion of the former theory had made Tucker laugh out loud, and the latter made even less sense; Big Frank's tools were always crammed like boat people into the back of his truck, which lived outside. White Bluff was too remote to draw thieves, and locals knew not to cross Big Frank.

The garage door was painted a drab brown that didn't quite match the house. *That's just like the old man.*

"Grow up here?" the driver asked.

A wave of depression had settled over Tucker. *Grow up here?* Not hardly. More like *thrown into here.* Back when he'd had a mom, or at least the fresh memory of one. Back when he didn't have a brother. Not really.

"Since I was eight," he said from his distance. "'Til I was seventeen or eighteen. Somewhere in there."

"Bet it looks small, huh?" the driver said as he stepped out to stretch his legs. "That's what everybody always thinks. Home's never the way you remember it."

"Yeah, well," he said softly, "I don't remember it being home."

Tucker, his mouth suddenly very dry, tried to swallow. For a moment, he couldn't understand why he'd even come back. The place felt as foreign as it did the first time he had seen it, which, as now, had been through a car window.

⁂

It had been his sixth birthday, he remembered that.

He was still a month away from starting first grade, just a boy who didn't understand why his mother seemed so upset, driving around in this strange town he'd never seen, intent on finding something or someone. His entreaties that he was hungry, tired, bored and wanted to get home before his friends began arriving for the birthday party had for two hours fallen on deaf ears. She barely seemed aware of his presence.

For the previous few weeks, his mother had been on edge, growing increasingly unreachable to Tucker and irritable toward Big Frank. The old man had done something to piss her off, but whatever it was hadn't crossed over into the usual shouting and throwing things. That in itself was odd, as far as Tucker was concerned. Louise wasn't a woman to hide her emotions; they flailed like tentacles all around her, embracing or embroiling anyone within range. God help you if you incurred her wrath while dining at a restaurant—there would be no waiting until you got home. You heard about it right away, in no uncertain terms, regardless of who might be within earshot or how mortifying such a public flogging might feel. But she was just as effusive with love and praise, both for the people in her life and the things that made it worth living. You always knew where you stood with her. And she, not Big Frank, was the epicenter of Tucker's emotional world.

All of which had made the past few weeks hard for Tucker to comprehend.

He hadn't heard his mother screaming at Big Frank, though most of the time she looked like she wanted to scream, period. Whenever they got into it, Tucker would be shooed from the room and a door would be slammed behind him. When he'd see them later, they'd still look just as pissed off as before, but each in a different way. Big Frank was just mad and closed off; Louise's anger seemed more like pain and confusion.

Tucker had seen the truck even before she did. His father's blue Chevy pickup was easy to spot, with the **Driveway Dodd** logo in fading paint on the side and the tools of his concrete business—long two-by-fours, shovels, concrete rakes, wood stakes—jutting out at angles from the truck bed. The Chevy was parked in front of a house—the same house in front of which Tucker would find himself, mired in memory, in the back seat of a taxi nearly two decades later.

"Look, there's Dad's truck," Tucker had announced. He'd been glad to see it, too, until his mother stomped the brake pedal so hard he nearly slammed into the dashboard. Until he heard his mother suck in her breath and then catch, as if there wasn't enough air in the car. Until he heard that awful sound, almost a moan, that came next.

"Mom? What's wrong?"

She didn't answer. She just stared at the truck with this funny expression, then at the little sedan in the carport, as if she didn't believe what she was seeing … but had known it all along.

She pulled in behind the truck and ordered Tucker to stay in the car.

"How come?" he demanded.

"Just *sit.*"

He recognized the tone and obeyed. Louise got out of the car, marched into the yard and hammered several times on the front door.

The next several minutes would change Tucker's life.

And not for the better.

⋏

"So ... is this the end of the line?"

The cabbie's voice and hisinterrogation still felt like a violation, but this time Tucker welcomed the respite from the blackest memory of his life. Although he later experienced far more painful days, it was upon this one the seeds of those days were sown. This was his personal hell, the moment he could revisit whenever the shame became too much, whenever he felt the need to beat the heavy bag in his garage, gloveless, until his knuckles were a puffy, oozing mess and the bag was painted with the blood of his penance. This was the start of everything turning to shit.

"The end of the line," Tucker said in a hollow echo. "You might call it that."

The cabbie reached inside and pulled the trunk lever. Tucker, immersed in his emotional quicksand, felt the car shudder as the cabbie lifted his duffel bag from the back. *End of the line,* he thought. *Ain't that the fuckin' truth.*

He heard a dog barking and spotted the dark shape pushing between curtains, its nose to the front bedroom window. Micah had apparently gotten himself a dog, which Tucker thought seemed pretty appropriate for the kid: Get yourself a man's best friend and you don't actually have to have any friends. You can just hide from everybody your whole life, and the dog won't mind a bit. *Or maybe it belongs to the old lady. Maybe that's why this piece-of-crap fence.* But even if that was Connie's dog, it wouldn't be for long. Of that he was certain.

"You want me to wait while you see if anybody's home?" The cabbie was back at the driver's door, leaning in.

Tucker shook his head, stepped out of the car and paid in cash. As he peeled off an extra twenty for the tip, he heard the house door open. In no hurry to step into the morass of his past, Tucker slowly handed the bill to the cabbie with a nod, then watched with something like regret as the cab did its U-turn and left.

Finally, he turned.

Micah stood at the threshold, wearing jeans and a sweatshirt, holding open the screen door. He'd grown a moustache—and looked pretty good in it, Tucker thought—but that wasn't all that made him appear older. It was the simple renovation of time; Tucker hadn't seen him in six years. Had the old lady not gotten so sick, it might have been another six years before Tucker saw either one of them. If even then.

Tucker sighed, glanced back at the cab no longer there, and closed the physical distance to his half-brother.

"Well, what do you know?" Micah said, reaching out a hand.

Tucker shook it, feeling odd about it. As the muffled yapping continued, he assessed his brother's face and frame. Standing so close, it surprised Tucker to be looking up just a bit; somewhere along the way, his little brother had actually become taller than he was, though still as thin and knobby as a foal.

"I wasn't sure you'd come," Micah said.

"Yeah?" Tucker cocked his head. "Think I'm that much of a jerk, huh?"

"That's not what I said."

"Sure it is."

Micah shook his head. "Same old Tucker. Still have to make everybody else feel stupid."

"Excuse me, Mister Valedictorian?" He hated Micah's smug superiority. "You a little bit confused on that one? You want me to find you a mirror?"

"I didn't get valedictorian."

"And who gives a herkin' shit? That was high school, man. Get over it."

Micah sighed. "Boy. Some things don't change."

Ain't that the truth, Tucker thought. *Always so much better than everybody else.* "I gotta tell you, Einstein, I got better things to do than spend six hours getting here just to have to put up with your holier-than-thou routine. Jesus, does that dog ever shut up?"

"Six hours? You're kidding me. It took you that long to fly here from Nevada?"

"Hey. Those six hours include *waiting*. Every step of the way. The plane didn't pick me up at my place and it damn sure didn't drop me off at Connie's doorstep. Speaking of which, where is she?"

"Sleeping. She does a lot of that."

"Sounds like a great life."

Micah's eyes became a squint. "She's dying," he bleated.

"So you said in your letter." Tucker's expression, a facade born at this very site so many years ago, gave nothing away.

"It wasn't easy finding your address, either," Micah said.

"Can't have been all that hard," Tucker said. "You found it."

"You know, you could have called to let me know you were coming today. What if I hadn't been here?"

"Well, sounds like Connie would been here either way, so what's the problem?"

Tucker rolled his eyes and looked away. Connie. Dying. All the way here, Tucker had managed to skirt that specific subject—the very reason for his trip back to White Bluff—but now it found a foothold. He found himself trying to imagine Connie the way she had looked on one of the last times he had seen her, at Big Frank's funeral more than six years ago—the nuances of her expression, sorrow no doubt infused with anger at the pointlessness of his death.

But Tucker's memory of her graveside countenance was, in fact, imagination; even his perfect vision couldn't have discerned so much as a quivering lip that day, since Tucker had not been close enough to see it. While Big Frank's cronies, Connie's friends and even some of the boys' classmates stood around during the graveside service, fidgeting uncomfortably in stuffy garments exhumed from the recesses of their closets, Tucker had watched from a nearby copse of Douglas firs, camouflaged within its brushy understory.

He hadn't chosen that cold distance for fear of the accusing eyes he would have faced. He simply wasn't willing to wade through the simmering stew of his own conflicted emotions. And every inclination to wallow in loss and regret over the old man's death—and his own role in it—had been tempered by a conviction that some dark justice had been served.

He knew Connie—the dutiful churchgoer whose insistence on the boys' regular Sunday school attendance had been precisely halfway successful—would tell him that kind of thinking without confession would consign him to hell.

He would have told her he was already there. And he knew exactly when he arrived.

⅄

Seeing Big Frank open the door had confused six-year-old Tucker.

It was wrong, somehow, and he knew it in that instant. This was a strange house, and he'd never seen his father coming out of any house but their own. Even those times Tucker had gone with his mom to other people's houses, the old man almost never went with them. Of course, Big Frank was gone a lot of the time anyway. Sometimes he wouldn't be around for days, and Tucker would ask his mother where he was. Doing a big parking lot in Sedro Woolley, Louise would say. Or a driveway in Arlington, maybe a tennis court in Everett. *Why don't he come home at night,* Tucker would ask. *He don't work all night, does he?* Your father is working long, late days on this contract, she'd say, and it's easier for him to stay near the job site than to drive back home on that road.

That road. Only years later, when Tucker was old enough to grasp the dangers inherent along that winding blacktop snake, its lanes only occasionally delineated in fading paint and routinely populated by logging trucks late for the mill, would he begin to understand how the old man had been able to fool Louise with that line of crap for so long.

That's where Big Frank was supposed to be at that very moment—at one of those long-hour jobs over in Sedro Woolley, Arlington or Burlington. Yet there he was, opening the door of a brown house as if he lived there.

But Big Frank didn't open the door for Louise to come in. Instead, he stepped out onto the stoop with an oddly defensive expression.

"What are you doing here?" the big man demanded. Tucker rolled down the window to hear, but stopped halfway when his mother started screaming at Big Frank.

"Who lives here? WHO LIVES HERE?" she was yelling. "Who's inside there?" She tried to step around, but Big Frank blocked her path, closed the frame and screen doors behind him and attempted to shepherd her to the car. He might as well have tried to harness a flood.

"C'mon, Louise, don't be acting crazy now," he said, grabbing her to keep her from getting around him. She was rambling on about something, but Tucker couldn't make it all out. Stuff like *wanna know what's going on* and *goddamnit* and *lemme by.*

"What're you doing here? What, you following me now?" Big Frank said, half-pushing her toward the car. "I'm the one oughta be pissed here." It was then he saw Tucker watching through the car window. "Aw shit, Lou, whadaya gotta bring the kid here for, he doesn't need to be seein' this."

"What, he's your son, you got something to hide from *your own son?*" Louise shouted, the last phrase rising to train-whistle shrill.

Tucker noticed a motion—a curtain in one of the front windows moving. He focused his attention on the curtain, using that distraction to shut out the screaming. There was definitely someone in there watching what was going on. A friend of his father's? Somebody he worked with? Big Frank obviously wasn't doing a job here—there were no forms set up anywhere for a concrete pour, and all of the old man's work stuff was still sticking out of the back of the truck.

"I want to know what's going on! Whose house is this?" his mom kept shouting.

"Settle down, settle down, come with me to the car," the old man said gruffly, trying to keep her away from the house.

They were in each other's face so intently neither noticed the small boy, much younger than Tucker, edging timorously around the corner of the garage into view. So focused was Tucker on the movement behind the curtain he didn't notice the boy until he was within just a few steps of the combative couple. In the instant Tucker saw him, their eyes met, and Tucker sensed a familiarity—a feeling both odd and unwelcome, as it was a face he knew he had never seen.

The boy was clearly even more perplexed and upset than Tucker, for whom a parental shouting match was nothing new, though the vehemence this time was reaching epic levels. As Tucker continued to take everything in from the open car window, Louise saw the boy for the first time. That alerted Big Frank to this new presence, and his reflexive anger disappeared, replaced by what looked like resignation.

The front door burst open and a woman hurtled outside, hesitated only briefly and then quickly wrapped the small boy in protective arms, as if Louise presented a possible threat to him. Tucker thought the woman looked younger than his mom—barely more than a girl, really, though with a melancholy weariness about her.

This latest development had sucked the wind from Louise. Her mouth fell slack as her shock coursed through its phases, from bewilderment to suspicion to barely contained fury.

"Mommy, who's that?" the boy blurted, cocking his head up at his mother but looking at Louise. Then, looking up uncertainly at Big Frank, the boy spoke again, in a timid voice Tucker could barely hear.

"Daddy?"

The wrongness in that one word in that context—by that little boy to Tucker's father—made Tucker want to shout out in anger. But it was all too strange for him even to move.

"Daddy?" the little boy said again to Big Frank. "Who's that?"

Tucker saw his mother's knees buckle.

CHAPTER 2

BIG FRANK'S BALL

It would be two years before little Micah truly understood what had happened that day in the front yard, when that woman he had never seen was yelling at his daddy like she knew him.

Until that day, his father had not lived in the house with Micah and his mom. The occasional nights he stayed until morning were times Micah cherished, not because Big Frank was a particularly warm and endearing father—he was neither—but because those were the times when Mommy seemed happiest. And, after all, he was Daddy. That's what his mom said, and she was the only one who had always been around, so he believed her.

After that day in the front yard, though, everything changed. Daddy had stayed in Mommy's room every night since. Mommy, noting Micah's anxiety over the new living arrangements, made sure the boy was involved in everything she and Big Frank did together.

Except at night.

Before, Micah had slept with Mommy on the nights he got scared by a clap of thunder or the boogeyman. But the first time he tried to climb into bed with the two of them, just days into the new living arrangement, the big man had lifted him up and laughed—though it didn't seem to Micah anything was funny.

"Whoa there, little man," Daddy bellowed behind that laugh, holding him close enough for the beer breath to smell. "What do you think you're doing?"

"I'm scared." In a small voice.

"What are you afraid of, bub? I ain't gonna hurt you."

Connie put a hand on Big Frank's forearm. "He just gets a little scared of the dark sometimes, Big. Sounds, things like that, they bother him," she whispered. "I let him sleep with me when—"

"Whoa whoa whoa. Nuh uh, no way. He ain't sleeping in this bed," Big Frank avowed, planting the boy on the floor in a sweeping motion as decisive as his tone. "That don't happen at home ... I mean, that didn't happen where I ... was before. And it ain't about to start here."

"Big, honey, this is still new to him. We're all still kind of figuring this thing out."

"Yeah, well, you can figure all you want, but I'm gonna be the rule-maker on this deal. I been paying the rent for this place—OK, fine, most of the rent—and I'm not having that kid climbing around in our bed, messing up my sleep and probably peeing all over hisself."

"He hasn't done that for a long time, honey. You know I told you that."

"Well, I ain't about to take that chance. Hell, he's afraid of the dark, ain't he?" Big Frank shook his head derisively. "Gimme a break. What kind of little wuss are you raising?"

Micah didn't know what that meant, but he was beginning to think maybe the boogeyman wasn't so scary after all. He began edging toward the door.

"Micah is your son, too. You are his father," his mother said in as authoritative a tone as she could muster. "Don't forget that."

"*Forget?* Hard to forget something that's cost me as much as that little shitter has," he said, reaching for a cigarette from a pack on the bedside table.

Micah slipped quietly into the hall and stayed by the door to hear what was said, standing where he could see Mommy but not Daddy. He watched Mommy cross her arms as she said, "He doesn't need to hear his father calling him names and hurting his feelings."

"Hurting his *feelings?* The only reason he gets to have feelings is because I *paid* for 'em! I've been paying that kid's bills since before he was born—right down to the last stinkin' diaper," Big Frank grumbled. "I haven't forgotten that, either."

"What did you expect? I couldn't work fulltime and raise a baby, and part-time waitress wages weren't going to pay the rent." Even when she had a point, Connie kept her voice level, its tone always leaning toward obsequious. Big hadn't hit her. So far.

"How many times I gotta hear that? Nobody told you to get pregnant."

"Ex*cuse* me?"

Big Frank lit the cigarette, inhaled like an asthmatic in desperate need of air and held it, savoring the nicotine rush. "OK, sorry," he said through breathy smoke. "I just … I mean, having another kid, you know … I already have a kid. Had."

"I guess you must've forgot that, though, huh. 'Cause you sure forgot to mention it to me that first night at the tavern … before …." She cocked her head to make the point.

"I didn't think it needed to come up."

"Well, something else sure did."

That struck them both funny and the bit of laughter helped ease the tension. But the lie upon which their shared history had been founded would always be there: Big Frank had pretended to be available when he was not, had told her he'd been married and his wife had died, and Connie had bought his act.

But he hadn't had a condom, she hadn't been on the pill and in their breathless fumbling around with this button and that zipper, neither had brought the subject up. And when Micah had shown up—welcomed or un-invited, embraced or abided, depending on the fumbler—Big Frank had had to come clean. Then, in an awkward stab at atonement, he had agreed to live a lie for her and, by extension, for the boy. A second life.

"It's just been tough," Big Frank said, softer now. "I been busting my ass on the job, taking on extra contracts all that time so I could keep making payments on two different places and tryin' to keep our little secret. So much for that."

"I never wanted you to keep it."

"And I never asked you to keep—you know."

"You know that wasn't an option," she said. "If you'd have shown up again sooner, maybe. But when you finally did? Wrong."

"Yeah, well, ain't nothin' right about me sneaking away from my wife and son to be with you, either, and you didn't have no problem with that."

"I wanted you to tell them."

"Yeah, tell 'em and leave 'em. Just blow 'em off and move right in over here, from day one. Tucker is my *son*."

"So is Micah."

"I couldn't just leave him. I'm not the sorry-ass excuse for a man my father was. I couldn't just turn my back on my family."

"And so instead, you did things your way, like you always do, and instead of you leaving them, they've left you," she said. "Same difference. Now we're all the family you have left."

Micah peeked around the edge of the door, hoping to glimpse the expression of this man called Daddy. What he saw wasn't what he hoped for.

⋏

To Big Frank, the boy's pedigree worked against him: He had been created by boredom, the progeny of beer buzz and last-call rationalization. The boy had been an unwelcome gift, and that just didn't work for a man accustomed to taking what he wanted.

Before becoming Big Frank, he had been the youngest of six children, always having to scrap to hold his own—and, worse, having to do it as the only boy in a houseful of females. The only male, in fact, after his old man took a powder when Frank was still in elementary school. Just left one day, saying this raising a family deal wasn't for him, and that was that. Frank grew up being ordered around by women and thinking men were pretty much assholes; that seemed to be the prevailing opinion of everybody else in the Dodd household, and the only man around who might have refuted the appraisal had instead already confirmed it. The chip on Frank's shoulder grew into the Rock of Gibraltar, a trait he would one day recognize in his first son. And the sense of abandonment spawned by his father's exodus made him determined not to do the same to any kid of his.

He became Big Frank early in his high-school football days in Sedro Woolley, when he broke into the starting lineup as a beefy freshman after making a couple of quarterback sacks during garbage time of a lopsided victory. In the locker room following the game, the coach tried to light a fire under his older players by extolling the first-year boy, saying, "You guys could take a lesson from big Frank here. He doesn't waste a single play when he's on the field. Big Frank always has his motor going." Naturally, the older players wouldn't let go of that, riding him with belittling repetitions of "big Frank"—out of the coach's earshot, of course—until he busted the nose of one of the senior linemen for saying it one too many times. That essentially guaranteed the nickname would stick, though for reasons profoundly more to his liking.

Big Frank left home the day he turned 18 and joined the Navy, where his experience from summer jobs as a construction laborer made for a natural transition to the Seabees, the naval construction battalions. Half of his four-year hitch was spent working on base expansion at Subic Bay in the Philippines, where copious amounts of beer helped persuade him to lace his biceps and shoulders with the tattoos that would one day fascinate the little waitress at the tavern. Subic Bay was also where he learned about sex from the Filipina whores whose squalid dwellings seemed to proliferate, like hungry dogs, just outside the main gate. Two years of their cold tutorials guaranteed that his afterglow interaction with either of the two women he later married would never get much more emotionally endearing than a cigarette and a beer.

Then came Vietnam.

For most of the nine months he was there, Vietnam was a tour no different than his last—muggy, interminable days of back-breaking labor, no-see-ums too many to swat and *Me so hawny* ten-dollar hookers too many to ignore. He and his buddies were always hearing about Seabee teams who had been fired upon while building this tactical airstrip or that Special Forces encampment, but it never felt real. This was still two years before the shit really hit the fan in Vietnam, and for the most part their assignments seemed designed to straddle the rickety fence between public relations and preparedness—trying to come off as road-building good Samaritans amid a suspicious citizenry while shaping an infrastructure for the full-scale military campaign everyone assumed was coming.

Most of his time in country he spent unarmed. Although his entire Seabee unit had been issued firearms, few of the men remained diligent about carrying them after their first few months. The work was punishing enough, the weapons got in the way and, frankly, they were just more weight to have to lug around. Even the omnipresent and heavily armed Marines sent along on every mission to protect them seemed unnecessary; they spent most of their time smoking cigarettes and playing cards while the Seabees were busting their butts.

But one day eight months into his Vietnam tour, while buttressing a roadside berm south of Danang, Big Frank's team came under heavy fire for the first time. He hunkered down in the ditch, gunfire coming from all directions, no weapon with which to return fire. The Marines detached to protect them were blasting away, but it was all just noise, fear and motion to Big Frank, a disorienting strobelight nightmare in full daylight.

"The big circus" was how he'd heard it described by one Marine lifer sergeant, a veteran of Korea, and now Big Frank was smack dab in the middle of center ring.

His face was mashed into a mud bank as he prayed to a God he had neither known nor sought, feeling a terror he had never experienced and was absolutely helpless to do anything about. For the first time in his young life, his size, strength and capacity for directed anger were no help to him; he was powerless to affect his fate. The madness was in full flower around and over him, pieces of death flying through the air looking for places to land, and whether one landed on him, perhaps snuffing him out in mid-thought, was entirely beyond his control. Nothing made sense. He was halfway around the world, digging a ditch in a country full of little brown people who squawked in a silly language he didn't understand and would sooner spit in his face than thank him for his troubles, and now whether he lived or died was a prospect reduced to dumb luck. He would either be perfectly fine in five seconds or five minutes, or he might be missing a leg or a face or simply be no more. Flip a coin, take a number, pick a card, choose a color …

But he couldn't wrap that pointlessness around him like a warm blanket and settle into it. Oh no, no can do. The circus was in town. With each kaleidoscopic second potentially his last, all of his synapses were firing and receiving at full blast, his senses taking everything in with every breath of extended life.

He could feel the blood throbbing against the tips of his fingers, jammed as they were into the mud, grasping in vain for sanctuary.

He could see a beetle wriggling across the mud just inches away, oblivious to the lethal malevolence exploding all around, having just another day at the office.

He could hear the anguished cries of an injured buddy and listened as the pathetic wailing rendered its vivid portrait of torment. He heard the sparky barking coordinates, calling base for backup. Realizing he could make out what the Marines' radio operator was saying in the vortex of this insanity seemed important, so he focused on that staccato delivery right up until he heard the sparky pause in his appeal for air support, then blurt, "Alpha mike foxtrot … shit." Followed not two seconds later by an explosion that brought the circus down upon Big Frank.

Alpha mike foxtrot.

Adios, motherfucker.

Certain his own death was imminent, Big Frank pissed in his pants.

Which is pretty much where the shrapnel got him.

⅄

Big Frank did not die that day in that muddy ditch near Danang, though his heretofore unassailable sense of immortality was gone forever. So, too, was his left testicle.

The physical wound wasn't nearly as debilitating as its emotional consequence.

As he lay in a stateside hospital bed in the days after the circus, Big Frank considered himself a freak. He was the product of a small town, where status among peers was largely determined by whether or not a guy had balls. *Balls.* Plural. Always. Now, he was feeling like half a man and acting as if his life might as well be over.

Even if he was physically capable of having sex, he was certain the only women who would willingly get close to him in his particular state of deformity would want to be paid for the experience, and that prospect wasn't appealing. He recalled only too well their contemptuous laughter at the two times when, in his teenaged eagerness, he had arrived prematurely at the dance. What if, in his current state, he couldn't arrive at all? The doctors all assured him otherwise, of course, but what did those assholes know.

Even the thought of having to reveal to a woman what Vietnam had taken from him made Big Frank want to pull the hospital sheet over his head and never come out.

⅄

Louise Boudreoux had been going to college part-time on the eight-year-to-permanent plan, enjoying those monthly care packages from the parents and the paltry alimony from a short-lived marriage, and picking up a few hours whenever she could at the V.A. hospital in San Francisco. It was at the latter, while dishing out a little TLC as necessary to the afflicted, she crossed paths with a burly trauma victim named Frank Dodd.

Although Louise was neither trained for nor expected to counsel victims of physical or emotional trauma, she was uniquely qualified to help the young man she came to know as Big.

Louise wasn't a classic beauty by anyone's standards, largely because her unfortunately equine nose preceded her into every room. But her limber body swayed with an unaffected sensuality when she walked, giving her thick, raven locks a life of their own, and her tawny, smooth skin and piercing green eyes had a magnetic effect upon many a wandering male eye.

She was not averse to the attention she stirred, nor shy about it. Although the era that would become known as the sexual revolution hadn't yet kicked into high gear, the recent advent of the birth-control pill had definitely stoked an appetite within Louise Boudreoux. In three or four years, young people with her sensibilities would be called flower children or hippies, but for now she was just a hands-on aide in a military hospital.

Her days at the hospital were spent helping provide whatever a patient needed outside of actual critical care, from cleaning up bedpans and puke to walking the grounds with the ones who could. What Big Frank Dodd needed most during and after his stay at the V.A was to feel normal again. And Louise Boudreoux was personally predisposed to assisting in that sort of transformation.

Because there was still no official war in Vietnam and the casualties by fall of 1963 numbered in the dozens, not the thousands, hospital staffing was still at peacetime levels and even a trickle of combat victims cut into the time doctors and nurses could expend on each patient. As a result, willing part-timers were given more latitude about the breadth of their duties, and Louise was young enough to identify with military wounded—at twenty-six, just three years older than Big Frank—and most assuredly willing.

She thought Big Frank was good-looking enough—ruggedly handsome, in the parlance of her guilty-pleasure romance novels—but for weeks she didn't give him any special attention. Then one day an annoying intern, who had for weeks been trying to get into her pants, joked about the seaman in the last bed of ward three having a semen issue.

"He's not a seaman, he's a Seabee," she retorted. "What do you mean, exactly? About his … issue?"

"He lost a testicle in Vietnam."

"I would have thought those would be hard to misplace."

"Ha ha. It got shot off."

She gave the intern a deadpan expression. "Why's he still here? I'm guess-ing that's not a life-threatening wound. Why hasn't he been reassigned?"

"Well, I thought you'd know that, you being this big expert on his Seabee status and all," the intern smirked in an awkward flirt. "He was coming up to the end of his tour anyway, so he'll be honorably discharged as soon as he's released."

"And they haven't released him … why?"

"Emotional distress. Whatever you want to call it. There's no shortage of beds, so they're willing to keep him until he knows he's OK. I think he's pretty bummed by this one-ball thing."

"Can you blame him?"

"Hey, as long as the equipment is functional," the intern cracked, "what's the big deal?"

What, indeed. The more Louise thought about this big country boy's humiliation over his testicular status, the more it piqued her curiosity. One afternoon a few days later, when the third ward was empty but for Frank Dodd and a couple of heavily-sedated sleepers at the far end, she sat on the edge of his bed. He was in his usual morose state.

"Hey, Frank, how's it going?" she asked.

His response was a wordless, leave-me-alone grunt.

"Hey, I've got some time," she said. "Want to play cards?"

"No." Sounding not much different than the grunt.

"Oh, come on. Why not?"

"Wanna be alone."

"Oh, I see. You're just determined to be the strong, silent type. Is that it?"

Apparently.

"Hey, now." She put her hand on his hip; he flinched at the touch. "What's wrong?"

"Go away. Please."

She moved her palm ever-so-slightly on his hip, a sympathetic touch. After a half-minute, he turned just enough to see her. "I said leave me alone," he said, then looked away again.

"Hey," she said, quieter now. "It's my responsibility to help you. If you won't let me, I won't be doing my job. And I need this job."

He was still looking away, but she sensed he wasn't closing her out.

"I think I have an idea what this might be about, you know." She waited for him to move or respond, but he did not. "I know about your injury."

She knew immediately it was the wrong thing to say, but she was committed now. "Do you want to talk about it?"

"What do you think?" he grumbled. But even in the bullish defensiveness in his rhetorical question, Louise sensed just the hint of Big Frank's hopefulness—that, just perhaps, against all odds, she might have some sort of answer.

"Well, I think … it never hurts to talk when you're hurting."

He was silent again, but now she was certain he wanted to talk about this.

"You know," she said, fabricating the white lie, "you're not the first enlisted man to come in here with a—a testicle wound."

She felt the slightest pulse of movement under her palm, followed by an adamant stillness.

"It's not a problem, you know," she said, glancing surreptitiously at the ward door.

He still didn't turn around. "How you figure that."

"Well, I know what happened to you bothers you. But it's not something that would ever bother a woman," she added.

"Women don't have balls to lose."

He didn't intend it as a joke, but she went with it anyway. She risked a chuckle. "That's pretty good, Frank," she said. "It's nice to see you've still got your sense of humor."

He cocked his head back a little to see if she was screwing with him.

"But I'm telling you the truth, Frank. Women don't worry about that kind of thing."

He grunted and rolled away once again.

"You know, we've seen this kind of thing here a lot," she said, making it up as she went along. "And I can tell you, losing a testicle almost never affects your … sexual performance."

Moments passed in silence. Finally he mumbled, "So the doc says."

"Well, there you go."

"So that's bullshit."

"No. It's not bullshit," she said. With another glance at the ward door, she shifted her body until it was between the door and Frank and pulled on his hip just enough to induce him to roll back over from his self-imposed exile.

Even flat on his back, though, he had trouble making eye contact.

"Tell you what," she said. "Let me just check the damage."

His eyes flashed *NO* at her, but she nodded assuringly and began gently pulling back the sheet, beneath which lay Frank's hospital gown. He grabbed her wrist, but she scolded him with a look that made him let go.

"It's OK," she said. "I'm just doing my job." She pulled the sheet down far enough, then reached to the edge of his hospital gown and tugged; he was lying on too much of it, though, so her expression requested that he shift his weight.

His response was wide eyes but no movement.

"Are you the doctor here?" she asked, neglecting the part about how she wasn't, either.

"Shouldn't a man doctor be the one doing this?"

"Well, Frank," she said, tilting her head just so, "wouldn't you prefer a woman?" She tugged once more on the edge of his gown.

She could see he wasn't at all sure what to expect but was at least finally becoming intrigued by the possibilities, and he shifted his weight enough to let her grip the edge of the gown. She pulled it around and out of the way, revealing that which so troubled Big Frank. He watched her eyes with a sort of anticipatory horror.

"Oh," Louise said. "Oh."

Frank was so tense he wasn't even breathing, much less moving.

"Oh, Frank," she said. "It's beautiful."

And, with that, something began to move.

CHAPTER 3

BECOMING BROTHERS

"**D**o you want to see her?"VEN

Micah could see his voice bring Tucker back into the thorny morning and the increasing urgency of its canine soundtrack as they entered the house.

He waited for an answer, but got none as Tucker took in the living room. Micah found himself hoping Tucker's silence might for once be the language of guilt, the thought of having to face a dying stepmother who had treated him like a son, only to see him push her away at every turn, and who had every reason to blame him for the death of her husband. *Atonement's a bitch, ain't it, big brother.*

"Well?" Micah insisted.

"She's asleep, right?" Tucker said breezily. "So what's the point?"

Micah did a double-take, and his answer came under his breath, as if his mother could hear them through her morphine haze, her dog and two walls.

"What's the *point*?" Micah shook his head and wanted to stalk away. "I'll never understand how you and I can come from the same genes and be so diametrically different."

"Diametrically. Huh." Tucker made a face. "Same old Micah. Still using fifty-cent words when you ain't got a nickel's worth of sense. We didn't come from the same genes, *little brother.* We came from the same old man, period, and I *do* understand how: He didn't know how to keep his zipper closed whenever some waitress would drop her pants."

Micah's eyes blazed. Tucker always knew how to find a soft and vulnerable spot. Making it hurt all the more, Micah could never seem to get under his brother's skin, despite his absolutely certainty he was far more intelligent and resourceful than Tucker.

He was the one who'd gotten the good grades, after all, while Tucker was the dyslexic jock. He was the one who had gotten all of the academic scholarship offers, while his brother, the Friday night hero and Barclay's icon, wouldn't even have been able to parlay his physical prowess into an athletic scholarship at one of the smaller northwest colleges. Even had Tucker stuck around, he could never have passed an entrance exam. Unable to read as painlessly as his classmates, Tucker had cheated his way through most of his high school classes by dint of his special powers of persuasion. When that failed, there was always the pressure brought to bear upon his teachers by every coach whose teams depended on Tucker's particular brand of channeled mayhem—until, finally, Tucker turned on his coaches as well.

The yapping coming from the front bedroom was incessant.

"So," Tucker said, "are you gonna kill that dog or do I have to do it." Spoken like so many of Tucker's questions: as a statement.

"He belongs to Mom."

"Yeah? Well, that must explain why she's checking out. Yapper like that'd make me jump out a fuckin' window."

"Why she's checking out?" Micah's voice got higher-pitched, as it always had whenever Tucker got to him. "What the hell is that supposed to mean?"

"You're the smart one, remember? Why don't you tell me?"

"Look, since you obviously don't care about seeing Mom," Micah hissed, "why did you come?"

"Who said I didn't want to see her? I never said that."

"You said …you just said …" Micah stammered the way he often did in response to Tucker's maddening ability to masquerade as brutally honest while remaining, in Micah's assessment, utterly guarded.

"You said she was asleep, and I don't see any reason for waking her up," Tucker said, dropping his duffel onto the living room floor. "It ain't like I'm goin' anywhere any time soon. Taxi's gone."

Micah watched as Tucker took stock of the living room and the combined kitchen-dining room, as he had done himself only six weeks before. The sofa that separated the dining and living rooms had been reupholstered, but Micah was pretty sure it was the same eight-foot beast Big Frank had purchased at a flea market. *That thing was probably ten years old when he bought it*, Micah thought, and felt a twinge of sadness. The recliner, ancient even then, still faced the television—this one a 19-incher upon which sat a large ceramic frog and a rabbit-eared antenna. The fireplace, once woefully inefficient, was now equipped with a blower that projected its heat at least throughout the living room, if not the house. The dining room table, a cheap oak veneer, was still surrounded by the same four ill-matched chairs. The pictures on the wall, poster-shop prints of landscape Americana, didn't seem to have changed.

As Tucker continued his inspection of the house, Micah tried to pinpoint when his father had bought that godawful sofa. Oh yeah. Autumn of his ninth-grade year, the year he caught up to Tucker in grade level. He had already surpassed him in academic ability, largely because of all the years Tucker's dyslexia went undiagnosed. But Micah's skipping the eighth grade— on top of his having bypassed third grade, the same one Tucker had to take twice—meant they would enter high school together.

And Micah remembered how demoralizing that prospect had been.

Not because of the step up in academics, though. Micah had long since decided the easy way to make up for his puny physique was to strengthen his mind, and, after all those nights his mother had read to him back when it had been just the two of them, language skills had come easily. No, the worst part was being a twelve-year-old high schooler and, worse, the wimpy brother of one of the toughest kids in east county—thus ensuring the teasing he'd endure would be perpetual yet clandestine, without even the mixed blessing of the cathartic bully punches that might allow everyone to move on. A guy would have to be crazy to do something to piss Tucker Dodd off, and punching his brother might lead to the possibility of having to punch Tucker himself—truly the height of insanity.

Unless, of course, the guy doing the punching was Tucker Dodd's father, and punch Tucker was precisely what Big Frank had done the day he arrived home with the sofa in the back of his truck. Connie had given it a long look and an indecisive little *Hmm* at its funky melange of ill-chosen colors. Tucker had laughed and said it's one thing to get drunk and puke on a sofa, but that didn't mean you had to bring it home. He was still chuckling at his own line when Big Frank's fist backhanded him across the mouth, chipping one of his teeth.

It had been the first time Big Frank had ever aimed one of his punches at anything other than the meaty flesh of Tucker's shoulder, and Micah remembered cringing at the sight. Now, recalling the punch and his brother's muted reaction to it, Micah wondered if Tucker had ever done anything to fix or replace that chipped tooth. Or whether he even remembered the punch that created it. Probably not. He had barely winced at the blow.

Connie sure had, though.

Micah knew his mother had always been a little fearful of the man she had, by happenstance and Catholic guilt, accepted as a partner to raise her child and, later, to marry and raise his. But the instant Big Frank's fist split Tucker's lip—and chipped the tooth, though that part would remain Tucker's secret for months—she had leapt in to protect the boy like a caribou cow taking on a pack of wolves to defend her young.

She would have defended him to the death, Micah knew. *My mother would have died for you*, he thought, glaring silently as his brother continued his casual inventory. *And you wouldn't even call her Mom. Was that too much to ask?*

He knew the answer: For Tucker, it had been. After his first full year in this house, when Big Frank decided it was time for him to begin calling her "Mom," Tucker had flatly refused. Every time it had been brought up. That intractable rebuff led to regular encounters with Big Frank's belt, but Tucker wasn't about to let anybody else step into a role occupied by only one woman.

$$\lambda$$

Before that bizarre, unhinging scene in that now-familiar front yard, Louise had been in love with the world around her. In love with Frank, too, though theirs had been a problematic relationship from the beginning, each too immersed within the excitement of the age and the exuberant sex to fret about an incompatibility that should have been obvious.

In the first few weeks after Louise had shown him he was still capable of snapping to attention, she gave Big Frank plenty of opportunities to field-test the equipment. The first time they did so convinced him he no longer needed to return to the hospital, and she was fine with him staying at her apartment until he knew what he wanted to do. What he mostly wanted to do was continue to field-test the equipment as often as possible, and she was happy to oblige. In her bed. On the sofa when her roommate wasn't home. On a blanket on the fringes of a park. Even a couple of times in her car.

He seemed so touched by and grateful for Louise's openhearted nature, she was surprised at how selfish he seemed to be in bed. She knew nothing of the hookers at Subic Bay who had trained him to be expeditious; she only knew as soon as Big Frank was finished, he was out of her and, usually, out of her bed. After the first few times, Louise had suggested Big Frank consider postponing his pleasure long enough so she might join him. He had no idea what she was talking about. She was amazed at how foreign a concept this seemed to him—a woman actually wanting to enjoy sex, and him having some responsibility in that. Still, he became a willing student, if not a particularly gifted one.

She also enjoyed smoking marijuana before sex, and though he hadn't taken to it when he'd tried it at Subic Bay, he went along for her sake. On the two occasions she asked him to join her in consuming what she called "magic mushrooms," though, he balked—just as he would later when she came home from class at Berkeley with something she called acid. He'd always hated mushrooms, he said, and now that he was a grown man, he wasn't going to eat them any more.

"And besides," he said, "I'm not puttin' anything in my mouth that looks like rat shit."

"It has to look gross or everybody will want it and there won't be enough to go around," she said, only partly in jest. "It's God's way of keeping it secret, so only the special people will be able to experience it. You should feel privileged. *C'mon.* It's like taking a trip."

"Hey, I'm here to tell ya, trips ain't all they're cracked up to be. I went on one halfway around the world and all I have to show for it is some G.I. Bill vouchers and one nut."

Soon enough, a son would be added to that inventory.

After the initial shock of learning she was pregnant—and bemoaning her fate of somehow falling outside the birth control pills' purported effectiveness of nearly 99 percent—Louise had undergone a transformation that surprised even her.

The candor and abandon with which she had been living her adult life had been a spreading of wings, a subconscious emergence from her upbringing within a family of impassive intellectuals. Now she could be impetuous and madcap and have to answer only to herself, flitting from one relationship to another with the random bliss of a hummingbird. But Tucker changed that with his first kick, engendering a sense of belonging that all but overwhelmed her.

When she shared the news of their impending addition with Big Frank, it hit him wrong at first, and he went into another room to stew. She half-expected him to flee back home to Washington state.

But he surprised her.

"OK, fine, let's do it. We'll get married," he announced in the tone of a man reconciled to making a great sacrifice for a noble cause.

"Married?" she'd asked in sudden wonder. That was a concept she hadn't considered. "Wow. Are you sure that's a good idea?"

"Well … yeah," he said, obviously disappointed by her reply. "Don't you want the kid to have a father?"

"Of course she will. Or he … if … you know. That's a given. You're the father."

"I know. That's what I'm sayin'. So we'll get married." He waited for affirmation of his stellar plan.

"I don't have *too* much experience at this," she said, "but isn't a marriage proposal supposed to have a question somewhere in there?"

"Oh yeah. So we'll get married ... right?"

That made her laugh. And, surprising even herself, she said yes.

But no sooner had she shared this exciting news with her parents than they turned their interrogative skills upon Big Frank and promptly ascertained his abundant shortcomings as a prospective husband and father. Although Louise knew their attempts to dissuade her were well-intended and well-reasoned, their disapproval only steeled her resolve, especially when her father—fully understanding why wedlock was even on the table—said he had doctor friends at the university hospital who'd be willing to take care of "that sort of thing."

In that moment, Louise realized she didn't care if her father ever saw her baby.

Then Frank told her he knew his family up in Washington would love her and welcome the baby. And that did it.

She moved with him from what she deemed the suffocating civility in the East Bay to a place Big Frank called east county, trading in a world measured by academic degrees and confined to cerebral observation for the untamed backcountry at the foot of the Cascades. All it took was one long, early-autumn drive with Big Frank over the North Cascades from Rockport to Winthrop to make her a Washington woman. She took in the flannel shirts, breathed the aromatic evergreen air, reveled in mountains still snow-capped after an Indian summer, and declared herself home. When they married, her parents and siblings came up for the ceremony, noted several guests at the reception chewing tobacco and spitting the dregs into styrofoam cups, and decided en masse they would never again need to venture this far from civilization.

Frank and Louise bought a place outside of Darrington, a double-wide with a garden, basically. He began working for a concrete contractor. She got a job at a long-term care facility, where she could do her TLC thing.

The next August, they welcomed their son into the world. And Tucker Jonathan Dodd became her world.

She had "rescued" his father, Louise became fond of telling the little boy.

"And then he rescued me," she would say, tapping the tip of Tucker's nose with her index finger, "by giving me you. The best gift *ever.*"

Micah eyed Tucker's duffel bag. His big brother either wasn't planning on an extended stay or he traveled light.

"How long you figure to stay?" he asked.

Tucker had opted for one of the kitchen chairs—the furthest away from the bedroom yapper, which had run out of gas or curiosity. "How long you think it's going to take her to die?"

He said it while looking at one of the posters—an old Maxfield Parrish—and so he completely missed Micah's angry stare.

"Man, you're cold," Micah hissed. "Are you just here to see if you're in her will?"

"Fuck you."

"Is that it? Because she hasn't got much to offer, I can tell you that much." Micah gestured around the room. "You're looking at it right here."

Tucker shook his head slowly. "Wow. Coming here for the will. Man. That's pretty cynical, Einstein. Even for you."

"*I'm* cynical? That's rich, coming from a guy who's never believed in a single thing his whole pathetic life."

"Ooh. I don't seem to recall you thinking my life was so pathetic when I was banging every cheerleader in school and you couldn't get a date to save your life."

"Yeah, and do you recall me not being old enough to *have* a date? And even if I'd been old enough to apply for a driver's license, you'd already have had the car. You always had Mom's car at night. And this—"

"Well, yeah," Tucker said, twisting the *yeah* as if this was all too obvious. "I needed that car. Where did you think I was banging those cheerleaders?"

"Thank you very much. That's a little more information than I wanted."

"Yeah, right. You're such a lyin' sack, Micah—you'd have paid a year's allowance to be takin' *pictures.* You think I didn't see you that time with Missy Klootchman, you little perv? Junior year?"

Micah felt a rush of embarrassment, made all the worse because he knew Tucker saw it.

"Oh yeah," Tucker crowed. "We were parked at that little clearing way back off the river road, remember? Oh yeah. We knew you were there by that tree the whole time."

"That was my turnaround spot. That was track season, remember? I ran out there all the time in training. It's a four-mile out-and-back, and that's two miles."

"Yeah, and you sure weren't in any big hurry to be heading back, were you? Did you like it? Did you ..." And he made the jerk-off motion with his right hand.

"Oh, go to hell. I was just taking a breather at the turnaround."

"Yeah, I'll bet you were breathing pretty hard, too. Hey, I gotta tell ya, Missy was getting off on it, knowing you were watching. She was really riding high in the saddle –"

"Oh, Jesus, Tucker ..."

"Hey, I'm serious, man, she was really trying to give you a show." He cupped his hands at breast level as a visual aid, recalling Missy Klootchman's most obvious attributes.

"Well, I'll make sure to thank her next time I see her," Micah snapped. "That's just great. Now I know why Dad had to be the one to come pick me up sometimes after band over at N.C.—and I'm sure you can imagine how happy he always was about having to do that, by the way. Mom almost never had her car, because you were out getting laid."

Tucker shrugged.

"You ever thank her?" Micah asked pointedly.

"Missy Klootchman?"

"No, dickweed. Mom."

"Oh, yessuh, massah," Tucker said in a mocking tone. "I thanked *Connie* every day of my whole pathetic life. Gimme a break."

They were getting louder now, and that got the dog yapping again.

"She loved you, you know," Micah spat out. "Even though you never treated her like a mother—and I gotta tell ya, you were really a jerk to her.

She loved you like you were her own son. Why do you think she stood up for you all those times when Dad was on one of his rampages? And why do you think she always let you use her car?"

"That's an easy one: She felt guilty."

"Guilty? What could she possibly have to feel guilty about?"

"Are you kidding me? Plenty, and she knew it, too, you little shit. She knew she owed me for ruining my life."

"Oh, really? She ruined your life, how'd she manage that? By cooking your meals and washing your clothes for all those years? By trying to get you help for your dyslexia—"

"I didn't ask for any help."

"—when Dad didn't want to have anything to do with it? He just thought you were lazy."

"And as usual, Big Frank didn't know shit."

"It wasn't Mom's fault, what happened to … your mother. But you blame her for that."

This time it was Tucker's eyes that blazed in anger. "I don't blame her for my mother. I blame him."

They heard a sound from elsewhere in the house that wasn't the dog. Both brothers went still, each looking at the wall through which the sound had come. Even the yapping stopped.

"And I blame you," Tucker said softly into the silence.

Micah was just beginning to react to that statement when they both heard the sound again. It was Connie's muffled voice. And what she was saying— the noises she was making—made no sense at all.

⚔

The night Big Frank Dodd had walked into the Come Right Inn, he'd been wearing a faded military fatigue jacket he then removed to reveal the T-shirt underneath and the muscular physique that comes with years of concrete work. The waitress had been wearing a mini-skirt that did not flatter her and a low-cut blouse that did, both of which Big Frank later removed to reveal the hot little body that comes with being twenty-one years old.

Big Frank was twenty-six. In a few months, his wife would be thirty. The big three-oh. She hadn't gotten chunky like he'd feared she might after having Tucker, but the rack was definitely sagging and her ass was becoming more than a handful. So was she, not entirely to his liking. It turned out not only had his family welcomed Louise with open arms, his sisters had practically gone into cahoots with her—telling her old stories about him, figuring out ways to embarrass him and getting her to act as high and mighty as they'd always been.

He didn't think he deserved that kind of disrespect. Hey, he'd been married for more than two years, and in all that time, even with his wife getting a little rundown and a lot snooty, with his buddies always going on about this piece of ass or that horny honey, he hadn't even once tried to score some strange. He hadn't so much as grabbed a waitress's ass.

He didn't grab Connie's ass, either—and neither did any of the other horny toads in the tavern, once they figured out the big guy in military fatigues was taking an interest.

They reacted to Big Frank in much the same way, years later, men would respond to the barely contained volatility of his oldest son. A man like that always presents a line that should not be crossed with a glance held too hold, or a shoulder not retracted deferentially in passing to avoid contact. And when this kind of man is with a woman about whom he feels territorial, the line is even more defined: Don't eyeball her. That's just asking for a confrontation, and men like Big Frank, whose biceps danced under his tattoos whenever he so much as raised his beer mug, relish what happens next.

So when Big Frank began showing an interest in the waitress—cute but not pretty, perky disposition and even perkier breasts—the other prospective suitors all pretty much drowned their moustaches in their beers. He knew it, too; he had no competitors in this game.

So he played it cool as the gentleman caller, the generous tipper. And he was very smooth and slow in asking the kind of questions he thought would prime her pump. So, is this place treating you good? Been working here long? Your boyfriend mind you working here, knowing guys will always hit on a pretty girl like you?

Finally he got around to, "So, bein' as we're all friendly, could I buy you a drink when you get off?"

⅄

Connie Sidrow had known he had been working up to the question, of course; the routine of any even remotely attractive barmaid involves screening the advances of inebriated and amorous patrons near closing time. But her inner radar, which had always served her well, had been less than stellar that night.

She misread Big Frank's gruff brevity as depth; she mistook as gallantry his not copping any *'scuse me miss* feels as she made her rounds. And she found herself both unnerved by and drawn to the effect his presence had on the other men in the bar: The ass-grabbers and tipsy winkers had noted his interest and uniformly assumed a hands-off policy.

Damn, she liked that about this big guy.

But she'd spotted his wedding ring in the first minute, and when he asked her the big after-work question, she asked him about the ring.

Big Frank did a little *oh-shit* double take, which nearly ended it for Connie. But then he recovered with what would ultimately turn out to be the first piece of Big Frank's Big Lie.

"My wife died two years ago. I haven't been able to bring myself to take it off."

And she bought it.

"Oh no. I'm so sorry."

"No, no, it's … I'm all right. I'm getting better, anyway. I'm not used to … you know, talking about my wife."

"You've been keeping it inside all this time?"

"Yeah."

"And you haven't … been able to … um … take it off?"

He shook his head.

The poignancy in Big Frank's Big Lie got him into her pants.

And got her into the predicament.

When Connie found out she was pregnant, her first reaction was profound disappointment in herself. *So stupid*, she thought. *You know better than that. No rubber, no lover.* She was only twenty-one, barely two years into her own adventure, determined to make it on her own and with a plan to make it happen. Nowhere in that blueprint was there a pregnancy before she even made it out of east county.

As for the life growing inside her, she was ambivalent; having a baby had been something she had hoped to put off for a long time. The plan certainly hadn't entailed having a baby with some guy she took home from a job she only intended to keep until she'd saved up enough money to move a thousand miles from here.

She wasn't without options. One of her cousins had gone up to Canada to get an abortion, and Connie knew she could do that if she had to. But her cousin still carried a lot of regret over her decision, and Connie wasn't sure she wanted to risk that—or the risks of the procedure itself.

She could keep the baby, of course, but this was a sticky wicket. Her roommate worked a forty-hour week, too, and paying for a babysitter or daycare would make it impossible to save any money. Connie lived twenty minutes from her parents, but that wouldn't be a drive she would choose to make. She was the fourth of five children, three of whom still lived at home. Each of her two older sisters had already gotten pregnant, unexpectedly and unmarried, and each had done the prodigal daughter thing often enough to make their parents fed up with the whole thing. When Connie learned she was pregnant, she didn't even consider her parents an option.

So she decided she'd find Big Frank.

She didn't have his number, but she didn't think that would be an issue. She expected him to stop by the restaurant any day now.

Any day came. And went.

The next day the same. And the next week.

Connie went through the early-term nausea, grateful the worst came in the mornings, hours before she went to work. She asked the other waitresses if they knew Big Frank, or where he lived. She had called the three Frank Smiths she found in the county book; none of them were him, none of them knew a Smith that met his description, and she had begun to believe that he had made up the name. *So stupid.*

A month went by. Then two.

She still wasn't really showing—Sidrow girls tended to carry their babies light and show late—but her jeans had begun to fit her a mite comfy by mid-December, nearing the end of month three. That was when Big Frank finally moseyed in, all swagger and expectation, a big bull out to stud in a pasture that had proven fertile once before.

Can we get together after your shift? he asked. *You bet we can*, she answered, although the trouser tent her answer gave him was thoroughly tempered by the news she imparted at her apartment.

His first response was automatic. "How did this happen?"

"You're kidding, right? How old are you?"

"What? Why?"

"Because even a six-year-old knows the answer to that question."

"Hey, don't be getting smart. This ain't my fault. Shit. Merry fuckin' Christmas. So. How much is this gonna cost?"

"How much is what gonna cost?"

"You know—the abortion deal."

Her glare registered her disgust.

"It's a little late for that."

"How you figure that?"

"I'm almost at twelve weeks."

"Okay. And ..."

"My God, you don't have a clue, do you? Do you know what it looks like in your womb when you're three months pregnant?"

Frank looked pissed at being challenged, but Connie thought he was simply embarrassed at being asked a simple question for which he had absolutely no answer.

"It's like a little person, Frank. OK? Fingers and toes, the whole deal."

"Yeah? How do you know that? How do you know what it looks like in there?"

Connie sighed heavily. "Because I can read, Frank." She put a hand on her stomach. "OK, how about this, maybe this will help you understand: If I got an abortion now, there's a real chance I could die, Frank—if that is your name."

"Of course that's my name."

She glared at him. "*Smith?*"

"OK. I guess … you know it's not Smith. Sorry. It's … Dodd. Frank Dodd … uh, Big Frank. That's what everybody calls me, I mean. Big Frank."

"So, Mister Big Frank Dodd, why'd you lie about your name?" She grabbed his left hand, splaying the fingers to display his ring finger, where the pale strip bespoke of the wedding ring he had obviously removed for the occasion. She pinched the finger between thumb and forefinger. "This one's not dead, is she."

He was silent.

"And you're still married to her."

Now he wouldn't even look at her.

So stupid. "Does she know you screw around?"

"I don't screw around," he muttered defensively. "It was just that one time. And, you know, tonight, if …"

She gaped at this almost adolescent gall. "*Tonight?* Are you kidding me? Is that all you can think about? Whether you're going to get laid tonight? What about the baby?"

Although the baby had been at the center of this entire conversation, this was the first time that word—baby—had been said out loud. *I'm pregnant,* she had said, and then there was a lot of *pregnancy* and *it* references. Even the fingers-and-toes thing hadn't done it to him, but she could see it on his face now: That single, spoken, four-letter word arrived like a fistful of sand in a balloon. His face absolutely sank.

"Shit," he said.

"That's not an answer," she said, sitting up straight to ask the question she'd been dreading. "Do you have children? Already?"

"Shit," he said again.

"Well," she said, her sigh nearly lapsing into a sob. "The hits just keep on coming. I get screwed, your wife gets screwed, your kids get screwed. And now *my* kid gets screwed."

"There's just one," he said sheepishly. "One kid. A boy."

"How old is he?"

For the moment, it looked like Big Frank had no idea. *Good Lord*, she thought. *I had sex with a man who doesn't know how old his son is.*

"Uh …two. He's two."

Connie raised her eyebrows. "Huh. Well. He's not going to be an only child."

Big Frank would hardly look at her, but she held the gaze long enough that he would have no choice but to recognize the inevitability of his situation. "So … I mean … you want to have the kid," he said finally. "That's what you're saying."

"I don't see as I have much choice."

"Huh."

Grunting seemed to be the best Big Frank could come up with at the moment.

"Hey, listen," he said finally. "We'll figure it out. I'll do the right thing. If it's gonna be my kid—" He paused to eyeball her. "It *is* my kid, right?"

She nearly slapped him. *No, better not,* she decided. *He might just hit me back, and where would I be then.* She let her silence deliver her answer.

"Well … shit," he said. "Guess I'm gonna have to start making more money."

And Big Frank actually tried to do what he thought was the right thing. He put Connie up in a cheap little clapboard house ten miles away in White Bluff, the last thing resembling a town before east county was swallowed up by the Cascades—on the way to nowhere and far enough out in the boonies to ensure Louise would never accidentally come by and see his truck. He began bidding on more contracts, gave cut-rate deals to anyone who'd pay in cash so he could keep it off the books, lied to his wife and son about his whereabouts, lied to the Internal Revenue Service about his income, and lied to himself about how he was being a good, decent family man making the best of a difficult situation.

Right up until the day Louise banged on Connie's front door.

CHAPTER 4

AMANDA

Amanda Devlin hit the FM scan button on her twenty-fourth birthday present to herself, hoping to rescue herself from the depths of a sadness nearly as bone-deep as the dampness outside the car.

The first couple of days after buying the dazzling Blaupunkt receiver and cassette player she hadn't been able to stop gawking at it, as if it was a work of visual rather than auditory art. Such a high-end stereo might seem out of place in her five-year-old Mazda, and it was definitely out of place in her otherwise judiciously-crafted budget. But sometimes you just had to go for it. And after somebody broke into her car and ripped out her old factory stereo, she did just that—and got the Blaupunkt. Along with a credit card bill that made her wince.

Over the few weeks since buying it, she had gawked every time it ran through its array of station choices, with its auto-scan readout listing the station frequency as it bounced along: too cool for words. And the clarity of reception was incredible—except when she was in the dead zone southeast of Concrete on her way to Darrington, as she was now.

Not that it made much difference what she could pick up on the radio. She had long since gotten outside of the measly range of the very few Seattle and Everett stations that ever played the kind of music she wanted to hear, bands like Green River and Soundgarden. Some radio jocks and magazines were starting to call their pulsating sound grunge, which made no sense whatsoever to Amanda; grunge was what you found in the corners of your toenails, not on your favorite radio station.

She watched as the frequency scan paused on a light rock/pop station in Bellingham and hit the button to keep it there, one she knew would fade out as soon as she cut south from Rockport. It didn't take much in the Cascades to wreak havoc on a radio signal—especially, it seemed, if the song was any good. She listened: This one was Madonna. *Next.* The receiver bounced through a country station ... then to the NPR feed, which she often listened to but wasn't in the mood ... a Mount Vernon rock station playing ... what. She hit the button to stop it and see if she could make out the song. She didn't recognize it, but it was catchy enough until it ended a half-minute later and the station went to a commercial. *Next.* Country. *Next.* More country. *Next.* "—because forgiveness may not come easy for you, but it comes easy for Him." One of those radio mega-preachers.

Forget it, she thought. She pushed in a Green River cassette and, with its first note, accidentally did the one thing she had been trying to avoid for as long as possible.

She thought about J.D.

God, he used to love this song, she thought, and began to cry again.

John Dallman was the reason she was making the drive to Darrington, a trip she had made numerous times since he had come home from that hospital in California. She had argued against his moving back to east county, considering how difficult it was going to be for him to be able to get around now. He needed a support network—not only friends, but people who made it their job to make his life easier. J.D. wasn't willing to move in with his mom and her husband, who had returned to southwest Oregon after his brother died. Amanda told J.D. he should swallow some pride, go to Grants Pass and lean on them for a while, or find out if he could move back in with his dad. J.D. wouldn't have any part of either option. Even after he came back to Washington over her protests—and his mother's—Amanda continued trying to convince him to live in Seattle, where he would have far easier access to services, or at least in Everett.

But telling him what to do hadn't worked. Neither had begging.

The odd thing was the way he seemed so at peace with everything. Sad, yes. Destroyed, yes. But seemingly no longer at war with his fate. Somehow at peace with it … as if being miles and hours from the people who might be able to help him was precisely what J.D. wanted.

⚔

They had long since metamorphosed from ill-matched lovers to easy friends by that weekend the previous October when J.D. got the call that would change his view of the world—would, in fact, remove it.

They had met in the summer of 1986—she a forestry management student at Washington State University on a summer internship with the Forest Service, John Dallman a trail crew foreman seven years her senior. In what she recognized in retrospect as youthful idealism, she had been charmed by what she perceived as this sort of renaissance man, a rugged bohemian.

J.D. had an art degree and was a serious though commercially unsuccessful painter. To pay the bills and because he loved the deep-breathing freedom he felt in the outdoors, he spent seven months every year cutting trees for the Forest Service. Most of his time was spent with an antique hand saw miles within the Mount Baker Wilderness, where federal guidelines outlawed machines of any kind, including the very chainsaws that would have allowed J.D. and his trail crews to clear four times as many trails. He endured those long shifts in the backcountry, many of them in silence broken only by his own panting and the rhythmic rasp of saw teeth carving the meat of a tree, just as easily as his endless hours in front of a canvas. In the long nights Amanda spent imagining his arms around her over the early weeks of that first summer, the man in her dreams was a romantic soul, a tortured artist whose demons could only be purged when he felt the redemption within her arms.

Of course, that was before the final weeks of that summer, when she did hold him within her arms and realized just how impregnable was the chamber encasing those demons—and J.D. himself. Sharing his bed didn't grant access; she was only being allowed to pass through, a social respite from the solitary world of his painting.

After finishing her bachelor's the following summer, she hooked on with the Forest Service as an interpretive ranger at the Sedro Woolley station, an hour's drive from Darrington. She rented a place in Concrete, midway between her job and his place. And after a very brief rekindling stage, she and J.D. spent most of the next three months as something resembling a couple. But even when she was with him, each was still alone.

J.D. opened up only just enough to display his voluminous baggage, but never enough to cut any of it loose. He had come from a broken home, his mother having had an affair and left before he had even entered elementary school. His brother, born to his mother and her second husband, had died while still in high school. J.D. was a starving artist, but an artist nonetheless—immersed so deeply within his painting, anyone around was left feeling like an imposition. On the rare occasions Amanda stayed at his place, she would hear him leave the bed in the middle of the night and go to the second bedroom, where he did his painting. And that was a world into which she was never invited.

Their liaisons were usually in her bed, though, not his. His rationale was simple: It made sense logistically, preventing her from having twice the drive to work the next morning. But that seemed to her like gauze dressing to conceal the truth: Having anyone come into his home—filled with the accoutrements of the art that so consumed and complicated his soul—was too much of an invasion for him. And after three months of meeting him halfway, she came to realize this was as close as they would ever get to being a couple. She pulled back, and they settled for friendship. The canvas remained his mistress.

That, she thought, was probably why he didn't seem particularly upset when his trail-crew foreman contract wasn't renewed the following spring.

With conservation groups' concerns about logging impacts on northern spotted owl habitat and the resulting lawsuits already beginning to cut into the Forest Service's ability to support its own budget with timber sales, the handwriting was on the wall: Budgets were going to take a hit, and trail crew foremen were a dime a dozen. And a couple of months after J.D.'s position was eliminated, ironically, he managed to hook on at a lumber mill in a logging community down in Cowlitz County that wasn't yet reading from the same wall.

She remembered almost everything about the evening that October when J.D. had driven the three hours from his little apartment near the lumber mill. He made a big deal of coming up to "celebrate their anniversary"—the one year, almost to the day, since they had come to what Amanda had believed to be their mutual agreement to evolve from lovers to friends. Their celebration turned out to be a couple of nice bottles of cabernet from a Yakima Valley winery and a for-old-times roll in her bed—which felt a little odd in light of the "anniversary," she thought, while at the same time feeling really good.

But what J.D. had also come up for, it turned out, was to pick up some of his old trail-crew gear for a logging trip down to Humboldt County, heart of the old-growth redwoods. Even though he'd been working only in the mill, this was sort of a special job, he told her—not more than a few days' work, but long ones, with the potential of plenty of overtime because it was kind of a hurry job.

Amanda didn't like the sound of it, but J.D. actually sounded excited about it.

"I can definitely use the extra money," he told her. "Hell, I'm lucky they've gotta do this big push to get the job done in a hurry, so they're bringing in extra crews. That's the only reason I'm getting to go."

"Yeah, but I thought you worked in the mill."

"I do. I'm the off—"

"The off-bearer, right. First rough cut on the log. I know."

"Yeah. Well, there's lots better money in the field than in the mill. And they need lots of bodies at this California deal."

"How come?"

"Well, the stand we'll be cutting has been a big deal with the grape nuts— the, uh, environmental people. It's been in court, the whole deal. Company got sued, the grape nuts climbed in some trees to stop the logging, yadda yadda yadda."

"Grape nuts. I never heard that before," Amanda said. "Except, you know, Grape Nuts."

"Ewell whatsisname. From those commercials."

"Grape nuts. Sounds like a putdown."

He nodded. "Yeah, well. I work at a lumber mill, so everybody I work with hates 'em. A lot of the guys are second-generation in the industry. It rubs off."

"Sounds funny coming from you, though. You're kind of a Ewell Gibbons greenhead yourself." She smiled as she said it, but she was looking at him oddly. "Even when you were working with the trail crews, I always got the idea you hated even cutting the blowdowns off the trails. Like it was just a necessary evil that came with getting to work outdoors."

"Yeah, well, now I'm seeing it from another side. And when you're around a bunch of people whose lives depend on cutting trees, you start to resent it when somebody starts screwing with their livelihood because they like trees better than people."

"I don't think it's that simple. But what all are they doing?"

"Ah, you know. Sand in the tank. Slashed tires. Busted out windshields. They'll mess with the engines, cut hoses or belts, whatever."

"Any tree spiking?"

He shook his head. "Just rumors. From what I hear, that stuff was going on for months before the grape nuts' lawyers got a court order to block the logging, and then it pretty much stopped. But now it looks like the court's leaning in the company's favor. Ruling's supposed to come down tomorrow. And when the company gets the OK, they're gonna announce operations starting Monday. That way the grape nuts can call all their TV buddies to be out there first thing Monday morning and get pictures of these eco-heroes doing their thing, climbing the trees to keep us from cutting them down or whatever they're gonna do."

"And?"

"And we'll be going at it first thing Saturday morning. All weekend long, sun-up to sundown, with every crew they can fit on that contract. And I'll be there."

"You know that's not actually going to fool them, right? You know those people, the greenies, they've probably got people out there in the woods right now, watching for just this kind of thing."

"Yeah, probably. But the bosses think it'll at least give us a head start before they get out there in force. Give the security crews a chance to get dug in."

"Well, you just be careful out there. Even if those people aren't out there messing with you, logging's dangerous enough by itself. So you watch out for yourself down there. Watch out for widowmakers. And spikes. You never know."

"Don't worry. I'm not gonna be one of the fallers. I'm just gonna be buckin'."

"Well, that makes me feel a little better. But you be careful anyway."

According to everything Amanda was later told by the guys on J.D.'s crew, he had been careful. But there was no way he could have seen the spike.

Whoever had put it in had gone to great pains to camouflage it. It had been pounded into the tree at a sharp downhill angle a good forty feet up from the base, its entry point then deftly covered over with a little wood putty to hide any dark spot the metal might bleed into the wood. J.D. was cutting the downed tree into logs, just sweaty business as usual, when his saw hit the spike. The chain snapped and he instinctively recoiled, causing the chain to flail back like a poison tentacle. It raked him across the face, quickly pulling his ill-fitting, borrowed goggles aside and lashing his eyes in a terrible, shrieking moment that left him in shock.

And in utter darkness.

The goggles had been only marginally unfit for the task of defending the assault, and so only the cornea of his left eye was lacerated. The right eye instead received a shock to the retinal nerve from the blunt force of the chain reaction.

The ramifications on both eyes, though, had been the same. He couldn't see with either.

Doctors tried a corneal transplant they were certain would return vision to his left eye. The surgery didn't take.

They were still confident J.D.'s right eye would, in time, recover enough from its retinal damage to regain some or all of its sight.

They were wrong about that, too.

Amanda hadn't even knocked on the door when she heard his voice from inside.

"Come on in. It's not locked."

He was sitting on the sofa. He wasn't wearing sunglasses; that wasn't surprising. He didn't get a lot of visitors, and he didn't seem to care about how the blankness in his eyes affected the few he did get.

"You know you shouldn't leave the door unlocked," she said.

"Why not? You always do."

"That's different. What if I'd been somebody else?"

"I could hear you on the sidewalk. Who walks like you do?"

"What's that supposed to mean?"

"Nothing. Hey, you're still wearing Giorgio. Smells good. I like it."

Amanda felt a warm fuzzy, then banished it. She leaned down over him, put a hand on the side of his neck as she kissed him on the cheek, and sat next to him.

"Thanks," she said. "You gave it to me."

She watched him not quite watching her. His left eye, once a beautiful green, had a yellowish scar across the iris.

"I can't believe there's any left," he said. "That was two years ago."

"A little bit goes a long way."

As she took in the room, her eyes fell on a painting she hadn't seen before. She had never seen original artwork displayed in his house, an absence she had always found odd. This one was on the far wall in a simple frame, its image seemingly ordinary but, upon further study, anything but. In the foreground, but slightly off to one side, was a young man in a flannel shirt and a skull cap, jeans and high-ankle work boots. Gripped in one of the man's hands and cradled with the other was a chain-saw, and he stood, one foot resting against the stump of the tree he had apparently just cut down. He was standing at a broadside angle, side-lit with an alpenglow effect, and Amanda thought it looked vaguely like a self-portrait of J.D., only at a younger age.

"I don't remember seeing that before," she said.

J.D. emitted a short, sad laugh. "I can't see what you're talking about."

"I know that," Amanda said, trying to make it sound funny. "The painting. Have I seen that before?"

"Probably not, unless you've been digging around my art closet. I haven't had it out."

"When did you put it up?"

"Couple days ago."

"I don't understand. You just put it up?"

"Yeah. What's not to understand? I ... just ... put ... it up. Just because I'm blind doesn't mean I can't hammer a nail into a wall and hang something on it. I'm not saying I didn't smash my thumb once or twice doing it."

"But you can't ..."

"See it?"

"Well, yeah."

"Can you see it?"

She caught herself nodding. "Yes. I can see it."

"Do you like it?"

"Very much."

"Then what's the mystery?"

"It's yours, though, right? You painted it?"

He held his palms up: DUH.

"I've never seen one of your paintings before."

"Sure you did. You saw lots of them."

"Yeah, but nothing done. They were always things you started and didn't finish."

"They weren't good enough."

"Yeah, you really suck." Her timing was perfect and they laughed together. Her eyes fell on the painting again, the image of the logger. "This one here? It's really good, J.D. Seriously."

J.D. seemed to darken at the compliment. She waited for him to say something, but he had gone to another place.

"When did you paint it?" she asked.

"I just finished it."

Her breath caught and it took her a few seconds to see him concealing the hint of a wan smile. She gave him a jolt to the shoulder. "You jerk! That's not funny."

He cocked his head. "I thought it was."

"Well. You were wrong. As usual." She whacked him again, lighter this time. "For a few seconds you had me believing it."

She watched as he closed his eyes and reopened them, blinking, then just closed them. His head drooped forward.

"Yeah, that's pretty ridiculous, all right," he murmured. "Believing I could still paint."

"Hey. C'mon. Don't do that."

"Don't what? Be honest about what I can't do anymore?"

"You don't know that. The doctors said—"

"The doctors said a lot of things. They also said if I got some sight back, it would probably happen in the first few months."

"It hasn't been that long."

"Nine months, Amanda. It's been nine months. And one operation."

She opened her mouth to retort but couldn't come up with anything supportive.

"Last few months down in California," he said, "you know what I was doing, right?"

"You were at the hospital."

"At *A* hospital. The rehab kind. Where they teach you how to be a blind person. That's where I was when you visited me."

"I knew that. I just thought ... I mean I figured ... I don't know. But your sight could still come back in the one eye. And they could try another transplant. They haven't ruled it out completely, right?"

"No, not completely, but—"

"So you have to believe. You have to, J.D."

"Why."

"Because miracles happen."

"Yeah. Right." J.D. cleared his throat as if to change the subject. "You want something to drink? I've got Pepsi, some grape juice, I think. Nothing alcoholic, I'm afraid. A blind guy stumbling around his own place too drunk to find the bathroom—not a pretty picture. Ice water?"

"I'm fine."

He stood up anyway. In halting but determined steps, J.D. moved into the kitchen, his left hand reaching out for the wall, feeling it lightly as he went, the right held closer in front of him, like a boxer in classic defensive position. Amanda watched him, frustrated by his shell, at a loss for the right thing to say.

"You didn't answer my question before," she said. "When did you do the painting?"

J.D. stopped at the refrigerator and waited several seconds before opening it, as if weighing a response. "It was the last thing I did before I went to Humboldt County for that job. I wasn't even really done with it."

"It looks finished. I mean, it looks like something you'd see in a gallery."

"Yeah, well. That's never going to happen."

"Why not? It's good enough to be—"

"It doesn't matter how good it is," J.D. said, closing the refrigerator and turning toward the living room. "Galleries sell paintings, Amanda. It's a business. And they stay in business by putting up paintings that will bring people into their galleries to buy paintings, and then bring them back to buy more paintings by those same artists. And I won't be bringing anybody any more paintings. It doesn't do them any good to hang this one. You get it? *I can't paint anymore.*"

His outburst left the room bloated with sudden silence. J.D. opened the refrigerator again and reached in, pawing around until his hand landed on what he was searching for. He pulled up a Pepsi can, but didn't pop it open until he had made his way back to the sofa and deposited himself in the same spot he'd left. Finally, he took a couple of sips.

When he didn't turn his face to her at any point during this process, Amanda felt almost as if he was ignoring her. *That's ridiculous*, she thought. *Why would he look at you? He can't see you.*

"What's it look like?" he asked.

"What."

"The painting."

"You know what it looks like. You painted it."

"Yeah. A long time ago. Tell me about … the colors."

"Well … there's red and black in his shirt. His cap is red, too, not as bright as in the shirt though. There's green in the trees in the background."

"And his eyes, too, right?"

She studied J.D.'s expression, then rose and crossed to the painting. "Yes. Green eyes. Like yours."

He grunted softly. "Green. Yours are blue, right?"

"Yes."

"I'm not sure I remember what green looks like."

She turned back to him, stung. She had never thought to ask about what he saw in his darkness. If there were colors. If there was anything.

"Seriously?"

"I mean, I have an idea. I still know red. I can still imagine it, I mean— sort of see it. And blue too, I think. I can sometimes picture what the sky used to look like. And the clouds, of course. But it all comes and goes. It's so dark in here. In … my head. And what I do remember gets sucked down into the darkness, little by little. What people look like, even people I've known forever. You know how I remember what you look like? Those pictures we took in that photo-mat at Pike Place Market that time."

"You mean those little four-for-a-quarter things? Where we were making faces?"

"Yeah. Them. But there was one where you were just smiling, not acting for the camera." "Like you did in all of them," she said, jokingly accusatory.

"Guilty as charged. I don't remember those other pictures and my stupid face, but I remember yours because I can always pull up your smile on that one. I mean, I can sort of picture you now while you're talking to me, and even sometimes when you're not here. But mostly, yeah, I just see the expression in that picture."

"So how do you remember it? I can barely remember even taking them."

"The rest of 'em I don't remember so much. The smile one I remember because I kept it in my wallet."

"I never knew that. For how long?"

"I dunno. Since that time at Pike Place, I'm guessing."

Oh. Oh no, J.D. "Where is it now?"

"Why?"

"No reason. Just … curious."

"Still in my old wallet, I suppose. I don't exactly look for it any more."

"J.D. … Pike Place, that was a long time ago. I thought … we figured things out since then. Where we stood."

"Hey, sorry, some people can just turn emotions off. I can't do that."

"I didn't turn anything off, J.D. It just went away. For both of us. For you most of all, whether you want to admit it or not."

"Is that right? You seeing inside me now?"

"No. Not now, not then. I never could. You never let me in. Not into your painting. Not into your silence. You were always a mystery."

He nodded. "Kinda funny now, though, in a way."

"Tell me. I could use a laugh."

"Not that kind of funny."

"Tell me anyway."

"I wouldn't let you see inside. And now I can't see out. Can't see you. Can't see to paint. Can't see what I've already painted." He shook his head. "I want you to have that painting. Take it with you."

"I can't do that, J.D. That's the only painting you've ever liked enough to hang up. You need to keep it."

"How much sense does that make? I can't see it. Maybe if I could, I wouldn't like it any more than the other stuff I threw away."

"But it's good, J.D. Really good."

"Then take it."

"No. It belongs with you."

"It belongs to somebody who's been gone nine months. I hung it up to remind myself I'm a painter. What a crock that idea was. I can't see it, and now even knowing it's there, all it does is remind me I'm *not* a painter. Not any more." He took a big, sad sigh. "Amanda, I don't know how long I can do this."

"Do what, exactly."

"Nothing. Absolutely nothing at all."

"Then do something."

As soon as she said it, she wished she could take it back.

She would wish it even more when she got the call three weeks later that J.D. had indeed done something.

He had turned on the gas and gone to bed.

CHAPTER 5

GROMMAN WANDLE

At the sound of Connie's voice and whatever it was she was saying—Tucker couldn't understand a word of it—the yapping began anew from the other bedroom.

"You said that dog is Connie's, right?" he asked. "It's not in there with her?"

Micah took in a big breath and exhaled slowly, obviously measuring his words.

"Mom is ... not like you remember her. That's why I've been putting the dog in the other room. She's got some issues."

"Issues. Yeah, I'd say dying's a pretty big issue."

Micah shook his head. "Yeah, but it's ... worse than that."

"Worse than dying?"

"You'll understand when you see her. I've been trying to keep a home-care nurse with her a lot of the time, but for a while there she was really going through them. Not so much now."

"I don't understand," Tucker said.

"She's been sleeping more." Micah shook it off. "Come on. She's awake now, might as well see if she knows you."

Tucker wondered about that—*if?*—and followed Micah to the short hall-way. The moment Micah opened the door, his demeanor changed to one of alarm.

"Mom!" he called, rushing into the room.

Tucker hurried to the door and saw what his brother had seen: Connie—incognito at the moment—squirming around on the floor, struggling to pull an old nightgown off over her head, baring her lower body. Tucker tried to avert his eyes from her nakedness but was riveted, horrified by what he saw: pale, feeble legs, their muscle tone stripped, covered by faded blotches that spoke of disease. She remained frantic in her efforts with the nightgown as Micah hunkered beside her, gently pulling it back over her body. Tucker kept his distance.

Connie's face was almost unrecognizable. Her face looked skeletal and dry, as if flow of all blood and nutrients had ceased. Her hair looked as if it were trying to escape her head and much of it already had, her scalp being much thinner than he remembered. Her eyes were wild, seeming not to see Micah even as he was tending to her. Not that there was much else to see—a bare chest of drawers, a bedside table with a sturdy-looking lamp, and the bed itself, its sheets mauled into disarray.

Tucker watched his half-brother patiently work with his mother, obviously already accustomed to the nightmarish apparition she had become.

"Mom, we're going to stand up now," Micah said in a little voice, as if he were coaxing a one-year-old learning to walk. "OK? You're going to stand up."

"Going going," she said, trying feebly to shake away his attending grip. "Going going."

"That's right, Mom," Micsh said. "We're going over to the bed where you can rest."

"NO! GOING!"

Tucker was surprised to hear that kind of volume coming out of that disintegrating body.

"You're right, Mom, we're going," Micah said, never changing his steady tone. "We're going over there right now."

"Going home! Home!"

"Yes, Mom." He had succeeded now in getting her to her feet, though she still looked wobbly. "We'll go home right now."

"Home. Home. Gromman. Gromman wandle. Going home."

The dog's incessant barking added to Tucker's sense of being in an asylum. He had a mental image of Jack Nicholson's fellow patients in "One Flew Over the Cuckoo's Nest" and wanted nothing more than to be away from this insanity.

"Going going," babbled the woman who had once been Connie.

"Going crazy is what," Tucker blurted. "Jesus Christ."

Connie turned at the sound of his voice and for a few moments didn't seem to be able to bring him into focus. Then she screamed, loudly and repeatedly.

"GROMMAN WANDLE! GROMMAN! GROMMAN!"

Micah looked around at his brother and waved a dismissing hand. "Why don't you go outside until she settles down."

Relieved, Tucker escaped into the living room and listened as Connie's nonsensical shouts, interspersed with the sound of Micah's patient prodding, became more subdued and finally disappeared altogether. Tucker had thought very little about Connie in several years and would never truly have described his feelings for her as love, but nonetheless he felt a sense of profound sadness at what she had become—which he immediately buried behind a scab of dark sarcasm. That had always been his way.

It was several minutes before Micah came out of the bedroom, closing the door behind him. He looked absolutely spent.

"How long's she been speaking in tongues?" Tucker said. "Gromman wandle? What the hell is that?"

"Don't know. That started a couple of days ago. Stuff like that comes and goes. Sometimes she's pretty good. Making sense. Sometimes she's like that."

"Sounds like she's out of her gourd. Does she even know who you are?"

Micah seemed to consider the answer for several seconds. The dog's barking, which had ceased when Connie had stopped bellowing, was once again an unrelenting onslaught.

"Why would anybody keep a dog like that?" Tucker groused.

"She lived alone, Tucker. She's been alone for six years. I've visited whenever I can, but basically that dog's been her only companion." Micah stepped into the hall and jerked open the door behind which the dog's protests emanated. "GULLIVER!" he hissed. "Quiet. Shh."

The dog quieted instantly and, miraculously, or so it seemed to Tucker, stayed that way even after Micah shut the door.

"Gulliver?" Tucker made a face.

Micah shrugged. "Mom always wanted to travel. Never did. I don't think she ever left the state." He sounded on the verge of tears.

Tucker sat on the sofa and bounced, testing the springs. "Nah, she even left the country. Remember, we went to Stanley Park that time."

The waterfront park in Vancouver, British Columbia, was less than a three-hour drive from White Bluff. The family had gone once, Big Frank granting a birthday wish to his wife and then griping about it all the way there and back.

"I think this is the same thing the old man got at that flea market," Tucker said. "Different cover. Same piece of shit sofa."

Micah sat down on the other end of the sofa—which, being eight feet long, kept them at an appropriate distance. They sat in silence for nearly a minute.

"In answer to your question, yes," Micah finally said. "She does know who I am. Most of the time. Not always. At least she seems to understand I'm on her side. She's not afraid of me, anyway. Not usually."

"Jesus."

"Hey. Could be worse."

"I can't see how."

"She could be rolling around in her own shit and vomit at some state hospital where nobody gives a damn because she's just one of thirty patients on her floor doing exactly the same thing. I think that would be worse."

Tucker swallowed. It did sound worse.

"Well, that's probably where she'd be if ..." Micah's voice trailed off. "That's where she was headed when I got here. Aunt Judy and Aunt Patty, they'd been taking care of her the best they could but finally couldn't deal with it anymore. They were all set to turn her over to the state hospital when they called me. And I couldn't let her go there."

"How long you been here?"

"Month and a half, maybe."

"Jesus. With her like that? And that dog? I'd go apeshit."

"I don't stay here all the time. I rented a little apartment in Darrington on a month-to-month basis. Until … you know."

"Til she checks out."

Micah shook his head. "Man, you're cold."

"Says the coldest fish of all time. So what's she got, anyway? What's she … dying of?"

Micah didn't answer right away, and this irritated Tucker as if the wait was intended to foster that very irritation.

"So?" Tucker prodded. "You gonna tell me?"

"OK. The doctors aren't sure, but they think it's something called general paresis. It's basically eating away at her brain."

"So it's like a cancer of the brain?"

"No. I mean, yeah, it's killing her, but it's not cancer. It's also pretty much making her crazy. Paranoid. Hallucinations. Depressed all the time. Sleeps all day sometimes."

"Jesus."

"For a guy who doesn't go to church, you use his name a lot."

"Eat me. So how you get something like that? This general … paralysis or whatever."

"Well. It's pretty simple, actually. You have sex with someone who has syphilis."

⅄

It had, of course, been yet another unintended gift from Big Frank, this one exponentially more unwelcome than the first.

That it had taken Big Frank as long as it did to contract a sexually-transmitted disease was nothing more than chance. He had become bored with Connie—and fed up with the demands and trials of fatherhood —just as quickly as he had with Louise. The woman from whom he picked up the bacteria did not represent the first dalliance of Big Frank's second marriage, nor even the first in which he did not use a condom. By the time Big Frank first found the tiny, only mildly sensitive nodule at the base of his penis three months later, he couldn't even remember the name of the bar hag he'd gotten it from.

Big Frank had an inkling about what the bump might be, and any doubt was removed at his next medical examination. After prescribing penicillin for Big Frank, the doctor said he'd need to check Connie for symptoms. Big Frank quashed that notion in no uncertain terms. He and his wife had been on the outs sexually for months, he said, and he'd gotten it from some nameless skank on his solitary one-night stand. And since he knew his wife couldn't possibly have it, went his reasoning, Big Frank Dodd wasn't about to have anybody ruin his marriage by telling his wife he'd been unfaithful to her. *You gettin' my drift, doc?*

After which Big Frank promptly changed doctors. And, just to make sure the doctor didn't get any ideas about contacting Connie behind his back, added a second, unlisted phone line for the house. He kept the old number as his work phone line, with Connie and the boys on strict orders never to answer it. He wasn't about to go through another divorce and have to pay another money-sucking lawyer. Hey, the chances of Connie getting this shit were slim to none anyway, right? All he had to do was just ride this thing out.

He was, of course, wrong and right. Connie contracted syphilis, but its symptoms were minor, its initial ramifications nebulous and its persistence essentially overlooked until it was too late. Connie wasn't big on doctor trips anyway—a penchant not unrelated to Big Frank's woeful family medical insurance plan—and the condition advanced through its primary and secondary stages as if it were no more than recurring bouts with whatever bug was going around. After that, there was no one left at home to assess its spread by seeing the changes in her; Tucker and Micah had moved away, and Big Frank had gone to his death, his indiscretion undiscovered.

The only living soul around to watch Connie's descent from sanity and health was Gulliver.

⚔

"Ah. Syphilis. The gift that keeps on giving," Tucker said softly, shaking his head. "That motherfucker."

Micah had had a lot more time to come to terms with his mother's inevitable path and found an ironic humor in that. "Yeah. Literally and figuratively."

Micah went to the refrigerator and pulled out two beers from a six-pack. He held one up: *Want this?* Tucker gave him a thumbs-up, got up from the sofa and joined Micah at the kitchen table, sitting in two of those unmatched chairs.

"Thanks, bro," Tucker said as he popped the top. "So how come Connie got so sick with this shit? I mean, syphilis? Are you kiddin' me? It's a rash, for chrissake. They got pills you can take and it's gone like that. Or a shot, whatever." He snapped his fingers. "I know a guy in Vegas who got it and it was no big deal. Went down to the clinic, took care of it in an afternoon."

"Yeah, well, if you don't take the medicine, this is what can happen."

"That doesn't make sense. Why wouldn't she take the medicine?"

"She probably didn't know she needed to."

"What, like she didn't know she had V.D.? How would she not know?"

Micah had a number of thoughts about that but, for now, offered up only the less inflammatory possibilities.

"Well, apparently not everybody gets it in a real obvious way. Women, especially."

"Yeah, but the old man would have known he had it."

"Maybe he didn't have time to tell her he had it."

"Bullshit. How much time could it take? Uh, honey, I gave you the clap. Go to the doctor. Bingo. Done."

"Unless ..."

"Unless what?"

Micah took a sip of his beer. Waiting. *Come on*, he thought. *You can figure it out. Think it through.*

Tucker stood up, apparently frustrated with the whole thing. "You're a real pain in the ass, you know?" he said before taking a long swig on the beer, finishing half the bottle. He took a couple of steps around the kitchen before abruptly stopping.

Now you're getting it, Micah thought.

Tucker sat back down. "So you're saying he died before he had a chance to tell her."

"Maybe before he found out himself. Who knows. It's a possibility."

Tucker grunted his disapproval of this hypothesis. "And since you and everybody else blames me for the old man's death, if his dying kept him from telling Connie about the syphilis, that means this is my fault, too. Right?"

"I didn't say that."

"You don't have to. I can read it in your face."

"You never could read for shit, Tucker. I guess that hasn't changed." Even as he said the words, Micah felt that old fear of his brother's wrath—which Tucker had never actually unleashed upon him—creeping in again.

Tucker's eyes honed in on him as dark slits. "Don't push your luck, little brother."

Micah, his retort balled up in the knots of his reticence, looked away. Lacking the courage to curse his brother out loud, he cursed himself in silence.

Tucker drained the rest of his beer, his eyes never leaving Micah's. He set the empty bottle firmly onto the table, walked to the refrigerator and got himself another one—not asking for permission, Micah noticed, nor asking if Micah was ready for another himself. Just taking over the room as usual. Same old Tucker.

"You know," Tucker said, "I just thought of another possibility."

No. Don't even go there, Tucker.

"Suppose she didn't get it from him."

"You know she did."

"I don't know that."

Micah wasn't sure if his brother was just baiting him again, but still couldn't bring himself to challenge him. He'd always been afraid of his older brother. He could refute things Tucker said, could run logical circles around him, but couldn't get into his face and say, *I'm right and you're wrong.* He couldn't take a chance on his brother reading into it the tacit challenge: *You got a problem with that?*

He couldn't be Tucker. And that's how Tucker always beat him.

"Yeah you do," Micah said. "You know she got it from him because getting a venereal disease is exactly the kind of thing Dad would do and exactly *not* the kind of thing Mom would do."

Tucker made a face. "How you figure that? She screwed around with Big Frank when he was married to someone else. Exhibit One, your honor." He twisted the last four words for maximum effect.

"She didn't know he was married," Micah said, trying not to let his rising emotions make him sound whiny. "I can't believe you're even questioning who got it from who. I think it's just because you won't forgive Mom."

"Your mom."

"Yeah." Micah thought about the shriveling facsimile of his mother in the other room. "My mom."

"Not mine."

"Oh and brother did you ever make sure she knew it."

Tucker took another long swill, glared at him and walked slowly into the living room. He flopped onto the sofa, facing away from the kitchen.

"You just don't owe her a thing," Micah said in disgust. "Do you."

"I may owe some people. But not her."

Why did I even write you? Micah thought. *And why did you even come?*

"You know," he said, in as forceful a voice as he could muster. "You know as well as I do it wasn't Mom. It was Dad. He got syphilis, and he never told her. He just ... kept it to himself. And gave her a death sentence."

Tucker didn't move a muscle, but Micah knew that one got him. The stillness almost vibrated in the room.

"Jesus." Tucker craned back over his shoulder, checking Micah's expression. He stood. "Man, that's cold. Even for him. Jesus, she was his *wife*. Could he really be so much of a shit not even to tell his own wife he'd given her the clap? Especially if ... you know, this is what happens."

Micah shrugged. "Well, hey, you didn't think it was that big a deal. Syphilis, right? Just a rash? Maybe that's what he figured. She'd get a little sore or two, maybe a little irritation, and that'd be that. Maybe he just didn't want to have to explain to her where he got it."

"Didn't have the guts. Period." Tucker's words oozed of unresolved hatred. "Big Frank. Mister Big didn't even have the guts to be a human being. Killed my mom. Killed your mom. And didn't even have the decency to just take a gun and shoot 'em. Or himself."

Micah almost shuddered at the postscript and gaped at the brother who uttered it. But Tucker simply finished the rest of his second beer and walked to the sink, reached down and opened the cabinet below, still home to the trash basket. He tossed in the bottle—his first empty was still on the table, beside Micah's half-full first—and reached into the refrigerator. This time, though, he held it up for Micah to see—*you mind?*—before popping the top. He pointed into the refrigerator with the question—*you want another one?*

Micah shook his head and rose. "Well, this has sure been a lot of fun," he said. "But I've got things I've got to take care of. I need some stuff for my apartment. It's pretty bare. So: There's more beer in the fridge, but I guess you already know that. There's food in there, too."

He grabbed his jacket and went to the door.

Tucker sat up to attention. "Where you goin'?"

Micah made a production of pulling on his jacket. He couldn't come up with a clever retort. "Out."

Tucker looked around the room, looking confused and somewhat lost. "Well ... when are you coming back?"

Wow, Micah thought. *The great Tucker Dodd is afraid of being alone.*

Alone in a house with a crazy woman who had always considered him her older son.

"Don't know," Micah said, suddenly feeling a bit giddy over that prospect. "Later today, maybe." He opened the door, looked back with an odd feeling of triumph, and walked out, letting it slam behind him.

The dog began to bark again.

"Boy, that's just like you," Micah heard Tucker saying as he strode out to the Corolla. He paused at its door, knowing Tucker would want a last word.

"Typical Micah," Tucker said from behind the screen door. "The going gets tough, and Micah leaves."

Micah considered that. "Hmm. Leaving. I thought that was your department."

Then he climbed into his car and drove away.

CHAPTER 6

THE SCALES OF JUSTICE

Louise took the news of Big Frank's second family much harder than Tucker did. But she dealt with it with as much grace and strength as she could muster.

She kicked Big Frank out of their house. She took everything that could be perceived as essentially his and deposited it onto the front yard—right down to the 19-inch color TV that had become his mistress every night from six o'clock to last beer. She changed the locks and filed for divorce. With Big Frank too mortified to contest much of anything, Louise was quickly granted primary custody of Tucker, with his father paying child support and getting the boy for weekly six-hour visits. Louise asked for and received a schedule with more backbreaking hours at the care center, where many of the residents had to be physically moved on a regular basis. She safeguarded every penny to make up for the loss of Big Frank's paycheck.

She did her best to keep Tucker insulated from the pain and ugliness of the divorce. She even tried to put a good face on Big Frank's Big Lie by offering a little white lie of her own. When Tucker asked why Dad was at that other house and not coming home, she said some religions believe it's OK for a man to have more than one wife, and some of those men have children with those other wives, too.

"But I don't believe in those religions," she said, knowing full well Big Frank didn't believe in much at all, and certainly not anything involving religion. "And that's why I was so angry at your father earlier, because we … believe differently."

"Does Dad believe in those religions?"

"I guess he must," Louise said.

"How come he don't go to church, then?"

"Doesn't. Tucker, you know that. He doesn't go to church."

"How come? Isn't that what you're supposed to do when you've got some of those religions?"

"Well, it's not exactly in the rules that you have to go."

"Is that why we don't go?"

"Do you want to go to church, Tucker?"

"No. I was just wonderin'. Some of my friends go."

"Do they like it?"

"I dunno. Skelly Radich threw up."

"Skelly threw up in church?"

"I think it was outside. So if Dad has another wife, do his kids have other dads, too?"

"Well, you've got one dad. And that other little boy at that house, the little boy you saw, he has a dad, too."

Tucker darkened. "I know. And he's gonna get it, too."

"What do you mean? Who is?"

"That kid. I'm gonna kick his ass. Uh, butt."

Hearing that coming from her son's six-year-old mouth, Louise almost had to suppress a laugh. "No, I don't want you to do that. Promise me you won't."

"How come?"

"Promise me first."

"OK, I promise. But that's not fair."

"Life's not fair."

"Huh?"

"What you have to understand," she said, "is you and that boy both have the same dad. You both have Big Frank. And that's not the boy's fault. That's Big Frank's fault."

"Oh." Tucker nodded, being all grown up about this. "But you're my only mom, right?"

She almost burst into something between tears and laughter, and held it off by simply hugging him so tight he squirmed. "Yes, Tucker," she said, "I'm your only mom. I'll always be your mom. And you'll always be my baby boy."

"I'm not a baby boy."

"No, you're not, are you. You're my big strong man. And you're always going to be strong, you know that? We're going to be strong together."

"What about Dad?"

"He's going to be strong over at that other house."

Louise was devastated. It wasn't losing Frank that made it so hard; he had never become what she had hoped he would as a man, and as a husband he had actually regressed. What made the blow so bitter was how completely she had opened up, had created life with this man whose foibles she had accepted and whose marital devotion she had presumed. Having taken that emotional leap of faith meant there would be no net to catch her when the winds of Big Frank's Big Lie blew apart their house of cards.

In some ways, Louise was too strong for her own good. Although she yearned for a support system—somebody to talk to, preferably somebody who might also be able to pitch in if she came up short on rent money—she refused to run back to her parents in California. She wasn't willing to admit to them she'd made a bad choice, when she was having a hard enough time admitting it to herself.

Money was tight. The Superior Court judge set Big Frank's child-support payments high enough to feed and clothe Tucker, but too low for Louise to afford much else. Her paycheck for a basic 40-hour week, when augmented by the child support checks, was enough to pay the bills, but didn't leave a surplus for any eating out, any games or toys for Tucker, any trips to the zoo in Seattle or even any movies. The long-term care facility's management had approved her request for a 48-hour schedule—Sunday through Friday, but with the extra hours at her regular hourly rate, not as overtime. Louise wasn't sure that was even legal, but she needed the hours.

Louise's extra work day didn't change much for Tucker that hadn't already been changed. Big Frank's visitation schedule called for one day a week anyway, so Sunday, now a work day for Mom, became that day. The boy had long since made himself into a self-sufficient child, even before Big Frank's Big Lie. Years as a latchkey kid had taught him not to be afraid, alone in the house on those winter evenings when it was dark by four-thirty and neither parent would be back for hours. Now he learned how to do it without the welcome distraction of the television. He had already figured out how to cook himself the cans of chili and boxes of macaroni he found in the pantry—not by reading the directions, which stymied Tucker, but by trial and error and the willingness to swallow the failures as readily as the successes.

But the mother he welcomed home at the end of each work day was not the same.

Before Big Frank's Big Lie, Louise had believed her work enough of a noble calling —bringing grace and dignity into the final years of people's lives—to make bearable the aches and pains that came with it. Yes, perhaps she had accepted a smaller life than she had hoped for as a young woman in northern California. But doing her job with compassion and patience while improving others' lives, she believed, was valuable; it made her important. And she had long believed she could sense a thread of gratitude running through the residents—including the ones who were beyond speaking, and even those whose dementia made them cantankerous.

The fact she wasn't being paid much—certainly not commensurate with a job of such physically demanding and disagreeable aspects—actually helped her rationalize and stomach it. With Frank's contracting business now in its third year and beginning to generate enough word-of-mouth business to sustain itself, Louise's paycheck had been less of a necessity than a luxury. She didn't *have* to go to the care center, but she did—allowing her to view it as selfless missionary work, dedicated to preserving the dignity of the elderly.

Now that Big Frank's Big Lie had left Louise no choice but to do the work, though, those feelings of altruism were gone. It was a grubby job, too much of it spent cleaning up after the excretory lapses of wizened octogenarians who had become strangers to themselves and were just as apt to slap her as hug her. In the first several months following Big Frank's Big Lie, the gratitude she had allowed herself to imagine among the residents faded, making her feel as if she had been no less delusional than the worst of her dementia cases. They didn't care about her. Many even seemed to resent her, as if she was the face of their aged infirmity, the reason for their fading sense of self. And now she was subjected to that antipathy and incontinence not just for five days a week, but six.

Still, she poured herself into her work for the sake of her son, the best thing in her life.

And she poured into herself a great deal of the poison of man, one shot at a time.

I'm having a drink. After what I've been through, I deserve it. Screw it, make that a double.

And then another one.

⅄

Even when she wasn't drinking, Tucker couldn't help but notice the change in his mother.

For a few weeks, he missed his father. Later, as he watched his mother pretending for his sake her heart was still whole, he began to think of Big Frank only as the instrument of her pain. The purity of that sentiment, though, was contaminated by glimpses from five years as a family, memories of his father showing him how to bait a hook, wrestling with him on the living room rug, pretending to be tackled by a four-year-old in their front yard. That his mother's pain and that boyhood joy came from the same man stoked within Tucker hatred that was at once fervent and clouded.

Love and hate can share the same skin, but rarely are the consequences of their uneasy alliance confined within.

Barely a month after his mother had kicked Big Frank out of the house, Tucker began first grade, and his feelings about school quickly transitioned from excitement and curiosity to frustration and sullen anger. The sensibilities already roiling in his own emotional sea became an open wound. When he couldn't grasp the letters and the words as quickly as other kids, he took to joking around to hide his own embarrassment and frustration. After a few weeks of this, one of the other boys in his class made a crack about Tucker being a retard. The teacher scolded the boy and sent him to the principal's office, but that was nothing compared to what Tucker did to the boy at recess.

His offender's black eye and bloody nose sent Tucker on his first of what would become commonplace trips to the principal's office. When it happened again two days later—the second boy, this one larger by half a foot, faring no better than the first—Tucker was about to receive his first suspension from school. But when the principal couldn't get an answer at Tucker's home number—his mother being at work and unreachable, his father no longer taking calls at that residence—Tucker got the first of many reprieves.

Even as Tucker grew to dislike school, coming home was becoming even more difficult; no six-year-old wants to watch his mother slowly unravel. Often she would grab and hold him close without warning, as if she desperately needed him to be the anchor keeping her from drifting away. Sometimes she would hold him so long and hard he would eventually squirm to be released, and then feel guilty about it.

As Tucker began second grade, Big Frank started making noises about wanting greater visitation rights. Louise relented and actually tried to make it palatable to Tucker by saying it was good for a boy to spend time with his father. Tucker had no interest in seeing Big Frank—which was how he now thought of him, not as Dad—but went along with it to please his mother.

Usually the visits involved just the two of them. But sometimes Big Frank would take Tucker to that other house, where there was that woman and that little boy.

The first time Big Frank brought Tucker there, the introductions had not gone well.

"This is … this is your Aunt Connie," Big Frank said, as Tucker noticed an odd look being passed between the two grownups. "And this is … Micah."

"He's your brother," the woman called Aunt Connie said.

"He's not my brother," Tucker said. "I don't have a brother."

"Yes you do, big guy," Big Frank said. "Just because your mother never explained this to you doesn't mean it's not true. This is your brother."

"Bullshit," Tucker said.

Big Frank swatted him really hard on the butt. "Don't you cuss at me, boy," he snarled, leaning closer until his whiskered face was only inches from Tucker's. "And don't you ever sass me. I'm still your father. And that—" he pointed at Micah—"is your brother."

Tucker looked at the little boy they said was his brother and wanted to punch him in the face.

⋏

The custody battle turned out to be a short one.

Big Frank had been threatening Louise with a custody fight for the better part of a year. Louise suspected Big Frank was concerned less with the amount of quality time he got to spend with his oldest son and more with the amount of child support he was paying out.

Big Frank's lawyer, a Seattle sharpie named Everhart, managed to get it on the Superior Court docket at the county courthouse in Mount Vernon that next summer, less than a week after Tucker's eighth birthday. Louise was very much a child of her era, believing goodness would always triumph over evil, and so had hired the cheapest lawyer she could find. Any fool could look at the basic facts of the case and see it clear: She was the boy's mother and the father had sired another child outside of their marital union. It would be an easy call.

She was right about that. The judge had a remarkably easy time with his decision, after watching Louise get sliced and diced on the stand like a tomato on an infomercial. Big Frank's Seattle sharpie knew all the right questions to ask and just how to ask them.

"Miz Boudreoux, how many times have you been married? Does that number include Mister Dodd? So then, he was your second husband, is that correct? And your first marriage, when was that? Yes, and how long did it last? Until the divorce, yes. Oh. Really. Well, Miss Boudreoux, does six months seem to you like a short duration for a lifelong commitment? Did you have that part—the lifelong thing, I mean—was that part whited-out from your wedding vows? Yes, your honor. Withdraw the question.

"So, you'd had this six-month marriage, and you'd been attending college for … how many years was it? Well, it says here more than five years. Oh, some of that was part-time, well, that explains a lot, certainly. So, between fulltime and part-time, you were into your sixth year of university studies.

"How long does it generally take someone to obtain an undergraduate degree, say, a bachelor's degree? The average, then, whatever would be par for the course. Four years. So you had already obtained your bachelor's degree, then? Oh, you hadn't? Six-month wedding, six-year college plan with no degree. Huh.

"I'm sorry, your honor. I'll try not to wander. Miz Boudreoux, you were in the employ of a veterans hospital when you met Mister Dodd, is that correct? And is it true that he was a patient recovering from a combat injury when you sexually molested him?

"I'm sorry, your honor, I'll rephrase. Miz Boudreoux, when you rearranged Mister Dodd's hospital gown so as to expose his penis, did you begin stroking it because you did that for all the patients or because you felt it was medically necessary at the time?

"No, Miz Boudreoux, that's not what I asked. I just wanted to know if giving hand jobs to the wounded patients was included in your job description at the hospital.

"No ma'am, I didn't think it would be. And were you aware that in performing this sexual act upon Mister Dodd, a patient of the hospital in which you were on staff—yes ma'am, part-time, thank you for correcting me—were you aware you were acting in violation of generally accepted medical industry guidelines? And that you were breaking several state and federal statutes?

"Well, I'm not surprised you didn't know, Miz Boudreoux, because you have a history of ignoring laws, don't you?

"I'll rephrase, your honor. Is it true, Miz Boudreoux, that at the time you met my client, you regularly used marijuana?

"Your honor, I believe this is absolutely relevant, because it goes to the character of the witness and her suitability as a mother. I think if there's a history of poor choices and drug abuse, it's incumbent on this process to bring it to light, so your honor might be able to take it into consideration when you're determining what's best for the well-being of an eight-year-old boy.

"Thank you, your honor. Miz Boudreoux, is it true that not only did you smoke marijuana, but you also made a point of persuading my client to use it, and he resisted your efforts? I'll take that as a yes. Were you aware of the state and federal laws against the use of marijuana? Did you also smoke hashish? Were you aware the use of hashish is also against the law? Interesting. And isn't it also true you ingested psychotropic drugs for the expressed purpose of 'taking a trip'? Some of these were mushrooms containing the drug psilocybin, isn't that correct? And you also took lysergic acid diethylamide, commonly referred to as LSD or acid, isn't that also true? And were you aware the use of this drug was against the law? Wow. Marijuana, hashish, psilocybin mushrooms, LSD. You were a veritable pharmaceutical crime wave, weren't you?

"Yes, of course, your honor, I'll move on. Miz Boudreoux, to your knowledge, did Mister Dodd ever take any of these psychedelic drugs, the mushrooms or the LSD? No, in fact he refused when you asked him repeatedly, isn't that true? Repeatedly, yes, meaning more than once. You did ask him more than once, did you not? Yes. As I said. Repeatedly. And he refused. Repeatedly.

"Miz Boudreoux, were you aware when you met Mister Dodd that he was a decorated war hero? Oh, I'm sorry, was he not awarded the Purple Heart? Yes, thank you, that is correct, he was. And did he not receive that *medal* as recognition for his having been wounded in combat in Vietnam? When he finished his career in the United States Navy, do you remember the type of discharge he received? Honorable, yes. Thank you, Miz Boudreoux. An honorable discharge for an honorable man.

"Do you find that contrast telling in any way, Miz Boudreoux? That your husband—a member of the armed forces who proudly served his country overseas, a decorated war hero—felt strongly enough about the law of the land and the possible medical risks associated with these illicit drugs that he refused to participate? And that you went ahead and did it anyway?

"I'm curious, Miz Boudreoux. Since you were someone who had worked in the medical industry, did you take the time to read up on any of the research linking LSD to possible brain damage? No? Really. That's interesting. What about the potential for psychosis, or pronounced depression? Well, are you at least concerned about flashbacks? I'm sorry, your honor, withdrawn. Miz Boudreoux, did you happen to hear about or read any of the research findings that lab rats, while given LSD early in their pregnancy, very often resulted in stillborn or malformed offspring? You didn't see that? I'm surprised, Miz Boudreoux. I personally read about it in Time Magazine. As a mother, do you not feel compelled to at least try to do the right thing for your child? Withdrawn.

"Miz Boudreoux, I just have one more question: Is it true you ingested LSD on at least one occasion *after* becoming pregnant with your son?"

From that moment on, Tucker might as well have started packing. Because, in the eyes of the law of the land, Louise had lost him.

And that was the beginning of the end.

ᛤ

Whatever was in the bottles was making Tucker's mother worse.

He had smelled the contents of a bottle on one of those Saturdays the judge had said was all he could spend with her. Tucker could tell in one sniff it was that stuff that tasted like poison, like something you'd get from pirates or voodoo witches. One time, when he had been younger, his mother had made him take a sip of it, and when he gagged and spit it up, she grabbed both of his wrists and made him look in her eyes.

"There, you see? It *is* poison," she had said. "And now you know it's poison that tastes really bad. So don't you ever, ever, ever drink it. At least until you're old. Like me."

"C'mon, Mom, you're not old. Not like Missus Giese at school."

His mom laughed very softly. "Missus Giese is pretty old, isn't she."

"Oh yeah, she's all wrinkled. She looks like a lizard."

And now Louise laughed, out loud and long, and Tucker listened with a child's pleasure at parental recognition of his own cuteness until it seemed like her laughter changed and was no longer funny. It was the last time Tucker heard his mother laugh out loud. And by the time she finished, it sounded more like she was crying.

"Mom?"

Then she pulled him into one of those hugs that made him squirm.

And went right back to pouring herself glasses from the very same bottles she said were full of poison. The stuff the older kids called booze.

Tucker wanted to throw the bottles away. Or break them, or pour them out. Anything to keep his mother from becoming this other person, this stranger without color or life or joy, who seemed to love him not like Mom, but rather like a condemned person hovering over a last meal, not wanting that last bite to end for fear of what would come after.

But he didn't do any of those things. He didn't want her to have to feel ashamed, knowing her own son had done this for her own good. Nor did he want her to get mad and create a scene, which she did sometimes when she'd had too much of the poison.

So he began hiding it.

Over the five or six Saturdays he spent with her—even the last one—he managed to slip away long enough to go to the cabinet where she put the bottles and move them to a different cabinet, perhaps behind some boxes of cereal, anything big enough to hide them. Maybe then, if she couldn't find them, she wouldn't always look as if she hadn't slept in a week. Or had spent the entire week passed out.

She looked that way on their final Saturday. He had been so excited to see her, after another unhappy week at Big Frank's with that woman he was supposed to call Aunt Connie. But when he'd gotten to his mom's house, she had obviously been drinking already and he'd practically had to force her to get off the sofa. All she wanted to do was sit with him on the sofa and hold him.

"C'mon, Mom," he pleaded on that last day. "It's our only day together. I want to do something. We never go hiking any more like we used to. Remember when we saw those baby deers? Yeah, and that was right down the hill from where we found the huckleberries that time, remember? Why don't we go huckleberry picking? Isn't this the time of year when we're supposed to do it? Right after school starts?"

She nodded with a little, sad smile. When they'd first discovered the berry fields four years earlier, flourishing in some fairly new clearcuts just below the crestline of Benning Ridge, Louise hadn't even known what the pretty purple little berries were and she wouldn't let Tucker eat any of them until she knew they were safe. After she found out by asking some of the people where she worked, she and Tucker had become a crack huckleberry team, and the activity had been a seed she would plant in his mind weeks in advance to prime his excitement. *It's almost huckleberry time …*

As Tucker pleaded, his mother raised her glass to her lips again but paused, seeming to weigh his urging against the pull of the poison. And she set it aside.

"OK, tiger. Let's go."

"All right!" he exclaimed, clapping his hands. Maybe this meant Mom was coming out of that dark place. Maybe she could be herself again.

She drove them to a pullout beyond which they could not drive—a sign posted there said the road was closed for an **ONGOING TIMBER OPERATION**. They decided to take a shortcut up the back side to Benning Ridge, but the bushwhack was anything but fun; the underbrush remained thick and difficult to traverse until they reached the clearcuts. There, the going didn't get much easier but it got a lot more fun, because the huckleberries were pretty much everywhere. But only a couple of minutes after they started picking, Tucker could hear his mother crying in the bushes below him. *Geez, Mom, not again*, he thought, and kept right on picking.

After an hour, Tucker's bucket was filled five inches deep with huckle-berries, a major haul. He pretended to be excited about it because his mother did, but he noticed her own huckleberries barely covered the bottom of her bucket. She was usually a far more prolific picker than he was.

They decided to avoid the bushwhack back to the car and take the easy way down, following the logging road. It was a longer walk, but at least it wasn't thorny and scratchy.

He heard the truck long before he saw it.

They were on the road where it followed a ridgeline, near the bottom of a sweeping right bend alongside a serious dropoff. It was a great view spot, but a bad place to be in the middle of the road with a logging truck coming downhill around the bend.

Tucker had spent most of the descent walking a few steps in front of his mother, partly to give her the privacy to cry, and partly because her crying was just hard to be around.

At the sound of the truck, he looked behind even though he knew it was still way up around the bend. He saw his mother shambling along behind him, swinging her bucket in a gentle cadence with her sluggish gait, her eyes to the ground. Tucker stepped to the inside of the road and continued walk-ing, right up against the slope across which the road had been cut, out of the path of traffic. It's what his mother had always taught him to do on logging roads.

But as he continued walking, waiting for the rumble of the advancing truck to call for him to turn around once again, he responded to a sudden impulse and turned back, as if he knew his mother was not right behind him where she should be.

And she was not.

She was still walking in the middle of the road, her eyes still down, not hearing the rumble—or, if she did, not heeding its warning. Tucker froze, his mouth open to shout at her when her distant gaze rose to meet his. Her eyes were puffy and dark from the off-and-on crying and the months of poison; she looked absolutely wretched. And it was obvious to Tucker she felt that way, too. She'd been that way since he'd had to go live with his father.

It was also obvious to Tucker she was standing in the middle of a narrow road with a logging truck bearing down on her, and there was nothing he could do about it.

Her eyes were still on his, her expression unchanged, when twenty tons of metal and wood slammed into her.

⚔

"What's your name?"

The woman had sat down beside him in the hallway and introduced herself with a maternal smile, as if they were going to be friends and everything was fine and he hadn't just watched his mother turned into a bloody rag doll. Tucker didn't know who this woman was or why she was talking to him. All he knew was the police officer hadn't allowed him to go with his mother in the ambulance, saying there was nothing he could do to help her. The cop didn't say she was dead, but Tucker knew. After that, the rest didn't really matter.

So he hadn't answered any questions.

The police officer was sitting at a desk within view of Tucker, talking on the telephone. This woman had arrived, spoken quietly with the cop and then come straight to Tucker.

"That's not fair, is it? I told you my name," she said. "Why won't you tell me yours?"

"Why should I?"

"I'm sorry about your mother."

"Why? Wasn't your fault. You didn't do it."

"I know. I'm just … sorry it happened. I really want to help you, but you have to help me, too."

"How you gonna help me? You can't make my mom alive again."

"No. I wish I could, but I can't."

"Then you can't help me."

"Who can we call to take care of you? How about your dad, where's he? I know you don't want to stay here in the police station."

Tucker didn't answer.

The police officer strode into the hall and gestured to the woman. "We found the car," he said to her, then turned to Tucker. "Is your mother's name Louise? Louise Dodd?"

Tucker just glared at him.

The officer said to the woman, "I called the only L. Dodd in the book. Nobody home." He cocked his head in Tucker's direction. "How you doing here?"

She turned to Tucker, again with that maternal smile. "We're still just getting to know each other. Isn't that right?"

"There's a bunch of Dodds in the county book," the officer said, turning to leave. "Maybe I'll eventually call one who knows the family."

The woman watched him leave and turned back to Tucker. "You know, we could save him some work," she appealed. "I sure wish you'd tell me your name I can call you so I don't always have to get your attention by going, *Hey handsome.*" She grinned at him as if they were sharing an inside joke.

Tucker weighed his decision. Not sure it mattered one way or the other, he relented.

"Tucker."

"Tucker? That's your name? I like that name. Are you named after somebody? A relative, maybe?"

His stare got harder. "Who cares? How does that matter?"

She sighed. "What about the rest of your family, Tucker? Where's your father?"

"I don't have a father."

She studied him, assessing his veracity, and finally gave him a consoling look. "I'm sorry to hear that," she said, then looked up at something across the way. Tucker followed her gaze and saw the police officer, his index finger up, mouthing the words, *I found the father.*

Tucker looked at the woman as she considered this revelation. But he felt no guilt about lying to her. He had long since given up caring about lying to grownups, and he did so easily. Except with his mother. And now she was dead.

"He says he found your father. Is he ... a stepfather?"

Tucker didn't answer. He didn't see the point.

CHAPTER 7

OWNERSHIP CAN BE MESSY

Micah had found the estate sale ad in the free shopper rack outside a Rockport gas station. The sale wasn't far from the duplex he was renting, and after only a couple of wrong turns, he found it in a nondescript neighborhood of older houses. A computer-printed note with an agency logo was on the front door, with **COME ON IN!** emblazoned in bold letters. The exclamation point seemed tacky to Micah, who associated estate sales with someone's personal loss and considered such punctuation better suited to used car lots and bingo halls.

Micah was hoping to find a cheap dresser, anything with drawers to stow his clothes at the apartment. But when he rounded a corner from the living room into the small, windowless adjacent area that must have served as a dining room, he saw the painting.

It was a portrait of a logger, standing chain-saw in hand over a tree he had obviously just cut down. There was something familiar about the logger that intrigued Micah, an aspect he attributed to the artist's gift—creating a face and an expression that would have broad appeal, meaning different things to whoever looked at it, but with an eerie familiarity that brought it home. The way the light caught the logger seemed to impart a look of strength, a certain omnipotence, but the expression wasn't one of power or pride. It looked like grief.

Micah didn't see a price tag and looked around for a selling agent. He didn't want to let the painting out of his sight, certain that anybody else seeing it would have the same reaction he did. Finally he spotted a man with a paunch, an ill-fitting, poorly ironed jacket and a clipboard, and asked how much for the painting.

The man scanned a page on the clipboard and the page beneath it.

"It's not on the list."

"Ad I saw said everything in here was part of the sale."

"Yes, that's right, it is. It's just not on the list of items the sellers have set a minimum price on. Generally that has the more big-ticket items."

"And this isn't on it? Seriously?"

Clipboard Man shrugged. "Maybe somebody just missed it. Or maybe they figured art's a matter of personal taste."

"Yeah, most of it is. But every once in a while it's … art," Micah said, studying the painting's color and being sucked in all over again by the intriguing, almost haunted expression of the logger—who still looked somehow familiar. That's a good painter, he thought, to create a face seemingly unknowable and yet known. "How much will you take?"

The man shrugged. "Fifty dollars?"

Micah blinked. "Are you serious?"

"Too much? I don't know, you tell me—twenty? Including the frame?"

"You really don't have a clue about this painting, do you? You actually work for these people? These estate sales people?"

"I'm covering for somebody. I usually just help buyers haul out the heavy stuff."

"I'll give you a hundred for it."

"You're jacking up your own price? Fine. Sold."

"I'm doing you a favor, pal. If the sellers find out you let this painting go for twenty bucks, they're going to go ballistic."

He paid in cash and waited while the painting was wrapped.

"What's the artist's name?" Micah asked. "I didn't see a signature on the painting. Do you know?" Not a chance. "Why am I not surprised."

Micah carried the painting to his car, which was nearly a half-block up the street. As he was unlocking his trunk, he noticed a woman—mid-20s, dirty-blonde hair and quite attractive, even in the heavy work boots—stepping out of an RX7 across the street. It was one of the classic pre-1985 models, Micah noticed appreciatively, before Mazda screwed with the design. And as soon as she noticed Micah, she froze momentarily and gaped at him for several seconds before hurrying toward the estate-sale home. As she walked, she looked back and watched Micah place the painting into his trunk. He was quite interested in watching her, too, so that's what he was doing when she turned back to eyeball him one more time before entering the home.

What was that about, he wondered.

Then: *Ya know, I didn't really get to see everything they had in there.*

So he went back in. And got there just in time to see the woman from the parking lot looking frenetically through the living room items, then accosting Clipboard Man.

"What are you doing? Who gave you permission to sell all of J.D.'s things?"

Clipboard Man was clearly nonplussed, but trying to control the situation. "And … who are you?"

"Amanda Devlin, I'm a friend of J.D.'s. Where do you come off selling his stuff?"

Clipboard Man held up a *justasec* finger and called someone named Grant from the kitchen. Grant, who in his suit certainly looked more the part than the erstwhile driver, excused himself from a couple of perusers.

"Is there a problem here?" he asked Clipboard Man.

"Uh, this is Miss, uh … she has a question."

As Grant turned to Amanda and opened his mouth, she beat him to the punch.

"Yeah, I got a question: Where do you come off selling J.D.'s stuff to whoever wants it? Who said you could do that? What gives you the right?"

"The executor of the will did. We were hired to do exactly that."

"Executor … who's that?"

He reached into his wallet, pulled out a business card and handed it over. "This is the gentleman's name."

Amanda eyed the card, frowned and handed it back. "Never heard of him."

"He's a cousin of the deceased. The next of kin named him the executor."

"Did J.D. even know him? He never mentioned him to me."

"I wouldn't know. But legally, it's his right and responsibility as the executor to dispense or dispose of the deceased's estate. Your friend didn't leave a will." Grant shrugged. "Happens all the time. And we were hired to liquidate the estate."

"Liquidate the estate. Pretty fancy language for selling all his stuff to total strangers."

Micah was watching the interchange from just inside the front door. Watching her. She was incredible.

As if she felt his gaze, Amanda Devlin turned and spotted him. She took a step toward him, then turned back to Grant. "And this guy—" she paused, gestured at him and pointed at the wall. "Where's the painting that used to hang there? Did you sell it? This guy, I saw him carrying out something that could have been a painting, and that's the only painting he kept here. The only one he had up, I mean."

The woman flashed accusing eyes at Micah. "Do you have it? Did they sell it to you?"

Micah looked to Grant.

Grant looked to Clipboard Man. "Is this painting on the list?"

No, he mouthed.

"I don't know anything about a painting, miss," Grant said. "It's not on our list—"

"Well, it was *in his house!*" she barked. "It was right there on the wall. And now it's not."

"I bought that painting," Micah blurted, but his voice cracked in the instant he spoke and he had to clear his throat and repeat himself. "I ... bought the piece on the wall there."

She threw up her arms and turned her wrath back onto Grant. "You can't sell his painting. It's not a *thing*. It's not a dishwasher. It's not a TV. It's … a piece of J.D. It *is* J.D. Did you even know that's a self-portrait? Sort of?"

She turned to Micah. "I want that painting back. J.D. gave it to me."

Micah looked at the man named Grant. "Wait a minute. Whose painting is this?"

"It's mine," Amanda said.

"No, it belongs to this gentleman. It was part of the estate, and it sold."

"But it wasn't yours to sell," Amanda barked, and turned to Micah. "And just because you paid for it doesn't make it yours."

"Hey, wait a minute, all I did was buy a painting. I don't know anything about the guy who painted it."

"No, you just saw something that looked like it would be a perfect fit for that bare spot on the wall above your TV set," she said, twisting the words. "I'll bet there's just enough room in there between your bowling trophies. I'll bet you talked him down on the price, too. Garage saler." She twisted her face to match the disdain in her words. "Did you make a real steal?"

"Miss, this isn't getting us anywhere," Grant interjected. "I can call the executor for you if you'd like to discuss the matter of the deceased's estate, but in lieu of a will …"

"Yeah, that's a good idea, let's just call him right up. And he can have his people call my people and we'll call a bunch of other people and we'll talk all about *the deceased's estate* and in the meantime this guy's got the only thing that meant anything to J.D. hanging in his …" She paused, her hand fluttering for an idea that didn't come. "… bowling alley or whatever."

It didn't come out right and Micah actually thought it was funny, but he was also a little tweaked by the bowling reference. He hated bowling. Big Frank had been in a bowling league, and always came home smelling smokier and beerier, not to mention happier … or, on the rare occasions when the big man had a bad night, not so happy. On one or two of those times he had found reasons to take a little of that less-happy vibe out on the woman of the house.

"All right, that's it, I'm outta here," Micah declared. He stalked out, and as he heard the door slam behind him, in the next instant he heard it open again and he turned to see her following him out, the poster child of if-looks-could-kill.

"Hey, I'm sorry about your boyfriend," he said, "but I liked his painting and I bought it."

"Oh, you're sorry about my boyfriend? You didn't know him, never been in his house before today and you bought a painting and now you think you know something about him? What, automatically he was my boyfriend? Oh, right, of course, I'm a woman, a man and a woman can't be friends, good god. What, did you see Harry Met Sally or something? Never get past high school back-seat groping?"

That struck Micah funny and, even in the same instant he was thinking *uh oh don't laugh*, he was doing just that.

"Back-seat groping?" he echoed, unable to resist. "Actually, I prefer to save that for my bowling alley."

He tried to say it deadpan but failed miserably at banishing the laugh. He quickly turned and walked to his car before he gave it away; he didn't want her thinking he was laughing at her pain. But laughing he was.

⅄

Micah, the little shit, had been gone for a couple of hours, and the silence was starting to get to Tucker. Even the barking had stopped a long time ago, and Tucker was hesitant to turn on the television for fear it would get the little yapper charged up.

Now, though, Tucker was hearing a weird little sound coming from the hall. He padded softly toward it, hoping it wasn't Connie; he really hoped Micah got back before she went into another one of those crazy spells, or whatever they were.

It wasn't Connie. The dog—Gulliver, what a name—was scratching and snuffling at the door of the other bedroom and just wouldn't stop. It wasn't loud, but it was insistent. *Here goes nothin'*, Tucker thought, and opened the door in resignation, expecting the barking to commence.

Instead, a little salt-and-pepper dog with a bushy beard and heavy eye-brows rushed anxiously to his knees, wrenching his rear end back and forth in happy, tailless wagging and doing the exuberant panting that serves as a big doggy smile. Tucker recognized the little guy as a miniature schnauzer. Back when he was boxing in Vegas, his manager—a tough little hustler everybody called Rat—had a miniature schnauzer he'd named Tirpitz, after some German admiral he'd read about. Tirpitz. Tucker had thought it was a ridiculous name, but Tirpitz was the smartest little dog he'd ever met, and by the time Tucker's boxing career had collapsed into an ignominious heap around him, Tirpitz was the only thing he liked about Rat.

Now here was what looked like Tirpitz the Second. The painfully incessant yapper he had wanted to punt into the next county wasn't barking at all, just snuggly and grateful for some company. *Aww.* Tucker squatted down and began scratching the dog's neck.

"Hey there, little buddy," Tucker said in that hushed tone people reserve for their babies, animals, and the dying. "Bet you're happy to be out of that lonely room, huh? Yeah, there you go. Yeah, we might just have to let you live."

Gulliver kept on twisting his body, adding oomph to what little wagging he could do with his stump of a tail, as long as Tucker was willing to scratch and pet. As soon as Tucker stood up, though, Gulliver headed immediately to the screen door and nosed it just open enough to squeeze through. In that instant, Tucker blurted, "Hey!" and hurried to the door. He opened it just in time to see the dog urinating on a bush beside the house—while looking up at Tucker with what looked like a proud little grin. Then he walked around the yard, sniffing at patches of grass for only a few seconds before finding one suitable for his next little project.

Tucker grinned. "When ya gotta go, ya gotta go," he said into the empty room.

And he thought, *Shit.* What about when Connie has to go? No way was he going to deal with that mess. Micah had better hustle his ass back home.

Home. Shit. He doesn't even LIVE here.

This could be bad if Micah decided to be a dick and not come back today. Tucker didn't even have a phone number to call him.

Tucker glanced at the hall and the dreaded room. This could get ugly. But right now, he had to go, and the yard wouldn't do. He slipped quietly down the hall to the bathroom and took care of business. On the way back, he looked at the cheaply-framed photographs lining the back end of the hall. He only vaguely remembered there being photographs before, in his childhood, and he flicked on the hallway light to see what memories hung there.

Not many, actually. There were a couple of old snapshots of the boys' childhood and a couple of bad portrait shots of Big Frank and Connie in happier days, all relegated to the very back end of the hall. Toward the front of the hall, the rest of the artwork was exactly that: photographic art. Landscapes. Wildlife close-ups. Sunset-silhouetted wildflowers. Remarkable angles, some apparently taken from high in the branches of forest trees. Some black-and-white, some color, all arresting in some way—whether achingly beautiful or hauntingly melancholy. All nicely framed, too, especially compared to the old snapsnots, which were simply thumb-tacked to the wall. Tucker had no idea the old lady was into photography. She must have paid some good coin for all these shots, none of them smaller than 8-by-10 and all of them matted and framed.

He was at the front of the hall, almost to the living room, when he came to the photograph that nearly floored him. He was surprised he hadn't noticed it on either of his two previous trips into the hall, first to go into Connie's room and second to free the dog. It was, like the others, large, matted and framed. But it was nothing like the rest. It was displayed more prominently than the others, with more room around it than the others, the distance making it stand out. It was also the only one of the framed photographs that wasn't taken outdoors.

This one was in a smoky arena Tucker knew well, at one of the casinos that likes to amp up the gambling action by holding boxing cards, always anchored by a title fight or two at the end of the night. Many of the faces in the crowd, captured in the soft focus of the periphery, were faces he recognized. The same movers and shakers, the same film moguls and stars making the megafight scene, the same hangers-on, the same hustlers and wannabes, the same well-tended mannequin women of high cheekbones and higher price tags. Rat Bilsky was probably in the photo somewhere as well, because at the center of the photo—in the center of the ring, parrying a lazy jab and preparing to launch a left hook—was none other than the Rat's most dependable palooka, Tucker Dodd.

Or, as he was routinely announced in the ring after his first few knockouts got the promoters' attention, T.J. "the Bludgeon" Boudreoux.

His opponent had his back to the camera, which had Tucker as its focus—something Tucker found odd, as he knew precisely whose back that was: The red, white and blue shorts, the heavily muscled shoulders glistening from the profuse sweat on that black skin, the monumentally expensive, time-consuming weave, everything about him seemingly made for television and magazine covers. Why any photographer would frame Tucker in a photograph also inhabited by Olympic medalist Jammin' J James, then undefeated as a pro and being groomed for greatness, was a mystery.

It wasn't a championship fight—Tucker never got one of those—but it was as close as he ever came. Third fight from the last on a pay-per-view card, two bouts before the headliner title bout featuring "Hitman" Thomas Hearns, a fighter whose warrior mentality Tucker greatly admired. It should have been the most memorable night of Tucker's four-year boxing career. Instead, it was the one he most wanted to forget.

Still, it was a wonderful photograph, by far the best he'd seen of himself. He thought he'd seen every shot of "the Bludgeon" ever published, whether in newspapers, fight magazines or promotional posters. There hadn't been all that many. But he'd never seen this one.

Where did Connie find it? And who the hell took it?

⚔

Amanda had been sitting and stewing for nearly a half-hour in the only place in Darrington that served what she considered decent coffee, when the reason for her funk walked in the door.

"Hello," Mister Painting Robber said. "I saw you, uh, through the window."

She gave him a long look. "Yeah. Windows are funny that way. I think it's the glass."

His face went blank.

She waved it off. *Forget it.*

"Oh." He nodded, looking a little sheepish. "Got it. Guess I'm just slow."

"Could've fooled me. You got out with that painting pretty fast."

He sighed. "You mind if I sit down?"

Amanda, who was still pretty bent about the painting, looked around at all the open seats.

"I'm not sure," she said finally. "I just might hit you."

He pursed his lips. "Well. I guess that's your prerogative. Just, please, no scratching. I get a little queasy if I see blood. Especially my own."

She almost smiled.

He gestured to the chair opposite her—*may I?*—and she nodded.

"Look, I swear I'm not stalking you," he said, taking a seat. "I was just going to the grocery next door and I thought I recognized your car when I pulled in."

"You know my car? And I'm supposed to believe you're not a stalker?"

He laughed and shrugged. "I dunno. Maybe I am. I have a thing for those old RX7s."

She made a face. "It's not *that* old."

"No, I don't mean—I mean, before they changed the body. Forget it." He held out his hand. "My name's Micah Dodd."

Amanda wasn't much on shaking hands, but she shook it.

"Look, I feel bad about ... your friend's painting," he said haltingly.

"Having a little buyer's remorse, are we?"

"If you really want it, you can have it."

That made her suspicious. "You'd give it to me."

"Well, no, not *give*. But I'll, you know, I'd sell to you. For exactly what I paid, not a dime more."

"Wow. I might not hit you after all."

The waitress arrived and Micah ordered coffee and an English muffin. "You want anything else?" he asked Amanda, who shook her head, not sure what to make of this guy.

"So tell me," she said. "I'm curious what you paid for the painting. In case I could afford it, which ... I doubt."

"A hundred bucks."

"Whoa," she said, putting up her hands. "No kidding. That's a lot more than when J.D. was trying to give it to me for nothing."

"Sorry. That's what I paid. As far as I'm concerned, it's worth a lot more than that."

"So what are you saying, now you want to up your selling price?"

"No, no. Actually, I'm kind of wishing I didn't do that already."

"Excuse me?"

"The guy? The estate sale guy?" He leaned forward conspiratorially. "He was going to give it to me for twenty."

"I thought you said you paid a hundred."

"I did. I didn't feel right stealing a painting like that for twenty bucks. Especially now, with the artist being … dead and all."

Amanda felt her cheeks flush with emotion, and it must have been obvious.

"I'm sorry," he blurted. "He was a good friend of yours?"

She nodded.

"Hmm. Now I really feel bad," he said. "I wish I'd just paid him the twenty."

Amanda thought about her last conversation with J.D., and his certainty his paintings would be of no value to a gallery.

"So … is it … really a good painting?"

"Let me put it this way," Micah said. "The price tag—if there'd been one, anyway—probably should have had another zero on the end. Maybe two."

"Hmm." Amanda suddenly felt a bit like crying. "I wish J.D. could hear you say that. Just to know." She felt herself flushing and looked down, clasping her empty cup with both hands.

"How'd he die? If you don't mind my asking."

She grimaced. "I don't really know you well enough to get into that."

He held up a *Sorry* hand. "Forget I asked."

Amanda was anxious to change the subject. "So how come you know so much about painting?"

He shrugged. "Not so much about painting, specifically. Just kind of art in general. Studied it in college. It was one of my majors, and then I went on and got a masters. Fine arts."

"Wow. 'One of your majors.' Lots of education."

"Yeah," Micah said. He added, so softly it might have been meant only for himself, "I'm just full of fifty-cent words."

"What?"

He waved it off.

This guy was beginning to intrigue her. "So," she tendered, "are you like an artist now?"

He shook his head. "Not really. Some photography. Some music. I dabble."

"Photography. Really. What'd you say your name was?"

"Micah."

"Micah what."

"Dodd."

Amanda perked up. "Micah Dodd."

"I usually answer to one or the other, yes."

"You're that guy. I don't see how, you look way too young to be him, but … you're him. You're the photographer."

"I'm *a* photographer. Don't know why anybody would refer to me as *the* photographer."

Amanda grinned. A couple of months ago she had purchased a coffee-table book by a photographer named Micah Dodd, but she hadn't made the connection at first.

"You do … forests."

⅄

Tucker was still eyeballing the Vegas boxing shot, trying to pick out faces he knew or recognized in the audience, when he heard a sound from behind him. In the instant he turned, the door began to open—giving Tucker a jolt like a B-movie's cheap thrill—and there was Connie.

She was in her nightgown, thank God, and rubbing sleepy eyes that didn't change even when they lit upon Tucker, something that, until that craziness a couple of hours before, they hadn't done in six years. And they didn't linger on him for more than a second before she brushed past him down the hall. She moved awkwardly, as if a knee or a hip joint was out, but she made it to the bathroom and shut the door behind her.

Tucker felt a passing certainty he was asleep or daydreaming. The woman who just strolled to the bathroom was Connie—an emaciated, blotchy version with patches of scarecrow hair, but Connie nonetheless. Not that crazy woman. But as he thought that, he became aware of a stench coming from her bedroom and suddenly felt sure there was shit in there. And that it hadn't come from Gulliver.

Tucker suddenly felt out of place and intrusive, hearing the toilet tinkling coming from the bathroom and wondering if Micah's mother had crapped in her bed. It felt rude somehow to be standing there, and he took a step toward the living room. *No, no, she might need help walking. She might fall down.*

So he didn't move. His wait was only seconds, but they passed like gallstones.

Finally, the door opened and she emerged, still clothed, thank God. She shuffled up the hall with that same herky-jerky gait and, while passing Tucker with little more than a cursory glance, she said, "Cereal. Cereal." She went in and sat at the kitchen table. "Cereal."

She's doing it again.

Without looking up, she barked, "Cereal!"

That got the dog going. Gulliver came to the screen door, pawing at it and standing up and leaning against it with his paws, barking and doing his body-wag thing.

Oh shit. She's babbling nonsense, she's getting mad and the shit's about to fly. Micah, where the hell are you?

Now she glared at him. And spoke to him. "Are you deaf?"

Tucker was dumbstruck. "I'm ... not sure ..."

She was still glaring, her expression less like one of Jack Nicholson's nut-bar "Cuckoo's Nest" pals than Nurse Ratched herself.

"You don't know?"

"Uh ... no. I'm not."

She exhaled heavily, as if this had been an exhausting interview. "Then. Cereal."

Oh. "You want cereal?" No answer, but he took that as a yes. "Sure. You got it." He began searching through the kitchen cabinets, mumbling only marginally confident assurances about how there must be cereal here, sure, no problem, and looked until he found a family-sized box of off-brand corn flakes. He located a glass bowl, poured in some cereal, stuck in a spoon he saw on the counter and set the bowl in front of Connie, who seemed to be studying the table. As she reached with both hands for the bowl, though, she paused with an expression Tucker couldn't quite make out, except that it looked bad.

The dog was still going crazy on the porch. Tucker turned toward the door. "Shut UP!"

Gulliver was silent for a moment, barked twice more, then sat down to watch the proceedings. Tucker breathed a sigh of relief and turned back, only to see Connie glaring at him, her hands firmly gripping the bowl.

"Again. Not again. They do. They do." she muttered. "WHY?"

Tucker held up his palms in supplication. "What?" he pleaded. "Why what?"

She gave him a nasty little look. "Milk," she snarled, at which point she lifted the bowl and slammed it onto the floor, covering the kitchen with corn flakes and glass shards. Connie seemed to take a great interest in them, as if the arrangement were fascinating. Gulliver yapped briefly, watched her through the screen and continued to yap softly.

Tucker shook his head. "Nice move, Connie. Real nice."

She looked up at his voice. "Cereal," she said.

"Are you shitting me?"

"CEREAL!"

Gulliver quieted in mid-yap, as if the shout was meant for him.

"Milk," Connie added, sounding just as sane as could be.

Tucker thought about Micah putting up with this for the last six weeks. *Little brother, you're a better man than I.* "OK, fine," he said, going to the narrow door off the kitchen that he knew housed both the hot-water heater and also a broom or two. "I'll make you some more cereal. With *milk*. But this time? No glass bowl for you. It's a plastic bowl or nothin'. And if you bounce it around the floor with that milk in it, you crazy …"

He couldn't bring himself to say the word he was thinking. As much as he had always cussed up a storm, that's one that just felt wrong out loud. Motherfucker? No problem. But bitch … uh uh. Not out loud. And absolutely never the C word. They reminded him of those arguments he had to listen to as a little kid and got him angry all over again, because he remembered how hurt his mom would be whenever Big Frank called her one of those names.

That motherfucker.

He looked at Connie, who was simply watching him sweep the mess into a pile. And she smiled. Big as life. And she pointed at him.

"Box," she said.

"Right, crazy lady. I'll deal with your cereal box after I clean up your mess."

"Box."

And she smiled again, as if that made all the sense in the world.

⋏

You do forests.

Micah smiled, a little embarrassed. "I do. Never heard it described quite that way, but … yes. I do forests."

"So do I." At his quizzical look, she added, "I work for the Forest Service."

"Ah," Micah said, nodding in approval. "Now there's a job where you never have to dread going in to the office."

"I wouldn't go that far," she said. "Anyway. I have your book. I … bought it."

"No way."

Except for a few minimally attended book signings, Micah had never met anybody who has purchased "Mother Forest." It had been published by a small Seattle outfit specializing in coffee-table books but had never been sold in more than a few small, independent bookstores.

"Whoa. I think you and maybe six other people bought that book," Micah said.

"I just realized why I don't remember you from your picture in the book," she said. "There wasn't one. How come?"

He shrugged. "You know. All those autographer seekers all the time, people wanting to take my picture. Having to hire bodyguards. You know."

She made a face. "Seriously."

"I just wasn't interested in a picture of myself. Besides, I'm a wanted man."

"Yeah?"

"Speeding ticket in northern California. It was a speed trap, so I didn't pay it. Principle of the thing."

"Oh, so not only are you this big-time fugitive from justice, you're also a revolutionary."

That struck a sensitive chord with Micah. "No," he said softly. "Just a photographer."

"Without his picture in his own book."

"Didn't mean that much to me, I guess. The book, that was pretty much my master's thesis, basically. It just turned out to be decent enough to publish."

"You did it while you were still in college? Wow."

"Don't be too impressed. I don't think it will ever pay for the cost of printing."

"Did you have to pay for that part?"

"Nah, that's the publisher's problem. They own it. I didn't want to have to lug around a bunch of books and sell them out of my trunk. So they gave me a little bit of money for it and it's theirs now. That was fine with me."

"A little bit? You mean picture books with trees and animals don't make you rich? How much did you get?"

He gave an odd little chuckle. "I don't really know you well enough to talk about that."

She started to protest, and then gave him a deadpan glare. "You're bad."

"Well, I think the photo-book-buying public would agree with that assessment, based on their fervent interest in not buying my book." The waitress brought his coffee and muffin. "Actually, now that I remember, 'Mother Earth' made me precisely one hundred dollars. Which is why I was able to afford that fine painting by your friend."

"Ha ha."

"Seriously, though. I'd like you to have the painting. You can owe me the hundred. At least until you win the lottery. Then you gotta pay up."

She smiled at the line, but seemed discomfited by the offer. "No, that's fine, you keep it."

"No, really. Look, I like the painting a lot, but you have an emotional connection to it. It makes more sense for you to have it."

"That's really thoughtful, Micah. But I'm not really sure I want to be reminded of him being gone every time I look at it. Thinking about how he died, how sad he was." She looked at Micah, seeming to be weighing something. "It was suicide."

"Oh geez. I'm sorry."

She nodded. "You keep the painting. I just want to know it's … that it's OK." She gave him a wan smile. "I can't explain it. At least I know you're not going to turn around and sell it."

"Are you kidding? Sell it? It's going to look so great in my bowling alley."

"Shut up."

"Anyway." Micah felt a little surge in his heartbeat. *Say something*, he thought, and flashed back to those pathetic telephone calls as a teenager, hanging up the phone before dialing the final number or, worse, hanging up at the first ring, too gutless to say hello and ask the girl if she'd go out. *Say something.*

"Maybe we could, I dunno, take turns keeping it," he said. "You know: I take it for a month or whatever, then you take it … you know. Provided … we stay friends, I mean."

Well, it's out there now, he thought. And held his breath as she looked into his eyes, apparently considering the same possibilities.

"Staying friends, I don't know," she said melodramatically. "What with you being a stalker and all …"

And they both laughed.

Tucker had had enough of Connie by the time little brother got home.

She hadn't thrown her second bowl of cereal, but she'd begun playing with its contents, which were nearly as messy and significantly more disgusting, especially since the playing involved spitting out globs of it onto the table or the floor. When he'd tried to clean up her mess on the table, she had gotten really defensive, as if he were a stranger with bad intentions and partially-chewed cereal must be protected from thieves. Her first act after leaving the table was to sit down on the kitchen floor, either because of or oblivious to the soggy little mounds of masticated corn flakes, which then affixed themselves to the hind quarters of her nightgown.

Which, of course, was the first thing Micah wanted to know about when he arrived and went into her bedroom to check on her. He came out into the living room, where Tucker was sitting in the recliner and sipping on an Oly.

"What's with the brown stuff on her butt?" Micah asked. "Did she …?" And he made a stinky face.

"Oh, that's gross, man," Tucker retorted. "I don't know. Maybe. But that's just cereal."

"Cereal."

"Yup."

"OK. I guess that makes sense."

"If you say so."

Micah nodded. He looked distracted.

"Hey. I got a question," Tucker said. "When did she get into photography? And where would she have the money to have all those big blow-ups in the hall, all framed and everything?"

"Why would I charge my own mother?"

"You bought 'em?" Tucker rose and walked to the hallway.

Micah followed. "Bought?"

"Well yeah, good photographs can cost a lot of money."

"You know a lot about that kind of thing, do you?"

"No. I just know nobody gives you shit in this world unless you take it for yourself or pay more than it's worth. That's the way things work."

"Oh. Well," Micah said. "So that's how it is."

What a snarky little shit. "Yeah. That's how it is," Tucker said. "You gonna tell me those pictures didn't set you back some serious coin?"

"What makes you think I bought them?"

"You stole 'em?"

Micah laughed out loud.

Tucker didn't know whether to get pissed or laugh along. "What's so funny?"

"It's just interesting you think that would be my first option: If I didn't buy them, I must have stolen them."

"Yeah? So what's your point?"

Micah shook his head. "Just not possible I might have taken them?"

"You took them? No shit." Tucker nodded approvingly, studying the photographic array. "Who knew, little brother. You could be an actual photographer."

Micah shrugged with an odd expression. "Maybe so."

"So I'm guessing," Tucker said, "you also took this one." He pointed at the Vegas shot.

Micah cocked his head: *Well, yeah.*

"Huh. That was almost two years ago."

"And almost four years since you left."

"Since we'd seen each other," Tucker said softly. "That's a long time."

"Yep."

"I guess I should feel bad about that."

"Would have been nice of you to call Mom, let her know where you were."

"I did call, a few times."

"Twice," Micah said emphatically. "Mom got all excited both times."

"Yeah?"

"Yeah. Told me all about it both times. Tucker called. Wowee."

Tucker looked at the photograph again.

"I didn't even know you were there. Woulda been nice to see ya."

Micah considered that. "You could have done that any time, Tucker. You always knew where you could find me. Or Mom. I just figured you didn't want to see either of us. Figured you didn't give a shit."

Tucker took it like a punch, not quite wincing.

"No. It wasn't that. I just ... there was stuff that happened and I ... just couldn't come back here. I wouldn't be back here now, except ... you know."

Micah nodded.

"Would have been nice to know you were there," Tucker said. "Except why couldn't it have been for another fight? Why did it have to be *that* one?"

Micah nodded as if he understood. "Lousy fight."

Tucker answered with a slow nod of his own. "Yeah. Good picture. Lousy fight."

CHAPTER 8

LISTENING IN

On the tenth of November, 1977, the day before Veterans Day, Micah was sitting on the rocking chair on the small back porch.

It was upon this throne he often sat, listening to the rustle of yew leaves and the insistent murmur of the creek, while reading about heroes. Even if it was dark outside, as it was getting to be now, he preferred the porch, where his stories would not have to compete with whatever TV show or sports event his dad was watching.

Instead, he would go outside, in heavy coat if need be, switch on the single bulb directly above the screen door and sink into the pages.

He read voraciously. A lot of comic books—Sergeant Rock and Batman were favorites—but also book after book, most of them intended for boys and girls older than Micah, who was only ten. But he was in sixth grade, the result of having jumped from second to fourth grades, skipping third altogether, and already reading at a level far beyond even his older classmates.

And also far beyond Tucker, who by this time was only a grade ahead of Micah, though three years older. Five years earlier, the first autumn the two half-brothers were living under the same roof—after Tucker had watched his mother die in front of him—Micah had entered kindergarten and Tucker had been a third-grader for the first time. Tucker spent that entire school year in his own solitary world of torment and confusion, loneliness and anger; but he did not spend much of it in school. Some days he might last until lunch before disappearing. Other days, he simply wandered away from the bus stop, leaving Micah alone and scared. That Tucker had had to repeat third grade didn't seem to matter to him. At that point, at least to Micah, it didn't seem that Tucker cared much about anything at all except how mad he was at the world and everybody in it. He had no trouble finding scapegoats upon which to take out that anger and frustration, frequently and ferociously.

Though he was not the biggest or strongest boy in his school grade in White Bluff, Tucker never lost a fight. He didn't always win—Micah had seen his older brother fight much larger boys against whom he could barely get in a lick—but they would eventually get tired and decide it was OK for this fight to be over. And Tucker never quit. He was always ready to take a few more punches for the opportunity to get in a good one, and he was always convinced he had another good one in him.

What Micah couldn't quite understand was why Tucker never turned those furious fists upon him. Whenever Micah triggered his brother's wrath, Tucker invariably turned away, leaving Micah both relieved and weirdly disappointed. He always cringed at the sound of bone striking bone whenever a fight broke out near him; it frightened him. He had never even been in a fight—partly because he avoided confrontation and no doubt also partly because nobody dared risk Tucker's possible retribution. And the longer Micah went without experiencing a fight, the scarier the prospect became.

Unable to engender any sense of kindred spirit or even brotherhood with Tucker, Micah immersed himself in his reading. By fifth grade he already had his own card at the city library, where he would peruse the shelves for the kind of adventure books that stirred his imagination. They could come from any genre—westerns, pirates on the high seas, explorers in a hostile land, soldiers at war, even coming-of-age books, though it would be years before he did the same.

There was but one common theme running throughout every book that held Micah rapt for hours on end, often late into the night under the covers with a flashlight. There had to be the gallant hero, brave and principled, admired by all and preferably also adored by a beautiful girl. The thought of being someone's hero was the basic theme in Micah's every daydream. It certainly trumped being the invisible afterthought, which was pretty much his perception of himself. Even within his own family, few discussions were about Micah. He had the occasional lead role whenever Connie felt compelled to extol his virtues, often the "Micah's on the honor roll again" variety. But that one seemed to bear little interest for Big Frank; she might as well have proclaimed that Micah could cross his eyes longer than anyone in his school.

Micah didn't know why his scholastic successes didn't excite his father, but this personal failure only made him work harder in ways that wouldn't leave him being compared to Tucker. He took up the clarinet after his mother found one at a flea market in Rockport and was diligent enough at his practice—which usually took place on that same back-porch stoop—to become reasonably painless within a year and downright good within two. He won an art contest with a charcoal sketch. But his news was still not good enough, his accomplishments not large enough, his grades not high enough.

人

For Big Frank, they could never be enough. Oh, he was pleased when the boy made good grades because he knew it made Connie happy, so he pretended he gave a herkin' shit. As a boy, Frank had regarded the good-grades kids as mama's-boy showoffs who were also crybabies and tattletalers as soon as they didn't have a teacher or a mommy around to protect them. Nerds.

Now the fact that he had sired one made Big Frank a little queasy.

The boy's way was simply not his way. Micah's politeness in the face of Tucker's rebellion and his unerring overachievement in school, while bringing great pride to his mother, grated on Big Frank. The boy was small and weak, sensitive like a woman. He gave in and accepted things, just like his mother. Besides, there wasn't much fathering Big Frank had to do for the boy. Micah never had to be kept in line, while Tucker refused to accept there was one.

But there was also a selfish reason behind Big Frank's disregard for conversations involving Micah. If they weren't Connie's latest report on Micah's perfection, they usually resulted in his being badgered to drive the kid somewhere or pick him up—at the library or some school band nonsense. Or they could be the dreaded *I wish you'd talk to Tucker about being nicer to Micah,* which Big Frank translated to *I wish you'd teach your little monster some manners.* And, frankly, sometimes he was just too damn tired to have to put up with that crap.

He was tired that Thursday evening, the night before Veterans Day, when Connie's voice barged in on "CHiPs." Big Frank had busted his ass all day on a tricky, time-consuming job on which he had badly underbid, and he wanted to forget all about his aching back and his aggravation. Ponch and Jon were in hot pursuit of some bad guys in a muscle car, getting ready to kick some righteous butt, and this was not a good time to be interrupted.

"Big? Honey?"

She had this annoying habit of waiting for an answer.

"Can't you wait for a commercial?" he groused.

In that instant, the muscle car got across some railroad tracks just in front of the train, leaving the two "CHiPs" cops frustrated as a commercial popped on the screen. *Shit.*

"Big, I got a call today from one of the counselors at the school," Connie went on.

"Yeah?" Big Frank mumbled with no enthusiasm. "What'd Tucker do now?"

"Nothing at all. There's nothing wrong. I mean, it's nothing he did."

Big Frank could tell this wasn't going to go away quickly. "What, then."

"She wants—well, she thought it would be a good idea for Tucker to take some tests."

"It's a school, right? Isn't that what they do?" He made a grunt that came out like a laugh. "Dumbasses. Test away. Good luck with that, morons. Kid's just not interested in school."

"Well, see, Big, that's why they want him to take these tests, because maybe it's more than him just not being interested."

"What, then?" he said, wishing the commercial would end so he could bring this crap to a halt. "If they want to know if he's lazy, well, I'm here to tell ya, boy."

"This is a different kind of test. The people at the school think … well, the teacher said she doesn't think Tucker can read very well."

He grunted. "Well, hell, that's their problem, ain't it? What the hell are we paying taxes to them clowns for? They oughta start doin' their jobs better. Morons."

Connie sighed. He hated when she did that. It was like she thought something he said was stupid. Made him want to pop her.

"Big, they think maybe there's something wrong with him and … and that's why he can't read right."

He glared at her. "Wrong with him? Wrong how?"

"Well, I don't know, Big, I'm not an expert. But they have tests for it."

"For what? Tests for what?"

"I can't remember the name she said, but it's like he doesn't see the letters and words like everybody else does."

"Bullshit. He's had his eyes checked, he sees just fine. He's just lazy, that's all. And pissed off at the whole world."

The commercial ended and "CHiPs" returned, though now Ponch and Jon were in the sergeant's office. *What? Shit. I musta missed something.* Big Frank made a production of repositioning himself on the recliner, settling back into his conversation-free existence.

"Well, but what if there is something wrong with him?"

What a load of crap.

"What if he's got this … thing, this whatever it is that makes him different from the other kids? Dysplexia. That's it, I think. Something like that. People who have it see words and letters different from everybody else, so they don't read the same way. And they don't learn as fast."

"Is that what this teacher said? That my son's different from everybody else, he's got this weird thing? Like he's disabled? Gimme a break. What's her name? She wants to talk about reading, I'll read that bitch the riot act if she wants to start calling my son a freak." Big Frank got up and grabbed the phone book. "What's her name?"

⅄

From his vantage point on the porch, Micah watched his mother, wondering if she'd tell him the name and let Big Frank go off on some poor counselor.

"Big, honey, she's just trying to help," he heard his mother say.

"Help, my ass. They're just trying to blame somebody else because they can't figure out how to get him to pay attention in class. You gonna give me her name or not?"

"But what if he really does have this reading disability thing? I went to the library and looked it up. There's books about it. It's real."

"It's real bullshit is what it is. Just people looking for an excuse why they can't do somethin', so they find a disease for it. Hey, here's why Johnny can't read, he's different, he's got a *disability*. Like hell. My kid ain't no freak. You got that? He's just lazy."

On the porch, Micah muttered, "Or maybe he's just stupid."

The voice from behind him: "Yeah? You think so?"

Oh crap.

At thirteen, Tucker wasn't hampered by any of the awkwardness of adolescence. He moved with the grace of a wild animal, silently, as if he were walking on wind—especially when he was outside. Whenever Micah would attempt to follow him on one of the rutted, rugged trails his brother seemed to know so intimately, he would have to follow right on his heels or risk being left behind. Tucker simply couldn't be heard if he chose not to be.

He sidled up beside Micah, close enough to peek inside.

Micah moved aside to give him room, accepting his place in the brothers' hierarchy. Tucker was the alpha male in almost any group at White Bluff Elementary, and when he finished sixth grade and moved up to junior high with the older kids, Micah had no doubt his reputation would precede him—and that he would quickly live up to it. A kid who will never back down—ever, from anybody, no matter how big or how many—is a schoolyard legend in any small town.

Tucker stood at the door, where he had the good view and Micah was resigned to peering around him. The conversation had slowed in the living room, a simmering pot waiting to boil.

"You at that assembly today?" Tucker whispered.

"What?" Micah was surprised. That question was out of nowhere.

"That assembly after lunch. Did your class go?"

"Yeah."

"What'd you think of that colonel? Pretty interesting, huh," Tucker whispered, still gazing in through the screen.

Micah peered at him. "Were you one of the kids who asked a question? One of my friends thought it was you."

Tucker nodded.

"What was it, your question? I could barely hear it."

"Nothing. Just wanted to make sure about something. And now I am," he said. "So what's with them? That sounded like it was about my grades again."

"I think that was it."

"Shit," Tucker said, though the epithet represented neither anger nor defiance. Micah could see his brother's demeanor sag upon learning that, once again, his parents were talking about his academic shortcomings. It was a common topic, especially for Connie, whose entire focus seemed to be on Micah's success and, by extension, Tucker's failure.

Micah couldn't understand why Tucker did so poorly in school. He seemed to get frustrated with his homework and toss it aside, then lie about it later whenever Connie asked if he'd finished it. But Micah had a pretty good idea how Tucker was managing to get by in his classes with as little work as he seemed to be putting into it. Micah's best friend was Deano Slocumb, who was a year younger than Tucker but in his same grade, and he sat in front of Tucker during a couple of periods.

"I'm pretty sure he cheats whenever he can," Deano said once when Micah asked the question. "I've let him copy off my papers some."

Micah asked why.

"What, I'm gonna say no to Tucker Dodd?" Deano said. "Do I look stupid?"

Micah had no idea how many accommodatingly lowered shoulders Tucker found in his network of accomplices, and he presumed most of it was just a case of everybody being afraid of him. Which surprised him, because he didn't think Deano was the type of guy to be afraid—even of Tucker Dodd.

Deano probably just assumed Tucker was lazy or didn't care about school. That seemed to be the general consensus, but Micah didn't believe that. He had seen Tucker's frustration over his inability to read, and how angry and embarrassed it made him. Micah had even heard Tucker cry a few times, late at night—undoubtedly when he assumed Micah had long been asleep, since Tucker never cried in anyone else's presence, ever. Sometimes, Micah knew, those tears were about his mom being dead and how alone Tucker felt. But Micah thought part of it was about Tucker feeling like he must be the stupidest kid in school.

Micah couldn't understand it. He knew Tucker wasn't stupid. He just couldn't read worth a turd.

"Don't worry about it," Micah said softly to his older brother. "Whatever they're saying."

Tucker, who was pressed against the screen door, as if waiting for the conversation to be renewed, whirled around. "Why would I worry about anything they have to say?" he said in a hushed growl. "You think I give a rip about grades and all that crap, just because they do?"

Not about my grades they don't, Micah thought. *Or, at least, Dad doesn't.*

Tucker returned his attention to the screen, but not before softly adding a stunning little postscript: "It's good that you do good with that stuff, though. Keep it up."

Micah, who had ostensibly gone back to reading his book but was really still trying to listen in on his parents, was floored. He wasn't accustomed to receiving much acknowledgement of any kind from his older brother, much less positive reinforcement. That simple, almost begrudged sentiment gave Micah a surge of pride that rivaled any of his mother's gushing praise.

Big Frank's bellowed voice boomed from inside. "If something's wrong with the kid, it's because that stupid bitch took that acid crap while he was in the oven cooking. Either way, whether it's the drugs or the fact he's a lazy shit, she screwed him up but good."

Micah could see Tucker tense up, staring through the screen.

"There ain't gonna be any headshrinkers poking around at that boy, and that's final," Frank declared. "That's the way it's gonna be. Only person gonna deal with him not doing his schoolwork is gonna be me. He's just lazy."

"Maybe I am," Tucker whispered, barely loud enough for Micah to hear but clearly not intended for him. "But you're a liar."

Micah wanted to ask what he meant. But before he said anything, Tucker glanced back at him with a funny little grin, as if he knew a secret he just couldn't wait to share, and headed off to wherever it was Tucker went.

⅄

The following night over dinner, after a full day spent hiking alone up to and along the high ridges—without even having to skip out, since school was closed for the holiday—Tucker got a double helping of things he had little stomach for. First came Connie's favorite casserole, an unidentifiable glop de jour she called slumgullion, a hodgepodge of whatever was available in the refrigerator that, with the inevitable leftovers, inevitably endured like a virus for half a week. The second was the issue of his grades.

"Tucker, honey, I talked to one of the people at your school yesterday."

Big Frank grunted and, shaking his head, took a big bite of slumgullion.

"It was one of your counselors. Mrs. Wandering, I think she said her name was."

"Wandling. Mrs. Wandling."

Connie nodded vigorously at his willing participation. "Yes, that's it. She thinks she may have an explanation for your ... the troubles you've been having at school."

Big Frank grunted again, and this time filled his mouth with a swig from his ready can of Rainier beer.

Tucker looked sidelong at Big Frank, having already overheard the old man's philosophy on this issue. "Yeah? What's she say?"

"She thinks you may have what's called a reading disability."

Big Frank's grunt was now a full-fledged harrumph. Connie gave him a little glance of reproach, to which he responded with a *don't push it* glare.

"Yeah?" Tucker said. "What's that?"

"It means you can't read," Big Frank blurted, unable to restrain himself. "It means you'd rather spend time hanging around with those stupid-shit friends of yours instead of doing your studies like the little guy here. How come he's doing good and you ain't, huh?"

"Tucker, honey," Connie said, trying to get the train of conversational thought back on the rails, "Mrs. Wandling thinks it might not be anything to do with how hard you study. Mr. Grogan says the same thing. It may be something that's—well, your brain may do things differently. And they want to do a test to see if that's the case."

"Great. One more test for me to fail."

Big Frank grunted again, picked up his plate, a fork and his beer and carried them the few steps to the living room recliner, deposited them on the TV table that lived there, switched on the TV and plopped down.

Connie tried to regain Tucker's attention, which had stayed on his father. "It's not that kind of test, honey. It's the kind where they find out if there's something wrong."

In the living room, Big Frank grumbled, "I'll tell ya what's wrong. Gimme a break." He took another swig of beer and shoveled another forkful of casserole in his mouth while, on the TV screen in front of him, a man in a bad toupee read the news.

"So, Big Frank," Tucker said, knowing full well the response that moniker would get. "You want me to take the test?"

"Don't you be calling me that."

"But that's what everybody calls you. It's your name." Tucker was pushing.

"The guys who work for me can call me Big Frank. Your mom can call me Big Frank. You're my kid. You call me Dad. Or sir."

"Well. OK. *Dad.* You were in the Navy, right?"

"Uh huh," Big Frank grunted, returning his attention to the next overflowing forkful of casserole and the TV news.

"In Vietnam. Isn't that what you said?"

"Almost a year."

"That was before I was born, right? 'Cause you didn't go back, right?"

"Why would anybody with half a brain do a second tour in Viet-fucking-nam. And what's with the third degree." One a declaration, one a warning. Neither one a question.

"Come on now, boys," Connie said. "Tucker, you haven't touched your dinner."

She might as well have been speaking in sign language.

"And I was born in 1964."

Big Frank paused, a forkful poised in front of his mouth. He might not have known where this was going, but when he looked over his shoulder at Tucker, his glower said precisely into what kind of minefield the line of conversation would lead. Tucker gave a conspiratorial look at Micah, who clearly wasn't sure exactly what scab Tucker was picking at.

"So how come, if that's true," Tucker said, still looking at Micah while stepping calculatedly into the hazard zone, "how come at school yesterday they said the U.S. wasn't in Vietnam until 1965?"

"'Cause those idiots at your school couldn't find their ass with both hands and a map, that's why."

"It was a colonel said it. At the assembly."

"Your daddy was in the Seabees, honey," Connie interjected, ever the mediator. "They were building –"

"Wait a minute," Frank said, rising from the recliner in his delayed comprehension. "Hold on a minute, you little shit, what'd you just say? Did I hear you say *if that's true?* That sounds like you're calling your old man a liar. Where do you come off questioning me, you little bastard?" He was still in the living room, but the fact he was now standing meant a hard shoulder punch, or worse, could be on the none-too-distant horizon.

The prospect didn't dissuade Tucker, who was practically smirking at the big man.

"I ain't your little bastard. He's your little bastard," he said, with a cock of the head at Micah. "My parents were married."

Connie's sudden intake of breath was followed by what Tucker knew was coming: She reached out and flicked his ear with her middle finger.

"And," Tucker spat out, ignoring his stinging ear, "one of 'em actually *knew* that."

"For your information, Mister Smart Mouth," Connie said, "your father and I are married."

"Yeah, *now*. Little late, don't you think?"

She unleashed another clinically killer flick, and this time he couldn't ignore the pain. He flinched and rubbed his ear, then caught himself being a wussy and reluctantly removed his hand. Connie's finger-flicks always stung like hell. But Tucker never allowed his taunting glare to waver from the old man.

And Big Frank's eyes were blazing right back at him as he took a heavy step toward the kitchen. Tucker noticed Micah wince at the next motion: his father slowly withdrawing the thick, leather belt from his chinos.

Tucker never changed his expression, though he had actually been hoping for the punch, not the belt. The punches were usually on the meaty part of the shoulder and were over quicker. The belt whippings always took longer, and the marks lasted longer—especially when the old man used the buckle—but those he couldn't display proudly as badges of insolent honor.

Connie began to protest, as Tucker knew she would. Sometimes he almost hated her for taking his side and trying to defend him.

"Don't even say it," Big Frank said, pointing at her without taking his eyes off Tucker.

The same Big Frank glare that could make a grown man's knees quake, though, had no impact on Tucker.

Nothing his old man ever dished out hurt more than the seconds or, at most, minutes it took for the throbbing to stop. But Tucker could sense the punches coming with more on them, the belt whippings coming now with the buckle more often than not. Tucker knew why: He was getting older. Bigger. Stronger. More defiant with each new inch on the penciled-in height marks on the bathroom wall, every new tuft of manhood. His day was coming, and Tucker knew Big Frank was realizing the mounting need to tame him now. If already at the age of thirteen the son didn't fear or at least obey the father—respect being out of the question altogether—how much harder would it become as he grew older, stronger, more capable?

And Tucker couldn't wait.

"All right, boy," Big Frank growled. "Into your bedroom. You got somethin' comin'. Big time."

↓

Micah cringed inside as Tucker rose and began to walk toward the hall. But the older boy turned around for just a second to catch Micah's eyes, and Micah recognized the look—it was something like that same little *I've got a secret* expression he'd flashed him on the porch, only this time without the grin that had originally accompanied it.

When Big Frank closed the bedroom door behind them, Micah turned to his mother, who shook her head as if this whole thing could have been avoided.

"I wish your brother wouldn't goad him on so," she said.

Even behind the closed door, the first crack of the belt across Tucker's backside might as well have been a gunshot. Micah flinched at the sound, and Connie reached across to cover his hand with hers, as if he was the one being punished. The sound both mesmerized and horrified him; he had never been whipped, and it just seemed like it would be so painful.

Micah heard what sounded almost like a choking laugh. And then his brother's voice:

"Is that the best you can do?"

Micah removed the hand from his mother's protective grasp and covered his ears, so he didn't have to imagine the picture with the sound. But he couldn't drown it out. He never could.

CHAPTER 9

SHOWDOWNS

M icah found himself looking at the kitchen clock every two minutes or so. Even though he knew Amanda was on her way and it was only a half-hour drive from Concrete, the passage of time seemed to be taking forever.

It would have been much easier on Micah's nerves had he been the one driving to pick her up, instead of vice versa. But because their destination was in Darrington, Amanda had said it made more sense for her to come one way than for him to pick her up, drive them back to Darrington and then have to bring her back to Concrete when they were done. Micah naturally attributed that logic to the most pessimistic of reasons, presuming she wanted to be able to leave at any time—or to avoid a potentially awkward kiss at her front door.

His nervousness grew with each passing moment. He was glad she would be meeting him at his meeting him at his nearly bare duplex, not at the house, where there would be too much explaining and uncomfortable introduction. He also wasn't excited about the prospect of Amanda meeting Tucker; girls always seemed to be mesmerized by that bad-boy allure, and Micah knew any light of his own would quickly be extinguished under Tucker's suffocating shadow.

Micah had stayed at the house for all but two nights that week—always on the sofa in the living room, ceding to Tucker the one bed in what used to be the two boys' bedroom. And he also made a point of being at the house most of the time during the days; he knew he could count on the daily visits by the home-care nurses to give him a break, but they were short and he didn't want to leave his mother unsupervised. That's why he was so grateful for Tucker's presence, though he didn't want to jeopardize the arrangement by relying too much on Tucker; this was his mother, not Tucker's.

But that was the surprising thing: Tucker didn't seem to mind. In those few times they were all at the house together, Micah had watched his brother and was touched by Tucker's patience with Connie. For all of his unrepentant gruffness, Tucker seemed … of all things, kind.

But something was going on with Tucker. Micah could sense that. Maybe he was queasy about being part of a death watch. Maybe it was his unresolved issues with Connie. Maybe it was returning to a town he had seemed intent on relegating to a forgotten past.

Or maybe he was running from something.

If he was hiding, he was doing a good job of it, because nobody in White Bluff seemed to know he was even back.

Every time Micah had been in town, picking up his mother's meds at Albert Drug Store and doing the grocery shopping, he ran into people he knew. And nobody mentioned Tucker, other than to ask *What ever happened to that crazy brother of yours?* Which meant no one had seen him, and Tucker wouldn't be easy to miss in White Bluff. Among people his own age Tucker had always been either revered or feared, and in some cases both. But never ignored.

Micah, though, wasn't spending much time thinking about Tucker. His thoughts now revolved around Amanda Devlin, and he felt almost guilty about it. Here his mother was going through a slow, horrible death, and Micah was feeling more alive than ever. In barely an hour's conversation at that diner, he had become as enthralled with Amanda Devlin as any infatuated teenager.

In many ways, though not chronologically, that's what he was.

Throughout high school, Micah had sat in classes beside girls who were two years older, who either thought of him as a nerd or, at best, a cute little kid. He couldn't drive in high school, since he didn't turn sixteen until several weeks after graduation. And because Tucker was rarely interested in having his kid brother tag along, Micah spent most of his time hanging around his best friend Deano's group of friends, most of whom could drive. But, or so it seemed to Micah, the rest of them tolerated him only because Deano insisted. So more often than not, Micah just read, wrote, sketched and spent long hours learning to play that old clarinet.

He never really dated.

As a college freshman, barely sixteen, a prodigy attending on a raft of academic and musical scholarships, he felt socially out of place and even ostracized by his older academic peers. He buried himself in his studies. It wasn't until his junior year when, still only eighteen, he finally found himself in a sublimely compromising situation with a nubile and very willing freshman. Although his ineptitude was obvious, he succeeded in shedding the albatross of his virginity and thus became, in his own eyes, somewhat normal. But although he had managed to dip his wicket with a few girls since, not one of them had made him feel like he did whenever he thought about Amanda. The way her blonde hair draped across her forehead and shaded her moondrop eyes, the way her few tiny freckles seemed to dance when she laughed. The way her lips framed her words. Those lips.

All of which, naturally, made him nervous as hell.

⅄

When he heard Connie making funny noises in her bedroom, Tucker didn't worry much about it. He wasn't planning on staying around for much longer anyway, with the home-care nurse scheduled to arrive any minute. The old lady wasn't going to hurt herself in there.

She'd been asleep for most of the time he'd babysat her over the last week. He was thankful for that, because it meant he got to sit around and roughhouse with Gulliver, his new best buddy. But with Connie sounding as if she was about to get rambunctious again, and Gulliver whimpering at her bedroom door to see her, Tucker began wishing for Vera, the home-care nurse, to hurry up.

When the nurse did arrive, though, it wasn't kindly, maternal Vera. Instead, it was a woman younger than Vera, perhaps forty, monumentally stern in that manner of a woman who had never married, with posture that suggested military efficiency. The moment Gulliver came near her, she stiffened.

"Please put the dog in the spare bedroom," she said in a clipped manner.

Tucker made a little face but grabbed Gulliver, who was pleased with being picked up only until he realized what was happening. The little schnauzer gave Tucker a look that made him feel guilty as he closed the bedroom door.

"You allergic or something?" he asked her.

"No."

OK, then screw you too. "Where's Vera?"

"She's not available," she said, offering no further explanation. "Where's Mister Dodd?"

"He's not available."

"Well, that's unfortunate. I've got some papers he'll need to sign. I thought he knew the nurse would be bringing that today."

"He had a pressing engagement."

She sighed in a tone suggesting her disapproval of anything that disturbed essential protocol, and stopped to listen to the sounds Connie was making. "Has she been acting up?"

Besides being wacko? he almost said, but this woman didn't sound like she had a working sense of humor. He simply shook his head.

"Good." She looked around, taking in the living and dining rooms with what seemed to Tucker a very faint expression of disapproval.

Tucker was put off by her tone and the dismissive gaze. He heard Connie making some more noise, and waited for the nurse to do her job. She didn't seem to be in a hurry to do that.

"Are you going to check on her?" he said.

She turned that dour gaze on him. "Excuse me, who are you?"

Tucker had to swallow what he really wanted to say. "Actually, I'm Mister Dodd. Micah's my kid brother. And you are?"

"I apologize for neglecting to introduce myself. Nurse Brimm," she said, offering a tepid palm for a handshake. "I'm here to tend to Mrs. Dodd for the afternoon."

"Well, fine, I'll just leave you to your tending. You have yourself a real nice day now."

Tucker strode out the back door with no real destination in mind, mostly just wanting to get away from prim nurse Brimm and the thought of Connie's rapidly diminishing capacity. But as soon as he hit the creekside path, his mind went to a place he hadn't seen in six years, even though he'd been in White Bluff for a week.

He hadn't been down to the Under Look to see if the falcon stone was still there.

He assumed it would be. Nobody else would even notice the small rock wedged into a crack, when all a normal person would think about upon arriving at the Under Look was the power of the waterfall and the absolute necessity of getting out of there alive.

The only person who knew the falcon stone was there was his brother. Tucker had told Micah years ago he'd placed it in there—even pointed it out to him once from the top of the falls, though neither could see it clearly at that distance. Tucker had stashed their childhood treasure there as a challenge to his brother, because the kid was so afraid of everything. This would either force him to get past his fear and go out onto the Under Look, or it would take the smelly pile of his gutlessness and shove it into his face, like a dog that has pooped on the linoleum.

Tucker followed the trail alongside the creek, paused for a moment's viewing from the top of the falls, worked his way down to the *KEEP OUT* fence, got a good grip on some fence links and swung around into the forbidden land.

About halfway down to the gap, he paused for a moment to look at the nearly horizontal little nook he had found and used so often six years ago. It was perhaps 10 feet above and overlooking the barely-worn path—accessible only by that path, but at a spot no one following this route was ever likely to see, so focused would they be on every precarious step of the descent.

When he needed to think and didn't feel like taking one of his meander-ing, hours-long hikes along the ridgetops, he would simply go to that little spot, where he could stretch out almost comfortably and be absolutely alone. Unfound and unfindable. One couldn't see the waterfall from there—it was just around the final bend in the path—but the falls' crashing arrival below was in plain view. Tucker looked upon his years-old haunt with a sort of nos-talgia that was quickly erased by a much darker memory. Unable to banish it, he continued on.

As Tucker reached the gap, he looked at the little plywood bridge that now straddled the gap. He had always hated the idea of a bridge there; it seemed wrong to make the Under Look easier to reach. He had only left it in place those six years ago, instead of pitching it over the side, out of respect for the person who had put it there.

That didn't mean he had to use it, though.

He took the easy hop-stride over the plank-covered gap, then peered over the edge. The roar of the crashing water below reverberated back up the can-yon wall at him, creating a misty wind that ruffled his hair. It wasn't hard to understand why so few people wanted to come here. It felt like life and death, and most people feared the latter.

After soaking in the forbidding ambience of east county's most storied, yet untraveled destination for nearly a minute, he turned around and stepped to a depression in the back wall. In that nook was the crack into which Tucker had wedged the falcon stone.

And the stone wasn't there.

For a moment, Tucker wasn't sure he was at the right place. He stepped back, looked around. Yep. There weren't a whole lot of spots to choose from on the Under Look. This was it.

No falcon stone.

Just an empty crack.

Then it came back to him. He'd seen that void before. He knew the falcon stone was gone, because he'd seen it gone—and now the unwelcome wraiths of remembrance and regret came howling back like banshees in the wind. Within minutes after the last time he had navigated that precarious route to the Under Look and seen that vacant cavity, he had watched someone die, a fingertip away. Close enough to leave unwashable blood on his hands. Again.

He didn't want to think about that now. He had spent six years not thinking about it. And it was a full-time job.

So he thought about the falcon stone, and who must have taken it six year earlier.

What do you know, he thought. The boy's got some guts after all.

He headed back to the house, with an extra skip to his step. Being able to embrace a grudging respect for his brother actually felt good.

Upon reaching the back porch, Tucker stepped in through the door without feeling the need to announce his return. He saw Connie in the kitchen facing nurse Brimm, whose back was to Tucker. His arrival was just in time to see something both unexpected and disturbing.

⅄

Micah and Amanda were sitting in shorts and T-shirts on lawn chairs in a grassy field. All around them were longhairs, long-in-the-tooth tarheels whose granddaddies migrated from the Carolinas after the Civil War, east county honyocks in hunting camo, veterans in fatigues, pregnant mamas in granny dresses and twenty-something beer-gut boys in old football jerseys that recalled glory days. They sprawled on blankets, perched on ice chests full of Olympia beer, sat in toe-tapping homage to the music, clustered in gaggles of conversation and meandered through the crowd. Amanda's music history had been largely confined to grunge and its homogenous audience of the darkly caffeinated. But the Darrington Bluegrass Festival crowd was nothing if not eclectic.

She and Micah had arrived in the middle of a performance by a band she might have described as barely palatable country-rock: They couldn't sing a lick, but they could play their guitars, and in this case a mandolin and a banjo as well. When they finished what was apparently their final song and there was a break before the next act, Amanda couldn't help herself.

"So, was that bluegrass?" she asked.

"Not exactly."

She sighed for effect. "Good, because I was thinking this was going to be a long day."

He gave an injured grin with raised eyebrows. "Ooh. Tough crowd."

"I've been spoiled by a lot of good music," she said. "Ooh. I guess that sounded a little smug, huh, you being someone who 'dabbles in music' and all." Her fingers framed the quote-unquote.

"Oh yes, of course, let's not forget that, I do dabble."

They were smiling at each other in that lilting dance of tentative flirtation.

"OK, you tell me: Was that performance good?" She cocked a head toward the stage. "To a musician, I mean."

"That? Good?" He timed it perfectly. "Good god, no."

Amanda laughed.

"Well, then why did you want to bring me here, if that's what they do?" Realizing how negative that sounded, she backtracked. "I mean, if you don't like it that much either …"

Micah shook his head. "That's probably just some local guys. They could be from right down the road. All kinds of people play in this thing."

"They've had this before?"

Micah did a little double-take. "Seriously? You've never been to the Darrington Bluegrass Festival? So you're not from around here, then."

She shrugged. "We moved to east county before my last two years of high school."

"Yeah? Where'd you graduate?"

"North Cascades High, class of 1983."

"No shit. I played in your band."

"Band? Whoa. Nerd alert."

"Oh, thank you very much. You know, most of the people who make that 'good music' you listen to played in their high school band."

She grinned at his huffiness. "So then you went to N.C.?"

"No. Just the band. You guys had that performance-band program, and my school didn't offer music at all." He shrugged and thumbed his chest. "White Bluff. Class of '83."

"Huh," she said, sizing him up. "You know, I would have sworn you were younger than me."

He didn't respond to that.

"But," she said, filling the gap in case the age crack bothered him, "I guess you can't be all that young if you've had time to do books. And dabble."

"Book," he said, correcting her. "Just the one. So ... N.C. High, huh? You're a Grizzly."

She whirled a finger. Whoopy-do.

"You guys were in our league," he went on. "Maybe we saw each other at games. I'm sure I would have been the guy staring at you."

The peculiar compliment warmed her, but she played it. "And I'd have been the girl calling security on that stalker who keeps staring at me. Except I didn't go to a lot of the games. So you probably never saw me."

"You weren't into sports?"

"Wasn't into the jocks who played 'em."

"Not into band, not into sports. Some Grizzly you were." Micah smirked. "You know, we had a special little cheer for you guys: We're the Wolves, we got the goods, you're the ones with no fat chance. Grizzlies don't shit in the woods—"

"—they shit in their pants," she said with a little edge. "Yeah, I've heard that."

"I think our football cheerleaders got suspended for a week for cheering that my junior year."

"Yeah, well," she said, "I have it on good authority White Bluff Wolves don't use toilet paper."

Micah started to make a funny retort, then winced. "Gross."

She shrugged. "That stuff is high school sports in a nutshell, as far as I'm concerned. So they actually did that Grizzly thing during a game? The cheerleaders? Not real bright."

"No, but at least they were well-paid." He grinned. "A bunch of us chipped in to pay them to do it. Like a dare." He winked. "You'd be surprised what some girls will do for money."

And even before she had time to laugh or raise her voice in semi-righteous indignation, she saw him grimace at what he'd said.

"That's not ... I meant, you know, them doing the Grizzly cheer, and us paying them." He was stumbling all over himself.

She threw him a lifeline by touching a lengthy scar that ran down the side of his left leg, next to the knee. "So is this from football then?"

"No, I didn't … that's from something else. I didn't actually play sports. Not for very long, anyway," he said softly, obviously wishing to change the subject. "So how could you be from east county and never been to this festival? They get big stars here."

She gave a teasing little finger-point at the just-finished band which was clearing off the stage. "Like them?"

"Like Bill Monroe. He's playing later today." He said the name as if it meant something, and Amanda could only answer with a blank look that, in turn, left him with mouth agape. "So you've never heard of Bill Monroe. Or Jim and Jesse. You don't know who they are?"

She held up her palms. "Cousins of yours?"

He gave her a little dig on the arm. She liked the touch, and poked back.

"You're kind of a forward guy, aren't you," she said with tongue-in-cheek challenge.

He got quiet again for a moment. "No. Afraid not," he said. "Sometimes I wish I could be. I'm usually the shy, tongue-tied type."

"Yeah, right."

"Really," he said, raising his right hand in a three-fingered oath. "Scout's honor."

"Oh geez, I'm going out with a Boy Scout."

She knew instantly what she had said—*going out with*—but then decided she was OK with the way it sounded. She could tell he had taken note of the phrase as well, and was a little relieved he let it pass without comment.

"And a shy one at that." She gave him a teasing look. "So you say."

He nodded. "I really wasn't a Boy Scout for very long. But the shy part is right."

"Huh. Didn't stick with sports, didn't stick with the Boy Scouts. What does that tell me about you?"

"Uh … that … I'm narcoleptic?"

It took her a second to get his stab at humor, but then she laughed. "So what are you doing here, anyway?"

"Sitting with a pretty girl at a bluegrass concert?"

She warmed again at the compliment, but wouldn't show it.

"No, forward guy. Here. In east county," she said. "Your place looks like somebody broke in and stole all your stuff. Do you actually live there? Or do you just not believe in furniture?"

"I'm … I don't know how long I'm going to be staying. I'm sort of visiting my mother. Sometimes I stay at home—where she lives, I mean, where I used to live—and I've also been keeping this little duplex."

"Good," she said. "Nobody should have to live with their mother past the age of eighteen. That would drive me nuts."

"Oh, it's nothing like that. I'm just here because … well … she's dying."

"Oh God."

He held up his hands, a defense against a big thing being made of it. "It's … there's nothing anybody can do, so we're just sort of waiting it out."

"We?"

"Well, me mostly. My brother, he came back a few days ago to … help, I guess."

"You just have the one brother? That's it?"

"Half brother. Tucker's from the first wife. I'm from the second."

"Are you guys close, then?"

Micah seemed to weigh that assessment.

"We're very different."

⅄

By the fall of 1979 Tucker's dyslexia had still not been officially diagnosed, Big Frank having remained belligerently averse to having his son turned into a short-bus retard by some fruitcake test. Micah had continued to advance through his studies at such a breakneck pace he bypassed eighth grade entirely, as he had done with the third grade. He entered ninth grade at White Bluff High School at the age of twelve.

With Tucker also entering ninth grade that same September, the brothers had become incongruous classmates. Tucker was fifteen years old, solid as a young pine and blessed with a tensile muscularity that made him a natural for sports. Micah was twelve, a sprig among saplings, the least physically mature male in the school.

But while Tucker was becoming the only freshman to make the starting team in football that fall, Micah was taking extra-credit courses and getting semi-serious about music. He had already basically taught himself to play the old clarinet his mother had bought him, and when White Bluff High turned out not to have a band program, Connie helped make arrangements for him to take part in the high-profile after-school music program at North Cascades High.

"Let me get this straight," Tucker had said when he'd heard about Micah's music class. "You're going to be in band at N.C.? You know they play their school music against us when they play us. You'd be on their side."

"When you're making music," Micah retorted, "you're not against anybody."

"Listen to you. 'Making music,' whoo. Big composer. Just remember, N.C.'s our rival."

"Everybody's your rival, Tucker."

Micah's observation wasn't far from the truth. After becoming a 154-pound guided missile as a freshman defensive back, Tucker went out for wrestling and approached every practice session and match as if it were a personal grudge. And instead of cutting weight to wrestle at a lower weight class, he actually bulked up to wrestle at 158 pounds, where the hard guys were—the 175-pounders who for weeks would order cups of ice at the drive-in while their friends ate burgers and fries, until their powerful upper bodies had not an extra ounce of fat.

None of which helped anyone against Tucker.

Wrestling came naturally to him, for the same reasons that stoked his sav-agely triumphal sophomore season at middle linebacker: Tucker never tired of the violent, concussive contact of football, and thus was usually able to exert his physical will over the other team, its blockers and ball-carriers. He simply beat on them, play after play, until they relented. The moment they began to flinch just before the point of contact, he had them. It was much the same way with the wrestlers who faced him. They might not flinch from fear; it could be from exhaustion, from pain or from the realization the pain was not going to stop until they did flinch.

Though younger than almost every opponent, Tucker mowed through his season, losing only twice all year. The first came in the district championship against a senior from Tolt who had been in a wrestling club since third grade, and upon reaching the state championship match, Tucker found himself facing that same nemesis. The boy from Tolt spent the entire match on the run, risking nothing, but his conservative approach paid off when he edged Tucker 1-0 on an escape in overtime. As they shook hands after the match, Tucker leaned over close enough to him to whisper, "You're a real chickenshit, you know that?" The older boy's face flushed, but he simply—and wisely—turned away.

While Tucker was wrestling in that state final, Micah was playing second clarinet for N.C. High's performance band as it won a prestigious competition in Everett. Connie was in the audience in Everett, while Big Frank was in the wrestling throngs at the University of Washington, rooting Tucker on and boasting *That's my boy* to anybody within earshot.

Much the same scenario would play out the next winter, their sophomore year: Tucker starring on the mat, Micah continuing his growth as a musician and student. The one new wrinkle was Micah, seeing an opportunity in another athletic arena that didn't involve his older brother, turning out for basketball. He made the "C" squad, the very essence of athletic anonymity. "C" team games were held at the middle school gym, not at the high school, on Thursdays, the same night as most of the varsity wrestling matches. Those factors virtually ensured no cute girls would ever be in the audience at the "C" games, and neither would Big Frank, who wasn't about to miss any of Tucker's wrestling matches. Connie sat through every one of Micah's games, though he rarely left the bench.

When Tucker reached the state wrestling finals again, the event once again fell on the same weekend of Micah's performance—now as first clarinet, complete with a solo—with the North Cascades band at the big Everett competition. The band show ended early enough that Connie and Micah were back at home when Big Frank called with the big news: Tucker had won the state 168-pound title. Unfortunately, though, Big Frank had rushed out to a phone booth with the scoop as soon as Tucker had pinned his opponent, so he missed seeing what happened only moments later: After having his hand raised in victory, Tucker offered a handshake to the other boy, who sneered at the gesture. So Tucker shoved him with both hands and was promptly disqualified for unsportsmanlike conduct. And with that, his victory was null and void and first place at 168 pounds was vacant; only second- and third-place medals would be awarded.

By the time Big Frank and Tucker got home, Connie and Micah—not aware of the postmatch drama—had draped the wall with a paper banner painted with WAY TO GO TUCKER and another that read NICE MOVES CHAMP! Big Frank, who wasn't sure who he was madder at, the referee who DQ'd his son or Tucker for being such a stupid hothead, saw the banner and emitted a dark cackle. Tucker took one look at it, decided they were all making fun of him and stormed to the bedroom, slamming the door behind him.

⅄

"Pick it up."

It was nurse Brimm's voice. It wasn't loud, but it was very firm. Tucker paused on the back porch and peeked in. He could see her back; she was standing at the edge of the kitchen, looking downward. He couldn't see Connie.

"That's good. Put it in the bowl. Get the next one. No. Missus Dodd. There. No, don't do that. There. Pick that one up. No, not in your mouth. Put it in the bowl."

He could see her gesturing and pointing at the floor, and the mental image of what he couldn't see—Connie crawling around the floor, picking up something off the floor, cereal, probably—disturbed him. He burst into the room, realizing even as he did so that he might startle the both of them. When his anticipation became reality, he exploded.

"Whoa whoa WHOA!" he said his voice booming. "What the hell's going on here?"

The nurse whirled around. Connie simply looked up, eyes wide and confused.

"What do you think you're doing?" Tucker demanded over Gulliver's yapping at this activity he could not see.

The nurse regained her composure quickly and her steady, calm voice was an obvious request for him to follow in kind. "We're solving a problem together," she said evenly. Missus Dodd has put some of her cereal on the floor where she knows it shouldn't be, and we're picking it up." She smiled at Connie. "Aren't we, Missus Dodd?"

Connie had a hint of a smile, seemingly at the positive reinforcement.

It made Tucker sick. "Looks like she's the one doing the picking up and you're the one doing the ordering around."

"Dementia patients have to constantly be reminded there are limits to what they can and cannot do. It's like teaching a child or a pet, except with these patients it's a constant process."

"And except she's not a child and she sure ain't no dog," he said, not mollified in the least. "Anybody could see she ain't firing on all cylinders. So she spilled her cereal. Shit happens."

Nurse Brimm just glared at him. "Yes. *It* does. And *it* can be picked up, too. The action serves a purpose."

"Yeah? What's the purpose? To make you feel like you're fucking God?"

That did it.

She seemed to consider her response for long enough that the silence became galling. "I suppose I shouldn't be too surprised at your ill manners and your dirty mouth, considering."

"What the hell does that mean? Considering *what?*"

"Well. Your mother ... no." She seemed to backpedal. "We don't need to go there."

"Oh, by all means. Go there. Or get the hell out."

She glared at him. "I don't believe leaving Missus Dodd under your supervision would be the best thing for her."

"Well, that's not your call to make, is it?"

"Nor is it yours," she retorted, not missing a beat. "She is my responsibility, though I doubt seriously that's a word you're familiar with."

Her lips actually curled into something resembling a smile with the last few words, and he wanted to knock it right off her face.

He wanted to knock those buck teeth right down her throat and make her gag on that condescending smile. He knew he would always have to fight that impulse; such is the dark legacy of a father like Big Frank. Tucker had thus far managed to avoid ever striking a woman, but nurse Brimm had become very familiar. She was every asshole Tucker had dealt with his whole life—the people who had laughed at him, pointed at him when he wasn't looking or taunted him outright, because he couldn't read like everyone else. It was all his fault, he must be lazy, he must not be as good as everybody else.

One of the only ones who had never made fun of him, in fact, was Connie. He knew that.

"Get out," Tucker said. "Take your arrogant ass out of here. And don't come back."

The smugness bled out of nurse Brimm's face, leaving a mask of ashen indignation.

"Oh really? Why don't we leave that for Mister Dodd to decide who needs to leave."

"I *am* Mister Dodd. And I'm telling you to get the fuck out."

"Fine," she said, gathering her things from the kitchen table and heading to the door. She paused for a parting show of bravado. "Don't bother calling our service again. And good luck finding someone to help with your mother now. You won't find anyone."

As the door slammed softly behind her, Tucker flipped a middle finger in her wake.

When he did so, Connie laughed. Sort of.

He looked at her. Laughter?

"Gully," she said.

"Yes ma'am," he said, and let the little dog out. Gulliver ran first to her, his little body wagging, then to him, and then back to her.

"Goodoggy. Goodoggy," she said, reaching down to nuzzle the dog. Then she looked up at Tucker with an expression that looked somewhat hopeful. "Tattle lem," she said. "Gromman wandle."

"Aah," he said, nodding. "We're back to that, are we? Well then, you crazy old bat, you want some cereal?"

She smiled.

The day had been reduced to fading vestiges of pink and gold as Micah watched Amanda turn her RX7 onto his street. He had been watching her all day, casting surreptitious glances as she warmed to the music, nodding her head along with Jim and Jesse's performance and then actually standing up to sway and clap along with Bill Monroe.

Once she had glanced over as he watched and, even as he blushed for having been caught, she reached over to him to squeeze his hand. He leaned down in response and their cheeks brushed in that magical proximity. "I didn't think I was going to like this," she had said, before pulling back to display a smile that said *Isn't this great?*

He watched her some more, bobbing along with the music, her hair dancing across her cheeks with each movement, thinking *Yes, it most definitely is.*

As Amanda pulled to a gentle stop in front of Micah's little duplex, he listened to the purr of the rotary engine and hoped she would switch off the engine. She didn't, and he feared he would have to rush into some kind of muddled goodbye scene. But then she said something that allowed him to breathe in an intoxicating ambrosia of relief and anticipation.

She said, "Do you mind if I use your bathroom?" And turned off the engine.

This respite gave him another couple of minutes to think of just the right thing to say. And he still couldn't come up with it.

He was standing outside on the small concrete porch, looking up at the starlight-starbright first star he'd seen tonight, when she opened the screen door behind him and stepped out. They stood together in the dark, gazing into the sky.

"Well, this was a fun day," she said.

"Yeah. Me, too. I mean … I thought … it was fun for me, too." He smiled sheepishly. "Excuse me, my tongue seems to have grown to twice its normal size."

She gave a soft, understanding laugh, for which he was grateful.

"I'm glad you suggested the festival," she said. "I would have thought I'd rather poke sharp objects in my eyes than spend a day listening to Americana music sung by people with banjos, but it was all right. I mean, it ain't *Soundgarden* …"

"Oh God no," he said, playing along.

"But I guess I'm saying your music is OK."

"Who said it was my music?"

"Don't give me that." She gave him a playful nudge and was about to say something else when the telephone rang inside the duplex. *You're kidding me,* Micah thought. *Now?* He'd had the phone in for a month, and this was the first time he'd heard it ring. He and Amanda exchanged a little glance of resignation, and he held up a *justasec* finger.

The phone was sitting on the inverted milk crate he was using as a coffee table. As he answered it, his eyes stayed on Amanda through the screen door.

On the line was Tucker, saying something about being tired of babysitting for the day and needing to talk about the people Micah had watching out over his mother.

Micah answered in the brief utterances of the conversationally disenfranchised. He nodded at the phone, as if that would somehow speed up the process of getting Tucker off of it.

"—and that's when I told her to get the fuck out."

That part Micah actually heard. "Wait. You told who what?"

His focus had abruptly riveted to the telephone, so it was only in his peripheral awareness he saw Amanda motioning to him. Tucker was going on in four-part harmony and accompaniment about the day's drama with Connie and the nurse, and Micah, ever deferential, couldn't bring himself to break in.

So he stood helplessly as Amanda gave him a little wave. She mimed a phone to her head—*Call me.*

He watched her walk away.

$$\lambda$$

Amanda had been home for less than ten minutes when the telephone rang.

Well, now.

"Hello?"

"You made it home safely." It was him.

"Yes. Against all odds. I was able to drive the entire twenty miles without once running off the road or getting lost."

"Remarkable. I'll be alerting the media now."

"So …"

"So …?"

"Well … you must have called for something."

"Yes. I did. I did call for something."

"And that something is …?"

"I should have kissed you."

Well, now.

"Yes," she said. "You certainly should have."

CHAPTER 10

SYDNEY CARTON WAS AN ASSHOLE

Micah was sitting at his usual spot on the back porch—facing the river this time, enjoying the Indian summer of a September Saturday—when the screen door opened behind him.

"Whatcha readin', bookbrain?"

Aw crap. Tucker invariably made fun of anything he found Micah engrossed in, even though he hadn't read any of it himself. Although they were both in the eleventh grade, Micah was taking college-prep classes and Tucker was in his environment in shop class—where he could build or fix almost anything, something that amazed Micah.

"'Tale of Two Cities.'"

"Wait a minute. Isn't that the one you spent like a month reading last year? You kept complaining about how long it was."

"I wasn't complaining. I was just sayin'."

"Whatever. You're reading it again?"

"Yeah, so? It's a good book."

"Would I like the story?"

"Nuh uh."

"How come?"

"You wouldn't like how it ends."

"So how's it end?"

Micah sighed. "You'd have to know the characters. Besides, you'd just make fun of it if I told you."

"Yeah, and maybe I'll hold you down and give you an Indian rub if you don't." Tucker crossed his arms, willing to wait him out.

"OK. Fine. Just remember I told you you wouldn't like it. So there's this guy who's in love with this girl who barely even knows he's alive, because she's in love with this other guy, this rich dude, this nobleman guy."

"Ah. Figures. Chicks give the honey to dicks with the money."

"No, it's not like that. The nobleman's not a bad guy at all, he was just born into this upper class. And what's going on is there's this uprising against the upper class, and the poor people take over the city and they're going to start executing all the rich people."

"Sounds like a good plan."

"So this guy, this Sydney Carton dude, he's got it made in the shade. He's in the clear since he's not a rich dude, he's in tight with the poor people who have taken over the city. And now they're going to hang this rich dude his dream girl's in love with. And that'd leave her all alone again—so you think maybe he'd have his shot."

"Yeah, fat chance she gives him the time of day."

"That's right. There's no way. He knows she loves the other dude, who he's got no problem with. And so this Sydney Carton guy goes to the place where they're going to hang the guy—actually, cut off his head, is what they were going to do to him."

"Holy shit. What country is this in?"

"France. They did a lot of it in real life, actually. Guillotine. That's the thing they did it with. Big blade coming down. Whummph."

"Ugh. Pretty vicious people. Sounds like something they'd do in the jungle. France, isn't that where they drink tea?"

"That's England. You want to hear the story or not?"

"Doesn't mean shit to me either way."

"Well, you practically made me tell it."

"So TELL it, already."

"OK. So the Sydney Carton guy goes to where they're going to execute the guy, who's really sick, and he switches places with him. And goes to the guillotine himself."

"Bullshit."

"No. Seriously."

"What an asshole."

"No, don't you see? He knows it's the right thing to do. See, Sydney Carton hasn't always been very proud of himself, you know? He knows there's not a lot of people in the world who really care about him. And here's this other guy who's going to get his head chopped off just because of the family he was born into, and this guy's actually got some potential, some decency. And the most amazing woman Sydney Carton has ever met is totally in love with this other guy, and he knows if this dude got his head cut off, she'd never be the same. So he does the one thing he knows will make her happy. He switches places with the guy and goes to the guillotine."

"So his dream girl knows he died for her, huh? Well, maybe she'll repay him if they meet up in the next life." He pokes his tongue against the fat part of his cheek a couple of times, the classic blow-job reference.

"Nope. She'll never know he ever did it. At least I think that's the way it went."

"What, this guy he rescues, the guy he switches place with, is so much of a dick he doesn't even tell her who saved his bacon?"

"No, he's too sick to know what happened. He's, like, delirious."

"OK, you're right about one thing: I think this is a horseshit story."

Micah gave him the I-told-you-so face.

"The guy's too sick even to know somebody changed places with him?" Tucker said. "Jesus, did they trade clothes? How'd he manage to pull that off? Who's gonna buy that?"

"Hey, I'm just telling you the story, man. That's the way I remember it, anyway."

"Well, it's a crock of shit. This dude doesn't even get to go out a hero, after giving up on his own chance of getting the girl back and taking the blade for some other guy? That's horseshit, man."

"He was never gonna get the girl."

"Why not? You don't know that. Maybe he would have."

"But she would never have been as happy as she would have been with the other guy."

"Yeah, but he'd have been happy. The Sydney guy."

Micah was shaking his head. "Don't you get it? He was doing the right thing, and he was willing to die for it. The right thing."

"Yeah, well, let's face it. Something like that would only happen in a stupid book. Nobody in real life—nobody in his right mind—would ever do something like that."

Micah stiffened. "I'd like to believe I would."

Tucker smirked. "Well, I can damn sure tell you I wouldn't."

"That's because you don't believe in anything."

"Fuck you."

"Seriously, what do you believe in?

"Fuck you twice. Gravity."

"What?"

"I believe in gravity. I read all about it in a book. Some scientist guy named Sydney Carton had an apple fall on his head."

Micah nodded his head. *Ha ha. Real funny.*

"Hey. I'm gonna head out with Steelbarton and Skelly in a while. Probably go over to Darrington. You wanna go?"

Micah almost did a double-take. Tucker never asked him to join in when he went out with his buddies.

"Why you going to Darrington? Oh wait, don't tell me. Steelbarton wants to pound a few Darrington guys since they beat us last night."

Tucker laughed softly. "You may be right about that."

"Well, what are you asking me for? I wouldn't be any help in a fight."

"Hey, ain't gonna be no fight. Steelbarton just wants to drive around and look tough in his Trans Am."

"Those guys don't want me tagging along. Skelly's never liked me."

"Who cares? And Steel's got no beef with you. You guys are practically teammates now."

Micah frowned. "Yeah. I hand him a water battle and he spits a mouthful out on my shoes."

Tucker allowed a sardonic grin. "Steel can be a dick. But he's OK."

"Thanks anyway. I'm going fishing with Deano in a little bit anyway."

"Well shit, why didn't you just say so, you little twerp? Like you'll catch anything."

And he was gone.

⅄

Micah hadn't counted on this. He'd heard Tucker tell him something about it on the phone the previous night, but Amanda had been on the porch and he'd been distracted. Now, sitting in his mother's kitchen the next morning, listening to the clatter of the rain gutters all but drown out the faint sound of his mother burbling in some tongue only she understood, it was starting to sink in.

"So you fired the nurse."

Tucker seemed more interested in jousting with Gulliver than rehashing the obvious. "I told her to get the fuck out."

"Man. I wish you hadn't done that."

"She's lucky I didn't toss her bony ass into the yard myself. She had it coming."

"Well," Micah said, "you know what this means."

From the other room, Connie turned up the decibel level on her monologue, which sounded like a confluence of languages from several solar systems.

Tucker raised his eyebrows and sighed in resignation. "We're going to be sweeping up a shitload of Cheerios and Fruit Loops."

Micah nodded.

"Hey," Tucker said, changing the tone. "So you finally made it your turn, huh?"

Micah had no idea what he was talking about.

"You went to the Under Look."

"What are you talking about? When?

"A long time ago, I guess. I just went down there yesterday. Saw that stupid bridge across the gap. Was that thing there when you took it?"

Micah was shaking his head, still trying to figure out what Tucker was going on about. And what to say.

"You've only just found out the falcon stone's not there anymore?"

"Well, I guess you could say I just got reminded of it. I saw it was missing way back before I left. But. You know."

That created a long silence.

"Wait a minute," Tucker said. "You actually helped Deano put that thing in. I remember him saying that. Man. I never would have thought you had it in you."

"Thanks a lot."

The silence came back. Micah knew he didn't have it in him. But he resented Tucker for thinking so.

"Well, anyway. You've got it now," Tucker finally said. "The stone."

Micah gave a conflicted nod. "Yeah. I got it."

"Good for you. Glad to see you finally took the leap. Even if you had to use that stupid bridge to do it."

"That was a long time ago, man."

Micah and Deano spent most of that Saturday fly-fishing for steelhead on the Suiattle below the mouth of the Kacheel. Micah was a fly fisherman entirely because of Deano, who had taught him everything about fishing neither his father nor his brother had ever taken the time for.

They had gone on foot, which meant hoofing it down the three-mile path that more or less followed the Kacheel from the base of the falls. As usual, their creels were empty, because Deano's fishing policy was to keep only fish that bled when the hook was removed. Rather than condemn the injured fish to a slow but inevitable death, Deano would smash its skull on a rock and take it home. And since Micah, as the student, adhered to Deano's policy, he also rarely brought a fish home. Big Frank just assumed his youngest boy was a shitty fisherman.

"Hey," Deano said, glancing back as they followed the winding trail up-hill through the trees in the general direction of Kacheel Falls. "I still say you should have gone out for the team. We ain't got anybody who can kick worth a crap. You don't have to be big to be able to kick a football, you know."

"Yeah, but you have to know how to kick one."

"You could learn. You're good at learning everything else, aren't you?"

Micah shrugged it off. "Well, it's too late now, anyway. I'm team manager and that's it."

Deano grunted. "Whoopty do. Haul water and pick up towels. Bet that'll get you laid."

Micah would have blushed at the thought had they not reached the por-tion of the trail that emerged from the forest opposite the Under Look. Micah couldn't help himself; he had to stop and stare across at the little plateau that fascinated him even more than the falls. Even looking across at that slippery, sloping, pitiful excuse for a path leading to the Under Look gave Micah those scaredy-cat tingles in the knees.

Deano stopped ahead of Micah and looked back to see what his buddy was staring at.

"You ever been?"

Micah just shook his head. "You?"

"Nope."

"You scared to try?"

Deano cocked his head, as if the question made no sense. "To go to the Under Look? Don't know. Never had any reason to find out. Why? You want to go?"

The mere thought made Micah flush with the vertigo pangs again. He put his free hand out to the nearest tree, just in case. "No, I don't want to go," he said.

Deano gave him a quizzical look, then turned back up the trail. "Fine. Let's not, then."

But Micah didn't follow him, instead standing in place, his hand touch-ing the tree trunk, which served as an anchor more emotional than physical. Deano noticed and came carefully back down the trail.

"You OK?"

Micah stared across the chasm at the Under Look. "Why don't I have the nerve to go out there?"

"That's easy: because you're not stupid."

"Tucker's been there. A bunch of times, probably."

Deano made the face. "Well there you have it—case in point. Anybody who'd do the Look without a good reason has to be either crazy or stupid. Of course, he's both, so there you go."

He turned to leave again, and this time Micah followed. They worked up the switchback trail, and in another five minutes had reached the bluff. They walked to the top of the falls—on the opposite bank from Tucker's flat-rock throne, directly across from the Under Look.

Micah's eyes again strained to see the crack with the falcon stone.

"What's your deal with the Under Look, man? What's going on with you?"

Micah shook his head. "Tucker put something out there once. And I don't have the balls to go get it."

Deano gave the Look a good look. "There's nothing over there, man."

"Oh. It's there. I know it is."

Micah gave Deano a brief history of the falcon stone and its current resting place.

"That's interesting, but what the hell, Micah. Why do you give a shit about a rock?"

"I don't know. I can't explain it. Ever since I was a kid, ever since my dad told us about it and gave it to us, it's had this thing on me, you know? Every time I see a falcon or an eagle soaring in the sky, I think about that falcon stone. Like it means something. It's like an emblem or something." He looked at Deano and caught his friend's bemused expression. "Screw you."

Deano grinned. "Well, if it means that much to you, why don't you just go down there and get it?"

"Yeah, right." Micah said softly. "Sure."

Deano shook his head, clearly finding the whole thing amusing. "Well, screw it, then. I'll go get the stupid thing."

"Hey, no way. You just said you'd have to be crazy to go out there."

"No, I just said you better have a good reason to go." He shrugged. "Hey. A prehistoric philosophy rock, that sounds like a pretty good reason to me."

"OK," Micah said, still trying to talk his friend out of what Micah was certain was tantamount to suicide. "What should I tell your mom if you fall?"

Deano shrugged. "Gimme a break. I'll be back in five minutes."

And he was.

⅄

At precisely the same moment Deano was handing Micah the falcon stone, Tucker was sitting in his chosen spot in Steelbarton's Trans Am—in the back, legs splayed out the length of the seat, Skelly Radich in front of him riding shotgun and Steelbarton at the wheel. They had the time and, thanks to Skelly's older brother Wes, they had the beer. Now they were driving around Darrington, doing nothing more than looking for trouble.

The night before, the White Bluff football team, for which Steelbarton played defensive end and Tucker was middle linebacker, had lost to Darrington on a last-minute touchdown set up by a penalty on Steelbarton. He had sacked the quarterback on fourth down, which would have clinched the victory. But Steelbarton had driven that quarterback to the turf with such gusto the back judge had thrown a flag. Unnecessary roughness, personal foul, fifteen yards, automatic first down. Given a new set of downs, Darrington had scored the game-winning touchdown three plays later.

Twenty hours later, Steelbarton was still steaming, and Skelly was happily stoking the coals of that discontent.

"These Darrington pricks should have apologized to you guys for winning that game," said Skelly, who wasn't on the team.

"They didn't win, Skull, don't even be saying that shit," Steelbarton snapped. "We had that game won. They should have to put a asterisk on it, like the home run deal that time with that guy, whatsisname, Maris. Tee-man, tell me again how it's unnecessary roughness if the QB's holding the ball when I hit him."

Tucker was looking out the window, watching passersby, eyeballing the occasional cute chick. He was bored with the whole refs-screwed-us thing. "Steel, I just couldn't tell ya."

"Well shit, you saw it, did I rough the guy or not?"

Jesus, give it up, Steel. "Well, I dunno, man. If he's still pissing blood, I'm guessing maybe you did."

Steelbarton and Skelly both cracked up as the Trans Am pulled up to an easy halt at the one four-way stop sign in Darrington. An instant later a Mustang convertible stopped from the cross street to the left.

"Tuck," Steelbarton said furtively. "Tee, look at the driver. Isn't that Blake Slesk?"

Slesk was Darrington's star running back, who had scored the decisive touchdown the night before. Tucker craned his neck to see. "Nah. That ain't him."

It was Steelbarton's turn to go at the four-way, but he wasn't going. "I think it is, man. I think that's the fuckstick himself."

Obviously tired of waiting for Steelbarton, the Mustang driver began to pull into the intersection. At the same instant, Steelbarton lurched the Trans Am forward. The Mustang stopped. So did Steelbarton, who then gave the Mustang driver a little wave to go ahead. But as soon as the Mustang began moving again, Steelbarton gave it the gas. The cars jerked to a simultaneous stop.

"What the hell are you doing, man?" Skelly said.

"Just having a little fun, Skull Man. Tuck, I still think that's Slesk."

"Who gives a herkin' shit?" Tucker said. "Let it go."

The Mustang driver was now shaking his head and saying something to his three passengers, no doubt about the moron driving the Trans Am. He made a big production of waving for Steelbarton to go first.

But Steelbarton wouldn't go.

Aah shit, Tucker thought.

The Mustang driver finally gave up and went on through the intersection, even when Steelbarton tried once again to block him. The driver glared at him, shaking his head in disdain, when Steelbarton blared his horn as if he'd been cut off. The girl in the back seat, a blonde who looked good-looking from that distance, flipped a bird at the Trans Am.

Steelbarton immediately turned right into the Mustang's wake, urging his Trans Am upon the Mustang's rear bumper.

Tucker sighed, knowing exactly where this was heading. Steelbarton's explosive nature made him a terrific teammate on the field, but kind of scary off it. Keeping that simmering volatility in check was a balancing act only Tucker seemed able to accomplish—and sometimes even he simply moved out of the way and let Steel Bar take on the world.

"Did you see that shit?" Steelbarton said with something like righteous glee. He peered back over his shoulder. "Tee, you see that? They flipped us off."

"*They* didn't do anything," Tucker retorted. "One chick flipped *you* off because you were screwing with 'em."

Steelbarton quizzed him with a look in the rearview mirror. "What's your problem?"

Tucker just shrugged and resigned himself to having Steelbarton's back. Steel had done the same for him time and again.

"Stay on him, Steel Bar," Skelly insisted.

The Trans Am's grill was three feet from the Mustang's bumper at about 25 miles an hour when the brake lights came on and the convertible lurched to an abrupt stop. Steelbarton's reactions were nearly instantaneous, those of an athlete, but weren't enough to keep him from touching the Mustang ever so slightly.

"Son of a bitch!" Steelbarton blurted. "I'm gonna kick this guy's ass."

The Mustang started to peel out before the driver apparently realized the inevitable perils of such an action and pulled over off the shoulder. Steelbarton followed, and was throwing open the door almost before the Trans Am had stopped moving.

"Well, here we go," Skelly said as he opened his door.

Tucker shook his head. *Yeah. Here we go again.*

By the time Tucker extracted himself from the back seat, Steelbarton was looming loudly over the driver door of the Mustang. None of its four passengers, two guys and two girls, had moved from their seats. The girl in the back who'd given them the bird was the only one of the four who wasn't hunkering down in dread.

"What do you think you're doing, jerkoff?" Steelbarton snarled. "Slamming on your brakes like that with a car behind you? You could get somebody hurt real bad doing stupid shit like that."

Tucker could see the Mustang driver being careful not to make more than fleeting direct eye contact, while at the same time trying not to look too wimpy in front of the two girls. Tucker could tell in a heartbeat neither the driver, who looked to be seventeen or eighteen, nor the dude in the back seat was interested in getting into anything; they weren't the type. As an alpha dog, Tucker was always being met with the same sort of capitulation, in which the surrendering party wants nothing more than to come away without getting punched out and without looking like a wuss for avoiding it. Neither of these guys was Slesk, a tough kid who probably would already be out of the car and right in Steel's face. These guys weren't going to be jocks showing off for their girls at all, which Tucker knew was what Steelbarton had been hoping for.

The driver was saying something, a soft posturing of his own right to indignation that Tucker couldn't hear. Tucker watched Steelbarton's body, the way he had his weight balanced—forward, onto the balls of the feet. The only way Steelbarton played the game.

"Don't give me that shit," Steelbarton barked in response to whatever had been said. "Why don't you come out of there and we'll see if you did any damage to my car."

"EXCUSE ME? Damage to YOUR car? You just rear-ended us, you big dumbass!"

The voice, loud and livid, didn't come from the driver, whose head sagged at the sound.

It was the blonde in the back seat.

Tucker was riveted by the girl. She had balls. And she was dang pretty.

"You better put a sock in that mouth of hers, pal," Steelbarton said to her seat mate. "Before she says something you can't back up."

The blonde stood up in grand defiance, thereby revealing a faded pair of tight Levis she filled out quite nicely. "He doesn't tell me what to do, and neither do you," she said, true grit in her voice. "Don't you losers have anything better to do than bother people?"

As she asked the question she glanced back at Skelly, then at Tucker, who regretted his momentary eye contact with her as having been perfectly timed with "you losers."

"Losers. LOSERS. You stupid bi—" Steelbarton said, stopping short of saying something he knew Tucker wouldn't abide. "You should learn to shut your hole."

In that instant, the Mustang driver opened his door and stepped out. Tucker watched his ashen face. The kid was absolutely terrified, but had stepped out to defend the people in his car. *Hmm. Good for you, kid. Just don't ruin it by opening your mouth.*

"You leave her alone," the boy said in what little voice he could muster up. *Ah shit, kid. Shut the hell up.*

Too late. With no wasted motion whatsoever, Steelbarton threw a short, hard right to the solar plexus. The kid doubled over and dropped like a rag doll.

"Ooh! Knockdown! Score!" Skelly enthused.

In the next second, Tucker assessed the situation: The driver's buddy was even more scared shitless than bachelor number one, so he wouldn't pose a problem. Blondie was about to climb out of the car herself, he could see that, maybe even to throw a punch at Steelbarton. The other girl had begun to cry in stuttering little shivers.

Tucker stepped forward, hands out like a peacemaker.

"OK, Steel, you made your point," he said, stepping into the narrow space between his friend and the gagging boy on his knees. Steelbarton glared at him for intervening, obviously disappointed the punching portion of this meeting was now adjourned.

Or maybe it wasn't.

The blonde, now having clambered out of the car behind Tucker, tried to push around him and get to Steelbarton. Tucker slid over and blocked her path.

"You big stupid bully," she was saying, poking at him around Tucker, who then became the target of her righteous wrath as he managed to get her into reverse. "And you too, what do you have to say for yourself? You proud of yourself? And you?" she added with a glance at Skelly. "Way to go."

"Thank you very much," Skelly mugged, no doubt thinking he was so very clever.

The driver's gagging finally ran its course and he began to catch his breath. The blonde glared again at Tucker, shrugged free of his hand on her arm and walked firmly past him to the driver, helping him up and standing close enough to prevent round two.

Emboldened by this human shield, the driver muttered, "That was a sucker punch."

Damn it, kid.

Steelbarton closed the distance and shoved blondie out of the way for another go, bellowing "Oh YEAH?" She pushed him back in the same instant Tucker forced his way between them, pushing Steelbarton hard to put him on his heels.

"STEEL!" He boomed it just like Coach Tucker would at practice, whenever he saw his big D-end loafing, or worse, in a game whenever the Steel Bar had laid somebody out after the whistle. And Steelbarton froze. You had to give that to the guy: He took instruction well, as long as it was loud enough.

Tucker crooked a *C'mere* finger at Steelbarton and beckoned him toward the space between the two cars. Steelbarton followed only reluctantly, giving the driver a sidelong glare. When he got to the back of the Mustang, Tucker pointed at the bumper.

"Look at his car, you big dumbass."

He could see the blonde cocking her head at his use of her phrase.

Steelbarton obviously didn't like the way this was going, but he looked. "Yeah?"

"Not a mark on it. Right? Now: Look at your car."

Steelbarton leaned in to give it a decent inspection. The Trans Am was his baby, after all.

"And?" Tucker crossed his arms.

"I dunno. It looks OK, I guess."

"Of course it looks OK, said tucker, the peacemaker. Nothing happened to it. You guys barely touched. No problem."

Tucker headed to the front of the car, passing a somewhat , Skelly and stopping in front of the driver and the blonde.

"No problem, right?" he said. He said it as a question, but it was nothing of the kind. It was strong advice. "We're all good, right? We all just had a little misunderstanding, right?"

Steelbarton came up behind him. "Hey, hold up now. They flipped me off."

Tucker stopped him with a look. "Don't worry about it. They're going to apologize."

As he turned back, the blonde said, "I'm not going to apologize—"

He held up the palm of his hand: *Stop.* "Not you. Him."

The driver looked up in dismay, clearly having hoped to maintain his nonspeaking role.

"Don't you have something to say to my friend?" Tucker demanded.

The driver ignored the blonde's *Don't you do it* look. "Sorry," he said.

"Not to me," Tucker said. "To him."

"Uh, yeah, I'm sorry," he said, turning to Steelbarton. "For … stepping on the brakes."

Tucker held out his hands expansively. "OK then," he announced, turning his body so he could keep an eye on everybody. "No harm done. We're all good."

Steelbarton began to protest. "But …"

"Steel? You already kicked his ass. One punch knockout."

"Yeah baby," Skelly said.

"So you're good, right? You don't need to kick the other guy's ass too, do you? I mean, if you really got your mind set, I won't stop you."

Tucker could almost feel bachelor number two shrivel into his seat.

Steelbarton shrugged, a little sheepish. "I guess I don't need to."

From behind him, the driver whined softly, "But he sucker-punched me."

Tucker pointed at Steelbarton—*Don't*—and wheeled around. His face was so close to that of the driver, Tucker could feel it when the boy stopped breathing.

"Shut. Up."

Tucker's tone was soft. But absolutely menacing.

"Just couldn't leave it alone, could you. Had to get in a last word. I should kick your ass just for being so stupid." Tucker shook his head with absolute disdain. "Get outta here."

"And you," he said, pointing a finger at the blonde. "Steel's right. You don't know when to shut up."

Tucker turned and motioned Steelbarton and Skelly back to the Trans Am. As the three of them began climbing into Steelbarton's car, Tucker glanced back for one last look at the Mustang group. The driver was opening his door to get in, no doubt glad to have his body fully intact, if not his pride.

The blonde, a 16-year-old North Cascades High School junior named Amanda Devlin, was looking at Tucker with an intriguing blend of emotions.

⚔

Micah held the falcon stone, turning it over in his hand to study its every nuance.

Deano watched him, bemused. "Happy now?" he asked.

Micah looked up from the falcon stone. It seemed surreal to be holding it. Until this moment, he had never actually touched it.

"You know," Deano said, "that gap there at the Look is a little dangerous."

"A little? That was crazy. You could have died."

Deano made the *gimme a break* face. "No, seriously, all it needs is a little bridge."

"What, you're gonna build a bridge to the Under Look?"

"I dunno. Maybe."

"You're crazier than my brother." He looked at the falcon stone in his hand. "If he sees this thing is gone, he's going to know I got it."

"Good."

"He'll want to know how I got it."

"'Cause you went and got it, how about that?"

"Yeah, right. Like he'd believe that."

"Screw that, I'll tell him you got it," Deano said, grinning. "I watched you go get it, dude."

"I don't want you lying for me. Maybe he won't notice it's gone. Probably just kid stuff for him." Micah sighed.

"Then why not just tell him? You got the rock now. It's your turn."

"He'll just take it back."

"No he won't."

"Yeah? How am I supposed to stop him?"

"You just stop him. I'll stand by you."

"He'll pound you."

"You too."

Micah slowly shook his head. "Nope. He won't. I don't know why. But he'd pound you."

"Maybe."

"Maybe for sure."

"Well, but see, I got a plan."

"What's your brilliant plan."

"See, after he beats on me for a while, eventually he's gonna get tired." Deano nodded in deadpan gravity. "And then I got him right where I want him."

"Oh yeah? That's when you'll pounce on him?"

"No, dipshit, that's when I'll run away as fast as I can. Do I look crazy to you?"

⋏

It had been more than six years since Tucker had seen the falcon stone, and now he really wanted to see it. He couldn't possibly have explained why. "So where is it?"

"Why?"

"Why you think? Because I want to see it."

Micah did the one-eye-squint contemplation. "Well, since I know if I show it to you, I'll never see it again, why should I do that?"

"Hey, what am I going to do, carry it around in my pocket? I'll give it back."

"Or maybe put it back at the Look."

"So? You got it once, you can get it again, right?"

"I'm not so sure about this."

Tucker gave him a quasi-hard look and balled a fist. "Suppose I make you." It was an idle threat, and they both knew it.

This time, Micah balled a fist in response—and then started rocking it up and down.

"Paper rock scissors for it."

"Gimme a break."

Micah pointed at him with his free hand, while the balled fist continued to rock. "All right, I got another idea. I give you the falcon stone and you take care of Mom today."

Tucker frowned. "Screw that, I was here almost all day yesterday while you were at that concert deal. She's your mother, not mine."

"You want the falcon stone or not?"

"Hey, I just want to see it. It's not like I couldn't just take it from you if I wanted to."

"If you knew where I kept it."

"Ain't that big a deal to me either way."

"Neither is taking care of Mom. So it's a good trade then, right?"

"Hey, man, the rock don't throw cereal all over the kitchen and wet the bed. Gross."

Micah responded with a melancholy nod. "Tell me about it." He rose and went into the other room. When he returned, he offered an open hand to Tucker. In it was the falcon stone, its falcon side now green.

"What the hell is that? You painted it?"

"Kinda more like ink, actually."

"What's with that?"

"I sort of used it like a stamp. Like a coat of arms."

"A what?"

"Like a signature."

Tucker frowned. "You're one weird dude, bro."

"So you've been telling me my whole life. OK, so now you'll take care of Mom today?"

"I didn't agree to that deal. What the hell do I want with a green rock?"

Micah balled his fist again. "OK, you piece of shit," he said. "Paper rock scissors for it."

"Not a chance."

Micah started rocking his fist. *You in or out?*

Tucker shook his head. But with a little smile. Relenting.

"Dickhead," Tucker said, and began rocking his fist along with his little brother.

"Asswipe," Micah said.

"OK, shit for brains," Tucker said. "But if I lose, I keep the falcon stone. That's the deal."

"Eat me. You can have it."

"OK then. Here we go … one … two …"

CHAPTER 11

DISASTER STRIKES

P aper wraps rock.

So Tucker sat on the back porch, his brother's old throne, flipping the falcon stone up and back into his right palm. Every time he tossed the falcon stone up, Gulliver—his near-constant companion these days—followed it with his alert eyes and his head, as if on the verge of leaping for it. Tucker palmed the stone, turning it over and feeling the naturally rougher, ink-free texture. But holding it began to make him think of Big Frank, so he shoved it into his pocket.

Prehistoric falcon. Yeah, right.

He noticed Gulliver hearing Connie in the other room and so he listened, too. Sure enough, she was rustling around.

"You got good ears, little buddy," he said, tugging tenderly on one of them. "Listen, if you hear the cops, lemme know, will you?" He rose and went inside to listen from outside Connie's door. Rustling in the bed. No gibberish. Nothing to worry about.

As he walked to the edge of the kitchen, Gulliver watched him dutifully, ready for whatever was next on their joint agenda. Tucker squatted down to nuzzle the little guy's scruffy head, and that put him even with the lowest shelf on Connie's old bookcase. Most of its contents were magazines like

Cosmopolitan and Women's Day, along with some old crossword puzzle books and a few paperbacks.

On the bottom shelf, he saw what he recognized as some of the boys' old yearbooks. Micah's yearbooks, actually, since Tucker had never gotten one. He wasn't about to go around having people sign and write stuff all through it that he would then have to read in their presence to see what stupid crap they'd written. Nor did he want to have to write stupid crap in anybody else's yearbook. Too much of a hassle. Too much work. Potentially embarrassing. So he always made a point of skipping school on the day they'd be made available.

As he picked up the yearbook on top, he saw what was below it. He vaguely remembered it as a scrapbook he'd seen Connie perusing several different times, years ago—but only when he was in passing, and pass he invariably did, even when she practically begged him to join her. Sit on the sofa with Big Frank's wife to look at stupid pictures while she oohed and aahed over them? No chance. He refused to indulge her that.

The scrapbook cover felt a little bit like the upholstery in the old '78 Skylark convertible he used to drive in Vegas. He set the yearbook on the shelf and toted the scrapbook to the back porch. Gulliver was overjoyed.

"What do you think, little buddy? You wanna give this a try? Can't be any worse than watching TV."

Gulliver wagged his body in agreement.

Tucker opened the scrapbook. The first few pages were just class pictures from elementary school. Tucker scanned them, looking for kids he recognized, but there were only a few faces that looked even remotely familiar. Then he realized: Aha. Micah was in every classroom photo. He flipped over the page, hoping to see some pictures of his own classes, or of himself, but not quite sure if he was expecting either. On the next two panels, he was in a couple of photos, all right. But never alone. Always with Micah. Page after page, Tucker skimmed through report cards, fancy-looking certificates of various achievements, even a few little newspaper articles, most of the headlines including BAND, a small word Tucker had no trouble recognizing.

Nothing of Tucker.

None of his football stories. Nothing from wrestling. He'd never actually read about himself in the newspapers, but he knew he'd been in there a bunch of times. The high school sports guy from the Skagit Valley Herald had talked to him a few times after games and matches, asking him questions and then writing stuff down in a little notebook, and Tucker's friends would tell him they saw his name in the paper again.

But none of that was here. Working hard to figure out what every clipping was about, he saw Micah's name in there a bunch of times. He never saw his own name, though. Not one time.

I should have known, he thought. *None of 'em ever gave a shit. I get all-state or win a tournament, that just gives Big Frank a reason to get juiced and brag to the cronies. That's all it was good for. Connie's big scrapbook? All full of Micah. Like I don't exist.*

Fine. That's the way it is. I knew it all along. I was never part of this family. Fuck 'em.

人

"Ah, come on, I'm doing all the talking."

Micah was sitting cross-legged on a patchwork quilt on the living room floor at his apartment. Amanda was stretched across the far side of the quilt, leaning on her elbow and looking heartstoppingly natural and beautiful.

"Well, yeah," she said with a very subtle grin. "You're a guy. Guys like to talk about themselves, so … we let you."

"Oh really, so that's it, is it?"

"Absolutely. We know it turns guys on when they get to talk about themselves."

"Oh. It turns us on?"

She did the palms-out shrug. "The nature of the beast."

"To be egomaniacs."

"Basically. You're a guy. Ergo, you are your own favorite subject."

She was so deadpan he laughed, and she did, too. "That's OK. I have the time," she said with a smile, gesturing to the rain-drenched window. Her voice competed with the tinny hammering on the rain gutters.

"Sorry the weather didn't pan out. For the picnic."

"Why are you sorry? We're just having the picnic indoors, that's all," she said, looking around the semibare apartment as if it were a penthouse suite. "No ants here. Hallelujah."

"Yeah, but it's not the same as being outdoors. I don't get to pee in the bushes."

"No, but you're a guy. You'll just pee all over the sides of the toilet and then leave the seat up. Might as well be in the bushes."

"Ah, so that's why you suggested here instead of your place then," he said. "You don't want me peeing all over your bathroom."

"Absolutely not. You troll. That and it's just nice to … well, it's nice to have some control of things when you're … getting to know someone."

"Aah. If you decide it's time to leave, you can just leave."

"Exactly."

It was one of those reality checks that could feel uncomfortable, but Micah smiled; it didn't feel uncomfortable at all. He almost couldn't believe his ease with the conversation. Or how good she looked, at once utterly unaffected and gracefully feminine, with a playful glint to her eyes. He had spent a lifetime botching every get-to-know-you conversation with any girl he was interested in, tripping over the hurdles of nervousness and hope. Not Amanda. She made it all so easy.

"Or if I decide I have to leave before I die of thirst," she said. "There is that possibility."

Micah popped up to a ready squat. "Oh, shit, I'm sorry. What would you like?"

"That's a pretty big question. I have a list," Amanda said with a grin. "First, I'd like you to get me a beer of some kind, light beer if you got it. Or a glass of wine, whichever." As Micah rose, she added, "Then I'd like you to show me some of your pictures."

"Photographs."

She made a face at his correction and watched him stroll to the refrigerator. "And *thennnn*, after that—but only after that—I'd like you to kiss me."

Micah nearly dropped the two beers he had grabbed, which made her smile and then laugh. Micah laughed along, unembarrassed.

"So," she said through the laughter, accepting the beer. "Do I get to see my photographs? Or you can tell me one of your sports stories first if you want. You being a guy and all."

"And a egomaniac."

"Well, yeah. Goes without saying. What's your best sports memory?"

Micah blew out a little thoughtful air, then shook his head.

"I only have worst ones."

⅄

Two worst ones, in fact. They both came within a couple of weeks of each other in the fall of his junior year. And they both involved Deano.

The first came in the last regular-season football game against N.C. High. White Bluff led by two points in the final twenty seconds, but N.C. had the ball and was driving.

The intensity was at a fever pitch on the field and in the stands, with the season riding on the final one or two plays. If the Wolves could hold on defense, they would win and advance to the playoffs. Give up a score and the season was over. N.C. might be close enough for a field goal that would win the game. And might not.

Micah wasn't really watching the game. Although he was the team manager—which, in high school, meant managing absolutely nothing—sports in general bored him. He understood the rules, but couldn't fathom the attraction. The only reason he'd turned out for C-squad basketball had been to keep Deano company, and football was pretty much the same deal—though he often took a morbid curiosity in watching Tucker lay waste to opposing ballcarriers.

Much more interesting at the moment was Judy Jubb, a cheerleader with a wholesome prettiness, freckles and what Deano called "capital letters"— precocious maturity at that point across which a baseball's passage was once commonly referred to as a "strike at the letters." She was standing on her cheerleading box on the track, which enabled her to see over the players, coaches and one skinny team manager crowding the sideline.

Micah heard the collective whoop and groan of the crowd in the moment Judy Jubb's eyes met his, or seemed to. Mortified at having been caught ogling, he whirled back to the action and it was right in front of him: the ball bouncing toward him, Deano barreling after it with other players in fruitless pursuit. It was so far behind the line of scrimmage, he assumed at once it was a dead ball—incomplete, or being tossed out to the ballboy. Deano's rapid pursuit didn't register.

Without thinking, his mind's eye still focused on Judy Jubb, he stepped onto the field—intending to toss the errant pigskin back to his buddy on the field—and reached down to pick up the ball.

In that instant, he realized—by the referee's whistle, the collective gasp and groan of the home crowd and Deano's *What the hell did you just do* expression—he had screwed up.

It took the officials several minutes to determine their ruling. Because Micah was not a player but was on the sideline in an official capacity—team manager, towel carrier, gofer—White Bluff would be assessed an unsportsmanlike conduct penalty. That would move the ball half the distance to the goal line and N.C. would retain possession. With only two seconds remaining now, the penalty put N.C. in range for a short field goal. They kicked it on the final play to win by one point.

Only in the next few terrible minutes did Micah learn what had happened before his attention was ripped from Judy Jubb's capital letters. The N.C. quarterback had thrown a slightly backward pass toward a receiver and Deano, blitzing from his safety position, had deflected it and sent it bounding toward the sideline. Deano seemed destined to recover the ball for the victory, and even if he didn't, the clock might have run out before N.C. could get off a last desperation play.

Until Micah stepped onto the field and handed N.C. the victory.

He wanted to disappear. But, as team manager, he still had a job to do, and Micah was nothing if not responsible. He gathered the towels and water bottles from the sideline and made his way to the locker room in silence. He sat through the coaches' postmortem speeches with his eyes on the concrete floor, feeling others' eyes on him.

The second after Coach Tucker and his assistants left, Steelbarton kicked a locker.

"DAMN it," he shouted. "We had those fuckers."

A couple of other players turned to glare at Micah. Before long, it was more than a couple.

"It ain't the kid's fault," Thad Mohler, a tight end, said to nobody in particular. "We should have put this game away ten different times, and we didn't."

"Got that right," somebody grumbled.

"Yeah," groused Jody Beckman, a big lineman. "But then we 'D' up and the little shit hands the ball right over to 'em."

"Hands 'em the stinkin' game," muttered someone else.

"Hey!" Deano, a 150-pound defensive back much closer to Micah's size than Beckman's, stood up. "Don't be blamin' him. If I would've just caught the ball instead of knocking it down, none of this would have happened. It's as much my fault as his."

"Oh shut up, Deano," Beckman said, without malice. "You made the play."

"No, you shut up," Deano barked. "We win and lose as a team, and losin' ain't any one guy's fault."

"Yeah? Well, that kid ain't even on the team, and it's damn sure his fault."

"Screw you, Beckman," Deano hissed. "C'mon, Micah, let's go."

Micah, who was trying to melt into the wall, shook his head. "I gotta stay til after and do the towels."

Deano waved for him to leave. "They'll still be here in the morning."

When they walked out, only Deano looked back.

Micah couldn't have looked at a single face without tearing up.

⅄

"What a wimp," Beckman said after they were gone. "Can't even stand up for hisself. Deano has to stand up for him. Hey, Dodd, how come your brother can't be more like you?"

Tucker was shoving his shoulder pads into his equipment bag. "Drop it, Beckman."

"Oh, come on, man. Kid's gotta be able to handle the heat if he's gonna be around us while we're busting our asses. Little jocksniffer."

There were a couple of tentative snickers around the room, but they were quickly swallowed. Tucker didn't say anything.

"Besides," Beckman said, "just havin' a little fun. Since we didn't get to have our fun on the field."

"Well, it ain't fun any more," Tucker said with a tone of finality. "So drop it."

He hefted his equipment bag over his shoulder and walked out, then stopped outside the locker room to readjust its contents. He could hear Beckman's voice from inside.

"What a family, huh?" Beckman said. "One brother who's crazy—"

"—and dumb as a post," added a voice Tucker couldn't quite place.

"Hey," somebody woofed. Tucker recognized Steelbarton's voice. "Nobody puts down the man."

"And another brother who's a little pussy."

Tucker stepped back inside, and movement within the room stopped.

"Next guy to say something like that about my brother? I'm gonna break your fuckin' neck. If I even hear about somebody saying somethin'. I'll break your fuckin' neck. And that goes for everybody here. I don't give a shit who you are."

He stood there, glaring first at Beckman but then scanning the room, meeting eyes long enough to let them all know he was serious. Then he walked back out, leaving the locker room as silent as a tomb.

Ten days later, a neck would break.

CHAPTER 12

Every Picture Tells A Story

"**S**ounds like quite a friend," Amanda said, "to stand up for you."

"Yeah. Deano was my best friend. I wish I could have been more like him. I got a picture of him. Hang on a sec."

She shrugged. "OK."

Micah held up a *justasec* finger and went to his kitchen table, which served as a repository for all things relating to bills, correspondence and photography. It was a zoo, but the chaos was his own, so he understood it. He extracted a manila envelope and leafed quickly through its contents. "Ah. Here it is."

He handed her a 5-by-7 snapshot. In it were two smiling boys in basketball uniforms, one slightly taller but much more filled-out, the other obviously younger; each had an arm around the other's shoulder as they grinned in their bright, new, unblemished uniforms.

"That's him on the left," he said. "The other one ... well, that's me."

"Gee, I'd have never known," she said just a bit sarcastically. She eyed it again. "I swear he looks familiar. Looks older than you, too."

"Yeah. Two years. But we were in the same class."

"He flunk out a lot?"

"No, I ... moved ahead."

"Oh, a whiz kid. Wait, you graduated in '83, right? But you skipped a class to get there. Two? You skipped *TWO* classes? Holy moly, how old are you?"

I was afraid of this. He held up both hands with finger-V peace signs.

She mugged. "You're *four*?"

"Twenty-two."

"Duh. Wow, so I'm practically robbing the cradle here."

"Oh yeah, you're so old. You're what, twenty-four?"

"You can call me ma'am, sonny."

"So..." He felt compelled to ask. "Am I too young, then? For ... whatever?"

She put on a theatrical thinker look. "Mm. Jury's still out." After an intriguing pause, she gestured at the manila envelope. "So what else you got there?"

"Oh. Just a bunch of old stuff from when I was kid, mostly."

"None of it's yours? Pictures you took, I mean."

"Not in there. I got some," he said, with a casual gesture toward the table. "You know."

"Got some forest stuff? Stuff that wasn't in the book, maybe?"

He shrugged. "Tons of it."

She made a *gimme gimme* gesture with her fingers. He smiled and obliged, handing her an array of photographs, some black-and-white, some color, some in portfolio binders, some loose. She stopped at a shot of a couple of owls, one larger than the other with different coloring. Both seemed to be staring at the photographer.

"Spotted owls," she said. "First-summer fledgling."

He nodded. "That's right. You got a good eye."

"I've just spent a lot of time in the woods."

"Me too."

They took a moment of silence, a nod to their common calling.

"Amazing how relaxed they can be around you, isn't it." She was talking about the owls in the photo.

"Yeah," he said, gazing at her. "And vice versa." But as she went into another portfolio, he felt a twinge of concern and wished he had set that one aside. That one really wasn't for public consumption.

She lit upon a photograph of perhaps three dozen men and women wearing a variety of dress, from blue jeans and tees to flag-colored shirts, bandanas and business suits. Some looked directly at the camera. Some looked sharply away, as if avoiding the camera.

"What's this?" Amanda asked.

"I didn't take that one."

"Oh. Your college fraternity, right?"

"Ha ha."

She glanced over a couple more photos, then stopped at one of a man, wearing a green headband, green stretch pants, a blousy smock made out of an American flag, and what looked like rock-climbing shoes. Wrapped around his torso and upper thighs were a climber's harness, anchored with caribiners and rope to the redwood tree he was sitting in. Some people on the ground, barely visible through a web of evergreen foliage, appeared to be nearly fifty yards below.

And the photographer's vantage point was from even higher, in another tree.

"You took this?"

He nodded.

"Whoa." She studied the photograph some more. "You were way up there."

"Yeah. I used to be afraid of heights, too."

"And you took this? That makes you my new hero."

"Don't be too impressed. It took me a long time to get up the nerve, and all I did was go up the fixed ropes. This guy, and a couple others, they put the ropes up. They were the real tree climbers."

"What's he doing?"

"Sitting there so they can't cut the tree down. As long as he's in it."

She looked more intently at the photo.

"Oh. He's one of them."

"Them?"

"A greenie. An eco-guy. One of the grape nuts."

Her tone sounded critical and put him a little on edge, but he mouthed it for humorous effect: *Grape nuts?*

"Was he a tree spiker?"

Micah managed not to show how much that question stabbed him. "A tree spiker? No, good grief, of course not. Why would you ask that?"

She shook her head and set the tree-sitter photo aside. She picked up another high-tree photo. This one was different. It was taken from high in another redwood tree, a portrait of the tree trunk itself—one that appeared to have been charred by lightning.

A couple of chunks of blackened bark had been removed, revealing the lighter layer beneath which had then been rasped and sanded to a relatively flat face several inches across. On that layer was a green circle, maybe two or three inches wide, the color broken only by the lines that crossed it in which there was no green, only the color of the wood below. Three lines came from a center point, and a fourth pointed down. It looked vaguely familiar.

"Now this is interesting. A peace sign, upside down, at the top of a tree, in the middle of a forest. So out of place and yet so right."

"You think it looks like a peace sign?"

"Upside down, but yeah, what else?"

He gave a little shrug. "I dunno. Bird print, or so I've been told."

"Have to be a pretty big bird."

"Raptor, probably. Hawk. Maybe a falcon."

"You don't know? Did you put it there? Or did you just find it while you were up there shooting grape nuts?"

He took the photograph from her hand as if it were a fragile gem and replaced it into the folder. "You think I'm going to tell you all my secrets?"

"Well. Just so you know, I don't like secrets. The last time somebody I was close to had a secret, he killed himself."

入

Connie had been so quiet the entire day, Tucker had actually looked in once just to check and see if she was still breathing. The raspy snore solved that mystery.

By late afternoon, Micah had still not returned or even called, Tucker was cursing the little shit and Gulliver was wagging his complete agreement until, suddenly, the little schnauzer hopped off the sofa and parked in front of Connie's door. With a plaintive look back, he beseeched Tucker to the door.

"I don't think so, little buddy."

Gulliver encouraged him with a little body wag.

"She can walk if she has to."

Still another wag.

"Don't push me, you little shit."

The ears drooped.

And he heard the muffled sound of a heavy thud in Connie's room.

"Aah shit," he uttered, and headed into her room.

She was on the floor, just beginning to prop herself up on an elbow. She didn't seem to be hurt; she just looked a little dazed. The room smelled like a port-a-potty. He approached slowly, making sure not to startle her; he didn't want her to go off again, yelling and throwing shit.

As he leaned to her, her blank gape at him underwent a metamorphosis, first into vague recognition and then into warm memory, finally into joyful reunion. It stunned Tucker when he realized she was reaching up toward him, her expression looking almost like the old Connie he remembered, albeit in an ashen shell of a body. She clearly wanted to touch him, perhaps hug him. And that seemed, at the moment, sort of touching.

Right up until the first hand to touch his cheek felt wet. And then, an instant later, smelled like shit.

He recoiled with the realization that it *was* shit. "Jesus Christ!" he shouted with a revulsive stumble, losing his balance. The room wasn't well-lit, but he could see darker patches on her nightgown, as if she had been rolling around in everything she could no longer control. He began wiping frantically at his face with the front of his T-shirt, grimacing and gagging.

And he could see her expression, full of hurt and abandonment.

He almost felt sorry for her. He was about to help her back up to the bed, but changed his mind. "Wait right there, all right? Don't move. Just stay there." He turned back to her at the door. "And don't touch anything. OK?"

Tucker went into the bathroom and grabbed a towel from the dirty clothes hamper, Big Frank's grudging concession to Connie's feminine need for bathroom order. He started to wet it, thought better of it, and brought it back to the bedroom dry. Connie had not moved.

"Well, thanks for small miracles, you crazy old bat," he said, squatting down next to her and beginning the disgusting task of wiping her nightgown as much as possible. Then he realized he was wasting his time; what it was on the inside of the nightgown had to be a lot worse.

Using the towel then as a two-way protective grip, then, instead of a cleaning agent, he helped her to her feet and down the hall to the bathroom, where he turned on the hot water in the tub. While he waited, she stood in place, watching him and smelling like buzzard buffet.

"Do you need to go to the bathroom?" he said, pointing at the toilet. She just looked at him with that same funny look of gratified recognition.

"Box," she said.

He looked at her.

"If you think I'm getting you any cereal right now, forget it. You got to have a bath."

She didn't resist as he used the towel again as a gripper to pull off her nightgown, trying to avoid touching it in any way. He reached down to make sure the hot water was going, helped her into the tub, taking pains to avoid having to see her withered, dying body. He adjusted the nozzle spray to reach her, then held a washrag in front of her face until she took it.

"Use that. Would you do that for me? Please?"

"Box," she said, and began wiping her haggard body.

He took a towel into her bedroom and wiped up the floor. He dropped the towel on the bed, then pulled off the sheets and blankets and carried the foul-smelling bundle to the little washroom off the bathroom. After he got the load going—hoping the immense amount of soap he used would remove all evidence of what had been on the sheets—he went back to the bathroom, now in a much fouler mood about the woman he had returned to watch die.

She was stretched out on the floor of the shower, her eyes closed to the beating of the water and looking so shriveled the bathtub seemed huge. He looked away, not wanting to be haunted by the grotesque specter of whatever was consuming her from within. She must have heard him, because she pushed herself slowly and seemingly painfully to a sitting position.

"Cardle. Carman. Box."

He went out of the room.

⅄

Micah looked at the window and was saddened by what he saw. "It stopped raining."

"Oh darn," Amanda said without looking.

They were still relaxing on their "picnic table," the quilt on Micah's living room rug. They had regaled one another with Cliff Notes versions of life stories and played conversational kickball. The kiss suggested earlier had not yet transpired, but its portent was everywhere. The space between them had closed; it was beginning to feel very much like shared personal space. This truly was a place Micah had never been.

"Did you have enough to eat?" she asked.

He couldn't help what he thought of in response, and felt a little bit dirty for thinking it. Then wondered why.

"Everything was perfect," he said.

"Thank you," she said.

"No, thank you. You made it."

"I did indeed. I just must be something special. Chicken salad, a fruit bowl. Bread. Cheese. Wow. Haute cuisine."

"And wine. Don't forget the wine."

"I didn't have the wine, you had the wine."

"Yes, but you helped drink it." He nodded meaningfully, and got the little laugh he was shooting for. "Hey."

"Hey what."

"Which was your favorite photograph?"

"Of yours? The ones in this stack? Why?"

"Maybe I'd give it to you. As a gift."

She wormed over to him, very slowly, inching closer to him until they were stretched out facing each other, just inches apart. Her breasts were just barely grazing his chest, a feeling that reverberated within him with tectonic intensity.

"So," she said softly, her lips no more than six inches from his, "you think the way to a girl's heart is to give her gifts?"

Micah almost couldn't breathe.

She smiled. "'Cause it *wooorrrks.*" She bent in and gave him a very quick kiss, their lips only lightly brushing, before rolling away and resuming a seated position next to the stack of portfolios and folders. "Sometimes," she added mischievously. "And I know just the one I want."

He smiled at that elusive kiss and wished it had stayed longer.

She began rifling carefully through the stack until she found the portfolio she was looking for. As soon as she settled on that portfolio, he thought *Oh no* and began trying to come up with excuses. She scrolled through the pages until she got to the one encasing the photo of the tree-climber in green and the old red, white and blue, with the watchers so far below. "This one. I'm glad he's not a tree-spiker. But knowing he's not ... well, it's an incredible picture. Photo."

"Oh, I'm really sorry," he said, scrambling to come up with a good reason. "That's ... that's the only print I have of that one, and I've lost the negative."

"Oh. OK, then, how about the peace sign?"

"I'm pretty sure it's not a peace sign."

"OK, fine, the *talon* or whatever. It's interesting. Different. I could really see that on my living room wall."

Micah was cringing at the thought. "Umm, Amanda. I'm really sorry, but ... that one's ... kind of private."

She frowned. "Private how? There's no people in it. And I swear I've seen it before. It wasn't in your book, was it?"

He shook his head. He had no idea what to say.

"You know," she said, "giving me my choice of pictures and then telling me no to the first two I pick is not the way to set a romantic mood."

Micah jump-started. "Are we ... being romantic?"

"Well," she said, "don't you think that would be a much more appropriate mood for two people who are going to be kissing each other for the first time?"

"I thought we just kissed."

"That little thing? That wasn't a kiss."

"Oh." He was too dumbstruck to add anything.

"Don't worry about those pictures, sorry I asked," she said. "How about the owls?"

He felt a rush of relief. "It's yours. You want me to frame it for you?"

"Don't worry about it, I can get that done."

"No, let me. I know a frame place in Arlington and ... I have kind of a feel for framing. Hey, I'm a photographer."

"Yes, I know. You dabble."

They shared a smile and a bit of silence as they began gathering up the accoutrements of their indoor picnic and easing into the sobering realization that something was coming to an end, that air was beginning to escape the little bubble they'd created around themselves. She seemed to sense it as much as he did.

"So ... when will I get it? My framed photograph by the famous forest photographer?" She grinned. "Boy, try to say that one five times fast. Fee fi fo fum."

"I don't know, when would you like it?" He didn't want to be pushy, but he really wanted to see her again, and soon. "You free next weekend?"

She pursed her lips ominously. "Well, no, I'm afraid not." A perfect beat. "I'm quite expensive next weekend. But I have a midweek special that's to die for."

He was so relieved he actually laughed out loud.

"Just give me a call when you get it ready," she said.

"Do I have to wait until then to call?"

For a second, it looked like she blushed just a little. "No," she said softly. "You don't."

"Good. Because it might take a good half-hour to get it done. And I'm not sure I can wait that long ... if calling you means getting to see you again." This time, he was the one to blush.

She smiled. "Well, since it's going to take me a half-hour to get home, you may have to control yourself."

"I'll try," he said, closing her wicker picnic basket. "Can't make any promises, though."

"Well, I've got to go," she said, rising and stretching languidly, in that moment looking as sensual and sexually stimulating as any woman Micah had ever seen. "So what ever happened to your buddy?"

"I'm not thinking about him right now." He was looking at her lips.

"No?"

"No."

"So …"

"So this." And without giving himself a reason to procrastinate or chicken out, he pulled her to him, his hands reaching around her waist to her back. And when he leaned down to kiss her, her face was already there, her lips parting to welcome his.

She was right.

That other little touch hadn't really been a kiss at all.

CHAPTER 13

About seventy boys were filing into the locker rooms for basketball and wrestling tryouts, and Micah was among them only at Deano's insistence. After barely making the C-squad as a sophomore, he knew he was wasting his time.

"You only want me along to make sure you're not the worst one out there," Micah said softly as they dressed in the locker room surrounded by dozens of other prospective athletes. "So if we both make the JV team you're not the last guy on the bench."

"Damn straight. Only I want varsity," Deano said, grinning. He looked up and gave Micah a nudge. *Check it out.*

Tucker had come into the locker room and was standing behind some poor C-squad wannabe who didn't realize the locker in which he was hanging his school clothes had belonged to Tucker Dodd since his freshman year. Tucker didn't have to put a lock on it, because everybody knew it was hands-off. Except the newbies.

Tucker stood there until the boy noticed his presence, the last in the room to do so.

"I'm sorry," the boy offered meekly. "Am I in your way?"

"Nope. But that's my locker."

"Oh. I didn't know. Sorry." He grabbed his hanging clothes in a swoop of fabric and his shoes and padded away in his stocking feet.

Deano chuckled. "Yo, Tucker. You oughta put a sign on that locker, keep out the riffraff."

Tucker cocked his head. "So that's all I gotta do to keep you out, Deano, put up a sign?"

"Ooh. Ouch," Deano said, still grinning. "Hey, Tuck, guess what I did yesterday."

Micah grabbed at Deano's arm to shut him up. "Don't."

Tucker noticed. "I'm listening."

"Me and Micah put in a bridge at the Under Look."

Every head in the place swiveled at that one. Most faces looked curious. Tucker looked furious.

"You did *what*?"

Uh oh, Micah thought.

"What's wrong with a bridge to the Under Look?" Deano asked without a hint of disingenuousness. "Makes it less dangerous."

Tucker shook his head. "No. It just makes it easier."

Micah interjected, his voice going to that high, whiny place. "How's that a bad thing?"

Tucker glared at him. "Because now stupid shits like you will think they can do it."

"You'd rather have the stupid shits fall than be able to use a bridge?" Deano demanded.

"I'd rather not have the stupid shits there at all," Tucker said, stepping closer to him in a movement that drew rapt but mute interest around the room. "You make it easy, and people who have no business going down there will do it, they'll get sewing-machine legs and get all freaky from the falls and the dropoff and they'll make a mistake and that'll be it. Then the county will close it off for real, not with some stupid fence. All right? You get it now? You can't be scared and go to the Under Look, even if some dickhead puts a bridge over the gap. People who get scared have no business going to the Under Look." He turned his eyes to Micah. "Or ever setting foot onto a football field."

And he turned back to his locker, pulling off his sweatshirt.

Micah's face started to flush. He actually had to blink a couple of times to make sure no tears welled up. His own brother, revered or feared by almost everybody he knew, had just ripped out Micah's heart in front of fifty guys.

Deano glared at Micah: *Don't listen to him.*

"Well, I guess it's just too bad more people can't be like you, huh, Tucker?" Deano said in what sounded an awful lot like a challenge.

Tucker, his sweatshirt now off, whirled to face Deano, who stood his ground.

"Yeah. That's right. It's too bad. But they can't, so fuck 'em," Tucker growled. "And fuck you, Deano," he added, stepping into Deano's breathing space.

Deano stood his ground, a gesture less of challenge than of willing defiance. Tucker was 190 hard-hewn pounds of gristle, bone and meat, and there was no question about how this would end if it played out. Deano was simply willing to get his ass kicked if that's what it took to make his point.

They held each other's glare, neither blinking. In that extended moment, Micah saw the parallel of the very dynamic he'd been watching for nearly ten years—Deano now in the role of Tucker, Tucker in the role of Big Frank, both knowing how the confrontation would end, but the younger, smaller challenger refusing to back down one inch. And yet Micah admired Deano, and resented Tucker.

"You know I'm going to take that bridge down," Tucker said. "It's coming out. You know that, right?"

"Yeah. I know. And I'll just put up another one. We will," Deano said, nodding his head toward Micah. "You know that, right?"

Tucker held the hardness for just a moment more before softening into a little laugh. "You probably will, you little shit. I should pound you just for being such a pain in the ass."

There was a collective relaxation in the room, since Tucker's meaning was clear—he wouldn't be pounding anybody. He gave Deano a friendly little shove and even allowed one in return. Tucker turned back to his locker, quickly changed into his wrestling gear and turned to leave. At the door, he turned back to say something, then changed his mind and just pointed at Deano with a little grin, ostensibly derisive, yet anything but.

There was a tacit respect in the gesture that Micah, watching this interchange with a feeling something like envy, knew he had never received from his brother.

Micah knew Tucker wasn't kidding about the bridge, though. He had no intention of leaving it there.

But then came that afternoon's basketball tryouts.

It was a five-minute reds-on-whites full-court scrimmage, just to give the coaches an idea of who already had any skills worth developing further. Deano, playing with the whites, was backpedaling to set up on defense when someone on the reds broke long and a teammate's pass flew his way. As Deano leapt high to deflect it, somebody running downcourt clipped him in passing, just enough to get him twisting around in midair, the momentum carrying one leg higher and throwing his head back with increased centrifugal force.

Micah, sitting in the stands with the next scrimmage group to take the floor, was talking to the kid next to him and didn't see it happening.

But when Deano's neck and head hit the floor, Micah heard it. Everybody did.

It sounded like a tree branch snapping.

⅄

The first couple of weeks after landing on the basketball court landed Deano at Harborview in Seattle, paralyzed from the neck down, Micah was at the hospital nearly every evening.

For Micah, it wasn't an easy task; it meant bumming rides with Deano's mom or dad, or convincing a teacher or some older kid who could drive him to the hospital in Seattle. Micah knew in some cases he was playing on the guilt of any would-be driver. If you went to see the paralyzed kid in the hospital once, it pretty much ensured you wouldn't have to go again; if anybody ever asked, you could say how awful it was about poor Deano but he sure seemed to be handling everything well *when you went to see him in the hospital* ...

Micah knew they thought that way, because part of him did, too. He hated seeing Deano unable to move, tubes and wires coming out every which way. Absolutely hated it. In his heart, he would rather have been anywhere than beside Deano, being reminded he couldn't move. But everything he knew about doing the right thing came from books, and a sensibility weaned on gallant heroes told him he had to go. So he did.

He was there on the Saturday the entire varsity and junior varsity teams, coaches and all, stopped by to see Deano at the hospital on the way to a game. Micah hadn't seen any of them outside of class in two weeks, having dropped out of basketball tryouts as soon as Deano got hurt. Now, feeling like an outsider, he slipped into a corner away from all their awkward offerings of optimism. He watched them fidgeting, uttering nonsense like the stuff in the dozens of cards, some from people he didn't even know: Get well soon … Hang in there … You'll be back on the court before you know it.

Yeah. Right.

But at least they were better than Deano's mom. After the doctors determined he would likely be paralyzed for the rest of his life, she couldn't be in his room for more than two minutes before starting to cry again. Deano's father was a steady-as-she-goes ex-sailor, but Mrs. Slocumb became so perpetually morose even Deano found himself trying to console her over his own lousy luck. After a while, he began asking her to leave the room when she got like that, and not long after that she simply went back to work.

So most of the time it was just Deano and Micah.

Most of the cards Micah simply read to Deano. A couple of teachers brought a big posterboard get-well card signed by about half the White Bluff student body, and that one Micah spent the better part of an hour holding up and angling it so Deano could read every little inscription. He enjoyed the lift Deano seemed to get out of them, but even then couldn't stop thinking about how none of the inscriptions said what each writer was thinking: *God I'm sure glad it was you and not me.*

One afternoon, Micah was sitting with Deano when a young man came in. He was perhaps eight years older than either of them and Micah had never seen him before, but there was instant recognition on Deano's face.

"Jesus, Demon," the man said with obvious compassion.

"Whoa, dude," Deano exclaimed, his whole face lighting up. "You come up here all the way from California? Thanks, man."

"What, like I *wouldn't* come? You'd come if it was me lying in a hospital all banged up."

"Would not."

"You lying sack."

"You pathetic excuse for a big brother."

"Yeah, well, just don't forget, I was here first."

Deano gave him a wan smile, looking around at the array of tubes and wires and contraptions all designed to keep him alive. "Yeah, well. I was *here* first."

The visitor's glib persona washed away into profound sadness. "No lie. Jesus."

There was a heavy silence, and Micah piped up, "You guys are brothers?"

The visitor nodded.

"I didn't know you had any brothers, Deano," Micah said.

Deano made a face. "Johnny's kind of the black sheep. We don't talk about him much."

Laughs all around. Micah shook Johnny's hand. "I'm Micah. I'm just a friend."

Johnny gave Deano a funny look. "I didn't know you had any friends, Demon."

"Yeah, right," Micah said. "He's only the most popular kid at White Bluff High."

As soon as the sentence left his mouth, it sank like an anchor. It sounded patronizing. Like something somebody would say at a funeral.

The visitor, Johnny, rescued him. "That right? Demon is the man there? Whoa. That school must really suck."

The timing was perfect, and they all laughed, Deano most of all, and it was amazing. Johnny stayed for the rest of the afternoon, communicating and caring for Deano in a way that made Micah envious. He was gone by the next morning—he said he had to get back to California to fight forest fires—but it was as if the air had been cleared. Micah had wanted to give Deano the kind of friendship and support he needed, but he had been unable to get past Deano's paralysis. He had simply been stuck in *Oh my God how awful*, just another rubbernecker at an accident, while Deano had already moved past that.

And now, thanks to some brotherly love—something Micah had rarely experienced—Micah moved past it, too.

A couple of weeks later, Micah and Deano were staring at the TV in Deano's hospital room when, out of nowhere, Deano said, "You know what really pisses me off?"

"What."

"I wish I'd have put it to Dayla Brockman when I had the chance."

Micah couldn't believe it.

"You had a chance to put it to Dayla Brockman and you *didn't?* What are you, a homo?"

In that instant, Micah was doing something he hadn't done since the moment Deano's back had met the gymnasium floor: He was looking at his friend in exactly the same way he'd look at any fully functional, blue-balled teenager—albeit one who had evidently passed up a chance to give the big one to one of the juiciest chicks at White Bluff High.

That moment sort of crystallized, like something tangible. He and Deano recognized it at the same instant and locked into it; it had to be the first time anyone had forgotten Deano was paralyzed since he'd *been* paralyzed.

"She was so drunk," Deano said, his grin spreading, "she couldn't even move."

Micah's mouth opened and so did Deano's, and they both burst into cathartic laughter.

"She *couldn't move!*" Deano sputtered out between heaving hoots. "She couldn't move! Not a stinkin' muscle!"

Both of them were laughing so hard by this time Deano began to cough convulsively and couldn't stop, frightening Micah enough to rush down the hall and call for a nurse. Two came in, quickly strapped an oxygen mask onto Deano and asked for Micah to leave the room, but in the moment he was leaving, he caught Deano's eye. He saw gratitude. And friendship.

人

Tucker never went to the hospital to see Deano.

The kid was Micah's friend, not his own, after all, but that wasn't really it. He just hated being around sick people. He'd listened during his mother's last year of life when she talked about the place she was working, helping those old, drooling crazy people, who shit all over themselves and had passed the point of being people. It just made him queasy.

And now, just thinking about Deano not being able to move … ugh.

He tried not to think about it, but Deano's condition lingered with Tucker like poison oak rash. You could go along for an hour not feeling it until you happened to scratch it without thinking; then it wouldn't stop itching, even after you'd scratched it until it bled.

He'd been on three or four teams with Deano over the years, some Little League and Grid Kids football. Deano had tons of energy, just full of life. And now he'd be stock still for the rest of his life. Not able to feel anything. Not able to do anything. For the rest of his life.

Tucker didn't want to think about that.

He had never understood why Deano, who was pretty cool and had plenty of friends, had chosen to be buddies with his little brother. But he was glad about it; he sort of liked Deano for that. Made him feel less guilty for not always being there to watch out for the little shit.

Just like Micah's spending time with Deano now made him feel less guilty about not wanting to do the same.

He went about his business that winter. He fought some, banged some cheerleaders, copied enough assignments and test answers off his willing abettors to remain eligible for wrestling, and, of course, kicked ass on the mat. The only match he lost all regular season—now at the 178-pound class—was a close decision in the finals of a Christmas tournament to an undefeated kid from big-school powerhouse Sedro Woolley.

But then came the state tournament. And something came up. Again.

Tucker, who had already reached two state championship matches, seemed destined for another right up until the semifinals, when he found himself across the mat from a tough kid from Coupeville named Aubrey Burlingame. He had won a couple of medals at state.

When they shook hands at the outset, Burlingame muttered, "Fuckwad Dodd," enunciating and stretching out each syllable. Tucker was angry but went about his business, taking no time to shoot for a single-leg takedown. But he couldn't turn the Coupeville boy over for a pin, and the round ended with Tucker ahead by only two points.

On the coin flip for position in the second round, Tucker won and chose down. But as Burlingame slipped into the up position—the controlling position—Burlingame began to talk. Between heaves of exertion, he started in.

"Fuck-wad Dah-ah-ah-odd ...man with ..."

Tucker tried to push himself up to his knees, but Burlingame was strong enough to hold him down.

"... with the famous ... brother," Burlingame muttered between pants as they twisted and wrenched. "I heard ... N.C. wanted to ... give him a letter for ... winning the game for 'em ... course it ... would have to be ... S ... for shithead—"

Tucker bolted up and immediately tried to drive his hips up and into Burlingame, to try to gain leverage to rise. "Fuck ... you," he grunted.

The referee, a well-muscled, graying ex-wrestler, whistled and made it clear: Any more unsportsmanlike behavior or foul language by either wrestler would cost points.

"Yessir," Burlingame responded, quite sportsmanlike.

Tucker said nothing, and the two moved back into position. As Burlingame clamped on, wrapping his right arm around Tucker's torso and grabbing his left wrist, he hissed, "Most schools won't let retarded kids on the field."

Tucker was seething. Too anxious to take out his anger, he tried to walk up without establishing position; Burlingame was able to work him into an arm bar and roll him onto his back long enough for a three-point near-fall. Tucker managed to get back on his stomach and escape before the end of the round, which ended with the score tied.

When Tucker came over to the corner for the break, Coach Schutz was livid.

"What the heck are you doing out there?" he barked. "Is that how I taught you to walk out, exposing your arm like that?"

"He's pissing me off," Tucker stammered. "I'm gonna bust him up."

"Hey. HEY." Schutz got right in his face. "He's playing you for a fool. Everybody in this building knows you threw away the title last year by losing your cool. Be smarter than that."

When the wrestlers came out for the third and final round, Burlingame chose the down position. At the starting buzzer, Tucker relinquished his left hand hold, slid it quickly under Burlingame's stomach and grabbed his own wrist. He hopped to his feet, never relinquishing his grip as he wrenched up with all his might until Burlingame's hands were off the mat. Then, with all of the torque he could muster, he threw his own body back, launching Burlingame over and beyond him in a 180-degree trajectory to the mat, shoulders and head first. Burlingame slammed to the mat with enough violent force to expel all of the air from his lungs.

Tucker rolled and was on his feet in a heartbeat, but not before the referee blew his whistle and stood, waving his arms. As Burlingame rolled over, wrapping his hands over his head and writhing on the mat, the referee strode to the scorer's table and announced, "Red is ejected for flagrant misconduct. Green' wins by disqualification."

Schutz objected to the ruling, but the ref was having none of it.

"Gimme a break, coach," he said. "I got your boy for locking hands, an illegal throw, unnecessary roughness, unsportsmanlike conduct, intent to injure. What more do you need?"

In another second Schutz was in Tucker's face, barking at him over how stupid that was, how he would be wrestling for the championship in two hours if he'd just kept his head.

He might as well have been reciting the pledge of allegiance.

As soon as the coach's rant ended, Tucker simply went back to staring across the mat as Burlingame was tended to by a coach and trainer. Tucker's eyes didn't leave him, daring him to stare back.

The return stare never came. Not even a glance.

In that way, the only way he cared about, Tucker won.

⋏

Micah continued to find ways to get to the Everett rehabilitation center to see Deano as often as he could through the spring and summer, but when school rolled around again in the fall of 1982, his visits became less frequent.

Then Deano was transferred to a long-term care facility in Arlington, a half-hour closer to White Bluff. And since he was doing well enough now that he could be out in a wheelchair for longer periods of time, one of the school's paraprofessionals began periodically picking him up in a school van and bringing him to the final couple of class periods. Since Micah was Deano's friend and a straight-A student, the parapro often left him responsible for getting Deano from class to class and then back to the van at the end of the day.

In Mrs. Rosebery's literature class, Deano never hesitated to take part in class discussion, something Micah considered a situation rife with awkward potential. What teacher wants to embarrass the poor paralyzed kid by calling on him when he might not know the answer—and how could he be expected to know squat when he'd been out of school for so long? But Deano would just pipe right in. Following the last class, on the days when Micah helped lift Deano from the wheelchair into the van, Deano would invariably act as if it tickled, and Micah would fall for it every time.

But Micah found less and less joy in Deano's moments of grace and began to visit him less and less. Micah was able to rationalize this: It was difficult to find people willing to drive him to Arlington; it took a lot of time; and his school work load was more demanding as a fifteen-year-old senior taking college-level courses.

The truth was much simpler.

Deano made Micah uncomfortable.

And that made Deano inconvenient.

CHAPTER 14

A TURN FOR THE WORSE

S he had been home for less than five minutes when the phone rang.

He wasn't kidding about not wanting to wait. Amanda began the task of disentangling herself from Thistle, her affectionate tabby. By the time she could reach the phone on the third ring, she was laughing about both Thistle's claws of love and Micah's bashful persistence.

Last time, he wished he'd kissed me. Hmm.

"So what are you wishing we'd done this time?" she said in a sultry tone. She heard the intake of breath on the other end. *Oh, shy boy.*

"Um … hello?" A woman's voice. "Mandible?"

Only one person ever called her that. "Kari? Karen Frances?"

It only took a moment to pull up the memory of her roommate during her summer on the Forest Service trail crew before her senior year at Washington State. They had become fast friends over the first half of that summer, then drifted apart when Amanda and J.D. became an item, in the way friendships are often relegated to second-tier relationship status the minute somebody starts getting laid.

"Hey. I'm glad I found you, Manda. I hope it's not too late to call. How are you doing?"

"I'm great, roomie. I didn't know I was hard to find." Amanda was feeling a bit giddy. Interesting new guy in her life. Old friend calling. What a day.

"Well," Karen said. "I just wanted to make sure you were OK. About J.D., I mean. They had his obit in the Grants Pass paper today."

That sucked the air out of the room. For more than two weeks Amanda hadn't gone an hour without thinking about J.D. being gone and the way he did it, and then all weekend he had barely crossed her mind.

"I'm so sorry, Manda. I know you guys were close. How'd it happen?"

Amanda understood then. Karen didn't know how J.D. had died. All she knew was what was in the obituary.

"Oh. You know. He just was never the same after the … after he got hurt."

"I had no idea he was hurt that bad."

Amanda considered telling her and decided against it. "Yeah. It was bad."

"That's so sad. Hmm. Manda, honey, how are you doing?"

Conflictedly happy, actually. And, now, a bit guilty.

"Oh, Kare Bear, I'm doing OK, I guess."

"You sure?"

"Yes. Really, I'm fine. We weren't—J.D. and I hadn't been together like that in a while. We were just friends. As much as anybody could be friends with J.D."

They shared a little silent understanding.

"Did they have a service up there?" Karen asked.

"No."

"Really. That's sad."

"His family's back in Oregon, and he was born down there. They probably had one there. Besides, he didn't know a lot of people. You know how he was."

"Yeah. Always the strong silent type."

Amanda didn't know what to say. She actually didn't feel like talking about J.D.

It must have been obvious even through the silence of a telephone line.

"Well, then anybody out there who's more than friends, Mandible? Maybe somebody who talks a lot?"

They both laughed. "Well, now that you mention it, there is somebody just like that," Amanda said.

"Ooh. Talk to me, baby. What's he like?"

"Well, me, for one."

"OK, so who is he? What's his name? What's he do?"

"His name's Micah, and he's a photographer."

"Uh oh. I guess that means you pick up the tab, right?"

"Very funny. He's a very good photographer. He did a book, in fact."

"He wrote a book?"

"It's pictures, Kari. He's a photographer. There's some writing, yeah, but it's pictures. Amazing pictures. I have his book."

"He gave you a copy? Did he sign it?"

"No. I—"

"He wouldn't sign it?"

"He didn't give me a book."

"But you said you had his book."

"I already had it. Before I met him."

"Really. You bought it, like from a store?"

"Yes. Like from a store."

"That's actually pretty cool. So what's the story, Mandible? What do you guys do together?"

"Well, he took me to a bluegrass festival yesterday."

"Really. Bluegrass? Umm. Sounds fun," Karen said as if they were talking about a root canal. "Was the kid from 'Deliverance' there?"

Amanda laughed. And then began to tell her friend about Micah Dodd. About the estate sale, about the painting, about the tentative laughter, about the picnic on his living-room rug. About the beautiful nature depictions in his book. About some of the photos in his duplex.

About the shot of the colorful tree-sitter high in a redwood tree.

And about the arresting photograph of a green circle painted on lightning-charred bark with what looked like an upside-down peace sign in the middle of it.

"He says it's a bird track," she said with a little chuckle, the idea too silly to consider.

"A bird track?"

"Yeah, like a talon. You know, like from an eagle. Or a falcon."

⅄

Thursday was two days before Christmas, and the last day of school before the holidays. Tucker came home at the time he would normally have come home after wrestling practice. He expected he'd be eating warmed-up left-overs, as usual.

But things were definitely not as usual.

Connie was already at the sink doing what she could of the dinner dishes; Micah was standing beside her, a dishtowel in his hand. Big Frank was sitting at the kitchen table, his empty plate sitting Leave It Right There in front of him.

"I'll warm you up something, honey," Connie said.

Big Frank was smoking a cigarette, using the plate as his ashtray. He never looked over as Tucker sat at the table, just kept staring at the clock on the wall.

"So where you been?" Big Frank asked without looking at him.

"Nowhere."

"Yeah. I figured that."

Connie dished something onto a plate. Tucker watched her put it into the microwave, already sensing he probably wasn't going to get to eat whatever it was.

"See, I figured you weren't at practice."

Ah. I was wondering when this would come up.

At wrestling turnout two days earlier, Tucker had been paired off with Beckman, the team's heavyweight. Beckman had always been a mouthy prick, and when he started working his mouth about "that wussy little brother of yours" and enjoying it far too much, Tucker had quieted him but good. The fact that Beckman's elbow might require surgery as a result, though, hadn't set well with Coach Schutz, who suspended him from the team until he demonstrated sufficient remorse over his actions. Which would be when hell froze over.

Big Frank was still waiting for his answer. "Well? Am I right?"

Tucker thought about all the things he really wanted to say. "About what?"

"Don't test me, boy. Were you at practice?"

"No," Tucker said, twisting the word for maximum disdain. "I wasn't at practice."

"No, I didn't think so. I'll tell you why. See, I'm talking with Harve over at the hardware store, and I mention the Sedro tournament, and how I was really looking forward to see you get that Sedro kid again in the finals and this time kick his ass. You know what Harve says?"

"I have an idea."

"Yeah, I'll bet you do," Big Frank said. "Harve says, 'Oh, is he back on the team?' I'm like, what the fuck? And he says my son quit the team, or got kicked off, or something. Said you beat up one of the other kids on the team. Said he heard all about it from some guy down at Roy's Meats."

"Huh. Roy's Meats. No kidding."

"Cut with the shit. Is it true?"

"I didn't beat anybody up."

"Then what did you do?"

"Nothin'."

"Nothin'. Huh."

Tucker shrugged. "I was wrestlin' with a guy, he gave me some shit and I gave him some back. It was just wrestlin'. He got hurt."

Big Frank pondered that and it seemed to sit OK with him.

"So for that you're off the team?"

"Schutz got all bent outta shape about it." Tucker leaned back as Connie put a plate of something in front of him. "Said maybe he'll let me back when I feel remorse."

"What, when you say you're sorry?"

Tucker shrugged. The microwave dinged, and Connie hustled his dinner plate to the kitchen table, probably hoping to delay or derail the impending blowup.

"Well, problem solved," Big Frank said. "You'll march right in to see him first thing in the morning and apologize."

Not a chance, Tucker thought.

"When did this happen?" Frank demanded.

"Um. Monday, I think. Yeah. Monday."

"Monday. This is Thursday, you little shit. When were you planning on telling me?"

"When I got around to it."

"Oh, is that right? You don't think I might have a right to know?"

"OK, now you know. So what?"

"So you're going to do what I said. You're going to apologize to your coach."

Tucker shook his head slowly. "I won't do that."

"Oh yes you will. I'm your father, you little shit," Big Frank said, rising from his chair. "And don't you forget it."

"Oh yeah. That must be it. I musta forgot."

Big Frank took a half-step toward him and in one quick motion back-handed him across the upper cheek. It was an open hand, but it was the right, the one with that jagged old high school ring.

Tucker felt the sting, knew it had cut, but didn't reach up to feel the blood. He wouldn't give Big Frank the satisfaction. He could see both Connie and Micah recoil at the blow.

Connie stepped in, just long enough to say "Big, honey—" before Big Frank, with a motion something between a shove and a slug, pushed her out of the way. She lost her balance and fell to the floor, jarring her little book-case enough to dislodge a few books. Micah hurried to her, but she was more startled than hurt.

That didn't matter to Tucker, who rose slowly.

"You know, I've just about had enough of you knocking her around," he said evenly. "Why don't you pick on somebody your own size?"

Tucker wasn't remotely Big Frank's own size; the father had sixty pounds and a good three inches on the son, but Big Frank had been an untested bully for far too long. He was tired, out of shape and no longer in possession of the sort of burning intensity that consumed Tucker's entire being.

Without hesitation, Big Frank stepped toward him again, clearly about to backhand him again.

From the spot against the wall, Connie implored, "Big, no! He's your son."

"Shut up, Connie," Tucker said, his eyes never leaving Big Frank.

Big Frank's expression became even blacker. It was one thing for him to put the bitch in her place, but he wasn't about to put up with the boy doing it. "You don't talk to your mother that way, boy."

"She ain't my mother."

Big Frank cranked up for another backhand, but never got the chance to launch it. Tucker caught the hand with his own left and, in a single motion, pulled it down and through so that it wrenched Big Frank's arm in a near-vise grip. He held it just long enough for Big Frank's eyes to bulge out in a red, wild ferocity, and then let him go.

Perfect, old man. Get good and pissed. Gimme a good bull rush.

Big Frank granted his unspoken wish, coming at him like any one of the big offensive linemen Tucker had laid out, like any of the wrestlers who had believed their weightlifting muscles could overcome his own channeled fury, like any of his futile challengers over the years on the blacktop at Barclay's. Tucker shifted his weight subtly but quickly onto his back foot, giving Big Frank a quick open-handed shiver to the shoulder, just enough to put him off-balance and move the big man's near arm out of the way. Then, with Big Frank's face wide open, Tucker unloaded with a short right cross. He didn't even put everything on it—something made him hold back—but it was enough to deposit Big Frank on his fat butt.

Only then did Tucker reach up and feel his cheek to see if it was bleeding. It was.

Sonuvabitch.

Big Frank got up slowly. His eyes a frenzy of disbelief and rage, he rose to his full height, then dipped into fighting posture.

"Old man, if you come at me again ..." Tucker's right fist was still clenched. Now he clenched the left.

Big Frank's eyes flickered, registering his understanding. They had both known this time would come, their journey inexorable, its destination inevitable: The boy had become the dominant male in this relationship. But for this rite of passage there would be no celebration.

Big Frank reached into the firewood bin and grabbed a sturdy, foot-long chunk of lodgepole pine. His huge mitt gripped the pine so tightly the blood left his knuckles. He gave it a couple of slow hefts and took a tentative half-step toward his defiant son.

"Big, no!" Connie pleaded.

Tucker didn't have anything that would work against the club, but he wasn't about to back down. "Give it your best shot, old man."

Big Frank stopped. He was still brandishing the club, but something Tucker couldn't quite register kept him from using it. Shame, maybe. Fear.

Big Frank growled, "Get out."

Tucker answered his father's glare with his own, one tempered by the light of redemption.

"Works for me," Tucker said. He took a step back, grabbing his down jacket and pulling it on, keeping his eyes on Big Frank.

"Get outta here," Big Frank said. "You come crawling back, I'll be here waiting." He whacked the club into an open palm for effect.

"You better get used to waiting, old man. 'Cause I ain't comin' back."

Connie stepped forward into the fray. "Tucker, where will you go? Big, honey, it's the middle of winter, he's got nowhere to go, where will he sleep?"

"He can sleep in a ditch for all I care," Big Frank said. "Go freeze to death, you ungrateful shit."

Part of Tucker wanted to take that club right out of the big man's hand and beat him to death with it. "Oh yeah. I got so much to be grateful for."

Connie was still in there battling. "But Tucker honey, Big, no, he doesn't have anywhere to go."

"Don't worry about it, Connie," Tucker said to shut her up. "I'll just go live with Skelly. Him and his brother and sister got loads of room at their house. Their parents *died*." He glared at Big Frank. "Some people just get lucky, I guess."

He stormed out, slamming the front screen door behind him.

He wouldn't hear that same sound for six years.

λ

More than an hour had passed since Amanda had driven off, and Micah knew the same thing now that he'd known then.

He was falling in love.

And looking at a photograph.

The mark of the falcon stone high up a lightning-scorched redwood.

He had forgotten all about this photograph. He had taken it at a time when he was hearing the call of a cause, but hadn't yet seen its effect. Damage had been done. And it could not be undone.

He wanted so much to open the door to this wonderful new chapter in his life and rush in, locking away the pain of the past. It ached within him like a rib out of place, stabbing into the sternum, pressing against the heart.

But how could he allow anyone inside, to wander about freely and discover where his shame festered. The door to his past must remain locked, lest it threaten with its Pandora's box of atonement and retribution. Some memories can never be forgotten. Or forgiven.

Tears welled in his eyes.

He stared at the photograph, the one with which Amanda had been so taken she could envision it on her living room wall.

And he tore it into little pieces.

CHAPTER 15

DEANO IS DEAD

It was Christmas Eve, but Micah didn't feel like celebrating.

He didn't know how long Tucker's exile would be in force; he just knew the scary blowup that led to it felt like something out of a nightmare. And that all of Tucker's clothes were here, but he wasn't.

He got up before first light, got a paper bag from the kitchen and stuffed into it a few pairs of Tucker's jeans, some underwear, some shirts, a pair of boots and Tucker's heaviest coat, which his brother had regrettably left behind. He rode his bicycle over to the Radich house, all the while eying the ominous cloud bank settling in over the ridges to the north. Somebody at school had said there was supposed to be some huge snowstorm, and it sure looked like it.

The Radich house was less than a mile away and in a sparse neighborhood much like Micah's, but the similarities stopped there. The Dodd abode was a two-bedroom box in which Micah and Tucker shared the smaller bedroom like gerbils crawling over one another in a cage. The Radich house had a garage with automatic doors, a finished half-basement, a living room *and* a den, a deck in the back, and four bedrooms. That meant a bedroom for each of the three kids and the master bedroom for the parents, which now served as the "date room." That's what Wes called it, anyway, since at 24 he was the only one old enough to have dates likely to spend the night. It was also the only room in the house that hadn't achieved significant squalor in the two years since a drunk driver on Mountain Loop Highway had turned mom and dad Radich into charred meat.

Micah knocked on the door, wondering if anyone would even be up yet. He had to knock a second time and was about to leave the bag of clothes on the porch when the door opened. It was Cami. Although she was only a year older than Micah, they hadn't had a class together since seventh grade, when he skipped to the grade ahead of her. As he began to develop adolescent yearnings and she began to blossom into everything those yearnings generally entail, he had taken to stealing glances at her. A couple of times he'd seen her momentarily alone in the cafeteria at lunch and had attempted to talk to her, only to stumble over the clutter of his own nerves or the arrival of others' ears.

Now she was standing in front of Micah, wearing a man's extra-large T-shirt that draped as far as her upper thighs … and, apparently, nothing else.

Micah had no idea where to look without feeling like he was ogling her.

"Hey," Cami said.

"Hey, Cami."

Cami waited, but Micah was still a little dumbstruck. There was clearly not a bra under the T-shirt. *There might not be … anything.*

"I never knew you were Tucker's little brother."

Little. Crap. He nodded. "I need to talk to him."

"I don't know if he's up yet."

"Well. I got some stuff for him. You think I should just leave it?"

She frowned. "He's your stupid brother, just wake him up. C'mon. He's downstairs."

She motioned him to follow, and he did, marveling over how high up her thighs her T-shirt came.

"Michael. That's your name, right?" she asked as she led him down the hall, glancing back and nearly catching him in mid-marvel.

"Micah." For a hopeful moment he thought they might actually have a conversation, but she just banged on the door at the end of hall and opened it.

"Tucker! It's your kid brother!" she hollered down and went back up the hall to another door—her bedroom, Micah imagined dreamily—and disappeared inside.

Kid brother.

He heard footsteps coming up the stairs and Tucker emerged, looking at him sleepily.

Micah handed him the bag. "You didn't take anything when you left."

Tucker's eyes widened. "Hey, thanks," he said softly, and gestured for Micah to follow him into the living room. Once away from the bedrooms, he added, "That shirt was starting to get ripe even before I left."

"You OK?"

Tucker gave a flippant cock of the head. "Sure. Why. Plenty of room here."

"I mean, you know, about Dad and everything."

Tucker shook it off. "No biggie. Hey, this is great timing. I was planning to get me an elk, so this"—he held up the heavy coat Micah had brought—"this'll come in real handy."

"Isn't elk season over?" Micah knew it was, even though the cow Tucker and Big Frank had taken last month off Goat Mountain was still making regular appearances in Connie's stew.

"So? It's Christmas eve. No chance I'll see a game warden today. Besides, if I'm gonna be staying with Skelly and Wes, I gotta pay my way somehow. A big old cow elk, that'd give us enough meat for a month."

"Well, I didn't bring your hunting rifle."

"Wes says I can use his."

"But ... there's supposed to be a big storm coming in."

"Why you think I'm heading up, numbnuts? After no snow for so long, there's going to be a shitload by tonight and all them damn elk are going to be on the move to the lowlands. They'll come right to me."

"And where you gonna be?"

"Why?"

"In case something happens."

"Well, ain't nothin' gonna happen, and you ain't telling nobody where I went. Period. You got that?"

"But …"

"But nothin'."

"What if you get lost? You could freeze to death."

"You think I don't know every ridge within twenty miles of here?"

"C'mon. Just in case. Tell me where you'll be, just in case."

"I don't know where I'm gonna be. I'll go wherever I think the elk are on the move, and I won't know that until I feel the wind blowing through the draws. Might hike up Rocky Creek, or maybe follow Sulphur to Schreiber's Meadows. There ought to be a lot of herd movement up there. Or I might head up the back side of Goat, or work my way up the South Fork Nooksack. Depends on what I see."

"I wish you wouldn't go, Tucker. Those roads are going to be bad."

"Nothing's going to happen to me, bro. And remember what I said about keeping this to yourself. I ain't interested in no game warden getting wind of it, and I damn sure don't want the old man coming after me and screwing up my hunt. Or even worse, deciding he's gonna be the big hero and come save me. Don't be telling nobody. Period."

Micah was still looking for a reason Tucker shouldn't go. "You don't have a truck," he blurted as it came to him. "Is Wes loaning you his?"

"Nah, he's workin'. But I don't need a truck. I don't have to bring back whatever I kill. As cold as it's going to be, all I gotta do is quarter it and bear-bag it for a few days. If that storm does shows up, the meat'll keep. I can get far enough up there in a car. I'd use Skelly's if I thought there'd be any way it would start after a night in the snow. Gonna have to borrow one."

Tucker's eyes took on a mischievous glint.

Micah saw where he was going with this. "Are you kidding? After yesterday? There's no way they'd let you take Mom's."

Tucker dug into his jeans pocket and pulled out a key. It looked like Connie's without the key ring. "I had a copy made. Hey, it's Christmas Eve and it's about to snow. She probably won't even notice it's gone."

"You might have a hard time getting to it. Since you left, Dad closed in the carport. Made it a garage."

"You're shitting me."

Micah nodded. "He did it."

Skelly wandered into the living room, scratching his ass, and took a drowsy interest in the conversation. "S'goin' on?"

Tucker ignored him. "He did it in two days?"

"Him and a couple of his guys."

"No shit. Automatic door or manual?"

"Manual. With a padlock."

"Figures. Cheapskate." Tucker shook his head and gave Skelly a look. "He's been talking about putting in that garage forever. Guess I motivated him."

Skelly laughed. "Probably thinks you'll go back there and screw with her car."

Tucker laughed at that, too. "Fat chance. I'd rather steal it."

That unnerved Micah, but he laughed as it was obviously a joke.

"How big is the lock?" Tucker asked. "Can I cut it with bolt cutters?"

"Dad would kill you."

"Micah. Big lock, small lock. Yes or no."

As usual Micah was mowed down by Tucker's will, and he resented it. "Yeah. I mean no, it's not big, yeah, you could cut it. Probably."

"Good. Big Frank working today?"

"I dunno." That was true.

"Hmm. Well, even if he's home there's probably a bowl game on TV that will keep him occupied. And if it snows, he ain't coming outside anyway."

"Tucker, you can't steal Connie's car."

"I'm not stealing it, numbnuts, I'm borrowing it."

"What about Dad?"

"Fuck him."

✦

The Christmas morning gift-giving had gone over like the spreading of disease.

Micah had abided his mother's efforts to make the most of it. That morning he had awoken to find, at the end of his bed, an oversize stocking with candies, nuts and fruits and stupid little things—Pez dispensers, a dollar-store harmonica, one of those paddles with the ball attached by a rubber band, each as if he were still a little kid. It made him sad. But there was also a Sony Walkman, and that helped erase the gloom.

By late morning, the living-room gifts had been opened, Connie was bustling around in the kitchen, and Big Frank sat morosely in his recliner, staring at a football game. Four wrapped boxes intended for Tucker sat forlorn in front of the Christmas tree.

The worst, though, was the tension Micah felt about his mother's car, and whether Tucker had actually gone through with it. His mother had not attempted to take her car anywhere, and Big Frank had had no reason to go to the garage.

But by early afternoon, his mother's airy faux Christmas spirit had worn down and was replaced by an honest melancholy, and the inevitable began to take shape.

"This is ridiculous," she said. "Not to have our oldest boy here on Christmas, just because you two can't get along."

"Get along?" Big Frank slurred through his latest beer. "Woman, that boy assaulted me. His own father."

"And I'm sure he feels terrible about it. But Big, I'm sorry to have to say this, you were both at fault."

Man, that took some guts, Micah thought, almost cringing at such audacious truth.

"You better watch yourself, missy," Big Frank said in a low voice. "I get enough lip from the boy. I ain't about to start taking it from you."

"But it's Christmas, and he's our son," she said, still in that submissive tone. "I'm sure he feels sorry about everything that happened."

Micah seriously doubted that.

He watched his mother looking out at the snow. It had been falling since noon the previous day and there was nearly a foot in the yard. The weatherman on the morning news had said it was likely to dump all weekend.

"I want to go get him and bring him home before this gets any worse," Connie said in a tone that spoke of unwavering grit.

"Yeah, well, don't forget it's gonna get a lot worse for him when he walks in that door," Big Frank said, punctuating the last swig of his beer with a loud burp. "That's a fact."

"It's Christmas, honey. The day Christ was born. A day of forgiveness. Can't you forgive your own son?"

He went to the refrigerator and grabbed another bottle of beer. He downed half of it in a single swig, all the while glaring at her. He wiped the excess from his lips with a heavy forearm. "Looks like you're doin' enough of that for both of us."

"So be it, then," she said. "But I'm going to go get your son and bring him home. Our son. Christmas is a time for family."

"I'll go with you," Micah offered, and his mother smiled her approval.

The smile disappeared three minutes later when she and Micah found the garage padlock missing and the car gone.

"Oh my God," she said. "All that time we didn't have a garage, and the day we get one the car gets stolen? Oh my God."

Naturally, then Big Frank had to go out to investigate for himself, after which he stormed inside and went to the telephone to call the police. As he was dialing, Micah blurted, "What if it wasn't stolen?"

Frank had the telephone receiver to his ear, having already dialed. "What do you mean, not stolen?" he asked, just as somebody came on the line. "Yes, I think I need to report a ... hang on just a second." He cupped a palm over the mouthpiece. "What do you know about this, boy?"

Micah, flustered, couldn't come up with what to say. But now that he'd opened his mouth, there was no going back.

"Just a goddamn minute, all right?" Big Frank said into the phone. "Yeah, that's right. We're still figuring it out here. ... Yeah? Well, fine, I'll do that!" And he slammed the telephone down as hard as he could onto its cradle, knocking his bottle to the floor. Remarkably, it didn't break—the saving grace of ugly, thick, shag carpet—and simply spewed its suddenly aerated contents. Big Frank didn't even notice as he returned his attention to Micah. "Where's the car?"

"I don't know," Micah said, stammering. "Exactly."

"What *do* you know? And if you lie to me, God help you."

Connie was about to intervene gingerly, but Big Frank's hard glare stopped that.

"Start talking. And I mean right now," he growled to Micah.

"Well ... I mean I could be wrong, but ... well, I think Tucker needed a car."

"For what?"

And here they were at the crux point: the very thing Tucker had said not to reveal.

"Well?"

He tried to imagine Tucker in this situation, daring—even welcoming—the punch with his defiance.

"WELL?"

Micah wasn't Tucker.

"He was going hunting."

"For what? Ain't nothin' in season."

"He said something about maybe going after an elk."

"*WHAT*? In this weather?" He stopped abruptly and narrowed his eyes. "Hold on. He stole your mother's car to go hunting?"

"I don't know that. I know he didn't have a car to use, so ... I guess it's possible."

"Son of a bitch. That little thief," Big Frank said with a scowl. "Where was he staying? With that Radich kid, is that what he said? I'm going over there and—"

The telephone rang.

Big Frank glared at it in an angry realization. "Fuckin' cops. Musta traced the call," he said, ripping the receiver to his ear and shouting, "WHAT?"

It wasn't the police. That was obvious when his expression went from anger to an odd irritation. He held the phone out to Micah.

Micah took it, suddenly afraid of whatever was coming from this telephone. "Hello?"

He listened. It didn't take long. Maybe a minute was all. Mister Slocumb was a get-to-the-point man, especially when he clearly had other such calls to make. When this one was done, he simply said he thought Micah would want to know, and he said goodbye.

Tears rushed to Micah's eyes as he reached out to hang up the telephone and didn't quite get it to the cradle. He sank onto the sofa. His mother squatted in front of him and waited for him to say what was wrong.

"Deano's dead," he murmured.

Micah felt like he had drowned and was floating, suspended in an eerie darkness.

"Died in his sleep this morning," he droned, parroting what he'd heard with a vacant stare. "Probably didn't feel a thing. Doctors say that can happen with quadriplegics. System's so messed up anyway, some complication kicks in and the body can't fight it, maybe it affects his breathing. Or his heart. They came in to get him for … to open Christmas presents. That's when they found him."

"Oh honey, I'm so sorry," Connie said, kneading Micah's forearm. She looked up at Big Frank, his rampage on hold. "It's his best friend, Big. It's so sad."

Big Frank stood, his anger at Tucker frustrated by this awkward situation. "Yeah, that's too bad. Sorry, kid. That's a tough deal." And he went to the closet.

"What are you doing, Big?"

He pulled out a thick wool sweater and began to tug it on. "What's it look like? I'm gonna go find that kid and bring your car back." To Micah, he said, "The Radich place, right?"

Micah looked up at him, still weightless. His own voice surprised him. "He's not there."

That stopped the big man. "How you know that."

None of this seemed important now. Tucker's secret, Big Frank's need for reckoning. None of it mattered anymore.

"I called over there an hour ago," Micah said through the haze. "He wasn't back."

"Wasn't *BACK*? When did he leave?"

Micah felt an odd awareness that his father might actually hit him, and for once the prospect didn't frighten him. He just didn't care.

"Answer me, boy."

"Probably yesterday."

"He told you he was going up for elk. Yesterday."

Micah nodded.

The fiery slits of Big Frank's eyes were burning into him. "Did he also tell you he was going to steal your mother's car?"

Micah answered with his own dull gape. He shook his head slowly.

"You little liar."

Connie tried to intervene. "Big, honey, you don't know that …"

Those slits never softened. "All right. Where's he gonna go, did he say?"

"No. I don't think so."

"You know." Big Frank grabbed him by the shoulder with his meathook of a hand.

It just doesn't matter. "Maybe up west of Shannon or Baker. I think he mentioned Schreiber's Meadows. Goat Mountain, too. He didn't say for sure."

"As far as I'm concerned, you were in on this," Big Frank said in a slow and heavy cadence. "We'll deal with that when I get back. And it won't be pretty."

Big Frank went to the closet. Connie flitted behind him, touching at his shoulder.

"Big, you can't go out looking for Tucker now. The weather …"

"Well, *he's* out in it. With *your* car. That he took out of *my* garage. After cutting off *my* lock. To go out in a snowstorm." He shook his head contemptuously. "Shit for brains kid has no sense whatsoever."

"Let's call someone," his mother muttered. "The police maybe, somebody …"

"I'm not calling the cops because he took the car, Con. Don't be an idiot."

"Who cares about the car? I'm talking about finding our son!"

That one hit Big Frank like a slap in the face; Micah could see it in his eyes as he watched his parents act out the manifest schism in their respective senses of humanity.

"Yeah," his father said. "Of course. Why do you think I'm going? To find him."

Big Frank began pulling the rest of his heavy things out of the closet—boots, heavy coat, winter gloves, a heavy skull cap. Connie fussed around behind him, her attention torn between Micah and her husband.

"But the police have people who could look for him," she pleaded.

"Yeah? Where they gonna look? His sidekick here doesn't know shit. Even if they could find him, they'd probably slap him with a fat herkin' fine for hunting out of season, and who the hell you think is gonna end up holding the bill for that? Huh? And for all we know he's just shacked up in some motel with one of those little skanks of his."

"But then where will you look? In this weather ..."

"Well, if he's actually looking to take an elk, I have an idea where he might go. Place I took him once in weather something like this. Not this bad, maybe. The elk were thick in there."

"But Big, you've been ..."

Micah sucked in his breath, and she stopped short of the line that was never to be crossed.

Big Frank clearly knew what utterance had been averted. His response was to stalk to the refrigerator and grab the rest of the half-rack of beer. "This could take a while," he hissed, pulling on his winter clothing and daring anyone to say a word. He stormed out the door.

Connie and Micah watched through the living-room window as Big Frank unloaded work gear from the bed of his pickup and carried it into the garage, each furious trip resulting in loud clatter. Connie began crying and tramped out into the snow herself. She disappeared into the garage and after a minute she and Big Frank emerged. Big Frank was carrying something Micah couldn't quite make out—a crowbar, perhaps.

His father climbed into the front seat, slammed the door and drove away, the bottom halves of the truck's tires disappearing in the blanket of snow as he headed off into the white Christmas.

⅄

Micah, a sheriff's sergeant named Ansel and a search-and-rescue guy who'd been introduced only as Wayne hunched forward against the white wind as they tromped through foot-deep snow to the Radich front door.

Wes Radich let them inside and led them to the den, where Tucker and Skelly were watching a football game beside a roaring fireplace. Neither of them seemed too interested in the intrusion.

"Yo, Tucker," Wes said. "It's the man."

Tucker issued an insouciant glance at Ansel, then turned it on Micah and held it. "What a surprise," he said softly, holding his eyes on Micah before returning to the game.

"Tucker Dodd. I'm Sergeant Ansel. We talked on the phone."

"Yeah," Tucker said without looking up. "I remember."

"Either turn that thing off," Ansel said, "or turn down the sound."

Skelly turned the sound down with the remote control, muttering, "This is the playoffs, man."

"I need your help in finding your father," the sergeant said.

"You're too late. He's already dead," Skelly said.

There was a sudden stillness and intake of breath.

"My dad's been dead for two years," Skelly said seriously, then laughed as if it was the funniest thing he'd said all day. He looked at Tucker, who shook his head with a little smile that said he admired the chutzpah.

Micah couldn't believe they were finding humor in this.

Neither, apparently, could Ansel.

"When I want you to talk again, I'll let you know," he scowled at Skelly. This got Tucker's attention, and their eyes met. "I need to know what you know about where your father might be."

"What makes you think I know anything about it?" Tucker retorted.

Why do you have to play everything so cool, Micah thought.

"We think he went looking for you," Ansel said. "Out hunting for elk."

Tucker's gaze slid across the room to Micah again. "That would be illegal," he said. "Everybody knows elk season's been over for a month."

Micah saw Skelly suppress a grin.

"Look. I'm not a game warden and I don't give a rat's ass if you were hunting or not," Ansel said. "I just want to know where your father might think you would have gone elk hunting. Micah. What was it your father said? How did he describe that place?"

Micah stepped forward. "He said there was a place he took you to once where there was lots of elk."

"In snowy conditions like this," Ansel said. "That's what you told me earlier."

Micah nodded.

"That ring any bells for you?" the sergeant asked Tucker.

"Could be lotsa places. I been hunting these hills since I was twelve. Got me an elk every year, too."

"And who CARES?" Micah finally shouted. "I don't know why you're acting like this is a joke. Dad's lost, and it's because of you."

Tucker stared at him. Micah couldn't hold his gaze.

Ansel sighed. "Look, Dodd, I don't know what's your problem with your father and I don't really care," he said heavily. "But you're going to help us."

The two of them locked eyes, but Tucker was out of his league. This was a sergeant. Probably ex-military. A neck thicker than Steelbarton's. And a handgun.

Tucker finally ended the standoff with a shrug. "Best guess. If I was lookin', maybe I'd work up the South Fork toward Wanlick or Bell. Sometimes the elk'll move down off the back side of the Sisters that way."

"I know those drainages," the search-and-rescue guy named Wayne said.

"I've hunted them myself," Ansel said. "But no way could he get around Lyman Pass in this stuff."

"I don't know," Wayne said. "When he took off it wasn't this bad."

Ansel glared at Tucker. "I don't suppose you'd be interested in coming along, maybe helping Wayne and his guys pinpoint some specific locations."

Tucker seemed to consider it, then shook his head.

Wayne shook his as well, but with utter disdain. "I didn't think so."

"This where you're gonna be?" Ansel asked. "In case we need to reach you? Maybe keep you apprised as to the search, how things are progressing?"

"Oh, I'll be here," Tucker said, turning back to the television. "But you don't need to keep me ... apprised or whatever."

In that moment, Micah hated him.

CHAPTER 16

THE MISSING

By mid-day of the next day, the search was suspended. Other storm-related disasters—snow-weighted trees falling across roads, houses, and power lines, outages, missing people—had stretched the county's resources. The roads in the Big Frank search area were virtually impassable, and if temperatures took the predicted uptick and the snow turned to rain, those canyons would become avalanche corridors. And no one even knew where Big Frank had gone.

That afternoon, Tucker borrowed Wes's pickup and drove to a place he hadn't told the sergeant about.

It was another drainage north and east of the places the searchers would have been looking. He had rarely seen any trophy bulls up there, which was probably why it didn't get a lot of hunting pressure; but he always seemed to find the cows, which made for better eating anyway. He never could understand the hard-on so many hunters got over big antlers. It was one thing to enjoy the hunt and eat the meat, but keeping souvenirs of killing didn't appeal to Tucker.

Now he was simply hoping to coax the pickup up that winding old logging road to a good wide spot he knew about only a half-mile from his treasure: the remaining three quarters from the young cow he'd killed on Christmas Eve, bled dry, quartered and then hung up outside of the reach of anything that might smell the kill.

He'd discovered this hidden little meadow, a real elk haven seemingly undiscovered by other hunters, a couple of years ago; last winter he'd brought his father up there and they'd each taken a cow.

But the place Micah had described as big Frank's possible destination was a place Tucker had taken the old man, not the other way around.

That'd be just like him, taking credit for something somebody else discovered, Tucker thought. *Be funny as shit if he actually came this way and I found him.*

Well, Big Frank had, and Tucker did.

But it wasn't funny.

⅄

It looked like a big mass of snow-covered boulders at first. But Tucker was on foot by this time, pausing at a switchback for a water break. Eying the boulder cluster as he guzzled, he began to notice its angular nature.

And the tire jutting out from one of those angles.

A slurry of emotions welled within Tucker.

The truck had clearly lost traction as Big Frank tried to make the hard right turn at the switchback. The truck slid backward into the ravine, which was mostly dry in winter, and came to rest on its side thirty yards below the road. The first spring gullywasher would probably flush it even further out of sight.

Tucker stared at his father's snow-camouflaged truck for nearly two minutes, until his heart stopped pounding out the William Tell Overture. Then he slipped and slid down the gully to the truck, afraid of what he would find—and not sure what he was hoping for.

He had almost circumvented the truck when he saw his father.

From the waist down, Big Frank wasn't visible; that part was completely under the side of the truck. His upper torso, arms and head were free, and it was clear by the disturbed area within his reach he hadn't died in the accident. The uninterrupted blanket of thick snow had been replaced by a muddy muck within what looked like an arm's-length radius around him. He must have eaten every handful of snow without reach.

A wafer-thin coating of snow covered him. Death had clearly come.

Tucker unshouldered his pack and sat beside his father's corpse and considered the novelty of his father's snowy face: Even in death, nothing had changed. Big Frank's expression still looked angry, as if he had taken his last breath cursing at the injustice of his end, or at the son who led him to it. Looking at that frozen sneer, Tucker's uneasy sadness over his father's death was supplanted by his own anger that he hadn't been there at the end. Tucker couldn't remember a time his father hadn't been beating on him, trying to make him surrender in one way or another, and now he felt cheated.

He hadn't been there to see the moment Big Frank gave up.

He began to wipe the snow off his father's face. The odd thought hit him that it might be the first time he had seen the old man with closed eyes when he wasn't snoring, and he tried to find a black humor in that. He wished he could laugh.

As much as he wanted to hate Big Frank, the son of a bitch was still his father.

Big Frank's face had taken on a color that looked something between blue and gray. His bushy eyebrows were frozen, and Tucker knocked some ice from them.

The eyes beneath them opened.

"Holy SHIT!" Tucker exclaimed as he fell backward against a rock and caught himself. "Holy shit! Dad?"

Big Frank's mouth began to move, but all that came out was crackling gasps. His hand reached out and latched onto a wrist, which Tucker instinctively ripped free.

"Jesus, I can't believe it. You're alive," Tucker said as he regained his composure and pulled out the canteen he'd been drinking from just a minute before. He half-handed it to his father and helped him to drink.

"Easy, easy," he said as Big Frank guzzled. "Not too fast. All right, enough, that's enough."

Operating on wilderness instinct, Tucker began assessing his father's predicament, trying to figure how to get him out. Big Frank was trying to talk again, but Tucker couldn't make out the rasping sounds and held up a hand. "Save your throat, old man. Let me figure this out."

He considered the way the truck was balanced on its side, with Big Frank wedged underneath. There was no way to get the truck off him, but he felt compelled to try. Looking around for something to use as a fulcrum, he scrambled onto a boulder to look inside the cab of the truck through the shattered passenger window, hoping the old man had brought a crowbar.

He saw the half-rack box, immersed in a frozen pool of amber. And then something else caught his attention, wedged into the space behind the seat: Big Frank's Winchester hunting rifle, the old Model 94 he'd been toting around for nearly two decades.

"All right. This'll do better than any stick I could find," he said, reaching down to pull out the rifle. "We might actually be able to get enough leverage with this as a wedge to get this thing off you. It's a long shot, but we gotta try somethin'."

The old man was trying to mouth something, but still couldn't create words.

Tucker ignored him. He started to wedge the rifle under the bottom, driver-door side of the pickup; then stopped. He looked down at his father's gray face. "What am I doin'. What'd you teach me, huh? Always be sure."

He swung the finger lever open, expecting to find an empty chamber. But it wasn't empty.

"Holy shit, old man, this thing's loaded. What are you, nuts? This could've gone off in the truck." He removed the first .30-.30 cartridge from the chamber, then a second, finally a third. As he set them onto a relatively flat rock surface, the realization hit him.

And he stopped.

"Hold on now. Wait a fucking minute," he said to himself, and that heavy sadness returned. He sat down on a boulder across from Big Frank, the rifle across his lap.

"What did you bring the gun for, old man?"

His father's mouth was moving, but the rasping sound had stopped. He shook his head and motioned weakly with both arms.

"You weren't goin' hunting. Why'd you need a gun?"

The old man wasn't looking at him now.

"Did you need it for me?"

Big Frank's eyes widened with what looked like protest. He started grunting out negatives, but those vocal cords had nothing left after three days of screaming at the top of his lungs every time he heard a sound in the woods.

The more Tucker thought about it, the clearer the picture became. Big Frank never kept the Winchester in the truck, so he would have had to make a conscious decision to bring it.

Tucker's eyes welled up with tears, and he wiped them away angrily.

"It wasn't enough for you to kill the only other person I ever loved?" he said, shaking his head in anger and shame at the truth in his post script: "Besides you."

Big Frank's eyes looked like they were reddening, but he simply had no moisture left within him to cry.

Tucker stood and turned away to wipe his eyes dry. He didn't want the old bastard to see even that much of his heart. He stepped back onto the boulder with the vantage point to the truck, and reached inside for the icy half-rack. Some of the beer ice chunks broke away as he pulled it out, and the black humor finally began to seep out with them.

"Oh, bummer, old man," he said. "Not only did you wreck your truck, you broke all your beers. No, wait. One didn't break." He twisted off the cap and turned it up. "Frozen solid, though."

Tucker took several deep breaths, pushing his emotions somewhere he wouldn't have to feel them.

"You know, they called off the search," he said matter-of-factly, watching his father's response. "They're not looking for you anymore. They've all gone back to whatever they were doing before. There's no one else coming. No one within five miles."

Tucker watched Big Frank's eyes for the epiphany, his moment of understanding where this was leading.

"I don't think I can get you out. The truck looks pretty solid right there," Tucker said. "I suppose if I really hurried back down the mountain, maybe I could manage to get to somebody who mattered within, say, three hours. They're going to take an hour to get together somebody to come look, get all their gear together. Then maybe more than three hours to get back up here." He looked at the sky. "That's what, six, seven hours? Be dark by then. Be awful frickin' cold. Might not even find you in the dark. You can get disoriented in deep snow like this, especially at night. Might be morning before anybody gets here. You'd have to spend another … whole … night just like that." He shook his head. "Man. You gotta be hating the thought of that."

He set the frozen bottle down next to the three rifle bullets.

"You won't remember this, but I do," he said. "One of the first nights I stayed in that house after my mom died, I was crying. And then Micah started crying. We must've got loud enough for you guys to hear 'cause you came in. You know what you said?"

Big Frank didn't move or try to respond.

"You told us to shut up. You said you were tired of listening to us crying, and that you didn't want to hear a peep out of either of us for the rest of the night."

Tucker shook his head. He leaned the rifle against a rock and unscrewed the cap of his canteen again for another swig, being sure to dribble some of the excess. His father watched thirstily but did not motion for a drink.

"You know what you said to me then?" Tucker continued, slowly moving down onto his hands and knees next to Big Frank. "You got real close. You were almost whispering. I could smell the beer on your breath."

Tucker leaned in close to his right ear. "You said, *Well, little man? Think you can make it through the night?*"

He watched his father's Adam's apple bob in a dry swallow. He sat up and looked around at his father's death pit.

"Without your beer, I'll bet you been eating snow, haven't you?" he said, nodding. "Sure looks like you ate a ton of it. Mm. Not good. Makes your body get colder that much faster. Leads to hypothermia. Tell you what I'll do, though. I'll leave this one unbroken beer with you. Maybe if you can keep it warm somehow, you can thaw it out enough to get a drop or two. Maybe put it in your armpit or something. Naah. You're practically a popsicle now anyway. I don't think that's gonna work. That's too bad."

Tucker leaned in close again, next to Big Frank's ear. "So what do you think, big man? Think you can make it through the night?"

Tucker rose to his feet and grabbed the three bullets. He was just about to toss them into the snowy brush when he caught himself.

One. Not three. One.

He looked down at Big Frank, finally pathetic, weak and begging.

Tucker chambered one round into the rifle and, clenching the two remaining rounds in one fist, stepped up the gully. Well beyond the old man's reach, he squatted and stood the bullets on a flat rock. Then he rose, holding the rifle, and gazed down at Big Frank, whose tired eyes widened at what he must have anticipated.

Tucker read the expression and took a little pleasure in it. He shook his head. "No, old man. I wouldn't waste a bullet on you."

He turned the rifle around to the butt end and handed it that way to his father.

"You know what, Big Frank?" Tucker said, with a sarcastic emphasis on the name. "I'm gonna give you something I never got. I'm gonna give you a chance. And a choice.

"I'm leaving you the gun. With one round. Use it as a signal if you want, but you'll be wasting it. Nobody will hear it, and if they do, big deal. Just some rifle shot in the boonies. Hear that all the time. Or you could use it for something else.

"It's your choice."

Tucker hefted his pack onto his back and clambered toward the switchback. He turned back for one final look at the man he blamed for everything wrong in his life.

Big Frank was begging him through the voicebox too frozen and dry to speak. Tucker just didn't care.

"Personally, I hope you don't use it at all," Tucker said.

I hope you die slow, he thought, but kept that sentiment to himself.

And he began to work his way back up the ravine.

He was nearly at the switchback, just below the level landing, when he heard the rifle blast and, in the same instant, felt the projectile slam into the snow-dappled alder tree next to him. As bits of tree bark, snow and dust shivered out of the alder in a soft shower, he was aware of the sound of the bullet having whistled so close past him.

Tucker froze.

That was a choice he hadn't expected, even from Big Frank.

And you fucked that up too, you son of a bitch.

Tucker didn't turn around. Instead, he stepped up onto the switchback and continued on his way.

He thought he heard a keening, anguished wail from behind him in the ravine.

Or maybe it was just the wind.

CHAPTER 17

THE THIRD ROUND

A manda was on her way to see Micah for what would probably be nothing more than a short social visit and gift exchange. The one gift officially on the agenda was one from Micah to Amanda, the framed enlargement of the spotted owls. The other gift was one Amanda intended for both of them: a continuation of the passionate kiss that had ended their indoor picnic five days earlier. Imagining a reprise warmed her in places that had been without heat for far too long.

Since J.D., in fact.

Holy moly. Has it been that long?

Amanda wondered if that could be true. She remembered: Yes. She had been seeing someone from work for a couple of months, but that had died for mutual lack of heat even before that nostalgic, for-old-times-sake reunion with J.D. Now she was transitioning into what already felt like a new love—with a man inextricably linked with her old love, by way of J.D.'s painting. And her blissful anticipation at seeing Micah was tainted by knowing that feeling was made possible only because J.D. had killed himself. Guilt feeds on death.

She knew tonight probably wouldn't have the opportunity to get very tender. Micah was at his mother's house; he couldn't leave, he had said, because his brother was going to be gone for a while and somebody needed to stay with his mother. Even though pretty much all she did was sleep these days, he said, he still needed to be there for her.

Even while disappointed they wouldn't be somewhere more private, Amanda was touched.

Gotta love a guy who respects his mother.

Love.

She almost shook her head. It was way too early to start thinking like that.

But Micah's directions were easy and the moment she recognized Micah's Toyota, she got that warm feeling again.

⅄

Tucker heard the front door open and heard the footsteps coming down the hall.

It was a Wednesday, the third day of school after Christmas vacation. Tucker was in the Radich basement, which had become his permanent bedroom, staring at nothing in particular on the thirteen-inch television Skelly had loaned him.

Wes was at work, though it was hard to imagine what kind of roofing jobs were still being done in the dead of winter. Skelly and Cami were at school, leaving him alone. None of them had asked him whether he planned on returning to school, or to his old home, or anything. They let him be.

And now he wasn't alone.

Cami sauntered down the steps, taking her time. Her well-chosen sweater and blue jeans defined an amply precocious maturity. *And boy, does she know it,* Tucker thought.

"Whacha watchin'," she said, and sat down next to him on the ratty loveseat.

"Nothin'. Aren't you supposed to be in school?"

"Aren't you?"

"What're they gonna do, kick me out? Fine. Do it." He looked at her, slouching too sensually beside him. "But that's me. Why are you here?"

"I went home sick." She laughed. "Sick of school."

"Aren't you on the girls basketball team?"

"Yeah. So?"

"They could suspend you a game for skipping out."

"Yeah. So aren't you on the wrestling team?"

"Not any more. So they got nothing left they can take away from me. You they can still suspend."

"Oooh. I'm so scared."

"I'm just sayin'."

"They wouldn't suspend me. They need me too much. I'm the point guard." She held her hands out in a way that looked very suggestive to Tucker. "I always make sure to get the balls into the right hands."

I'll bet you do, he thought.

"Besides, I really need a break from practice for a day. I'm actually pretty sore. After all that time off over the holidays and then practicing so hard yesterday and Monday." She reached up behind her shoulder and squeezed, eliciting a dramatic wince. "Ooh. I'm just all balled up."

Jesus.

"Think you could do something about that?" she almost cooed.

Jesus. "Huh?"

"You know. A massage."

She was a little fox, and she sure knew it. But never shit where you eat, that's what Tucker had always heard. He shook his head.

"Pleeeeeease?"

She was making it hard for him. Literally.

"Oh, come on," she said. And she turned her back to him, slowly pulling the back of her sweater up and over her head. Keeping the sweater demurely in front of her, she left her back revealed, bare but for bra straps. She scootched closer to him.

"Can you unsnap that for me?"

"I'm not sure this is a real good idea."

"Oh. It's a very good idea. It'll feel a lot better with that thing out of the way."

He shrugged, and released the bra clasps with a practiced twist of thumb and forefinger.

She turned, still keeping her front side covered with the sweater, and said coyly, "Where do you want me? For the massage, I mean."

"Oh. Right. The massage."

She looked around as if there were actually any kind of a choice. The love seat barely had room for them to sit in. And there was the bed.

"Not a lot of options here," she said, rising. Still holding the sweater in place, she crawled onto the bed on her knees. She wrestled with her apparel until the bra miraculously appeared in her hand, with the sweater still strategically placed. She dropped the bra on the floor—looking back at him for just a moment as she did so—then leaned down onto her elbows, for a moment uncovering her young but quite developed breasts before she stretched out onto the sweater. On the bed. With that bare back, her blonde hair all a-tumble around her shoulders, looking really smooth and touchable.

"Come on. I know you've seen me when I've been sunbathing."

"Yeah? So?"

"Uh huh. In the back yard that time last summer. You were looking. Big time."

"That right?"

She peeked up over a shoulder at him.

"Yeah. That's right." She glanced back and bent her legs at the knees, raising her feet. "Oh. I'm on your bed with my shoes on." And with that, she reached back with one hand to remove one shoe and then the other, dropping each on the floor. Throughout this process, the sweater remained on the bed. Her breasts, of course, did not.

Jesus.

They were actually fairly remarkable. He hadn't seen anything like that probably since Missy Klootchman.

And she's just a kid.

"What are you, fifteen?"

"Sixteen. Or I will be next week, anyway. What are you gonna give me for my birthday?" She was back to lying, stomach down, on the bed, her face partly hidden by a shoulder.

Jesus.

"Guess it's gonna have to be a massage."

She peered up over the shoulder. "Well all right. You … up for it?"

At that moment, he certainly was. And she knew it.

"Besides, with the way you been moping around, after your dad and all," she said, "I figure you could use a little cheering … up."

Jesus.

"Well? You coming?"

Jesus.

He guessed he would.

He sat down next to her, bracing a foot on the floor for balance, and reached his hands tentatively toward her back. In that instant, she rolled over, naked from the waist up. And touched her tongue to her lower lip with a little giggle that said the waist down would be that way in no time.

Oh well, he thought. *The rollercoaster has started. Can't get off now.*

Time to ride the ride.

Eight minutes later, when they were done, Tucker watched Cami pull on her sweater and shake her hair.

And she looked really young.

Definitely still juicy, but not like the seductive chick of the past ten minutes. Now, with his small brain no longer doing the thinking, she looked to Tucker like somebody's kid sister. Like Skelly's kid sister. Who was fifteen. He had actually felt guilty that time he'd seen her sunbathing, because she had looked pretty hot then. And she was just a kid. And now he'd done a lot more than just look.

Shit.

As he began pulling on his pants, suddenly feeling uncomfortable being naked, he noticed her self-satisfied little grin.

"What're you grinning about."

"Nothin'."

"What. Tell me."

"I'm just thinking about how Shawna's going to freak out when I tell her at practice. And Angie in homeroom."

"Oh, hey, don't be telling people at school about this."

"Why not?"

"I don't want people knowing, that's all."

"Ooh, I get it. You just don't want me telling my brothers. What, are you afraid they'll beat you up for banging their little sister?"

"Yeah, right. I'm real afraid about that happening. Gimme a break."

"Well, maybe I'll just tell your creepy little brother. Maybe then he won't keep hanging around looking at me all weird if he knows I'm getting it on with you. He's creepy. Like I'd ever actually go out with a little dork like that."

Aw shit. You gotta be kidding me.

"Micah asked you out? On a date?"

"He *tried*," Cami said, making a face. "This morning. Came up to me at my locker. Geez, anybody could have seen us, the little dip. You know he doesn't even have a driver's license? What a creep."

"Hey. Give it a rest."

"Give what a rest."

"You can shut up talking about my brother."

"Yeah right, like you give a shit about the little creep."

"Hey. I'm just telling you: Knock it off."

"You can't tell me what to do. What, because you screwed me now suddenly you can tell me what to do?"

"I didn't screw you. You screwed yourself. I just happened to have a dick handy."

"You're really a jerk, you know that?" she said, storming up the stairs. "I'm gonna tell Skelly and Wes the whole thing."

"Good. Do it," he called up after her, raising his voice as she went. "They'll probably kick your ass for being a little skank. My kid brother's probably the only guy in school you haven't screwed."

He heard the telephone start ringing upstairs.

"Fuck you!" She was shouting from the hall.

"No thanks," he mumbled. "Once was enough."

The telephone rang again, and he heard her pick it up. "Hey, asshole!" she shouted. "It's for you!"

He pulled on a T-shirt as he shuffled up the stairs and heard her bedroom door slam. He picked up the phone in the living room.

"Hello."

"Tucker?" It was Micah. "They called off the search for Dad."

Tucker pondered that and tried to rummage up some emotion. None surfaced. "Again?"

"This time they say it's for good. They've had people looking all over for four days, and they don't even know where to look. They figure with all the snow up there, it may be spring before he shows up unless somebody spots the truck. And he's probably frozen anyway. So I guess that's it."

"I guess so."

Micah was silent for a while. Finally: "You haven't been at school all week."

Tucker was filling up with an anger he couldn't have put into words. "Yeah. So?"

"Well. You're not at school, you're not at home anymore. I dunno. Just seems weird. And Mom's just lying around in her robe all the time like she's dead."

"I'm not surprised."

"Well ... with Dad gone and all ... why don't you come home? I know Mom wishes you'd come home."

Tucker thought about having to look into her eyes, knowing what he knew.

"I don't think I can do that, little brother. I think I've already crossed that bridge."

⋏

Nor would Micah find him any more willing nearly three months later, when a couple of shed hunters looking for elk antlers down from Park Butte came upon a badly decomposed body half-buried by a pickup truck in a creek bed.

He was called to the office from honors English and was surprised when the principal handed him the telephone. It was his mother, who said she was sitting in the living room with Sergeant Ansel, and that his father had been found. She said after the police were done with their business—she didn't say body—they'd have a funeral, probably a week from Saturday. She asked him to give the news to his brother. And she sounded absolutely hollow.

When he hung up the phone, Principal Phalen told Micah was certainly excused if he wanted to go home. In fact, the principal would be happy to give him a ride.

"No, that's all right," Micah said. He felt numb. He'd known this day was coming, had almost wished for it just to know, but now the reality made him want to lie down. He felt too exhausted to go home and have to watch his mother wither. "I think I'd rather go back to class."

After last period, Micah rode his bicycle to the Radich house. He felt oddly neutral about his father's body having been found. Everybody had known he was dead. A couple of Micah's aunts had suggested perhaps he'd done a repeat of his father, simply taken a powder, but his mother hadn't believed it and neither had Micah. He'd always figured the mean old drunk was lying dead in some ravine.

As he reached the Radich house, he left his bicycle in the yard and knocked. He hoped he wouldn't see Cami; once she had let slip to one of her megaphone friends the tale of her dalliance with White Bluff's resident bad boy hunk, it had been all over. It didn't matter that almost immediately after that he began seeing her walking around the halls with Steelbarton, entwined in ways that indicated he, too, was visiting portions of Cami's body Micah would never see. Now he couldn't pass her in the halls without seeing the mental image of her legs wrapped around her brother or Steelbarton or both, and all of them looking up at him and laughing.

Skelly answered the door.

"Hey, kid," he said, thumbing him inside. "Yo Tee! It's your brother." Skelly led Micah toward the kitchen, where Tucker was standing at the counter in a grimy T-shirt, dirty jeans and work boots, looking as if he'd been wrestling a bear. Tucker flipped Micah a less-than-hospitable look. Micah said nothing.

Skelly watched them in silence for a few seconds, then said to Tucker, "Last chance, man. Steel's gonna be waitin'."

"Nah, I'm beat, you go on. If you see your brother, ask him to pick up some beer on the way home, would ya?"

Skelly agreed and left.

Tucker went back to making himself a peanut butter and banana sandwich, focusing on his task and not looking at his brother. Micah watched him cut the banana slices and arrange them on the bread.

"They found Dad," he said. "His body. Some guys found him with the truck. He had a wreck."

Tucker kept slicing.

"You don't have anything to say?" Micah asked.

Tucker took the second piece of bread, slathered in peanut butter, and placed it atop the banana-slice bread. After appraising his finished product, he finally looked at Micah. "What do you want me to say? We all knew he was dead."

What's the use, Micah thought. "Funeral's probably going to be a week from Saturday. Not that you'd go."

He started to leave, and he heard Tucker mutter, "You're right about that."

Micah wheeled at him. "Nothing's ever your fault, is it?"

"You tell me, smart guy: What's my fault?"

"You don't feel guilty at all?"

Tucker just glared. "For what?"

"You're unbelievable. He's dead because you just had to go hunting during the worst storm of the last ten years."

Tucker took a big bite of the sandwich, chewed and swallowed, the glare never wavering.

"No, smart guy. He's dead because you told him I did."

"*What?*"

"If you'd done like I said and not told anybody, he'd have gone back out to the garage the next morning and seen the car right where it was supposed to be. Or maybe he'd still want to break my neck. Either way, he'd be alive. So don't be putting that on me, little brother. This one's on you."

Micah's mouth had dropped open. "Now it's my fault he went out and got himself killed trying to rescue you?"

"What makes you so sure he was trying to rescue me?"

"Well, then, why'd he go into the hills in a blizzard? For his health?"

"That's a good question," Tucker said, taking his sandwich and heading out the kitchen and down the hall. He stopped and turned. "Now I got one for you. If he was just out to rescue me, why'd he bring his gun?" As he walked down the hall, leaving Micah alone, he added, "Think about that."

It wasn't until he saw Tucker on the day before Easter Sunday—lurking in the trees, watching Big Frank's graveside service from the distance—that Micah really thought about it.

That son of a bitch, he was thinking at the moment. *Doesn't even care enough to sit here next to Mom when she buries her husband.* And he considered Tucker's unrepentant anger ... and what the rifle might have had to do with it.

Micah and his mother had had lots of time to talk about everything that had happened the day Big Frank disappeared. So Micah knew about his dad taking the rifle.

How did Tucker know?

⋏

The sun was just beginning to dip below forested crestlines to the southwest when Tucker came out of the trail he'd followed through the woods and stood within view of the last place in White Bluff he had called home.

He'd been dreading this day since that taxi ride from Arlington two weeks before. He had come back because of Connie, but also because he needed to see an old friend. To make whatever peace could be made, after everything that had happened six years ago.

He stood outside the Radich place and tried to stoke a courage that now seemed foreign to him.

For six years he had wondered what ever became of Skelly, since the last horrible, blood-spattered moment before Tucker started running.

Tucker hadn't called on the telephone. Not once. He was certain he was a fugitive from the law, and uncertain how people back in White Bluff thought of him. Some, he knew, would be happy to finger him. For Steel. For Cami. For Skelly, maybe. For being Tucker Dodd.

Since he had been home, he had spoken to almost nobody in White Bluff, and certainly nobody in his old circle. Nobody who knew him, who knew why he had left, who knew what he had left behind. Nobody who might know something.

The lights were on. Tucker willed himself from his emotional inertia and strode across the patchy lawn. He didn't know who would answer the front door. He didn't even know for sure if either of the Radich boys still lived here. He knew for sure Cami didn't.

He rang the doorbell, heard footsteps coming down the hall, thought about a day six years past and regretted coming.

CHAPTER 18

Tucker had been crumpled into his usual raven's roost in Steelbarton's back seat when the Corvette wheeled into the parking lot.

It was one of those hot 1982 Stingrays, last year's killer model, two-o'clock-June-sun yellow, convertible top down. Everybody with half a clue knew Chevy had only cranked out something like twenty thousand of them last year and this year's model was changed up so it didn't look the same. That Vette right there in front of the 7-Eleven was the final classic, the one where when you were 60 years old you'd be looking back and wishing you'd sat behind the wheel of one of those babies just once. Just to feel it purr.

The driver's *Yeah I know everybody wants to be me* cruising attitude was embellished by the accessories—his mirrored aviator sunglasses and a passenger whose serpentine blonde hair flowed in the breeze like tresses of pleated silk. Tucker watched as the driver, a Bellevue blow-dry obviously slumming this far out in the sticks, strutted his well-pressed Calvin Kleins into the store. He reeked of exactly the kind of born-rich arrogance Tucker hated.

He'd been in a morose mood for more than two weeks, ever since the shed hunters had found Big Frank's pickup—and Big Frank himself, in a gruesome state of decomposition. Everybody had known the old man was dead, of course, but Tucker didn't enjoy having it shoved in his face all over again, first with the news stories and then the graveside service he wasn't about to attend. It made him want to be anywhere but here, and anyone but himself.

Tucker stared with the contempt of envy and muttered, "Check that baby out."

Skelly was watching lasciviously from the shotgun seat as a couple of high-school honeys sauntered from the 7-11 to a waiting Mustang. He turned to see what Tucker was talking about and whistled under his breath. "Whoa. She's hot. Nice car, too."

Steelbarton arrived with a half-rack and asked if they'd had seen the fresh meat.

"Yeah, we seen it, so what," sighed Tucker, whose attention was back on the Vette. His every verbalized daydream of escape from White Bluff had featured just such a getaway car.

Steelbarton finally noticed what had so gripped Tucker. "Whoa," he said, popping a can for himself. He guzzled half of it before passing one to Tucker, who popped his top and took a slow swig, never taking his eyes from the Vette. Steelbarton eyeballed Tucker.

"You're likin' that action, Tee-man," he said. "I know you. That Vette. That's you, my man."

The blow-dry came back out with a bottle in a brown bag and a pack of smokes he was unwrapping on the way. He got into the Vette, finding something to laugh about before he coolly closed the door, as if he knew he was being watched and was accustomed to others' envy. Tucker watched the blow-dry. Steelbarton watched Tucker.

The Vette's engine fired up, a jungle cat announcing precisely who would be king of the jungle tonight.

"Well?" Steelbarton's tone was pure challenge.

The Vette peeled out.

Steelbarton stared at him, dumbfounded at his buddy's failure to grasp the obvious. "That's the car of your dreams, bro. A man should get to see what his dreams feel like. Don't you think?"

Skelly expelled a beery belly laugh at what he presumed was a joke.

Tucker knew better. "How the hell am I gonna do that?"

Steelbarton glared momentarily at the infidel. "We'll talk to the guy," he said with a rogue's smile. "Explain why you need to borrow his keys for a little while."

Tucker gave Steelbarton the look. "You're crazy."

"Fuckin' A, Bubba."

"'Cause there ain't no goin' halfway on something like this."

"Oh shit," Skelly muttered, laughing now with far less mirth.

"When have I ever been the halfway type?" Steelbarton said, his grin growing.

"Then I guess it's on." Tucker shook his head. "Time to ride the ride, Skull Man."

"Oh shit," Skelly murmured again. "What are you guys doing?"

Steelbarton, shifting his Trans Am into the chase, burst into loud, cackling laughter. "Livin', Skull Man," he exclaimed. "Livin'."

In less than a minute Steelbarton had the Stingray in sight, and he quickly passed the only vehicle between them on the Mountain Loop Highway. As he closed in on the Vette's bumper, it became obvious the blow-dry had seen them and decided to dust them. But although he may have had enough horsepower under the hood, he simply wasn't crazy enough to use it. The blow-dry slowed the Vette going into every bend in the road and Steelbarton felt no such compunction, staying close enough on his bumper to read the vanity plate: 2KUL4YU.

"Look at this dickhead's license plate," Skelly said nervously, forcing a chuckle. "Too Cool For You. You believe that shit?"

Steelbarton, focused on maintaining the Trans Am's almost clinical proximity to the Vette, didn't answer. Tucker knew this wasn't likely to end well, but Steelbarton was a good friend, a teammate, and Tucker had his back. So did Skelly, although in this instance clearly without glee.

Tucker could see blow-dry boy watching them in the mirror, and just north of Arlington on Highway 9 the Vette pulled off to the gravel shoulder. Steelbarton pulled off just behind him and began to open the door. This was really starting to feel familiar to Tucker.

Steelbarton looked back. "You coming or I do have to do the talking for you?"

Tucker shook his head. "Big man, I think you *want* to do the talking."

Steelbarton laughed, got out of the car and approached the Vette. Skelly popped out of the passenger door and was just behind him. Tucker could see the blow-dry looking at the approaching pair in his wide window; the blonde had craned her neck around to see.

Ah shit, here we go again, Tucker thought, and followed as Steelbarton ignited the inevitable.

"Hey, I like your car," Steelbarton said in exaggerated appreciation.

"Yeah?" retorted the blow-dry, who seemed unafraid. "And you've been riding my ass just to tell me that?"

"I just wanted a closer look. So does my buddy here," Steelbarton said, glancing back at Tucker's approach.

"Well, now you've had your look," the blow-dry said, putting his hand on the gear-shift knob.

Steelbarton held out a cease-and-desist hand. "No, you don't understand. My friend wants a really close look. Like from inside."

Blow-dry and the blonde both wrenched their heads around at Tucker.

"What the hell are you talking about?" the blow-dry demanded, for the first time with a hint of uncertainty.

Steelbarton grinned. "My friend would like to test-drive your car."

The blonde put a hand to her mouth.

The blow-dry swallowed. "It's not for sale," he said.

"Oh, that's all right," Steelbarton said with a devilish grin. "We're not buying."

The Vette took off in a wheel-spinning roar, spraying Steelbarton, Skelly and Tucker with a scattershot blast of gravel and leaving the Trans Am in a cloud of dust. *Nice move,* Tucker thought. *Now put the hammer down and keep it there.*

Steelbarton, who took the brunt of the gravel spray, was cussing loudly as he touched places on his face to check for blood. Tucker saw this and started laughing as he headed back to the Trans-Am at an easy pace.

"I believe that boy got you, Steel. And good."

"It ain't funny," Steelbarton said, hustling past him to the driver's door and bringing the Trans Am to life while Skelly waited for Tucker to climb into the back before taking the shotgun seat. "That motherfucker is gonna die."

Tucker knew the speed of the blow-dry's Vette might match even his buddy's pathological need for payback, but then he saw the Vette take the cutoff to Lake Cavanaugh. *That was a mistake*, he thought. *Should have stayed on the main road.*

The Vette was more than a half-mile ahead by the time they caught a glimpse of it on a rare straightaway. Steelbarton floored it and closed some distance, gaining much more quickly as the road became more serpentine and his own willing abandon became an even greater ally. The Trans Am was back to within two car lengths when they reached the split in the road, the easy right and the hard left.

From the hesitation in front of them, Tucker sensed what Vette boy was considering. "Don't do it," he murmured. *Can't make that turn at this speed.*

Tucker was right.

λ

Of all the trails and backcountry roads Micah had tagged along behind his older brother on in those early years, he had never been on this one. Apparently, though, Big Frank had. Because it was up here somewhere, Sergeant Ansel had told him, that his father's body had been found, trapped under his own truck.

His father was no longer there, of course. The truck would be there until enough mountain snow melted to get a truck up there to winch it out, though, and that gave Micah something to look for as he followed Ansel's directions.

Micah was surprised at how little emotion he felt as he made his way up the drainage. He didn't even have a good reason for going, just a morbid desire to see where his father had died what had almost certainly been a very slow and painful death.

The rifle had been found right next to his body. It was empty, Big Frank presumably having fired off all of the signal rounds he'd taken up with him— three, his mom had said. But none of the people searching for him had heard even one.

Micah was working his way up the draw when he came upon the truck from below. The snow on and around the truck had largely melted or been washed away by the runoff. As he took in the scene, he tried to picture his father's dying position there; but it was just an effort to work up some heartfelt grief, and he had used his up two months before. He had come to this place expecting to reengage his sorrow, but all he had wrought was a wet pair of socks.

He was sitting on a rock next to his father's death zone, inspecting what Big Frank may have touched or reached for, when his eyes happened to fall upon something glinting in the sunlight.

That's weird.

He made his way carefully over the unsteady footing to get a closer view. There, on a horizontal piece of shale, nestled between some other rocks, were two .30-.30 rounds.

One was lying on its side. The other was upright. Micah considered every possibility of his father's imprisonment, and one thing was clear: This mystery had been well beyond his reach.

Yet these rounds had been placed there by human hand.

And he had an idea whose hand it was.

⚔

The Vette took the hard left without slowing sufficiently, sending it skidding across the far lane and off the road. It never rolled, instead slamming passenger-side-first into a ponderosa pine. After a violent shiver, it settled into its tremor cloud.

Tucker felt an urge something like nausea.

Steelbarton took the soft right fork, brakes screeching to a halt half a football field from the Corvette.

"Holy shit," Skelly muttered, then scrambled out.

"What are you doing?" Steelbarton yelled.

Skelly was already running back and across the road toward the Corvette. The door had slammed shut behind him.

"Skelly!" Steelbarton shouted.

Tucker struggled to push Skelly's seat forward and tried to open the door. It was awkward and difficult. "Goddamit!" He finally managed to get to the door handle.

"SKELLY!" Steelbarton turned and saw Tucker wrestling out of the back seat and battling the door. "What are you doing, dickhead, we gotta get outta here. SKELLY!"

Skelly kept running. Tucker got the door open and crawled out, managing to get to his feet just as Skelly reached the Corvette and stood, gaping inside.

"Oh shit," Steelbarton said. "Look!"

Tucker had to tear his eyes from Skelly and the Corvette to see what Steelbarton was talking about. He was staring out the windshield at a vehicle in the distance.

"Somebody's coming. Shit," Steelbarton said. He honked the horn twice and stepped out to shout. "Skull! We gotta go! Now!"

Skelly looked back, hesitated, looked into the Corvette again and came running back. He reached Steelbarton's Trans Am just as the approaching vehicle—a farm truck—passed. Its brake lights came on as it came abreast of the Corvette, now engulfed in a billowing cloud of dust. Tucker was still standing outside the passenger door.

"They're messed up. I think maybe the girl's dead," Skelly panted.

"Shit. Get in," Steelbarton commanded, and Skelly launched himself into the back. "No fuckin' way we're goin' down for this. TUCK! Get in!"

Tucker hesitated, wanting to run to the Corvette.

"Tucker!"

"But … those people!"

The driver of the farm truck was pulling off the road.

"That's right!" Steelbarton shouted. "Those people will take care of it. Get IN!"

In the instant that Tucker's butt hit the seat, Steelbarton peeled out.

"The driver," Skelly said. "I think … he saw me."

"Well, at least that means he ain't dead," Steelbarton said glumly.

Nobody said a thing for two minutes. Tucker was a flurry of roiling anger and helplessness. The road narrowed as it snaked along, but Steelbarton barely slowed down.

It wasn't until they came around a bend to a fork in the road and Tucker could see the glistening water in the distance that he realized where they were.

Big Frank and Connie had brought the boys out to the lake for a picnic once when they were kids and Tucker had been back with girls a couple of times since.

"Hey. Hey. This is a dead end," he said. "I know this place, we can't get out of here. We have to go back the way we came."

Steelbarton slammed on the brakes, leaving rubber, and turned around. His voice reflected his fear. "What are you talking about? It looks like the road keeps going around the lake."

"Yeah, but I don't think it goes anywhere. It just goes around it and comes back, like a big circle."

"Bullshit," Steelbarton said. And he kept going. The road followed the lake, passing a few large, lakeside homes. Steelbarton's vise-grip on the steering wheel seemed certain to crack it any moment now.

Minutes passed without conversation.

"Steel. We have to go back."

"Bullshit."

Skelly seconded that. "We can't go back that way."

They reached a fork in the road—the left following the lake and the right away from it.

"See, what'd I tell you?" Steelbarton said, taking the right fork. "We're outta here now, man."

In a quarter-mile they came to yet another fork in the road and saw the skidmarks in the road the Trans Am had left five minutes earlier.

"Shit," Steelbarton grumbled.

"What are we gonna do now?" Skelly said. "We can't go back. They'll see us."

"What, the people in the truck? They don't know what happened," Tucker said. "All they know is that Vette crashed."

"The driver sure knows," Skelly said, his voice quivering. "And he saw me. What if that girl's dead?"

"Get over it, willya, Skull," Steelbarton barked. "I'm the one who's gonna fry for this if they get me. You know how this is gonna play out, don't you? That rich asshole doesn't know how to drive, so we end up paying for it! Me most of all, because I'm the one at the wheel!"

"Well, what do you want me to tell you, Steel?" Tucker said. "There's no other road outta here. We either go out that way or we wait for them to come looking for us."

"This whole thing bites," Steelbarton said, and he took the right fork.

When they reached the accident scene, there were five vehicles and a slew of people clustered around the Corvette. Not one was a cop. And no ambulance yet.

"Don't slow down," Tucker instructed from the back.

"Are you kidding?" Steelbarton said.

As they went by, Tucker noticed somebody in the cluster turn and point at the Trans Am.

That isn't good.

A minute later, they heard a siren and saw the flashing lights of a police cruiser. State patrol, maybe, or sheriff's department coming at high speed toward them.

"Don't slow down," Tucker said. "They're going to the accident. They're not looking for anybody yet."

"I am so fucked," Steelbarton said.

The cruiser passed, siren wailing.

"Jesus," Tucker said.

A minute later, another siren, this one a fire truck. Paramedics.

After another minute, yet another siren. Another cop.

It passed, and Tucker turned around to watch it. He saw its brake lights come on just as it disappeared around a bend.

"Oh shit," Steelbarton said, his eyes on the mirror. "I think he's coming around."

"STEEL!"

Skelly's scream came just as a small boy with a fishing pole ran across the road in front of the Trans Am.

Steelbarton cranked the wheel to the left and the Trans Am flew across the oncoming lane, slammed through a guardrail, airborne for just a moment. Tucker slammed into the back of Skelly's seat in a rolling avalanche of wrenching violence that felt and sounded longer than it was. He heard metal grinding and tearing in that instant, experienced an epiphany that he was about to die, was aware of shattering glass and then an abrupt stillness that had an after-effect something like the settling of Fourth of July fireworks after the big-burst finale.

He wasn't dead.

He felt warm and wet and realized his eyes were clenched shut. He opened them and reminded himself: *You're not dead. Get out. Police. Get out.*

It was dark and he tried to rise, bumping something above him. He looked for light and it was off to the side. It was a window, the glass smashed out, and he crawled through it, surprised nothing was holding him in place. As he pulled himself out he felt searing pain in both of his elbows and some in his back, but felt weirdly whole. Unshattered. As he pulled his legs free of the window, he rolled over and saw that the Trans Am, what was left of it, was upside down. He was surrounded by trees and scruffy undergrowth. He scrambled toward what he thought would be the front and saw Skelly, hanging half-in and half-out of the windshield, the blood just now starting to pour out from a hornet's nest of cuts.

He couldn't see Steelbarton.

"Skelly," he rasped. "Skelly, can you hear me?"

Skelly opened his eyes. Tucker could see him trying to focus.

"I'm gonna try to get you out of here, man," Tucker said, raising onto his knees for leverage. But as he took Skelly by the shoulders and tried to pull, his friend was being held fast by something inside the car. Skelly also let out of a little cry of agony, and Tucker stopped.

He heard a siren in the distance.

"Gimme. Out." Skelly sounded half-dead.

Tucker braced himself and tried again. Skelly didn't budge, and this time his squeal of pain was louder.

The siren was still closing in.

"Shit, man," Tucker muttered. "Skelly, I don't think I can get you out."

"Tuck. Help. Me."

The siren reached a crescendo and, for a moment, began to recede.

Tucker heard the cruiser screech to a stop. It sounded muffled by the steaming metal of the inverted Trans Am and the trees. Tucker looked around. How the car had ended up this far into the trees was a mystery.

"Tuck …"

Ah shit. "Skull, I can't help you, man. I'm sorry. I'm really sorry."

And he started to crab walk away from the sound of the siren, moving deeper into the forest, when he tripped over a log and tumbled backward.

Only it wasn't a log. It was Steelbarton, face down into the dry, leafy forest floor. He wasn't moving.

Tucker froze, stared at the still life before him for only a few seconds and then scuttered away, before that final image became one he'd never be able to bury.

CHAPTER 19

Micah opened the door and decided Amanda had gotten more beautiful over the two-day eternity since he'd seen her. He smiled and drank her in.

Right up until she cracked a grinand said, "I do get to come in, right?"

He hurried to open the door as they shared a soft laugh at the silliness. As she came in, their bodies brushed.

"Mmm. You smell good," he said softly. He reached a hand around her waist and led her to him. She pressed her hands against his chest—not to push away, but to caress.

"You feel good," she said, her lips only inches from his.

He leaned in, until their lips were nearly touching. He began to say, "So do you," as her lips closed the distance.

In the moment of touch, a sudden yapping startled both of them.

Micah sighed. "Gulliver."

"Friendly, I hope?"

"Vicious. Man-eating."

She nodded. "Good thing I'm a woman then."

"Do you mind if he's out here? I didn't ask if you like dogs."

"Only vicious ones."

He smiled. "I think he'll settle down after he meets you. I just don't want him to wake Mom."

Amanda nodded. Micah had told her about the dementia.

He let Gulliver out of the bedroom and the little schnauzer became a wagging little lover at Amanda's knee. Micah stuck his head into Connie's room and listened for a few seconds, but his mother was quiet. He offered Amanda a seat on the sofa, where Gulliver quickly joined her.

"Well, here's what you came for," Micah said, retrieving the 18-by-12 framed photograph from the kitchen table and bringing it to her.

"I love it," she said, admiring the colors and the fledgling's almost comic appearance alongside its stately mother. "But this isn't what I came for." And she set it aside.

"No, but it was my excuse to get you here," Micah said, sliding down into place next to her, forcing Gulliver to abandon the narrowing crawlspace between them.

This time the kiss was interrupted only by more kisses as Gulliver began lapping at the necks above him. That made them laugh and kiss some more.

"So," Amanda said when they separated by an inch or two. "Your mother's sleeping really well, is she?"

He nodded.

"I guess that leads to the other question," she said.

He didn't hazard a guess.

"How long before your brother comes home?"

⅄

Tucker watched the door slowly open, prepared to face the demons of his past.

And there stood Skelly Radich.

Tucker watched his old friend's face run through the phases of recognition, surprise, arrival and baggage claim. Years of baggage to be pawed through. They stood, each eying the other through the filter of the last six years apart and what preceded that separation. Tucker considered Skelly's face, as hardened by life now as his own.

"You look like shit," Skelly said.

"You too."

Skelly looked around him to the street. "You walkin'?"

"Yup."

"Well, you might as well come in," Skelly said and headed into the kitchen.

Skelly stopped at the refrigerator and pulled out two Olys without a word. Each took a long draw on his beer without speaking. When Skelly sat at the kitchen table, so did Tucker.

"Long time," Tucker said.

"Yep."

They mulled that over.

"You been OK?" Tucker said.

That got a little rise. "Oh, just real peachy. You?"

The air in the room got heavier.

"You know the old story," Tucker said. "Win some, lose some. The losin's worse than the winnin's good."

"Ain't that the truth." Swig. Swallow. "Where you been, anyway? California?"

"Some of the time."

"Figured that."

"Sometimes Nevada. Arizona. You know."

"Long way from here."

"Always."

"Just curious about something."

"Yeah?"

"Did Cami go with you?"

That registered with Tucker like a punch to the stomach. "No," he said finally.

"She disappeared. Same time you did. You didn't know that?"

Tucker rocked his chair, balancing on the back legs. "I haven't talked to anybody back here in years. Since I left, basically."

Skelly nodded. "Yep. You left, all right."

Another punch.

"I didn't exactly have a lot of choices," Tucker said, a little defensive. "Did I?"

Skelly didn't answer. Swig. Swallow.

Tucker wanted the answer. "What would you have done?"

Skelly took another swig. That finished his beer. He rose and pulled out the rest of the six-pack from the fridge. He opened one as he sat.

Swig. Swallow.

"If I was you? And my best friend was lying there?"

"Hey, you weren't just lying there," Tucker said, his voice rising. "You were stuck but good, man. I tried to get you out, remember?"

"I remember you left."

The punches just kept coming. Tucker was steaming and ashamed, but didn't have a good answer.

"I didn't have a choice. I had to leave. The cops were on their way."

"Oh yeah. And they sure got there, too, thank you very much."

"I couldn't do anything about that."

"No, I guess you couldn't. 'Cause you were already gone. Thanks a lot."

"Hey. I ain't the only one who let somebody down here. All right? So you can drop that shit right now."

"What's that supposed to mean? Who the hell let you down, tell me that."

"I gotta spell it out for you?"

"What are you talking about?"

"Gimme a break. How about singing like a robin?"

"What?"

"It's a lot of fun being a wanted man, with warrants out on you up and down the West Coast. I gotta tell you, I about halfway expected that shit from my brother, but not from you," Tucker said. "He couldn't keep his mouth shut either."

"Hey, blow me. I didn't tell anybody jack. Nobody even knew who you were."

"Right. That's why they had the reward out on me, right?"

"Reward? You're outta your tree, man. I never even told them your name. Why you think I was the one they sent up? Because *I never even told them your name*. They got it from other people in town, but those people were guessing. I was there, and I didn't tell them dick."

Tucker felt his old brew of guilt and rage bubbling to the surface. "That's not what I heard."

"Yeah?" Skelly glared at him with a brassy toughness Tucker had never seen from him. "Well, you heard wrong. Screw you, Tucker. I could have given you up and walked away and washed my hands of the whole thing, man. They'd have let me walk scot-free. I told them it was Steelbarton's deal, it was his idea, his car and he was driving. The guy remembered seeing me, but he couldn't give a description of you and I didn't tell them shit. If they figured out who you were, it wasn't me who told them. Shit, if that chick had died, I'd still be at Wally World."

"But ... she did die."

"What are you talking about? When?"

"But ... they said ... she died and there was a reward out there for me."

"Who said?"

"Some guys I knew checked into it for me."

"Jeez, Tucker. You need to find some new guys."

"You got sent up to Walla Walla for that?"

"No. I got sent to county for four months, would've got out after three. But I got into a fight with some asshole in for DUI and busted him up pretty good. The judge looked at that and the car thing both and decided I was a *baaad* boy. That's what got me to Walla Walla." Skelly took a swig that left his bottle empty and opened another.

"Asshole," he said as he set it down.

"I'm sorry, man. I didn't know."

"Like I'd fucking talk."

"How long were you in Walla Walla?"

"Almost a year."

"Jesus. Is it as bad as ... you know. What you hear."

Skelly gave him a cold stare. "I didn't get gang-raped, if that's what you mean."

Tucker didn't say anything.

Skelly dropped his gaze. "They damn sure tried."

"Jesus. What happened?"

"I got lucky. I don't think I could've held them off. But I was fighting back so hard while they were reefing on me, trying to hold me down, my shoulder got completely pulled out of its socket. I guess I was screaming so loud 'cause it hurt so bad, they decided I wasn't worth all that much trouble." Skelly pulled up the sleeve on his tee-shirt and pointed to a scar. "Had the operation later."

As he pulled the sleeve back down, he added pointedly, "I didn't rat them out either."

"And they never came back for you?"

Skelly shook his head. "Nope," he said. "Neither did you."

A

Micah had long ago put Gulliver back in the boys' room, where his whimpering had not gone on long and would have gone unnoticed anyway.

As their tongues continued to dance, their hands began the tentative search for places to caress, breathily measuring each other's responses to every new exploration. Amanda sensed Micah's uncertainty in the way his hands roamed but never seemed to encroach on her breasts or, below her waist, on anything other than her waist, hips and outer thigh. *He's so nervous,* she thought. *He doesn't know if he's allowed to touch me.* It was sweet, she thought.

And it made her want all the more for him to touch her. Anywhere. Everywhere.

"You know," she said in a brief moment of air, "I never thought I'd say this, but I'm starting to wish your brother would hurry up and get home."

Micah misunderstood. "How come?"

"Well, at the risk of seeming unladylike or forward, then maybe we could … I dunno … go somewhere else. More private."

Micah's eyes widened.

"Really?" he asked, like a child who's been told all of his Christmas wishes are going to come true, but can't quite believe it.

"Well," she said, "haven't you been thinking the same thing?"

He looked at his watch and then glanced back at his mother's door. "I don't understand what's keeping Tucker. I thought he'd be home by now.

It's almost dark, and he's walking, so I'm sure he'll be here soon. And she is sleeping. Maybe we could … if you wanted, we could … go over to the duplex."

"What if your mom wakes up?"

Micah shrugged. "She just goes back to sleep. Amanda, I've been here for almost two months, and been in this house probably sixteen to twenty-four hours every day of that time. Worst case scenario, she'll go into one of her fits while we're gone and I'll find her on the floor."

"Oh no."

He gave a little wave of his hand. "Sleeping. Trust me. It'll be fine."

"You're sure? Well, then. OK. Let's do it."

Micah seemed almost dumbstruck by her choice of words.

They rose, unwrapping themselves from each other, Amanda enjoying a delicious sense of anxiousness. But not apprehension. Anticipation.

"Oh. My picture," she said, tossing her hair, feeling somewhat free now that whatever was going to happen seemed to have been put into motion.

"Photograph," Micah said just as his voice cracked, making him clear his throat.

"Oh, that's right," she said with a little smile. "I forgot. You didn't use crayons."

"So," he said tentatively, following her out to the car. "Do you … want to follow me to the duplex? Or do you remember the way?"

"Well," she said, deciding to jump all the way into the pool, "I have to work in the morning."

She could see his immediate deflation.

"Oh. Yeah. It's … yeah," he stammered. "That's … yeah, you probably need your sleep."

"Actually, sleep wasn't what I had in mind," she said breezily. "I have to work in the morning, and it will save me a half-hour if I didn't stay at your place …"

She paused to let that sink in.

"… and you followed me to mine instead."

Micah blinked. And double-blinked. "Me come to your house? Now?"

She leaned to him and gave him a light kiss, just a touch of butterfly wings. "Umm hmm."

"And ... stay?"

"Don't worry. I went to the dentist last week," she said and enjoyed seeing the confusion cloud his woozy euphoria. She smiled. "Now I have an extra toothbrush."

CHAPTER 20

When he heard the tapping on the window, Micah was taking a break from an evening of studying for a calculus exam and making a grilled cheese sandwich. He dropped the spatula.

He turned to the window and saw movement. His heart pounded until he saw enough of the face in the glow of the kitchen light.

"What are you doing?" he asked as he opened the door for his brother.

Tucker didn't immediately come in. Instead, he peered around Micah into the house. "Has anybody been here looking for me?"

What a weird question, Micah thought. "Why would they? Everybody knows you're at Skelly's."

Tucker squinted hard at him. "Who knows? What do you mean? Are they watching for me there?"

"What are you talking about? Who's they?"

Tucker's demeanor eased. "So you haven't heard anything."

"About what? You're not making any sense." Micah wondered if his mother could hear any of this. "Are you gonna stay?"

"Why?"

"What do you mean, why? This is your home. Remember?"

Tucker stared at him as if he were speaking in Latin. "No, I'm ... I have to leave."

Micah made a face. "Why? You still have a bed here, you know."

Tucker looked like he was considering it. Then he shook his head. "No, that's not a good idea. But I'll tell you what, though. I could use a flashlight, maybe a couple of blankets. I'm gonna stay outside tonight."

Micah did a double-take. "Where?"

"Where I can be alone. And nobody will … see me."

"Are you crazy?" Micah listened for sounds of his mother being awakened, and was confident she hadn't. "Who's gonna see you in your own bed?"

"Anybody who comes here. I know a place."

"Who's gonna come here?" Micah was adamant. "What place?"

"You don't need to know. And I don't need anybody else to know."

"Who the hell you think I'm gonna tell?"

Tucker glared at him and walked past him into the kitchen, grabbing the heavy flashlight from under the sink.

"So go to your secret place," Micah said. "Freeze to death. Whatever."

"It's not even cold. But tomorrow afternoon after school, I'm going to need you to do me a ."

"You act like a a nutbar and then you want me to do a you a favor. Nice."

"It isn't for me. It's for your mom. Get somebody to drive you to the Greyhound station in Everett."

"Why?"

"That's where you'll be able to pick up her car."

"But it's in the garage."

Tucker peered out the window. "It won't be tomorrow. I'll leave my extra key in the trunk. I'd go tonight but I'm too tired. I've been on my feet for must be thirty miles."

Tucker's unwillingness to explain himself was making Micah angry. "You're not making any sense."

Tucker sighed. "Something bad happened."

"What."

"It's nothin' I did, but I didn't stop it. It's bad. And it's gonna get worse."

With that, Tucker walked out the back door. As he disappeared into the deepening darkness—without turning on the flashlight—Micah could tell which direction his brother had taken. Downstream. Toward the falls.

As he had so many times years ago, Micah began to follow him, this time keeping his distance. There was only a three-quarter moon, but the sky was cloudless and there was enough light. Tucker reached the cross-over rocks but didn't cross, instead continuing on the trail. This led to only two places: the opposite-shore viewpoint atop the falls … and the Under Look.

Tucker stopped suddenly, turned on the flashlight and wheeled back, cutting into the night with its swath of light. Micah froze, not knowing if he was too far back to be illuminated.

When Tucker turned the light back off, Micah was too blind to see.

⅄

It was barely dawn when Tucker stirred from his semi-sleep in his fern-covered cubbyhole overlooking the scramble path to the Under Look, where he had spent a near-sleepless night planning his next move and listening for sounds in the night.

He clambered out of his haven and was about to head back up the trail and away when he remembered the falcon stone, something he hadn't thought about in months, perhaps years. He remembered it crossing his mind when Deano had told him about putting in that bridge at the Under Look, but when Deano had broken his neck that same day, it had simply been forgotten.

Today, though, Tucker was leaving. So he headed down to the Under Look to take the one thing that was his.

Except that it wasn't there.

Son of a bitch. The kid took it.

Naah. Can't be. Deano must've got it for him.

He stood at the precipice and looked down into the churning froth below. Even at this time of year, when many waterfalls were reduced to dripping, the Kacheel still had a steady flow. But he didn't stay long. Anyone who showed up at the falls could see him there, and he knew he had to leave unseen. People were looking for him. He knew it.

He stepped back to the gap and set himself to jump across it, refusing—as he had upon arrival—to step on Deano's stupid little bridge. He paused, and squatted down to study it. The top looked like double-ply plywood, but it had to be stronger than that if Deano had expected it to hold a person's weight. In a move fraught with peril that didn't even remotely frighten Tucker—who had no fear of heights whatsoever—he reached to the center of the wood piece and wrenched it free. He looked at the 2-by-4 braces underneath, shaking his head at the almost excessively detailed workmanship.

Fuckin' Deano, he thought. *You probably measured the gap and cut this stupid thing to fit. Tried to save people you maybe didn't even know. And look what happened to you.* He thought about throwing it over the edge, thought again about Deano, and instead replaced the bridge, wedging it back into place where Deano—and Micah, according to Deano—had put it.

He scrambled his way up the trail to the fence and was about to swing around when he detected movement from the periphery. His abrupt start made him slip just a bit and he grabbed the fence to keep himself from plummeting to his death.

It was Cami Radich, perhaps ten feet from the edge, rising to her feet on the uphill, safer side of the fence.

"Jesus," Tucker blurted, his heart pounding as he swung around to her side. "You scared the shit out of me. What are you doing here?"

Cami gaped at him dully, as if she were in a trance. Tucker waited. She looked like she was trying to formulate words that just wouldn't come.

"Cami?"

"Yeah?" As if they'd been having a conversation.

"What are you doing here?"

Cami seemed to have a waking moment.

"What do you think? I've been waiting for you."

Tucker looked beyond her, half expecting to see her leading someone else to him. But she was apparently alone.

"You need to get out of here," he said, pointing the way up. She took a tentative step toward the top of the falls but stopped and waited for him to follow. "C'mon, let's go," he urged. "This is a dangerous place."

"Who gives a shit."

"How'd you know where I was?"

"Your brother gave me a pretty good idea."

Fuckin' Micah.

They were on the wide trail now, and they walked in silence up and around to the top of the falls, across from the waterside expanse of flat rock Tucker and his brother had shared so many times, so many years before. Cami stopped, just a couple of feet from the edge.

"Steel's dead," Cami said.

The pounding of the waterfall below muffled her words, but they slammed him like a left hook to the solar plexus. He had feared as much in the moment he had paused over Steelbarton's motionless form in the forest, but there had been hope in the not knowing.

He tried to swallow, but the sudden lump in his throat wouldn't budge.

Tears welled up in Cami's eyes. Tucker took her arm to lead her away from the water's edge and began moving upstream, pulling her with him. She was just too close to the river, and that water was moving fast toward the falls.

She pulled her arm free, seeming to stumble just a bit toward the water as she did so, nearly making Tucker reach for her again. "He's dead," she said again, in a toneless drone. "He's just … dead. And Skelly's in the hospital."

That snapped Tucker back to attention. "How bad is he? Is he gonna be OK?"

"I don't know. They won't let me see him."

"The doctors?"

"No," she said. "The cops. There's a couple of cops sitting outside his room. I guess 'Cause of those people in the other car."

Tucker was almost afraid to ask. "Did they die?"

"Who cares? Probably, since they won't even let me see my brother in the hospital." She shook her head vehemently. "Everything is so fucked up."

Tucker was struck how much she talked like her brother.

She studied his face and finally focused on the gash outside his right eye.

"What happened to—oh my God. Oh my God. You were there. In the car."

He nodded. "That's why I gotta get out of here."

"You son of a bitch. You're not even hurt."

"Hey. I don't know how. I should be dead."

That made her tears rise again.

"It's not fair," she mumbled

He shook his head. *It's not. Not at all.*

"What am I supposed to do now?" she wailed.

He looked away, his eyes falling on the rushing current beside them. "You should go home. C'mon. You're making me nervous."

"You son of a bitch. What am I supposed to do now?"

"You can stop acting crazy, for one thing. C'mon, I gotta go."

"Steel's *dead.*"

"Yeah, and I'm not, I'm real sorry about that."

"What am I gonna do?" She thought of something and her expression sharpened. "Where are you gonna go?" Then, before he could answer: "I'm coming with you."

"No you're not. C'mon, get going."

"Steel's *dead.*"

"Goddamn it—"

"And I'm *pregnant.*"

"Oh. Shit."

"What am I supposed to do now? Steel's dead. If you leave, what do I got?"

"I don't know what to tell you. He was my friend, too. I feel as bad as you do."

"Yeah, but I'm the one who's gonna be stuck with a baby."

"Well, that's up to you. C'mon. Let's go. This is nuts standing here."

"Oh, what, now big brave Tucker Dodd is a pussy after all? Afraid of falling, gonna run away from everything, run out on Skelly, run away from the cops, run out on Steel, run out on me—"

"Hey, goddamn it, I'm sorry about Steel. He was my friend but he's a lunatic and he always was. And I'm not going to stick around and have the cops lock me away just because he knocked you up and then got himself killed."

"What makes you so sure it was him knocked me up?"

"Well, who the hell else?" Then her meaning sank in. "Oh now wait a minute, wait a stinkin' minute. We did it one time and you been banging Steel for weeks."

"And we always used a rubber, too. Steel was a lot smarter than you."

"Yeah. Now he's a lot deader than me and I ain't about to join him. I'm outta here."

"Well, I got news for you," she said, not budging an inch. "I'm coming with you."

"Like hell you are."

"And your baby's coming, too."

"No it ain't, and it ain't my baby either."

"Yeah, well, I guess we'll find out when they do the blood test, won't we?"

"Good idea, let's take a blood test of every guy in east county dumb enough to check your oil. Probably take the grange hall to hold 'em all."

Her left fist flew at him and he weaved and parried, his fighter's instinct taking over. The weave allowed him to slip just outside the punch, and the parry was the slightest push by his right, chin-protecting hand, on the outside of her outstretched forearm as the fist missed its mark.

It doesn't take much, really.

In a fight—something at which Tucker was well-versed and naturally skilled—any time a puncher has overextended, the parry pulls him the slightest bit off-balance. His lead foot must adjust forward with the slightest lunge-step for him to regain solid footing, and that momentary lapse in balance leaves him susceptible to the counterpunch.

Tucker didn't throw that counterpunch, but the damage had already been done.

Propelled by Tucker's slight but critical deflection, Cami's balance shifted. Her left foot instinctively stepped forward to establish a new base, but her shoe caught on one of the riverside rocks and she stumbled. Without solid footing, the momentum from the missed punch and the parry carried her further to the outside. Toward the water.

The next second or two—and, chronologically, that's all it was—became a series of freeze-frame mental images Tucker would never forget.

With her curled, fisted left arm leading the way, she did a complete revolution as her left foot swept outward, trying to find purchase. Instead, it came down wide of solid ground and found only air—and then water.

In that instant, as Cami continued to revolve, Tucker was aware of both of her arms reaching up toward his left hand.

Instinctively, without thinking, the wrestler in Tucker pulled his hand away, as he had done some so many times in so many matches, in the split-second before the opponent could affix a grip.

He felt the slightest touch of one of her fingers in the instant before her revolution carried her back-first into the water. Only then did he see her mouth open to scream, but the sound was swallowed up by the river in the same instant she was.

She bobbed up a moment later, already halfway to the rim of the falls. Her eyes, as wide and round as silver dollars in the instant her head broke the surface, somehow found Tucker's in a horrible instant of realization. She opened her mouth again for what might have been a scream.

And then she disappeared into the froth over the edge, her final sound already fading into the pulsating drumming of the falls.

CHAPTER 21

What Ever Happened to Cami?

The conversation had pretty much died.

The six-pack was gone. If there was another, Skelly made no attempt to get it. They sat in the kitchen chairs, each dealing with the weight of his own revelations.

And Tucker pulled out the one skeleton he could no longer keep buried.

"Skelly. When you asked me if I'd heard about Cami ..."

"Yeah ..."

"I thought you'd know by now what happened to her."

"What do you mean?" Skelly's head turned, on full alert.

Tucker stared at his beer, not ready to step into the minefield. "I thought she'd have turned up by now."

He could feel Skelly holding his gaze, studying Tucker for more information. Finally, there was an easing and Skelly turned away.

"For all I know she's turning tricks in Seattle or Los Angeles," Skelly said darkly. "Or dead."

Tucker swallowed, but it wasn't beer. It was now or never.

So he said it. "She's not turning tricks anywhere."

He felt Skelly's stare and had to force himself to meet his old friend's eyes. Skelly's expression didn't seem to change, really. It was as if he had known all along Tucker knew the truth.

Tucker's mouth felt so dry, he needed another beer. But this wasn't the time for that.

"She came to see me when I was hiding. After ... you know. I was down near the Under Look." Tucker took in a big breath, slowly let it out. "She fell."

Skelly didn't say anything for a half-minute. If he was flushed with emotion, he was hiding it.

"That doesn't sound like something Cami would do," Skelly said. "Going down to the Under Look. She's not that crazy."

Tucker shook his head. "No, she didn't go down. She waited at the fence."

"That's where she fell?"

"No. We were by the falls. That's ... where."

Skelly frowned as he pondered that.

"By the falls. You mean on the trail?"

It didn't sound good. Tucker knew that. He had to force himself not to look away when he nodded. It would look too guilty.

Skelly was silent for a while. Finally: "You saw her fall?"

Tucker nodded.

"But you couldn't save her."

Tucker shook his head. "It happened too fast. One minute we were talking, the next she was falling."

Skelly tended. "You were talking to her when it happened?"

Tucker swallowed again. He'd had three beers and yet his mouth was absolutely dry. He nodded, this time looking down at the table.

"Talking about what."

Tucker shook his head. "About you, I think. I don't remember exactly. She was acting kind of crazy. She was freaked out because the cops wouldn't let her see you at the hospital."

"Huh."

"And she told me Steel was dead. She was pretty freaked out. She was talking about leaving town, wanting to get away, something like that."

Skelly's expression never changed. "And then she fell."

Tucker nodded. "Yeah."

"Over the falls."

Tucker didn't want to get too specific. "Into the river. Just above the falls. And it just sucked her over."

Silence filled the room again. A minute passed. Two.

"My sister's been dead for six years," Skelly said. "And I'm just now finding out about it. And my best friend has known about it. For. Six. Years."

"I'm sorry, man. I was on the run. And I ... I just didn't know how to tell you."

Skelly didn't even seem to hear him. His expression was still that ghostly calm, but now his eyes were glistening with ready tears. "For six years I haven't known if my only sister's lying in some shallow grave somewhere, chopped up into little pieces by some sicko. Haven't known if she was broke or in trouble and needed my help. Haven't known if she's just a phone call away but maybe doesn't even care enough to spend a quarter. And you knew the whole time."

"I thought—" Tucker started, and swallowed his protest. He had no right.

"You couldn't make one phone call," Skelly said. "You used to be my best friend, man. And you couldn't make a simple phone call to tell me my sister's dead."

"People ... they told me not to call back home."

"People told you not to call."

"Because of ... you know, the cops."

"Oh right. That again. So because of somebody else's lie you couldn't call your friend and tell him his sister is dead. Is that about right?"

Tucker had always managed to rationalize his secret and even the guilt it spawned. Now, hearing his crime of silence testified out loud, he felt like a coward.

Skelly never took his eyes from Tucker's face; he seemed to be studying it as he came to grips with something.

"Did you know," Skelly asked, speaking slowly, "she was pregnant?"

Tucker had to fight to remain expressionless. ·

"Me, I didn't know," Skelly continued softly. "Not until after, anyway. She was gone by the time I ... well. She told Wes, though. That same day you and me and Steel did our stupid ..." He softly slammed a fist into a palm and mouthed a soft exploding sound. "Did you know? Did she tell you? At the falls?"

Tucker couldn't say the truth. He knew how it would look.

"She maybe tell you it was yours?"

Tucker couldn't even move.

"That's what she told Wes," Skelly said. "What she thought, anyway."

Tucker couldn't quite shake his head. "It … couldn't have … no. There was just the one time. Just not …" His voice trailed off. He hadn't gone a day in those six years, or even an hour, without thinking of that final moment with Cami, her face receding into the abyss … his fighter's instinctive parry as she swung, then his wrestler's instinctive reaction as she grabbed at his hand. Had he not pulled it away, he knew, she would certainly have pulled him to his own death. But not once in those thousands of mental reruns did he feel relief at having eluded her grasp.

Tucker could feel the blood of shame rushing to his face.

"I don't see how she could just fall into the river," Skelly said. "She wasn't clumsy. And she sure wasn't stupid."

Tucker didn't respond. The air in the room was so thick and heavy. He knew what Skelly had to be thinking. And finally it came out.

"Did you push her?"

The question was a knife blade. And Skelly twisted the hilt.

"Is that how she slipped?"

"What … hell no," Tucker stammered. "Jesus, Skelly. I wouldn't—shit. She took a swing at me and she … missed. She … it threw her off balance. And she fell in."

Each word and phrase got slower as Tucker realized how much deeper into this quagmire he was sinking. He looked at his feet and tried to plead his innocence to a jury of himself. *But I didn't push her, I didn't mean …*

"She took a swing at you. Huh. That's interesting. She tried to hit you and she ended up dead. And you never told anybody. That's real interesting."

Skelly rose and stepped to the hall entryway. "You know the ironic thing?"

Tucker didn't want to know.

"For a long time," Skelly said, "the whole time I was in jail and then later at Walls, and she was gone and you were gone and I never heard from either one of you, I hoped maybe the two of you had run off together."

In that moment, Tucker wished they had.

"Get out of my house," Skelly said softly, and walked away.

⋏

The drive from White Bluff to Concrete was no more than a half-hour, but for Micah it seemed to take forever.

A half-hour is a long time for a person to reconsider something, and as Micah followed her tail lights into the deepening dusk, he couldn't push away the nagging certainty that Amanda would change her mind.

Over the final five miles, he forced himself to breathe deeply and just enjoy the moment, not to presume the worst. When Amanda finally turned into a driveway, he pulled in behind her, and they exited their cars at precisely the same time, each door shutting at the same instant.

"Well, this is it," Amanda said, and Micah considered the momentous finality of the statement. And its tenuous frailty.

"Your house. Yes," he said, fumbling thoughts and words. "This is where you live."

Holding her framed photograph with both hands to her bosom, Amanda moved close to him, and he stopped breathing.

"This is where we *are*," she said softly, and leaned into him with a kiss, their bodies separated by nothing but the photograph.

Oh ...

She opened the door without a key, Micah noticed, and led him inside. Thistle yowled her feline plaint and quickly entwined herself around every available ankle.

"Thistle," Amanda said in introduction to Micah. "The boss."

"Hello, Thistle," Micah said, a bit awkwardly.

She held up a finger. "Bathroom," she said. "Why don't you ..." She pointed to her stereo cabinet. "Why don't you see if you can find some nice music."

"Anything in particular?"

"Surprise me."

"I'm already surprised," he said.

She paused. "Nice surprise, I hope."

"You have no idea."

She went down the hall. Thistle, upon being left outside the bathroom door, quickly bored with trying to seduce this interloper and eventually resumed her throne atop the sofa. Micah ignored Amanda's few CDs, preferring the comfortable familiarity of record albums. She had a bunch of music he had never heard of, some he knew well and a small but tasty selection of jazz. He picked out John Klemmer's "Touch" album, and the title cut was just beginning when Amanda returned. Her blouse, which had been tucked in moments before, was untucked now.

Oh my.

"What are you thinking right now?" she asked with a heartstopping smile.

He blushed at what he had been thinking, but had a ready answer. "How much I want to be here."

She smiled. "Good."

"And how nervous I am."

"Why are you nervous?"

No sense in lying about it. "Well ... I've had kind of a, um, short sexual history."

"Well," she said, her heartbreaking smile slipping into something more comfortable, "it's about to get longer."

⋏

Connie shambled from her bedroom into the living room, focused on a search she only barely understood but seemed to grasp instinctively. She knew she would recognize what she was looking for when she saw it, though she couldn't have put a word to it.

She was oblivious to the soft, runny excrement dribbling from the hem of her soiled nightgown, leaving a sporadic trail from her bedroom past the back door toward the kitchen and finally, stopping at her destination: the bookshelf.

She squatted down before it, mumbling in a language only she understood, pulling outbook after book , studying each with what an observer might have considered an apelike curiosity, and tossing it aside. She went through the top shelf, leaving its contents strewn across the floor around her. She coughed, emitting a gurgle of greenish, viscous liquid that bubbled down her chin, and went back to her search.

When the books from the second shelf had all found the floor, each having failed to pass her cursory visual test, she reached the larger books at the bottom. She was nearly at the bottom when she reached what she was looking for. She held it up, verifying it to what little remained of her conscious understanding, and smiled.

Clutching it to her bosom like an elementary schoolgirl walking between classes, she stood and considered going back to her room. Something fleeting in her mind made her turn instead to the refrigerator, and she opened the door wide. But instead of looking in, she was distracted instead by a box of cereal on the counter. Leaving the refrigerator door standing open—it had long since lost the ability to close on its own—she tried to open the cereal boxtop with her one free hand, refusing to release her grip on the scrapbook. Not being able to open it with the one hand, and the thought of putting the scrapbook down not occurring to her, she became frustrated and swung the box at the cupboard. In an instant, she was briefly showered by Cheerios. She stared at them, dropped the box onto the floor, scooped up three Cheerios off the countertop and put them into her mouth.

And she carried her prize back into her room, shutting the door—unlike the refrigerator—behind her.

She rolled onto her bed, clutching the book. She curled up in a corner of her bed, the little safe nestling haven she had created with her pillow wedged between the headboard and the wall, and held the scrapbook before her, staring at the striped-fabric cover. She felt a passing image of automobile upholstery, but it found no purchase on her slippery grasp of reality and memory.

She opened the cover to the first page of the book, unveiling its first four photographs. They were of a young boy not more than ten or twelve wearing what looked like a forced smile and a remarkably clean football uniform.

"Tucko. Ahmay tattle lem. Gramman wandle," Connie cooed in a raspy voice, marveling at the photograph. "Tattle lem." She smiled, and abruptly began to cough violently, each cough spewing out more greenish fluid.

After several minutes of this, she slumped into her little corner with a cough, shuddered and stiffened, emitting a breathy sound like air leaking from a badly punctured tire.

CHAPTER 22

ON THE RUN

Steelbarton's death, Skelly's legal entanglement and the dual disappearances—Tucker Dodd and his dead running buddy's main squeeze—became quite the *cause celebre* in the high school halls. Speculation ran rampant about Tucker's whereabouts and what he might be wanted for, even though none of the newspaper or television stories ever mentioned his name and everybody who should have known fell into a de facto conspiracy to remain silent. And most people presumed Cami Radich had simply decided to leave east county after Steelbarton died.

The only two people who might have put two-and-two together about the seemingly simultaneous disappearances of Tucker and Cami were Skelly, who wasn't saying anything to anybody, and Micah. And Micah simply hadn't done the math.

Cami had seemed so out of sorts on that last morning on Micah's porch, he thought she was very likely running away from home—though, with no parents to escape at home, what would be the point? She'd been known to skip school for days at a time anyway, so when she didn't show up for a while nobody really thought much about it. With Skelly in custody and Wes dealing with his brother's legal problems, Cami being missing just hadn't been that big a deal. Until a week went by. And then a month. And then the rest of Micah's senior year.

He was still a month shy of his sixteenth birthday when he graduated second in his class from White Bluff High, having already accrued enough scholarships and student loans to guarantee his college education. He had decided on Western Washington University in Bellingham, a ninety-minute drive away—close enough to make laundry trips home in Big Frank's old Chevy truck, but far enough that commuting from home would be impractical. He couldn't bear the thought of another year smothered by his mother's increasingly grasping sadness—or its alternative, her role as abandoned martyr.

On the day Micah left home, she kept going on about how proud she was of him and how she was going to miss him, but how he shouldn't worry about that and should just go be the best student and the best person he could be.

"I'll be fine, Mom," he kept saying. "I'll call a lot. I promise."

"I know, honey," she kept saying. "It's just going to be so lonely here. You off at school. Your dad gone … but don't you worry about me."

Micah watched for tears but there weren't any.

"And with your brother gone off to God knows where." She shook her head sadly. "I just want to know if he's all right. Just a call. That's all I ask."

"I know, Mom," Micah said, growing impatient. "Listen, I gotta go."

"I think he just feels too much shame," she said. "About your father."

Micah bit his lip. "I'm sure you're right, Mom." And he left.

⋏

After leaving Connie's car at the bus station in Everett, Tucker hadn't a clue where to go. The guy in line ahead of him at the ticket counter asked the fare to Tacoma, and the price and the destination sounded OK to Tucker, who bought a one-way ticket.

He caught a job first at a burger joint, where he was found to be sorely lacking in patience for indecisive customers. Then he found a day-to-day gig as a grunt-level laborer for a concrete contractor, where the money was decent, the work was steady and the foreman was willing to pay him off the books—until the boss received a lucrative government contract, for which he would have to document every worker's social security number and address.

Tucker had the former but was loathe to use it, fearful the police would trace him that way. His fluid inventory of domiciles, though, was light on actual addresses—this freeway underpass on wet days, that park shrubbery clearing on the dry ones, this flophouse when he had a couple of bucks.

But when he went into a boxing gym in a rough section of town to answer a help-wanted sign for a janitor, he found a home. Always a fighter but never a boxer, the mindset that built his reputation in his small town gave him a profession in the big city. Not long after the boxing impresario who co-owned the gym saw this muscular kid pounding on the heavy bag after his first janitorial shift, he was fighting on amateur cards as T.J. Boudreoux, employing his initials, his mother's maiden name and his father's heavy fists.

He spent his first few months searching the crowd for familiar or ominous faces. Nobody asked for his social security number, and he met a guy at the gym who could get him a fake driver's license, so he got one using his mother's last name and a variation of his first. Still, every new day meant another day unfound but not unfollowed, as his certainty of pursuers in his wake never waned.

Within a year he was fighting on professional undercards as the crowd-pleasing "Bludgeon" Boudreoux, who never stopped moving forward and whose bouts against the ham-and- chosen to oppose him nearly always ended in a knockout.

By the time Tucker got to Vegas not long after turning twenty, he had achieved enough ring success to afford a cheap manufactured home on the edge of town. When he signed the papers and gave his social security number, he halfway expected that to bring the police to his door within a week, but they didn't show. He wanted to believe they had stopped looking, but part of him still believed they were simply waiting for him to return home. And he wouldn't even call home. He couldn't take that chance.

In Las Vegas, he had a manager to direct his career: Delroy "Rat" Bilsky, aka the Rat, a colorful flesh peddler of uncertain lineage and unverifiable mob connections. Tucker decided it might help to have some connected guys check into his legal status, and asked Rat if he could do that.

"Shouldn't be a problem, kid, but I'll need some information," Rat said. "Why you think the cops are looking for you?"

Tucker told him the tale of Steelbarton and Skelly, how Steel died and the cops would have grilled Skelly until he gave them Tucker's name, and if the couple in the other car died or were crippled, well …

A month or so later, while Tucker was taking a break between bag work and shadow-boxing, the Rat pulled him aside.

"Kid, I got some bad news and I got some good news," he said. "What do you want to hear first."

Tucker asked for the bad.

"OK, kid, here's the deal. One of the people in that car you was talkin' about, the one you were racing—"

"We weren't racing, we were—"

"Shut it." The Rat shook his head. "It don't matter what you were doin'. Only matters what your local boys in blue think they can prove. You want the goods or don't you? OK. As I was saying before I was so rudely interrupted, those people in that car? One of them died, like you thought."

"Which one? The girl?"

"I think so. And that buddy of yours, whatsisname …"

"Steelbarton."

"Yeah, he's dead too. And the other guy, the one who lived?"

"Skelly Radich."

"Yeah, Radish, that's right. I was trying to remember that name the other day when I was talking with my people and I kept coming up with rutabaga." The Rat thought that was funny and laughed, and was obviously disappointed when Tucker didn't join in. "Yeah, whatever. You said you haven't been checking in back home, right?"

Tucker shook his head no.

"Well, don't. Your boy Radish is some friend, all right. My sources tell me he ratted you out big-time. There was a reward on your head."

Tucker sighed. "So I'm fucked, basically."

"Well now, wait a minute. You gotta ask for the good news." And Rat held his arms wide: Remember Who Ya Talking To Here.

"You was only fucked until the Rat stepped in," he said. "You know the Rat takes care of his fighters. Ask anybody, does the Rat take care of his guys? It's taken care of."

Tucker couldn't believe what he was hearing. "What's that mean, exactly? How's it taken care of?"

"Well, suffice it to say the constabulary ain't looking for you any more." The Rat rubbed his fingers and thumb together: *I greased some palms, kid. Am I great or what?*

Tucker, who had spent two years waiting for a badge to come walking into his dressing room before a fight and plunk down a warrant for his arrest, felt nearly lightheaded at this news.

"So … it's done?" He was almost afraid to ask.

"Well, I don't think you should be matriculatin' back to Washington any time soon or checking in with anybody back home—somebody who might not be adversed to coming into a little hard reward cash, if you get my drift," the Rat said. "But the cops ain't gonna come looking for you here. Only in Washington. You go home or draw them a stinkin' map by calling home, you lose your Get Out of Jail card, do not pass Go, do not collect two hundred dollars. Here, you're free as a bird. The Rat has seen to that."

"Huh," Tucker said. "I guess I owe you one, Rat."

"That's right, kid. You do."

⅄

Micah's transformation into the role he most regretted began innocently enough.

After finishing his B.A. at Western in three and a half years, Micah had gone to get his masters in fine arts at Humboldt State, to which he had received a grant and where he became a bit infatuated with a coed named Petra. Pretentious and clinically beautiful, Petra always seemed to be protesting something, and Micah was a moth drawn to her exotic glow.

His timid advances, though, were quickly rebuffed: "I have a boyfriend; he's in *Greenpeace.*"

Still, he jumped at an offer to join her at an anti-logging rally, where she remained largely oblivious to him. She gravitated toward people who seemed more principally involved, including a couple of wiry climber types she introduced as Petey and STP. "They're tree-sitters," she said in a way that sounded like name-dropping.

He had never heard of tree-sitters, but within a month he saw Petey and STP in action at an old-growth site, and Micah spent enough time at that and ensuing protests—taking photographs with every breath—he became another one of the recognizable faces within the save-the-old-growth movement. Some of this group loosely calling itself the Green Brigade initially took him to be FBI. After he free-lanced to newspapers a couple of his photographs—ones showing the brigaders in a positive light, as eco-warriors defending trees—some of the others in the group began to accept him for what he was: an idealist with a camera.

Petra never got around to giving Micah more than the time of day—though she certainly seemed to be giving STP the tree-sitter a lot more than that, her alleged Greenpeace squeeze notwithstanding. Nevertheless, as weeks passed and Micah continued to come around and even take part, he gradually began to feel accepted by this community of the outraged. And that feeling was profound; it was the first time in his age-skewed life he had felt that way.

Over several beers at a tavern one evening with a couple of younger brigaders—who went by the whimsical names Zee and Snarkle—they mentioned they'd be going on "a little midnight madness" the next night. He asked what they were talking about, and—with hushed enthusiasm fueled by beer and camaraderie—they regaled him with tales of pouring sugar and sand into various engine-block orifices at construction or logging sites.

Micah was fascinated. "And you never get caught?"

"Never say never," Snarkle retorted.

"They have security guards, but we've been lucky," added Zee, who seemed to view himself as an intrepid renegade. "Keep it quiet, get in, get it done and get out. And poof—we disappear."

"Wow," Micah said. "What's your calling card?"

Zee frowned. "What do you mean?"

"You know," Micah said. "Your mark of Zorro."

"What the hell is that?" asked Snarkle, who always struck Micah as being pretty cynical for an environmental protester.

"You know: Something you leave behind to let them know you were there."

"That's the whole point," Zee said. "We don't want them to know."

"Until they try to start up the ignition the next morning," Snarkle said.

"Fuckin' A," Zee laughed, slapping palms with Snarkle.

"Of course they're going to figure out you were there," Micah said. "But you want something to strike fear into the heart of the enemy. A signature."

Snarkle shook his head in disdain. But Micah already had just the calling card in mind.

The next night, when Micah rode along with Zee and Snarkle on his first "midnight madness," he showed them the four blank business cards he'd green-stamped with the mark of the falcon stone, and gave a little of its background. Snarkle's reaction was predictable—*You're kidding me, right?*—but Zee loved it immediately.

"You think we should sign it?" he asked Micah. "You know: the Green Falcon?"

"That sounds stupid," Snarkle said.

"You think every idea that isn't yours is stupid," Zee snapped.

"How about just the Falcon?" Micah mused.

And the Falcon was born.

⋏

Tucker knew he was never going to be a champion.

In the big-time fight game, he was at best little more than a middle-of-the-card club fighter. He could hit a ton, but what had worked on the black-top at Barclay's didn't go far against the pretty boys fast-tracked for the bright lights of pay-per-view shows.

He hoped he might one day get a shot at one of the lesser alphabet-soup titles, the continental this or the regional that, something that might earn him a little more money and respect. But he developed new scar tissue with every thirty-thousand paycheck, all in the hopes of a six-figure fight—or better yet, the boosted-by-television-bucks million-dollar night against one of the golden boys.

But although he won twenty of his first twenty-five pro fights, most of them by knockout, he still didn't have much to show for it in the bank. First his manager and trainer would take their cut, then his promoter would take out his locker and gym fees, and a twenty-grand payday was suddenly sixty-five hundred in the bank—before taxes on the twenty thou. Unable to wade through his contracts, full of legalese that read like a foreign language even without the dyslexia, Tucker often went home more discouraged after winning a fight than he had been hungry before. He took out those frustrations on the heavy bag in his garage over long, late-night sessions that had nothing to do with fight preparation.

One afternoon, the Rat called him over during training to tell him he was going to fight in five weeks for his biggest paycheck on the undercard of a Thomas Hearns title fight.

"This is it, kid: your candy-bar fight," the Rat said with his toothy grin. His reference was to the 100 Grand, the one chocolate sweet-tooth vice Tucker always allowed himself, even during training.

The opponent would be Jammin' J James, a former member of the U.S. Olympic team clearly being groomed for the big-time, right down to his fashionable one-letter, no-period first name. He had won all ten of his professional bouts against handpicked opponents whose faults he could easily exploit, which made Tucker wonder: Had Jammin' J's handlers seen some fatal flaw in him?

Because Jammin' J had quite a following—each of his fights having been televised—Tucker's training sessions were moved from his usual sweathole gym to one associated with one of the casinos. That way, the gamblers, the betting public and the fight fans who only turned out for the ones involving boxing "personalities" could see the training without having to cross over into the wrong part of town. The single-minded, almost fanatical fervor of Tucker's workouts began drawing crowds and affecting bettors. By fight night, the odds were down to 5-2 against him, a lot better than the opening 10-1 odds when the fight was announced.

In the locker room before the fight, Tucker was getting his hands wrapped by the trainer, Bonjo Delp, a pretty decent welterweight from the '50s and '60s and now a Rat employee. Rat watched quietly until Bonjo was done, then asked the trainer to leave the room for a few minutes. Tucker wondered about that, since Rat Bilsky wasn't one for pep talks, but he was feeling great. He had watched enough tape on Jammin' J to know precisely what he had to do to beat him. He'd told Bonjo about it, and the old man had seemed enthusiastic about the prospects.

"Hey, this must be what the big time feels like, eh Rat?" Tucker said with a smile. "My own locker room. Ain't this some shit?"

"Glad to see the kid's not nervous," the Rat said. "Don't want to see you go out there and lay a turd. Got to put on a good show. Name of the game."

"Oh, I'm gonna do more than put on a good show, Rat. Are you kidding me? I'm not nervous at all."

The Rat nodded. "Good. This is big-time, T.J. That's why you're getting the big money."

"Don't worry. I'm gonna earn it. I'm going to knock that golden boy right into next week."

"Hey now, let's not get overexcited," the Rat said. "Let's just stick with the game plan. I want you taking the fight to him from the opening bell. Never a backward step."

That caught Tucker by surprise. "But didn't Bonjo tell you what I picked up on J's tape? He'll counterpunch me all night long if I do that—that's what he does best. But if I do a quick retreat after a flurry, especially if I don't catch him good, he'll come forward way too anxious-like and throw that big overhand he likes so much."

The Rat nodded, but it wasn't one of agreement. Tucker knew it was a Yes But.

"Yes, Bonjo told me about this theory of yours, but …"

And Tucker came back with the counterpunch. "He's done it three times already, Rat. Leaves him off-balance and wide open for a left hook or an overhand right every time, but the guys he's fighting didn't take advantage of it. They aren't looking for it because they're afraid of getting hit, and he hasn't fought anybody who can take a punch and punch back. He pulls that on me, I'll take him out."

"I'm sure he's noticed the error of his ways by now, kid," the Rat said. "In fact, I'd bet on it."

That was a weird thing to say.

"What do you mean."

"I mean, if I was taking odds, kid, I'd be betting J's been working on that very thing."

"Bullshit," Tucker spat out. "Why's he suddenly going to figure out something that ain't cost him yet? Tell me that."

"I'm just telling you," the Rat said, weighing his words slowly, "if I was a betting man, I'd bet he'd have that all figured out and that he's going to be too fast and elusive for you to keep up."

Tucker studied him. "You *are* a betting man."

The Rat nodded. "Exactly."

Son of a bitch.

The Rat nodded again. "And you should be, too. If you get my drift."

"I already put down a bet," Tucker said. "Five grand. On *me*."

The Rat nodded. "I know you did. I know who you gave the money to lay the bet. He works for me." He shook his head slowly. "Not a good bet, kid."

Son of a bitch. "You bet on me to lose."

The Rat didn't answer. He didn't have to.

Tucker shook his head slowly. "Not a good bet, Rat."

The Rat cocked an eye. "I'm afraid it is, kid. It's going to have to be."

"No fucking way. I'm not taking a dive, Rat."

"Who said anything about taking a dive?"

Tucker did a double-take. "Then what are you talking about?"

The Rat shrugged. "I'm talking about you fighting a good hard fight, following my game plan."

"Wade into him and get chopped up like an apple."

"And be very well-paid for it."

"I'd get paid just as much if I win."

"No. You wouldn't. Not in the long run. This is one fight, T.J. Don't make it your last one by doing something stupid."

"You can't make me do that. Who do you think you are?"

"I'm somebody I would think you'd want to show a little appreciation to."

"Appreciation. For what? You been getting your cut. What do I owe you appreciation for?"

The Rat shrugged with an open hand: *C'mon, kid.*

"I ain't gonna take a dive because you took care of that stuff back home. I don't owe you that much."

"Yes," the Rat said, in a matter-of-fact, unthreatening voice. "I'm afraid you do. They wanted your ass bad. I had to call in some markers on that one. That one cost me. The difference here is you can equal that score without it costing you a thing. It's gonna make you richer."

"How you figure."

"We lay off a bet for you."

"I already … I'd just be betting against myself. And against my own bet."

"Don't worry about your other bet. It never got made." At Tucker's flared eyebrows, he gave an *It's OK* nod. "I told you. He works for me."

"I got a lot better odds betting on myself."

"Yeah, but that's because most people know Jammin' J James should win this fight. And when you think about it, you know he should, too."

"How the fuck you figure that?"

"He's the Olympian, kid. He's the golden boy. Lots of people will make lots of money off him before he's done. Who's gonna make money off you, kid? You ain't got what it takes to be big-time. That's just the facts. Don't get me wrong, kid, I love ya. But you ain't big-time. J's big-time. He's real money. You're not."

"So even if I happened to lose to this pretty boy—which I won't—how would I be making any money betting short-odds on him? I don't got much to bet."

"Sure you do. How about your purse? Before expenses. A hundred grand. You make that bet, you net nearly forty large, and that'd be on top of your cut—and ain't no expenses coming out of that part of it. All yours, kid."

Now Tucker was starting to see a larger picture. "And this wouldn't hurt me in getting some other good fights? Losing?"

"Hey, kid. Like I said, nobody wants to see you go out there and lay a turd. Hey, no shame in losing to a golden boy, right? Look good doing it, and it'll pay off down the line. If you get my drift."

Tucker chewed on a lip. He was reduced to rationalization.

"You couldn't lay off a bet like that in time."

"I already did."

"Wait, WHAT? Without my say-so? You can't do that."

The Rat shrugged. *Yes, I can.*

"That's my money," Tucker insisted.

"Technically, no, it's my money. That's in your contract. My hand's in the big pot, and yours isn't. I pay your purse out of *my* purse. And in this case, I've taken the liberty of doing you this big favor—"

"Without my OK."

"—this big favor because I want the best for you, kid. 'Cause I'm in your corner."

"Betting on the guy in the other corner."

"It's the right bet."

"What if I kick his ass? I still get paid my purse, but you lose the bet. Because that was your money, right? You just said so."

"Kid. Listen to me. Listen real close. You. Do. NOT. Want me to lose this bet."

Tucker knew he could kick the Rat's ass all around this locker room. And a couple of days later there would be a story on the cover of the metro section about a body found in the desert, believed to be a fighter nobody gave a shit about named T.J. Boudreoux, but police wouldn't know for sure until they found all the pieces.

That night, in the eighth round, T.J. "the Bludgeon" Boudreoux was caught by an overhand right and went down for the count, then was up and gone. Even as Jammin' J James was parading around the ring in victory, his victim was already walking out the fighters' aisle, his head down, unwilling to meet any eyes, even those offering consolations.

How did I get to this, Tucker was thinking.

I'm just a high-priced whore.

⅄

They were on their way out, climbing back out the chain-link fence protecting a nest of logging trucks and backhoes. It had all seemed so daring, so like a highwayman, like something out of the epic period dramas he had read as an adolescent. Micah felt almost like a romantic character.

Right up until a shout shattered his almost comical calm.

"FREEZE!"

Micah was halfway up the fence when he heard the voice coming from what sounded like halfway across the lot. Zee, just ahead of him to the right, threw himself over the top and hissed at Micah, "C'mon, man! They won't shoot!"

SHOOT? WHAT?

Snarkle, to his left, never slowed and pulled himself to the top of the fence and began to cross over. Micah, his heart having gone from adrenaline-rush pounding to pulmonary overload, scurried up the fence. As he hauled himself to the top and slid one foot to the outside, he felt something heavy and hard smash him on the left shoulder—knocking him over the fence but catching his jeans, and his left calf, on a sharp fence snag. He heard and felt both of them rip as he left the fence, in the instant before thudding to the ground.

Micah was bloodied and dazed as Zee and Snarkle hauled him frantically to his feet. He looked around to see the shouter sprinting toward the fence, yelling "STOP! STOP!" The shouter was running in light that illuminated his power and size, his wide face made memorable by a bushy Fu Manchu and an expression that looked capable of mayhem.

Micah glanced down by his feet and saw the wide ray of light from a sturdy industrial flashlight—the instrument of his hasty descent from the fence. Next to it, he saw his last two Falcon cards on the ground.

And then the three of them were sprinting away, in the instant he heard his pursuer slam into the fence and shake it in fury.

Thirty minutes later they were in Zee's apartment having a beer as Zee bandaged up the six-inch gash on Micah's calf.

"You think I might need stitches?" Micah asked.

"Take the scar," Snarkle said. "Gives you a great story later when somebody asks you about it. Besides, I don't think it's a good idea to go to the hospital right now. They might be there on the lookout for a guy looking to get his leg all stitched up."

"Oh come on," Micah said. "You're not serious, right?"

"I wouldn't put it past 'em," Zee said. "This ain't a big city. There's just the one emergency room. And this is Mad Bull we're talking about."

"Yeah, dude," Snarkle said, raising his mug. "That's right. You've now been officially initiated. You've had the Bull after your ass. Congratulations."

"Mad Bull?" Micah said, then took his obligatory gulp. "That's what you guys call that rent-a-cop?"

"Everybody calls him that. Somebody told me it sounds like his name or something, I don't know," Snarkle said. "But I can tell you this, he ain't no rent-a-cop. Those logger security guys are some serious badasses, and they do not like us wrecking their stuff."

"And Mad Bull's the worst."

Snarkle nodded. "He's mean."

"Last time one of our night raiders got caught," Zee whispered, "they worked him over but good. He was blindfolded the whole time, but everybody knows it was the Bull did it."

"Busted ribs. Concussion. Knocked out a coupla teeth," Snarkle said. "He's mean."

"Don't forget the lacerated kidney," added Zee.

Micah winced. "I'm not interested in getting maimed just to save some trees."

"You just take your lumps and you fight back," Zee said. "It's a war. We're on the side of saving the world, and they're destroying it."

"Yeah, but that's some pretty scary shit."

"Hey," Snarkle said, "you're the one who said we needed to be scaring them."

"What about that guy they beat up?" Micah asked. "Is he OK now?"

"Sure. He's fine," Zee said. "He's done with night raids, though. The Bull saw to that."

"Did he press charges?"

Zee made a face. "The Bull?"

"No, dickhead. The *guy*."

"Are you serious?" Snarkle said, frowning. "What's he going to tell the cops? I was fucking up some guys' shit and they caught me? You know what their story's gonna be: Sorry, officer, he fell down a flight of stairs while we were chasing him. He slipped and hit his head on the toilet. And the cops will smile and say thanks for your help, boys, because they don't like us either. Fuck 'em: You just have to strike where you can, don't get caught, and if you do, take your lumps. Only a few of our guys have ever been caught and none of them's ever been turned over to the police, as far as I can remember. Those guys' attitude is definitely an eye for an eye."

"But the ones that did get caught," Micah said, "none of them died, right?"

"Not so far," Snarkle said, then added with a laugh, "but if you can't run any faster than tonight, you could be the first."

They all laughed, but Micah's wasn't born of humor. It was more a feeling of having stepped into one of his books. He was in a war, and not just any war. A war against tyranny, a war of wills against the evil Mad Bull. He knew it wasn't that simple, but for the first time he was reacting to aggression not with fear but with excitement. It was more intoxicating than the beer.

"They gotta catch me first," Micah said ominously. "So when do we strike back again?"

And Micah's life changed. The same months Micah spent exercising and honing his photographic talent with intimate portraits of the forest and its array of permanent and temporary inhabitants, he also spent creating a public enemy number one for the timber industry.

The Falcon's calling card became infamous as it became ubiquitous. Those little calling cards with the green, emblematic stamp and its talon outline were found on the dashboard of many a logging-rig cab that had been sliced to ribbons, or rubber-banded it to the radiator cap of an engine rendered useless. Many of them were left not by Micah but by others who saw no literary gallantry in what they did, but felt like they were fighting a war. And the cards were simply another weapon.

So were the large spikes the night raiders hammered deeply into the trunks of several old-growth trees marked for removal, each with a Falcon card wrapped around and taped to the shank. The spikes, carefully camouflaged, were intended to strike even more fear into the enemy, as well as bleed them for the price of a few new saw blades.

One of the spikes, as it turned out, cost more than that.

⅄

Tucker left the ring following his complicated defeat to Jammin' J in a whirlpool of shame so palpable it was evident in every freeze-frame moment of his flight.

Micah knew this. Because he had captured every one of those moments.

As he went through the hundreds of negatives he had taken with his motor-drive Canon—which he was allowed to use in the casino arena because of his press pass as a freelance photographer on assignment for a boxing magazine—he saw nothing but pain. Not physical pain, Micah knew; he had never seen his brother wince from a punch over years of fights with other boys or his defiant rebellion against Big Frank. This pain was emotional. And every photograph depicted it.

These weren't the photos he'd be sending to the boxing magazine, which would be interested only in photos of Jammin' J looking spectacular. Nor would any of these be in the packet of photos he would send to his mother, as he had done numerous times over the past couple of years since he had traced his brother to the boxing circuit in Las Vegas and began offering himself up as a free-lancer to boxing publications.

Micah's photographic forays into his brother's world remained observations from afar; he was just another faceless cameraman in the photo pit that Tucker never saw. Each time, Micah wondered whether this would be the time he broke the silence Tucker seemed so intent on maintaining.

But the right moment never materialized.

So the right words remained unspoken.

CHAPTER 23

How Money Works

Tucker had walked home at dusk via a route he hadn't followed since he returned to White Bluff. Alongside a paved road. Right through town. Visible.

Growing up, he had strolled, hiked or scrambled every path, game trail, ridgetop and gully within ten miles of home, all for the simple joy of the journey. Since coming back, though, he had traveled them for the anonymity.

For six years he had believed he was a wanted man. Coming back to the place where all of his troubles lived, died and lived again had been a leap into darkness amid a prayer for penitence. He yearned to see familiar faces, yet dreaded what he might see in familiar eyes. So he had avoided them, choosing instead to revisit the treks of his youth while awaiting a death and stoking some courage.

Now he had spent the courage, and felt the worse for it. Releasing the weight of his secret had brought on an even greater burden, and the only benefit was that of being free once again to walk the streets of White Bluff. And not one of those streets felt like home.

He walked past houses and wondered if the same people still lived there. He walked past the road Steelbarton used to live on and didn't turn to look, not wanting to see the house. When a car drove by, he lowered his gaze to the street, just a silhouette of a man walking down a road. Nobody special. Nobody anybody knew anymore.

Even his boxing career had added to his transformation into a sort of ghost. It had ended not with the loss to Jammin J, but after a desultory half-dozen more performances, as many losses as wins, all for decent but not big-house money. After that, his job qualification became his vaguely recognizable face, his job to schmooze gamblers at the couple casinos the Rat had a financial interest in. One of the other greeters would make a point of introducing him at the tables as "You all know the Bludgeon, don't you? Cruiserweight contender, you saw him on TV or down the street, or maybe when he fought Jammin' J on pay-per-view. Tough fighter, the Bludgeon was. Big time." They talked about Tucker like he was fifty, punch-drunk and shaking with Parkinson's, just passing through on his way to the buffet. But the sunburned tourists and wannabe high rollers ate it up, and Tucker would clench a playful fist for the camera and pal around with small-town visitors to the big city who wanted to be able to say they were hanging around with that fighter, you know, whatisname, white guy, had a heck of a punch ...

And if somebody got out of line at one of the tables and didn't like being reminded of it by the staff, Tucker was also the bouncer.

He went home in the early mornings, drank until he passed out and slept until he was awakened by dry mouth and highway traffic. By his twenty-fifth birthday, the day on which he had received the letter from Micah telling him Connie was dying, Tucker was already there. He couldn't remember the last time he had cared about anything.

When Tucker reached the house after his illuminating conversation with Skelly, he was pissed Micah wasn't home. That meant he'd be alone in the house with Connie. Again. She slept most of the time anyway, but it was kind of creepy knowing she was in there, a spooky presence only occasionally heard as a knock or a whimper in the dark. And there was no telling when she might come out, or what she might look or smell like when she did.

Great. I get to spend another night babysitting for this woman who never gave a shit about me, he thought. *I'll bet there's no beer in the house, either.*

As soon as the front door shut behind him, he heard Gulliver going ballistic in the boys' bedroom and quickly let him out. He picked up the little schnauzer and pulled his head away from the thankful licks as he headed to the refrigerator, with beer as his quest.

The refrigerator door was open. As he crossed the kitchen floor, he felt and heard crunching beneath his feet. He saw the Cheerios then, all over the countertop and floor. *Great*, he thought. Since he'd been back, cereal cleanup had become routine.

He shook his head—*Crazy old bat*—and grabbed one of the two remaining beers, closed the refrigerator and sat in the kitchen, allowing Gulliver to sit on his lap and survey the top of the table, a landscape view he very rarely enjoyed.

Tucker felt tears rising up and closed his eyes to squeeze them back. He didn't want to face whatever sadness was seeping out. Sadness and knowing.

Knowing his best friend had stayed true to him and gotten no truth in return for six years. Knowing he might have prevented three deaths, and hadn't prevented even one. Knowing he had been afraid. And had run. Knowing he'd been bought, and had nothing to show for it but shame.

He wished he had even once in his life been able to take joy in those days when he had mattered to almost everyone whose path he crossed. The girls who wanted to be with him, the guys who wanted to be him, the teammates who depended on him and the coaches whose jobs depended on reining in young men of his particular wiring. None of it, though, had ever brought him any real or lasting pleasure. The anger colored everything like a photographic filter, twisting bliss into cynicism and dousing another's open sincerity with distance. Even the gushing gratification he had enjoyed with so many of White Bluff's prettiest young things had lasted no longer than it took to zip up and drive home. He could remember their faces, most of them; but he didn't associate real joy, or even mere poignance, with the memory of even one. Nor did he try to remember any one in particular, because Cami's face would seep into the mental picture.

She had even stolen into some of his dreams and each ended the same way, with her falling away into a scream he never heard. The only one he heard was his own, upon waking in a clammy sweat from Cami's first nocturnal haunting. She had had a far greater impact on him in death than she had in life.

Death. *Better check on Connie.*

He rose to go to her door and was in the process of setting Gulliver down when he slipped. Gulliver was immediately drawn to something on the floor and that's when Tucker saw the greenish-brown skid mark he'd made. He leaned over and was about to dab it with a finger to smell it when he stopped and pulled back. He could already smell it.

That's SHIT, he thought, relieved at having stopped short of touching it.

He gave Gulliver a hard look. *No, he was in the bedroom.* He set the beer on the table—it suddenly wasn't appealing—and began to look around the floor. He saw another, smaller dab. Then another. He rose to assess the extent, and found a larger pool beside Connie's bookcase, around which it appeared that most of the books had been strewn—some of them smack dab in the putrid ooze.

"Ah Jesus," he grumbled, spotting more greenish-brown splotches closer to Connie's door. He checked his hands for anything disgusting he might already have touched without knowing it.

Figures, he thought. *Everything's fine until Micah takes off. THEN she comes out and shits all over everything.*

Something like anger swelled and then dissipated.

He listened at Connie's door, then peered inside. It was dark, but he could see the lump of her shape on the bed. The smell was awful, so he carefully closed the door again.

Jesus, Connie. You're probably lying in it, he thought. *Oh well. If you can sleep in that, you might as well sleep. Nothing we can't take care of in the morning.*

He began looking for rags and disinfectant to clean up her mess, shaking his head—but not in disgust. In an empathy he wouldn't have expected.

I feel for you, old girl.

⅄

Amanda was climbing out of the shower the next morning when the phone rang.

It struck her as odd. It was barely seven, and she only had a half-hour to get ready for work. The nearest telephone was on the bedside table, and before stepping out of the shower, she pulled the towel down from the rack and wrapped it demurely around her. When she stepped out from behind the opaque shower door, she saw Micah, stretched on his stomach on the bed, grinning at her. He wasn't under the covers, he did have a cute ass in that position, and he looked like a really good reason to call in sick right now.

She considered his vantage point. "Have you been watching me shower?"

Riiiiiing. Number two.

"I wish," he said. "Couldn't see through the glass."

She glanced at the opaque shower door. "Well," she said, enjoying the dichotomy of feeling both morning-shy and morning-ready, "if you really wanted to watch, you should have joined me."

Riiiiiing.

"I didn't know if I was invited."

"You didn't ask," she said, and picked up the phone. "Hello."

"Hello." A man's voice. *"Is this Amanda Devlin?"*

"Who's calling?"

"This is Matt Bullard. You probably don't remember me."

"Refresh my memory." Wearing only a towel, looking down at Micah's nakedness, made it hard to concentrate. The deliciousness of the moment was made comic by the fact that she was on the phone talking to a stranger at seven in the morning.

"We met at the hospital after Johnny Dallman got hurt."

She turned away from Micah at the sound of J.D.'s name.

"Who are you again?"

"Matt Bullard."

"Were you a friend of his? I don't remember meeting you."

She suddenly felt as if she should have more clothes on, or even a larger towel. Micah must have sensed it, because he chose that moment to rise from bed and pass around her into the bathroom. He gave her a quick look back and pointed to the shower. She nodded, now oblivious to the cute ass.

"Not exactly. I'm employed by the wood products company he was working for at the time of his injury. I may have met him once, but I can't say for sure."

The voice was deep, heavy. And it did sound vaguely familiar.

"I was sorry to hear about his death. I know you were close."

She heard the shower come on. She was suddenly glad for the privacy it afforded.

"And just how is it you know that? Did you say we've met?"

She looked to the bathroom and saw Micah's vague, soft-focus form in the shower, and reflected momentarily on how Micah had been watching her in much the same way.

"At the hospital. I came to see you and Mister Dallman's mother after he received the card."

"The card? The—oh."

J.D. had received dozens, maybe hundreds of cards, but only one really stood out. The card had so disturbed her she had tried to bury it out of emotional recall, yet she still remembered its every word. All seven of them.

"I told you I would keep you informed if we were able to find the person responsible for Mister Dallman's injury. And that we would find him."

She was still staring absently at the shower, focused on the conversation and the memories it was stirring up, when Micah slid the shower door open just a bit in mid-shower and peeked out at her. He gave a silly look that might have been intended to be cute or sexy but at the moment was neither. She gave him a little shake of the head with an apologetic smile—Not now—and turned away before he had a chance to respond.

"Have you found him?"

"Well, that's why I'm calling, Miss Devlin. I'm wondering if perhaps you have."

"OK, you just lost me."

"We'd already been looking for this terrorist, the Falcon, for a while when your friend was hurt. Almost a year. He cost the company millions of dollars."

"Huh. That much?"

"Oh yes. The machinery he and his gang ruined does not come cheap. Plus you have millions of dollars in contracts lost, that couldn't be fulfilled because of the damage done by the Falcon."

"And you think that's the guy who caused the accident that hurt J.D.?"

"I don't think it, I know it. And that was no accident. It was intentional. They had to know, this Falcon had to know it was only a matter of time before one of those spikes did more than ruin a saw blade. And then they ruined a life. They killed a man."

"He killed himself."

"No. They killed him. He just finished the job."

"So where's the Falcon?"

"I understand you recently saw some photographs that showed something like a talon print on a round ink blot."

She sat down heavily on the bed, suddenly unable to catch her breath. That was why the photograph of that symbol on the tree had seemed so familiar. She had seen it on the card. "Like a peace sign," she said softly.

The shower turned off. She heard the shower door slide open, and she saw Micah stick his head out and look around. He caught her eye and mouthed TOWEL.

She had to turn away.

"That's the same mark the Falcon left behind at all of his acts of terrorism. It was on a piece of paper wrapped around the spike that injured your friend."

She heard Micah padding around in the bathroom, then opening the towel closet.

No.

Micah came into the room, a towel wrapped around his waist. He reached over to kiss her cheek, and without thinking she recoiled. She saw the hurt in his expression and reached a hand out in tacit apology, but still turned away.

Not possible. This was all wrong.

"How did you find out," she said softly into the phone, choosing her words carefully, "about the ... what I saw recently?"

Micah made a point of tiptoeing around her to the other side of the bed, where he dropped the towel on the edge of the bed and hastily pulled on his briefs. He glanced over with a shy and confused smile, his blithe giddiness now put on edge. She tried to give him a little smile in return, but she was too upset and her expression came out stilted and stiff. She would never forget that card. Two seemingly kind words on the front, five terrible words inside.

I'M SORRY
I DIDN'T FINISH THE JOB.

"You said something to a friend who mentioned this something to somebody else who then called me. So is it true? You have seen photographs of the Falcon's mark? Including one up in a tree?"

She looked at Micah and then away. He couldn't be the Falcon. He couldn't.

"Yes. I have."

"Can you describe what you saw?"

Micah pulled on his T-shirt and then sat on the edge of the bed to tug on his jeans. He glanced again at Amanda and she happened to glance over at the same instant.

"No. Not at the moment," she said.

"Can you tell me his name?"

She and Micah shared a grin that was awkward for each. "I'm late for work," she said, bending in self-conscious secrecy over the phone. "So ... not at the moment."

"Is he there?"

It felt like he could see her through the telephone line.

"I don't believe that's any of your business."

She noticed Micah's head perk up at the tension in her half of the conversation.

There was silence on the other end. She listened, awaiting his next move.

"Look. I understand this may be difficult and a little awkward. But I really need your help. This man who showed you the photographs, I gather he's a friend of yours."

She looked at Micah.

"Yes."

"Well, I'd like to be able to eliminate him as a suspect. He's probably not the man I'm looking for, but he may know him. Will you help me?"

"Maybe."

"I'm going to express-mail you a photograph. It should be there tomorrow by noon."

She looked over at Micah, who was watching her, looking very protective. Trying to do the supportive guy thing, she thought abstractly. To be the hero.

Or the Falcon.

"Where?" she asked, feeling awkward at having to choose her words in Micah's presence.

"At your Concrete address. On Glade Road. It hasn't changed, has it?"

It was a little disturbing that he knew the address. It wasn't listed. "No."

"I need you to look at the people in the photograph. It's a group of environmental terrorists who called themselves the Green Brigade. We believe the Falcon is in the group. We've been able to eliminate most of them as suspects, but there are a few we can't identify."

"How did you get this ... information?"

"It doesn't matter how we got it. What matters is who's in it. I need to know if the man who showed you the Falcon photograph is in the picture."

"Why? How would that—how would you know—what would that tell you?"

She was trying so hard not to give anything away, she felt sure Micah must sense something was wrong. She didn't want to look up and see him staring at her. What if his expression looked different, looked off ...

"If this man who showed you these photographs is in the picture I'm sending you, he can lead me to the man responsible for your friend's injury and eventual death."

Amanda breathed softly. Yes, that would be it. If he was in the picture. Surely.

"Or it could mean he's the man responsible."

And she caught her breath again.

"I would find that difficult to believe," she said, as evenly as she could.

"I hope you're right, Miss Devlin. Either way, I'm going to find the Falcon, whether it's your friend or not. I've already got a guy checking bookstores and publishing houses for a landscape photography book by somebody named, lessee ... Micah Wood. Or a name similar to that. If we find the publisher, we'll find your friend. I'd just like to do it easier, not harder."

She looked at Micah, who was ruffling his wet hair and watching her intently with just the hint of a hopeful smile. No. Micah could not be the man they're looking for.

"So, the photograph. Can I count on your help?" When she wasn't quick with an answer, he added: *"Miss Devlin, the Falcon will not get away with what he did. I have pledged my word on that."*

Amanda remembered then. A thick-set man at the hospital. A hard man, with a hard edge. She couldn't remember much about what he looked like, but there was something ... what was it ... something about his face.

"So I'll talk to you tomorrow? At this same number?"

Oh yeah. The fu Manchu.

"That's up to you, isn't it," Amanda said, and hung up.

⅄

Micah was so overflowing with the rampant energy of a young man in love he simply couldn't go back home right now, filled with its painful past, a dying mother and a bitter brother. He didn't even want to think about them right now, so he decided to go shopping. Since the bigger stores were all closer to I-5, he drove along behind Amanda as far as Sedro Woolley, even waving at her once or twice in giddy abandon, then continued south to the mall at Mount Vernon. He bounced his head in time to whatever song he could find over the static on the radio, singing along with Smokey Robinson to the classic "I Second That Emotion," caring not a bit whether anybody could hear his hysterical warbling.

He stopped at a greeting cards store and bought a bunch of silly cards designed for the smitten. At a specialty clothing shop, he bought a couple of T-shirts for himself and very nearly bought one for her that said I'M WITH STUPID, but thought that might be just a bit presumptuous. Then he stopped at a music store and, while looking for a CD he might give her, he spotted a Darrington Bluegrass Festival T-shirt and immediately took it up to the cashier, laughing at what Amanda's reaction might be.

It was nearly ten-thirty by the time he decided he was hungry, so he had a late breakfast at Denny's. He couldn't remember food ever tasting so good. Or smiling while eating.

After eating he headed home, stopping at a grocery to stock up for the long haul. He thought about Tucker probably being all bent out of shape about his having gone out for the night without leaving a note about where he'd be, and then laughed out loud at the concept. Who would read the note? Tucker? His mom? He laughed again. And he realized he didn't much care what Tucker thought.

He drove back to White Bluff by way of Concrete, turning to look at the high school—force of habit—and also at the turn he knew led eventually to Amanda's house. He got warm again just thinking about last night, and hoped she was feeling the same way.

Kind of funny, though. Their parting kiss. She'd seemed preoccupied. He figured it was just because she was running late for work. That was probably it. But ...

He wanted to go to the duplex first to change his clothes, but some of the frozen groceries would be getting pretty soft by then, so he drove directly to his mother's house.

Tucker was sitting at the table eating cereal. He didn't look up as Micah walked in, laden with bags.

"Mornin'," Micah said. "Got some groceries."

Tucker nodded.

"There's more bags in the car," Micah offered hopefully.

Tucker took another bite of cereal.

Micah balanced the first load of bags on the countertops. "Well, I guess I'll just go out and get them then," he said, just the tiniest bit snarky but feeling too damn good to be bothered by his brother's lethargy. He bounded out, got another double armload of groceries—leaving the bag with the gift T-shirt in the car—and hauled them inside.

"What time you get in last night?" Micah asked, only mildly curious to see how much time of his mother being alone he should feel quietly guilty about.

Tucker paused in mid-mouthful, then resumed chewing until he swallowed. "That's an interesting question. Coming from you."

Micah grinned sheepishly, his euphoria creeping in. "Sorry about that. I, uh ... I went out."

Tucker looked at him dully. *No shit.*

"They made me an offer I couldn't refuse," Micah said, trying to be clever.

Tucker didn't find any humor. "They?"

Micah wondered if he'd ever seen the movie. "OK. Her."

"The girl from the bluegrass deal."

"Yeah."

"Well, bully for you, Master Dodd. Glad you got your jewels polished. I'm happy for you. Only next time you pull that, make sure you take the old girl on a bathroom run before you go."

Micah frowned. "What happened?"

"Smell like Pine Sol in here?"

Micah sniffed a couple of times. "Yeah, I guess."

"Then you know what happened."

Oh. "In here?"

"Oh yeah."

"Ah. Shit."

"Oh yeah."

"When? Were you awake?"

"Awake. I wasn't even here."

"So when did you get in?"

"It wasn't even dark when I got here, man. And it was all over the place."

Micah gave the area a quick scan. "Well, thanks for cleaning it up, I guess."

"Next time I'm leaving it for you."

"Well, is she OK? She didn't fall down or anything?"

"How would I know?" Tucker's irritation was obviously rising. "She was sleeping in her bed when I got in. Shit all over the house, and sleeping like a baby."

Tucker was still sitting at the kitchen table. He pushed the cereal away. "Thanks for ruining my appetite. Again."

Micah walked to the top of the hall and listened outside his mother's door. He listened so long Tucker turned to see what he was doing, and Micah shook his head.

"I can't hear her," Micah said softly.

"Good."

Micah shook his head at his brother's response. He twisted the doorknob slowly. The smell in the room hit him almost immediately. Shit. And something else. He stuck his head inside to listen closer and still couldn't hear anything. Soft ambient light from the kitchen brightened the room enough to see and he crept into the room, not wanting to wake her and create a problem where there wasn't one. But with every step, the only sound he heard was his own hushed breathing and the creaking of the floorboards.

He stopped beside the bed. Now he heard no sound, not even himself. And certainly not his mother. She was absolutely silent. And absolutely still.

He knew even before he turned on the bedroom light.

She was gone.

CHAPTER 24

SCRAPBOOK SCARS

Tucker didn't want to have much to do with the business of the dead, so he let Micah deal with it. She was Micah's mom, after all, and he was just an outsider visiting to pay his respects. Or so he told himself.

Connie had always been the one person to whom he couldn't respond with an unfettered emotion: hatred, anger, resentment, disdain, distrust and even, only very occasionally, conditional acceptance. His feelings about her had always been muddled, so having to think about her or respond to her had always made him edgy, like a shirt that chafed at the collar.

Now that Connie was dead, that chafing was cutting to the bone. So he stayed on the porch while Micah dealt with the nuts and bolts of a death in the family. Micah called it in to the sheriff's department, who dispatched a deputy to ascertain that, yes, there was a dead woman at that address. Then came the coroner, whose ruling on the cause of death was necessary because nobody had actually witnessed it. Then came an irritatingly upbeat young man from a funeral home in Darrington, and Tucker could hear them from his vantage point on the back porch as they discussed the pros and cons of open-versus-closed-casket services. He was pleasantly surprised when he heard Micah ask, "So how much if we just have her cremated?"

The Sidrow family—the aunts and their mangy mom, a broomstick scarecrow with gray hair and grotesque Jackson Pollock makeup—arrived as the funeral-home crew was loading Connie into something that looked to Tucker like an ambulance. Why Micah had even called them Tucker couldn't comprehend; neither brother could stand those biddies, and he was fairly certain Connie hadn't thought much of her sisters either. They fussed around the boys like buzzards too late for the carrion feast, and Tucker was ready to bolt when Micah said he was on his way to the funeral home to continue taking care of the paperwork and arrangements. Micah being the nice nephew—the only *real* nephew, Tucker imagined them carping—that sent them quickly on their way. Tucker was simply glad to see them leave.

And it was getting to be time for Tucker to leave as well.

He knew that. He had come to fill a few holes in his heart—to see Connie before she died, to determine if there was distance worth closing with his brother, and to come to terms with the ghosts of his past. And all he had done was excavate even deeper wounds.

Not that leaving held any great appeal, either. The only place with any hold on him was his house on the edge of Vegas, basically no more than a double-wide with a yard of dead grass, rocks and weeds that probably wasn't worth what he owed on it. His job? Gladhanding drunks at a casino when they're losing, helping them find the door when they get pissed off about the losing. One of his buddies, another ex-fighter, had told him once during a mutual bitch session, "Yeah, but don't forget, bro, these losers? They're never gonna stop losing. Throw them out on their asses tonight, they'll be back next week. Or next month. Or tomorrow. That's job security, baby. Job security. And face it, my man, where else are you gonna have this much fine pussy around to choose from?"

None of which meant a thing to Tucker.

Vegas felt foreign and cold. So did this house—and now it also had the faint but unmistakable stench of death.

The smell made him think of Connie's last night of life. Sick. Weak. Dribbles of her own shit dropping behind her as she shuffled around the room. Not sure who she was, or who her son was. Sons. Or whatever he was.

Tucker reached up to scratch an itchy eye and found the eyelid wet with tears.

He looked around the kitchen, which he had cleaned up the night before. And the odd thought poked in: *Anybody clean her bedroom?*

Who gives a shit, he thought. *She's gone.*

But he couldn't push the thought away. He couldn't have explained why it was suddenly important to him to see to it that her legacy wasn't a room of shit smears across the floor. Maybe he owed it to her. Maybe he even owed it to Micah.

Maybe he simply owed it to himself not to leave until this deal was done.

So he opened her door—presuming it had been shut to keep in as much of the stench as possible—and turned on the light.

It wasn't as putrid as he feared. Not quite.

He went immediately to the window and opened both the blinds and the window itself, to air out the stagnant stench. The floor seemed not to have any telltale splotches—perhaps Micah had cleaned it earlier—but the tarnished sheets were still on the bed, so he began pulling them off. He'd put them in the washer and be done with it.

As he tugged the sheets from the side against the wall, something came part of the way up with them. A book that had slipped down into the crack between the bed and the wall.

No, he thought with just a hint of contempt. *Just that Mighty Micah scrapbook.*

But when he pulled it out from its temporary nest, he realized it wasn't the same one. It had the same type of car-upholstery cover, but it was a slightly different color.

He opened it with just a bit of dread.

And saw himself.

The four photographs on the first page were all of him in a football uniform. He remembered the uniform; it had been his first team back in sixth grade. Looking at that clean uniform, with not a grass stain on it, he began to smile at the memory.

And then the smile went away and was replaced by confusion and, finally, deep shame.

Shame for his anger and resentment upon finding the other scrapbook, the one full of Micah. Shame for years of thoughts and emotions just like that.

He turned to the next page.

More pictures of him. Newspaper clippings, with his name color-high-lighted in every one in fading yellow or orange. Football. Wrestling.

The next page was more of the same.

And the next.

As he turned the pages, his face flushing with remorse, he saw the first boxing photograph. Tucker had never seen the picture and tried to place when and where it had been taken, and he was stunned when the location came to him. It was the armory down in Tacoma. *Shit, I wasn't even in the pros then.*

Micah was keeping tabs on me? Even back then? How'd he even find me?

He turned the page and there were more boxing photographs, plus a couple of newspaper clippings from the early part of his pro career.

He flipped the page again and came to a complete halt.

He was looking at a single sheet of notebook paper. The top and the bottom—just above and below the message on the page—had been cut off to fit the scrapbook.

Dear Mom, it read in a hand-printed but unsteady scrawl.

> **I'm sorry I didn't write before. It's hard for me. I just want you to know I'm OK.**
>
> **I'm a pro boxer. Please don't worry about me, I'm being carefull and doing well. I don't know when I will be able to write more. I'm pretty busy. But I will try to send pictures and maybe a postcard when I can.**
> **Love,**
> **Your son, Tucker**

Tucker read it once. Then he read through it again. It wasn't hard, because it was written in words he could read if he really focused. No really long ones, nothing in odd tenses.

It was exactly how he would have written it, had he actually written the letter.

Until now, he'd never seen it.

As he came to the realization of who had written the letter and why, his shame began to make room for another emotion. Something like brotherly love. And something like pride.

⋏

Amanda dialed the number she had written down several nights earlier. Karen Frances answered on the third ring.

"Kare, it's Amanda."

"Mandible? Hey, two times in a week, what a great surprise! How are you doing?"

Karen's peppy response was a little surprising. Amanda had been considering conspiracy theories since the early phone call that morning from the fu Manchu guy, whatsisname. Bullard.

"Well, I'm not sure but I think maybe I'm mad at you."

"What? Why?"

"I got a really weird phone call this morning."

"Oh." Karen's one-word response spoke volumes.

"I thought that was just you I was talking to, Kare Bear. What'd you do, put out a news release?"

"I'm sorry, Manda. I don't even know how it happened. I was talking to a friend of mine, she's into photography, and I told her about this Micah Wood guy to see if she'd heard of him, and she asked what kind of pictures he took and I told her."

"Who is she, your friend?"

"Just somebody I know. She works for one of the timber outfits."

"You told her, and I get a call from this Bullard guy? Just like that?"

"Well, he called me, too."

"Why? What did you tell him?"

"Nothing. Just ... you know, he asked about the pictures you told me about. He was real interested in that one, you know ... the thing on the tree."

"The one that looked like a peace sign."

"Yeah. Only he said it was a bird print."

"So he called you."

"Uh huh."

"Do you know him?"

"No, not exactly. But my friend knows him."

"So even though you don't know him, you just told him whatever he wanted to know?"

"Well, I didn't realize I was supposed to be keeping a secret."

"It's not a secret, it's just …" Amanda had no idea what it was *just.*

"Besides, he wasn't asking about you. He was asking about this guy. Your friend. And the pictures."

"What do you know about him, Karen? This Bullard guy."

"I don't know anything about him. I've never even seen him."

They got quiet then.

"Manda? Your friend? Is he the guy they're looking for? This bird guy?"

"No," Amanda said. "He's not."

"Good. Oh, I'm really glad."

"Why?"

"I talked to my friend after this Bullard guy called, and she said he was pretty serious business. And that he's seriously got it in for this bird guy. She thinks he'd throw him off a cliff if he could get his hands on him."

A

By the time Micah returned to the house, he felt the life had been wrung out of him.

Only five or six hours before, he'd been singing along with Smoky Robinson in the car. Now he felt emotionally and physically beaten. The woman who had been his emotional center his entire life had died and was well on her way to becoming ashes in an urn. And he was the only person who truly seemed to care.

When he walked in, he felt a little déjà vu: There was Tucker at the kitchen table, this time nursing a beer, once again having done nothing to help. Gulliver, at least, raced across the floor for a wriggly hello.

Micah decided in an instant he had made a mistake in coming home at all. He should have just gone to the duplex. Why put up with Tucker's crap?

But then Tucker spoke, surprising him. "Hey. How you doin'." Spoken not like a question but, surprisingly, like an offer of empathy. It threw Micah just a bit.

"Oh, I'm having a great day," he snapped. "Couldn't be better."

"I know it's tough, man," Tucker said. "But you knew this was coming."

Micah turned around to glare at him. "Is that supposed to make it all better? My mother just died. That may not mean shit to you, but it means something to me. So yeah, I'm gonna feel bad about it for just as long as I want. That all right with you?"

Micah said it with more forceful venom than he could ever remember addressing his brother, and he girded himself for Tucker to take umbrage.

But Tucker did not. "So how much is all that gonna cost? The funeral-home and all."

Micah frowned. "Why you want to know?"

He kept waiting for Tucker to get mad, but it just wasn't happening.

"Why do you think, dumbass?" Tucker said with no rancor. "So I can help with it. I got some money in the bank."

"Why would you want to help? That's not like you."

"Thanks a lot."

"Hey, if the shoe fits."

"Why don't you calm down and cut me some slack here, little brother. I'm on your side."

Instead of placating him, Tucker's seemingly newfound humanity only struck Micah as condescending. "Who said I wanted you on my side?"

Tucker rose, actually looking a bit hurt by that.

"Well, you little shit," Tucker said, setting his empty beer can on the table. "You don't want me on your side? Fine, I quit."

"Yeah," Micah said. "That is what you do."

Tucker glared at him, but the expression seemed more bruised than angry. And he walked out the back door, leaving a disappointed Gulliver, ears drooping, pressing his nose on the inside of the screen door the second after it slammed.

CHAPTER 25

MISSING PERSONS

Micah hadn't seen Tucker since he had stormed out the back door the previous evening, and when he heard a knock on the front door—triggering Gulliver's all-too-ferocious yapping—he thought it might be Tucker reaffirming his status as an outsider by not just walking in.

But it wasn't Tucker. It was a man in a uniform with a badge.

"Good morning, sir. I'm Deputy Rowan with the county sheriff. I'm looking for Tucker Dodd."

For Micah, that came out of nowhere. His instinct was to say he'd never heard of Tucker Dodd, but then Micah had rarely gone with his instinct.

"Uh ... well ... he's definitely not here."

The deputy seemed to consider the oddness of that response.

"When was the last time you saw him?"

"Mmm." Micah frowned like a kid in a spelling bee confronted with a word he'd never heard. "I'm not sure. Been a while. Why you looking for Tucker?"

"Who are you?"

"I'm Micah Dodd. His brother."

"We believe he may have some information on a missing persons case."

Micah frowned again, this time for real. "Who? Who's missing? Tucker's been gone for six years, so I don't know how he could be any help to you."

"This case is six years old. We got a tip from somebody who said your brother may know something about it. "

Micah knew at once who Rowan was talking about. Two people disappeared six years ago. Tucker was one. And now the cops wanted to talk to him about the other one.

Cami.

He felt rumbles of that same old gnawing suspicion,

The deputy leaned in. "Are you saying you haven't seen him in six years?"

"What—no. I mean, yes. I've seen him … recently. He came back to see my mom before … well. She was dying. And now she's dead."

Deputy Rowan seemed to soften. "I'm sorry for your loss. I do need to talk to your brother, though. Do you know where I can find him?"

Micah shook his head. "No idea."

"When do you expect him back?"

Micah shrugged. "I'm not even sure I expect him at all."

Rowan sized him up, then reached into a pocket and pulled out a card. "If he does come back, have him call me. And if he doesn't call, then you should. We just need to talk to him. He's not a suspect."

Sure he is. Or you wouldn't be here.

After Rowan left, Micah considered his choices.

He could wait until Tucker got back to tell him about the sheriff's department looking for him, but he might have to wait a long time. He decided instead to go see Amanda first, to tell her about his mother's death. He could have told her last night, but that wasn't a conversation he wanted to have over the phone.

He wanted her arms around him for that.

ᴧ

The package had been nestled in the space between the screen and front doors when Amanda arrived. She typically didn't come home for lunch—the nearly half-hour drive each way pretty much negating any opportunity for a "lunch hour"—but today she couldn't wait until after work. She was just too antsy. She had to know.

But with the contents of the envelope spread on the coffee table before her, the only thing she knew was that she wished she had simply thrown it away unopened.

What she had seen did nothing for her or for Micah. All it did was render her uncomfortably numb. It was proof of nothing. But she knew whatever Micah had or had not done, he was in trouble. He was about to become a target.

Was it possible? Could the man she was falling in love with be the man who indirectly brought death to the last man she had loved?

Misgivings and doubt scrabbled at her edges, trying to forge a foothold. But even though she didn't know what else was true, she knew his feelings for her were.

As were hers for him.

She picked up the telephone and called in sick for the rest of the day.

She stacked the papers and began to put them back into the envelope, then, on second thought, just set them on the table.

She didn't need them. She just needed to ask him herself.

⅄

Tucker was squeezing the last of his stuff into his duffle bag, intending to head out, when he heard a car door outside and Gulliver start his caterwauling. Micah must have left the little guy out in the yard, he thought as he walked to the door, grousing over the possibilities. *What now?*

At the fence gate was a very attractive blonde wearing what looked like a uniform shirt over a pair of jeans. As she got closer he recognized the Forest Service insignia on the shirt, something he'd seen on numerous trail crews on his trips into the boonies.

But who the hell was this?

"Hey, Gulliver," she was saying, leaning down to let the schnauzer sniff her. "How's it going, buddy? Yeah, there you go ..."

She looked up as he came out, and her expectant expression disappeared. "Oh. Hi," she said.

"Hello."

"You must be the famous Tucker."

"I must be."

When he added nothing else, she said, "And I must be the famous Amanda."

"OK." The name meant nothing to him, because Micah hadn't said her name or anything about her—and clearly there was much to say.

"Oh. Not so famous, apparently," she said. "Micah hasn't mentioned me?"

"We don't talk much."

"Oh." She seemed to consider that. "Is he here?"

"Nope."

She seemed to be puzzling over something. "You look familiar," she said.

Although he'd heard that as a line a hundred times, he knew this wasn't one. He studied her. She looked familiar, too. But he couldn't place her.

Gulliver was pacing anxiously around the gate.

"You can wait for Micah if you want. I think that'd make Gulliver's day."

She shrugged and nodded, opening the gate and giving Gulliver the excited-doggy-dance defense as they went into the house. Tucker held the door open for her, and as she passed, she studied his face again.

"I know I've seen you," she said. "You went to school at White Bluff, right?"

He nodded.

Amanda sat on the sofa. In seconds, Gulliver has his head in her lap. "When did you graduate?"

That was a painful subject for Tucker, who hadn't graduated and, after six years on the run, was a bit unnerved at being recognized. "Senior year was '82-83."

"Me too. N.C. High."

"Huh." He could read people, and even though she was hiding it well, he could tell she was in emotional turmoil of her own.

"Must have seen each other around somewhere." She sniffed. "Something smells funny."

Tucker didn't want to go into what she must be smelling.

"So you and Micah aren't close, then," she said. "If he had a secret, you probably wouldn't know it."

That's interesting. "Wouldn't be much of a secret if I did." He sat on the recliner.

"Do you know about the Falcon?"

"I know there's more than one," he cracked.

That seemed to confuse her, but she was undeterred. "Tucker, I think your brother is in trouble. Really bad trouble. I think he may have hurt somebody … really bad."

Tucker stiffened. "What, like an accident?"

She shook her head.

"Well, what then."

"Not an accident."

"On purpose?"

She said nothing. To her surprise, her solemn seriousness made him smile. "Micah?" He actually chuckled.

"There's nothing funny about this," Amanda growled.

His smile dimmed. "Hurt somebody? Micah? Shit, he wouldn't hurt a yapper dog." He glanced at Gulliver, who wagged his rump. "He's like the most pacifist guy you ever met. Trust me. I know this for a fact."

"I believe you. I do. But I also believe there are people who are going to be coming here to get him soon. They could already be on their way."

"What do you mean, exactly. Get him."

"I wish I knew."

"OK. Who are these people?"

"People who would like to see him put away in prison for some things he did."

"Micah? That kid never did anything to anybody. These people got him mixed up with somebody else. So: What did he supposedly do?"

"They think he was this, this Falcon."

"Micah's a bird? These people are retarded, right?"

His flippancy made her smile. "The Falcon was, I guess you'd call him like an environmental fanatic," she said. "Destroying logging trucks, things like that."

"Micah? No way. Why would he give a shit about logging?"

"I don't know. But these people down in California or Oregon think Micah's the Falcon, or maybe he knows who is. They're pretty sure he was in with these environmental people."

"And that he hurt somebody."

"The Falcon did."

"Bad?"

She gently set Gulliver aside and rose, getting emotional. "Somebody I knew."

"Knew?"

She looked unsure about telling him. "He committed suicide. He was an artist. And he was blinded by ... in a logging accident. Incident."

"The Falcon. Jesus."

"Yeah."

"Well, Micah didn't do it, I can tell you that much. And if anybody's coming for him, fuck 'em. They can deal with me."

She cocked her head then, studying him until she seemed to realize something. She lifted a finger and wagged it. "Your hair used to be longer."

That threw him. "What?" He still couldn't place her. "OK, you got me. When was this?"

"High school. I was in the back seat of a Mustang convertible. You were in the back of a ... a Trans Am."

Ah hah. He remembered her now. Steelbarton at the four-way stop. The blonde with an attitude.

"You," he said. "You were crazy."

"You were an asshole. But you were also pretty great."

"OK, so you're still crazy."

She smiled. "Maybe I am," she said. "I think I'm in love with your brother."

Tucker's eyes opened wide. "Wow. No shit?"

The smile again. "No shit."

"This is *my* brother we're talking about?" *How about that, my little brother has found himself a real woman.* He felt an odd rush of emotion, that brotherly love and pride thing again. "Well, that's it, then. You're certifiable."

The softness lasted for only a few moments before Amanda's expression darkened.

"I think it's my fault. That people are looking for your brother," she said, and gave him a short rundown on the photograph and the people so interested in Micah.

"Because he had a picture of this falcon thing," Tucker said. "This mark." She nodded.

"What did it look like, exactly?"

"Like a upside-down peace sign, kind of. Like two—no, three claws coming up one side and one going down the other. You know. Like a falcon claw. Er, talon. Falcon talon."

Tucker leaned back in the recliner and wriggled something out of his blue jeans. He held it out in his flat palm—a flat, round rock, nothing more. Until Tucker flipped it over, revealing the other side.

"Something like this," he said.

It was obvious she recognized it. Her jaw went slack.

"Well," Tucker said, "I don't know anything about him having pictures of it, but this happens to be mine. It was never his."

Amanda was stunned into silence.

Tucker shook his head slowly and pocketed the stone again.

"And if anybody's coming after somebody, like I said before, fuck'em. They can deal with me."

Micah was half-hoping he'd be able to see Amanda the moment he entered the ranger station in Sedro Woolley, but there was only a receptionist at a forbidding front desk who said she wasn't in the office. She asked who he was, obviously recognized the name, and told him Amanda had gone home for lunch and then called in sick.

He thanked her, left and drove immediately to Concrete.

At her house, he was dismayed at not seeing her car out front but knocked on the door anyway.

After a second knock went unanswered, he tried the door. It was unlocked, so he opened it, calling out softly, "Amanda? Are you home?"

He went into the living room and waited for an answer.

"Amanda?"

Thistle trotted out from the bedroom and hesitated. Thinking Amanda might simply be at the grocery or the drug store getting something to deal with whatever flu she must have come down with, Micah paused, wondering whether he should wait. He saw the stack of papers next to a manila envelope on the table and leaned over to read what was written on the envelope in heavy black ink.

AMANDA DEVLIN
PERSONAL

That made him peer closer at the handwritten sheet next to it.

It was on business stationary. He looked at the letterhead and nearly gagged.

PacRim Wood Products.

It was a name he had seen dozens of times—on protest placards and on no-trespassing signs, on fences he had climbed and in newspaper stories.

His past was staring at him in black and white.

MISS DEVLIN, the letter began in penned script. *Here's the photograph we discussed. Please see if you can identify the individual we're trying to locate. I've included a couple of things I hope will remind you why we are so intent on locating this individual. I'll call you this evening at your home. I look forward to whatever information you may have.*
—Matt Bullard

With his sense of foreboding growing by the second, Micah set the letter aside, revealing the photograph beneath it. One glance gripped him with sudden fear. It was a group shot he had never seen, though he recognized where it had been taken and had a good idea about when. Nearly everyone in it was a Green Brigade activist—including Micah, standing near the back.

Seeing the photograph made him feel ill.

He looked back at the second sheet.

Matt Bullard. Something about that name ...

On the next sheet was a photocopy of what appeared to be the cover of a greeting card, with a picture of a pretty scene and a handwritten message below. It said simply: I'M SORRY.

He went to the next sheet, apparently a copy of the inside of the card. It contained these printed words: I DIDN'T FINISH THE JOB.

They didn't mean a thing to him.

But underneath them was something that did.

It wasn't in color, but he knew the original would have been green. And round.

With four lines coming out from a central point. Three going up. One going down. The way the talon of a prehistoric falcon might look, had there been such a thing.

He looked again at the words on the card, taking the message in full.

I'M SORRY I DIDN'T FINISH THE JOB.

A message stamped with the Falcon seal. But not one he had ever sent.

Somebody had sent this to Amanda. For help in identifying the Falcon.

With a photograph that included Micah.

His insides twisting like a wet towel, he let the contents of the envelope slip from his grasp, and they splayed across the floor. He stared at them blankly, his world too askew to see. When he finally took notice, he saw the last sheet, left partially uncovered. It looked like a column of newspaper type.

He reached down and picked it up. He had to concentrate to focus on the words.

It was an obituary column. The name on the top was John Dallman.

Oh God. He was dead.

Micah knew the name only too well.

It had never crossed Micah's mind that the spikes would ever do anything more than ruin a saw, and the whole campaign felt righteous somehow, even gallant. It had thoroughly enthralled him and made him feel more alive than he ever had, right up until he read the account in the Eureka newspaper of John Dallman, a logger blinded by a tree spike in an old-growth stand. "Someone close to the investigation" was quoted as saying an ecoterrorist known as the Falcon had claimed responsibility for the tree-spiking.

The story so distressed him, he immediately stopped taking part in the night raids and stopped associating with his erstwhile Green Brigade buddies. He continued his forest photography, though always by himself, confining himself to—and within—the world of nature.

Micah stared at the obituary photograph. The face looked familiar, though that was probably from having seen the same picture in the newspaper after the accident.

For Micah, that's what it had been. An accident. For John Dallman, he knew only too well, it had been anything but. Micah hadn't known he had died, and he began to read the obituary with a morbid fervor.

John Dallman had died unexpectedly, the first paragraph, and it gave the date of the death as July 4, 1989.

Fourth of July? Micah thought. *That's less than a month ago.*

He continued reading. The obituary wasn't long. It said there was to be a memorial service at a church in Medford. The next to last paragraph listed survivors. The last paragraph said he was preceded in death by a brother, Dean Slocumb.

He felt a sudden urge to vomit.

Dean Slocumb.

Deano.

He looked at the papers on the floor. Both sheets with the copies of the card were visible. I'M SORRY I DIDN'T FINISH THE JOB.

The obituary. The face. The man in the painting.

Amanda's friend.

John Dallman. J.D. Amanda's friend J.D. Who committed suicide.

Deano's brother.

Dead.

Suicide.

Because of the Falcon.

I'M SORRY I DIDN'T FINISH THE JOB.

Micah ran to the bathroom and threw up into the toilet.

CHAPTER 26

I'M SORRY I DIDN'T FINISH THE JOB

They were both standing at the edge of the kitchen, where the conversation had taken them. Amanda glanced at her watch, wondering where Micah was, and that reminded her of his ailing mother. She gestured at the closed door at the end of the hall and said, softly, "We're probably being loud. Your mother."

Tucker stared at her, clearly not understanding. Then: "Oh. No. She … uh, she's gone. She … died."

"Oh. God."

He cocked his head. "Well, she hoped so."

"I'm so sorry."

He seemed to cloud up then, and Amanda was sure he was about to cry. And that it was not something he did easily.

Without a moment's hesitation, with the simple empathy of a woman's heart, she reached out both arms for a hug. In the moment he accepted it, she felt him choke off what would have been a sob. In the embrace, she felt his strength, and felt it shaken. She barely heard Gulliver bark briefly at something and race to the door.

But she heard the front door opening to Gulliver's wiggly excitement, and her heart raced and sank in the same moment. She whirled and saw Micah's emotions roiling in his eyes.

The look in those eyes was very different and yet very much the same as a look she had just seen: a man on the verge of tears.

Micah tore his eyes from hers and turned the glare upon his brother. "You don't waste much time," he said with a virulence that shocked Amanda. "Some things sure don't change."

His eyes returned to Amanda, filled with a hurt she knew could be allayed with a simple explanation. But he didn't give her time. Before she could say a thing, Micah marched out the back door.

"Micah!" she called out after him and took a step to follow.

Tucker touched her arm in a soft restraint and shook his head. "Give him time. He just needs to clear his head."

"But he doesn't understand—"

"He will."

"He needs to know—"

"I'll tell him."

"About everything."

"Yeah. And he's gonna tell me everything, too. Then I'll know what to do."

Amanda studied Tucker's face and believed him. "I'm really worried about him."

"Don't be."

Something in his strength made her feel better. Somehow, she was sure, it made Micah safer. "Micah's lucky to have you as his brother."

Tucker's expression gave something away, but she couldn't place it.

"I'm not so sure about that," he said quietly.

"I am," she said. "If he comes back—"

"He'll be back. He's just clearing his head."

"You said that before."

"Yeah. He thinks way too damn much. I think his head gets so full of facts he can't see what's in front of him. Or who."

"You got him all figured out, do you?"

He shook his head. "Kid's been a mystery to me his whole life."

"OK. When he comes back, and you guys talk or whatever, have him call me. I don't care how late it is. I'll be up. Or … just tell him I'll leave the door unlocked."

He nodded. "He'll be there."

"You sound so sure."

"Kid may be an idiot sometimes," he said. "But he's not stupid."

Amanda smiled and almost gave him another hug, this time one of gratitude, but held back. She gave him an awkward little wave as she backed away. "Nice to meet you," she said, not sure what to say.

"Likewise," he said. "Never thought I'd see the day I wished I was my brother."

⋏

Tucker was standing with Gulliver on the back porch when Micah traipsed up the river trail and turned into the yard. The reversal of roles struck Tucker.

For so many years of their mutual discontent, the trails had been Tucker's escape when life crowded in on him. Micah simply withdrew from his own life to the porch and his books, his fantasy world of other lives. Now Tucker was the one on the porch with nowhere to go, while Micah was the one whose life was exploding all around him.

The two stared at one another until Tucker broke the silence.

"You got some explaining to do, little brother."

"*I* have explaining?" Micah's voice got higher, the curse of his emotion. "Screw you. How about you start."

"Fine. I will. Two things. You better go find Amanda, that's number one."

"Looks like you already found her."

"Oh grow up," Tucker said. "She doesn't care about me any more than whether or not I can help you."

"Oh, you help me? That's a good one. The same guy who's spent his whole life ruining mine." Micah wasn't backing down an inch.

"Ruining your life?" Tucker stepped off the porch. "Don't you have that backwards, junior?"

"Go to hell. You stole my childhood. You stole my father. You—"

Tucker stammered. "Your childhood … what?"

"—you stole Cami, when you knew I liked her."

"Hey, I didn't want her."

"But you stole her anyway. I hope you're proud."

"Hey, Einstein, how is it stealing if you never had her in the first place?"

"Go to hell."

"You said that already. Smart guy like you should be able to come up with something new."

"OK," Micah said, his voice rising again. "How about *THIS?*"

And he cocked and threw a punch.

Even in his instant of reaction, Tucker was amazed. He was pretty sure Micah had never thrown a punch in his life, while Tucker had spent a lifetime dodging them and then retaliating. This one came as such a surprise, though—*Micah? Throwing a punch?*—and Tucker's reaction was awkward. Although he turned enough at the last moment to escape the brunt of the blow, it knocked him off-balance and he tripped over his own feet. He nearly went down, but stumbled backwards into the wall and caught himself. His instinctive response, that of the experienced fighter, was immediately overridden by something else. Big brother's need to protect little brother, even from himself—just a little bit of that. And a hint of grudging respect.

Well whadya know, he thought, and the little frown that furrowed his brow belied the smile lurking beneath. *Who'da thought the kid had it in him.* The glancing punch had mashed his upper lip into his teeth, and he dabbed it with a couple of fingers to see if any blood had been drawn.

Micah set his feet to ward off a counterattack, and Tucker—who hadn't even considered launching one—suppressed a smile at how silly and short such a battle would be.

"You gotta work on that a little bit," Tucker said, doing a slow-motion demonstration of a right-cross followthrough. "Thrust your weight forward, onto your lead foot. Give you more power."

"Go to hell."

Tucker cocked his head, shook it. "You wanna blame me for Cami, fine. Maybe I got it comin'. You wanna blame me for Big Frank, fine. I went out in the big storm, whoopty fucking do, I screwed up. But Big Frank, he screwed up even worse. The difference is I took care of myself."

"Yeah. You're real good at that. And Dad, he got killed because he was more interested in taking care of you than himself."

"He wanted to take care of me, all right. You got that part right."

"He came after you because he loved you."

"Loved me. That's rich. That's a good one, Einstein. Yeah, I'm sure love was the reason every time he came at me with a punch or a belt, since I was eight years old."

"Good lord, Tucker, how stupid are you? Yeah. That's right. Every time. It was all because he loved you."

"Yeah? Well, he never fuckin' punched you, did he? How you explain that?"

"Because he didn't love me. Not like he loved you."

"You're a whack job. You were his little glory boy," Tucker retorted, though with diminishing certainty. "Yessir, nossir, oh yeah my homework's done, always got the good grades, meanwhile I'm the dumbshit who can't read while the little scholarship boy here, he —"

"My grades meant nothing to him. You were the sports star, not me. Everything you did mattered. You were the first son, you were the oldest, and you were the one who pushed him away. You refused to surrender, and that just made him have to go to war with you that much harder, fight you that much harder. Because he just had to win you over." Micah shook his head. "And you didn't give a shit about him."

"He ruined my fucking life."

"Join the club."

"Oh right, Big Frank ruined your life, uh huh. That must be why he moved from our house to your house, leaving my mom and me —"

"And regretting it every day."

"— for your mom and you."

311

"He made my mother miserable," Micah said. "I spent all those years trying to make him care about me, and now sometimes I wish he'd never met her."

"Then you'da never been born, Einstein."

"Or maybe I'd have just had a father who actually wanted me, instead of one of who pretty much only wanted you. And died trying to save your sorry ass."

They glared at each other, but Tucker's conviction was wavering. He had worn his own long list of grievances as blinders, giving short shrift to the ways their abruptly mutual family had impacted Micah. That the kid could have felt unloved or even underappreciated by Big Frank would have been unfathomable to Tucker. But now, under the stark illumination of time and perspective, it made a weird kind of sense.

"And you probably saw it happen," Micah said in what sounded like a challenge.

Tucker, lost in his enlightenment, missed the connection. "Saw what happen."

"Dad dying."

Well, what do you know.

"How you figure that," Tucker offered.

"He had three bullets in the rifle."

"So?"

"So I found two near where they found him. Somebody put them there. Not him."

"That right?"

"Uh huh."

"Oh, I see. You're a detective now. And how is it you know he had three rounds?"

"Mom told me. She watched him load the Winchester. We talked about everything that happened that night so many times over the next couple of months, everything we remembered about the last time we saw him, as you can imagine. Or maybe you can't."

"Fuck you."

"So why did Dad have the rifle … with two rounds out of reach?"

Tucker had long since perfected an absolutely unreadable, insolent gaze, one he had used to face down authority figures for most of his life. But as he stared at his kid brother, who had somehow become no longer a kid, Tucker was surprised to feel an odd pleasure in surrendering this particular secret. The kid had the right to know.

"Because I only gave him the one."

Micah looked devastated by the truth he must have suspected.

"Why? Why not just save him?"

"He was almost dead when I got there. It was still snowing good. Couldn't have got him down in time, even if I coulda got the truck off him."

"Did you at least try?"

Tucker remembered his anger when he'd discovered the loaded rifle, and now the bile arose anew. "At first I was going to. But no. I did something else. I gave him an option."

"One bullet."

"Yeah. It's all he deserved."

"Doesn't sound like much of an option. For someone who came to save you."

Tucker uttered a hateful chortle. "Yeah. That must be why he brought that loaded rifle, huh. Two days after I punched his lights out in the living room."

"What?" Micah's mouth dropped agape. "He brought it for signal fire."

"Bullshit."

"Three rounds, three shots: That's an S.O.S. Three shots, one right after the other, evenly timed. That's a distress signal. He learned that in the military. Didn't he teach you that when you were hunting?"

"Big Frank didn't have to teach me shit."

"Well, what did you think, he was going to shoot you? Are you crazy?"

They were standing in each other's face, the volume escalating with each sentence. The three-shot distress signal suggestion hit Tucker hard. The justice of those final minutes with his father had remained pure and unfettered in his heart; having those emotional waters muddied made him roil.

"You got it all figured out, do you?" he demanded. "OK, then you tell me what he did with the one round I gave him. C'mon, smart guy. What did he do with it? You're so sure he wouldn't use three rounds on me, WHAT DID HE DO WITH ONE?"

That silenced Micah. He shook his head, refusing to believe. "He did not."

Tucker nodded.

"He didn't shoot you," Micah insisted.

"No. He screwed that up, too. Just like everything in his miserable fucking life. He *missed*."

Micah sank onto the porch. "I can't believe it."

"Believe it."

Micah was shaking his head, but not in denial. "I can't ... oh my God. I'm sorry."

"Don't worry about it. He won't come looking for me again." He sat down on the sofa beside his brother.

Micah straightened up a bit. "The police are looking for you."

Tucker's breath caught in his throat. "The police? For what?"

"Deputy came by this morning, wanted to talk to you about a missing person case. Said it was six years old."

Ah. So you rolled on me after all, Skelly.

And in that moment, Tucker knew he would be on the run again. If his one-time best friend didn't believe him about what happened to Cami, the cops sure wouldn't. Neither would a jury.

"What happened to Cami, Tucker?"

Tucker shook his head, flush with bitterness.

"I know she came looking for you that day," Micah said. "After Steelbarton died. What did you do, Tucker?"

"WHAT? Nothin'," Tucker spat angrily, lurching to his feet. "I didn't do anything. The question is what did you do ... Mister Falcon?"

Tucker saw the immediate deflation, blood rushing to his brother's face. Micah buried his face in his hands.

"Oh God," he said, sounding on the edge of tears.

"She was right, then. You are him."

Micah nodded. "I used to be."

"Jesus. Amanda thinks they're coming after you."

Micah sat up, emerging from the cocoon of his hands. "Yeah, well, I think that's because she's helping them."

"Oh shut up. If that's what you think, you're a bigger dumbass than I thought."

"Look, I saw some stuff at her house."

"Oh. You mean, like pictures? Letter from some Fu Manchu guy? Stuff like that?"

"Fu Manchu guy?"

"Yeah. Matt Bullard, I think the name was. She said she met him once. At the hospital where that guy was, her friend. The one who got hurt."

"By a spike. By the Falcon. I know."

"Why would you do that, man?"

Micah shook his head. "I don't even know if I did. That spike could have been put there by a lot of people. We were leaving the Falcon stamp every time we did anything."

"Wrapped around spikes in the tree."

Micah nodded. "Other stuff, too, but yeah. We did some spikes."

"Well, this one worked. But good."

Micah choked back what sounded like a sob.

"And this Matt Bullard guy, he's still after you."

"The mad bull." Micah seemed to slip into a memory. "He almost did catch me, once. I barely made it over a fence. Got a good look at him."

"So he got a good look at you, then?"

"I don't think so. I was in the dark. Flashlight was right on his face. Big guy. Mean-looking. Or maybe that was just the Fu Manchu."

"And the fact that he wanted to tear you a new asshole."

Micah nodded with a wan smile. "That, too."

"OK, little brother of mine. I'm going to give you some advice, and you damn well better listen or I will kick your ass. I've let you ride all these years, but you screw this up and you're meat. You got it?"

Micah nodded, wide-eyed.

"One. I'm on your side here. Maybe you don't want me on your side, but too fucking bad. Got that?"

Micah nodded again.

"Two. Amanda is on your side."

"I'm not so sure—"

"Oh give me a break. She loves you, you little dick."

Micah was dumbfounded. "She said that?"

"Amazing, ain't it. She didn't mean for these people to find out who you were, but somehow they did. So here's what you're going to do, little brother: You will go to her place. And the both of you will then leave her place and go stay at a motel. I don't know if you guys are sleeping together or what, but now would be a good time to start."

"What if you're wrong about her and she doesn't—"

"Jesus, would you just shut up and listen to me for once in your life?"

"Well ... why a motel?"

Tucker shook his head in exasperation. "How did you live to be twenty-two years old and still be so stupid? If these people, this mad bull and his people, if they're already on their way, they got her address and they know this one. So it'd be good if they didn't find you just yet. Got that? Not until we have a chance to figure this deal out. Figure out our next move."

"Oh. Yeah."

Tucker began pacing the yard, thinking about all of the new developments. He glanced back at Micah, still sitting on the porch like a man in a daze.

"What do you think you're doing?"

Micah looked up, surprised at the tone. "What?"

"Aren't you supposed to be going somewhere?"

"Right now?"

"Yeah. Right now. Get the fuck out of here."

"All right already." He got up to go inside. "I should call Amanda, let her know I'm coming."

"What did I just tell you? Go. She knows you're coming."

Micah seemed to understand, and went inside. Tucker followed. He could hear a drawer being opened and, seconds later, shut. Micah came out carrying what looked like a T-shirt and a change of underwear. He stopped at the front door.

"Hey," he said softly. "Thanks for being on my side."

Tucker shook his head in mock derision. "The things a guy's got to do for his brother. Now get the hell out of here before I change my mind and kick your ass anyway."

CHAPTER 27

VENGEANCE FROM THE PAST

As he watched Amanda sleep, Micah was struck by how beautiful she looked, bathed in the soft light of the early dawn filtering through his duplex window. He knew this might be the last time he would experience that sublime vision.

He had concurred immediately with Tucker's idea of laying low, but on the drive to Amanda's house he had reconsidered the motel aspect: Why do that when nobody could possibly find either of them at the duplex? He hadn't had to sign a lease, it had been a handshake deal and he had paid three months in cash.

So they had gone to his duplex, where they had enjoyed their indoor picnic in a much happier time not that long ago. They did not make love, though they held each other close for a long time. Somehow, she managed to drift into a fitful sleep, and he was thankful for that. He knew when light arrived, his past would be coming for him.

They hadn't even really talked about what led to these men coming for him, only that they were coming. She hadn't asked for an explanation or justification for his culpability. When he tried to bring it up, to stop ignoring the elephant in the room, she had said it didn't matter. The man he used to be, and whatever that man did, she had said, was not the man she fell in love with. And she could forgive the man he was now.

He had cried and held her, all the while knowing he would have to let her go.

His past was about to consume his future, and he couldn't let it destroy hers.

He could run, but they'd find him sooner or later. Maybe it would be Bullard, the mad bull. Maybe it would be a sheriff's deputy, or a detective. He'd keep looking over his shoulder until one day there would be someone there. And that would be that.

He would be tried. Sent to federal prison. Or, worse, state prison. Considering the media attention John Dallman's injury—his maiming—had commanded, Micah's sentence would likely be at the higher end of the sentencing guidelines. Twelve to fifteen years, maybe. If the prosecution decided to charge him with culpability in J.D.'s death, he could be looking at twenty years. Maybe life.

He couldn't put Amanda through that.

Especially since he knew whatever sentence he served could never outlast his grief. And his guilt.

As he watched her skin being painted with the morning's first strokes, he wanted nothing more than to kiss her, to hold her tightly, to feel her body against his, to take that warmth and that heartbeat and keep forever an imprint of that love. But that would be wrong. It would give her pause, would make her linger within his world in hopes of reprieve or pardon, an official forgiveness of his sins. She would be dragged into court to testify against him, at least about what little she knew, and it would tear her apart.

No, he would harden his heart. And he would push her away.

He knew what he had to do.

⅄

Although Tucker was awake when he heard the car doors shutting outside, he was still surprised at how early it was.

Gulliver was up and barking vigilantly before Tucker heard the knock on the door. There were two men. The first one was perhaps forty, husky but solid. His jaw had just the hint of a thick shadow, as if one shave a day simply wasn't enough. He was definitely the lead dog. The other was younger, less assured, standing back a step. Both were in jeans and work boots. Definitely not sheriff's department. Tucker noticed they were both wearing light jackets. It was almost August.

These were the guys coming for Micah. He knew it before either spoke.

"I'm looking for a Mister Dodd," the lead dog said through the screen door.

Tucker studied his face. That heavy beard would work for a Fu Manchu. He opened the door and stepped out onto the concrete porch pad, using his foot to keep Gulliver inside the screen door. "And why would that be?"

"That's a matter for Mister Dodd."

"Yeah? Well then, he ain't here."

Lead dog glanced back at young dog, then at Tucker, then down at the real dog. Gulliver was still going ballistic.

"Who are you?" lead dog asked.

Tucker looked at their car. Looked like a rental. "Who are *you?*"

"My name is Bullard. I'm a security specialist. I'm also licensed as a private investigator, I do contract bounty work with bail bondsmen and I have a concealed weapons permit. This here's Cannon. He works for me. Now. Who are you?"

His partner, Cannon, tapped him on the arm and subtly shook his head: *It's not the guy.* Bullard frowned.

"Well, since you're not cops," Tucker said, "I don't have to tell you who I am, do I. I could even tell you to go fuck yourself."

Bullard began to turn again to his backup man, but in the same motion slipped his right hand into his jacket and produced a handgun. He didn't point it at Tucker; its mere presence made his point.

"You could do that," Bullard said evenly. "But we're going to need to go inside now. Will you control the dog or do we need to?"

"What's that supposed to mean? You so scared of a yapper dog you're gonna shoot it?" he asked derisively. He shooed Gulliver back from the door and stepped in, holding the door briefly for Bullard. "Better back off, you big bad dog. You're scaring the guests."

As the two men followed him in, Tucker sized up the situation, his boxer's mind immediately breaking down the opponent and developing a game plan. It was a tossup as to whether he could take the gun from Bullard. All it would take would be getting a hand on his wrist before he pulled the trigger; after that, the takedown would be simple. Or he could simply parry the gun hand with his left and take him out with a straight right. His odds with Bullard alone were good. Fifty-fifty, easy. Maybe even sixty-forty.

But what about bachelor number two? Even if he got the gun, Cannon was probably armed as well. Taking both of them out would be a long shot.

"Are you Micah Dodd?" Bullard demanded, brandishing the gun only as a visual aid, without pointing it.

Tucker laughed. "Micah Dodd? He wishes. Why do you want that little twerp?"

"That's really a matter for he and I to discuss."

"So if you're a bounty hunter, what's up? Big bad Micah jump bail?"

"Nope, this is not a bond issue. But there is a reward."

"For Micah? You gotta be shitting me. What'd he do, jaywalk?"

Bullard raised the gun a little. "Who are you?"

"Peter fucking Pan."

Bullard gestured with his free hand. "I want to see your driver's license."

Tucker gestured disdainfully to the T-shirt and boxing training shorts he had slept in.

"Does it look like I have it on me?"

"Where's your wallet?"

"Haven't seen it today." Behind his facade, Tucker's mind was racing. He had to separate the two of them, so he was only dealing with one. Get the gun from him.

The next one will have a gun, too, he thought. *Maybe a couple of buddies with guns. Maybe even badges. Micah, you dumbass.*

Ah, shit.

"You guys aren't looking for Micah," he said. "You want the Falcon."

That stopped all traffic. Bullard and Cannon exchanged a glance.

"OK. You got my attention," Bullard growled. "Where can we find him?"

Tucker shrugged. "Not far from here. I could take you."

"All right. We'll take our car."

"Can't drive there," Tucker said. "We have to walk."

Bullard frowned. "Where is he? And what's his name?"

"You're the one getting paid. Ask him yourself."

That seemed to amuse Bullard, who raised his gun, pointing it at Tucker's midsection. "All right, mister tour guide. Lead the way."

Tucker eyed the gun and said wryly, "And here I thought we were getting all friendly."

He put Gulliver in Connie's room, pulled on a pair of sneakers and led them down the river trail he had ambled so many times. Instead of crossing over to his old viewpoint, though, he continued on the path that passed the apex of the falls and wound down to that forbidden place of his childhood, all the while weighing his options.

At the fence, Tucker pointed at the edge. "You swing around the edge there to the other side. The Falcon's down there."

"You're out of your mind," Bullard said.

Tucker gave him an ironic little grin. "Probably. But it's the only way you're gonna get to the Falcon. It's his hiding place."

"Is there another way out?"

"Nope. One way in, one way out."

"Well … maybe I should just wait him out. Call for the locals."

Cannon chimed in. "And give up the reward? Not a chance."

"So what are you saying?" Tucker teased. "The Falcon's got the stones to go down there but you don't?"

Bullard glared at him. "OK, you go first. And then you don't take another step. You try to take off, I'll shoot you in the back."

"Ooh, you're scaring me," Tucker said, and swung around the fence to the far side with the ease of someone who had made the same move a hundred times.

Bullard eyed the fence, the edge, the dropoff and Tucker. "If he's not down there after this shit? If we don't find him?" Bullard shook his head. "You better be taking me to him. Now back away. Cannon. Cover him. If he so much as moves an inch towards me when I swing around, blow his head off."

Cannon grinned, pulling out his gun and pointing it at Tucker's face. "Gladly."

Bullard holstered his gun under his jacket and swung around. He gave a good look down only when he was on the downhill side of the fence.

"Christ almighty," he said, pulling out his gun again. "I may shoot you anyway after this." He turned to Cannon. "No use in both of us risking our lives on a fool's errand. Go back to the house in case Micah Dodd shows up."

"Which would mean this guy's lying."

"It's crossed my mind," Bullard said.

Tucker shrugged innocently.

"All right, but you watch yourself," Cannon said, and headed back up the trail. With a leer at Tucker, he added, "I don't think he has to be alive for the reward to be good. This could be our man right here."

Oh yeah, I'm your man, Tucker thought, considering the laughable irony.

And if I'm your man ... Micah isn't.

⋏

For Amanda, waking up was no easier than falling asleep had been the night before. And when she finally awoke, Micah wasn't beside her.

She called his name out softly, but got no answer.

She called in sick to the ranger station, and showered up to go look for him.

Where would he go?

And why, with everything that was going on, would he go without her?

⋏

Micah walked with a determined gait into the sheriff's substation in Darrington and asked the uniformed woman behind the front desk if Sergeant Ansel was in. She asked what this was about.

"I'd rather tell him," Micah said.

"Well, he should be back within twenty minutes," she said.

"I'll wait."

He sat on the middle of three chairs braced against the front wall. He and the woman at the desk were the only people he could see, though he could hear someone speaking in another part of the building.

He breathed slowly and deeply. He tried not to think about what he was doing, because he had made his decision and didn't want to talk himself out of it. He would wait for Ansel.

If he was going to turn himself in, it was going to be to somebody he knew.

⅄

Tucker had been following the precarious route slowly, but not entirely out of caution. As he reached the point at which he could see up to the top of the falls, but before the Under Look was visible, he was watching to make sure Cannon didn't stop at the falls and look back this way. He didn't want a witness. Only when he caught a glimpse of Cannon passing the falls and continuing on his way back to the house did Tucker round the final bend.

"Watch your step along here," Tucker said over his shoulder. "It can get slick."

"I can see that." Bullard's voice had a tremulous edge. "Where are we going?"

"He's got a cave. It's just around the bend here."

"This better not be a trick."

"Hey, you're the one with the gun. What do you have to worry about?"

"Breaking my fricking neck," Bullard muttered.

Tucker carefully worked his way around the last bend, and there in front of him was the Under Look.

Bullard held up behind him. "What now?" he asked, almost in a shout to be heard over the roar of the waterfall.

Tucker pointed out to the Look.

Bullard looked doubtfully at Deano's bridge. "I ain't going across that."

"Yeah. You are. If you want to find the Falcon."

Bullard gaped at the Under Look. "There's nobody there. There's nothing there."

"You can't see it from here."

"There's nothing to see."

"Yeah? Then I guess you came a long way for nothing."

And before Bullard could respond, Tucker leapt across onto the Under Look, ignoring Deano's bridge. He looked back at Bullard with a palms-up gesture. "See? Nothin' to it."

Bullard pointed the gun at him. "OK. Back up."

Tucker did as he was ordered. Bullard jumped across, as he had. And in the moment Bullard landed, throwing up his arms to balance himself, Tucker took a quick step toward him. With balance and fluidity wrought from years of physical combat and the easy confidence that comes with having nothing to lose, he shot out his hand as he had done so many times on the wrestling mat, instantly arrested Bullard's arm and gun hand and wrenched him into such a position that Bullard had to surrender the gun or withstand a broken arm. It wasn't even difficult.

A moment later, Tucker was holding the gun, pointing it at Bullard's head. Bullard was back against the wall, as far as he could get from the precipice, holding his hands out in protest of what he obviously believed was going to be the last thing he ever saw.

"Please don't shoot," he pleaded.

Tucker was ready to do just that. "Step away from the wall," he ordered.

Bullard cringed. "No! I won't! If you're going to kill me, you're going to have to do it right here. I'm not going over that side."

"What difference does it make? Either way, you're dead."

Bullard straightened up. "Fuck you. I'll choose how I die. Not you."

Tucker's finger was poised on the trigger, but he hesitated. *I'll choose how I die. Huh.*

"If I meant to kill you," Tucker said, "you'd already be dead. I'd have pitched you over the side."

"So you were never going to take me to the Falcon."

"You still haven't figured it out. Some investigator you are. Or maybe you're like that Samson guy. Wasn't he the one who lost his strength when they cut off his hair? Yeah. Shoulda kept your Fu Manchu."

Bullard straightened up a bit, taking in this new evidence.

"Yeah, that was a good look for you," Tucker said. "By flashlight anyway. Remember? That night at the fence?"

Bullard dropped his hands. "You're Micah Dodd?"

"Oh, would you stop with that shit? You think Micah Dodd would have the stones to pull something like that? To be the Falcon? Gimme a break."

"Why should I believe you?"

Tucker pursed his lips, studying the gun. "Did you like my card?"

Bullard squinted one eye. "What card?"

"You know what card. I was wrong, though, what I said. Turns out I finished the job after all."

Bullard shook his head in disdain. "Why? Who *are* you?"

"Who cares what my name is? You know who I am." Tucker took a step past Bullard, raising his gun hand as he did it. Bullard recoiled, expecting the shot, but Tucker simply tossed the gun well onto the far side of Deano's bridge. It came to rest, wedged gently against the high-side slope.

Tucker watched it stop, then—noting that Bullard hadn't moved a muscle from his spot against the wall, except that his mouth had dropped open— reached down and got a firm two-handed grip on Deano's bridge. In one swift and brutal motion, he ripped it free and hurled it over the edge. He watched as it tumbled, topsy-turvy, into the roaring crash of water below. He stood at the edge, danger in front and behind. He felt no fear.

When he turned back, though, it was obvious the Mad Bull was feeling some.

"Why'd you do that?" Bullard blurted. "That's a hundred foot drop."

"Oh, it's more than that. But that there"—he pointed to the gap—"that's five feet. You afraid you can't long jump five feet?"

"But screw up and you die."

Tucker cocked his head. "Don't screw up."

"You're crazy."

"Well," Tucker said, reaching into his pocket, "I've got a reputation to live up to. Remember what it looked like? My reputation?"

Bullard didn't answer, clearly unsure where this was going.

Tucker pulled out the falcon stone, with its now readily recognizable talon mark across a green circle, and held it up for Bullard to see.

"Looked like this, didn't it."

CHAPTER 28

The Falcon Must Fly

Micah was beginning to have second thoughts about his plan when the phone on the woman's desk buzzed. She answered it and, after a quiet conversation, directed Micah to the door at the end of the hall.

"So, Mister Dodd," Sergeant Ansel said, rising briefly from his desk chair. "What can I do for you today? Is this about your brother?

"My brother?"

"Tucker Dodd?"

"No, why would it have to do with him?"

"Oh, I'm sorry, I just assumed that's why you're here. Deputy Rowan told you yesterday we believe he may have some information on a missing-persons case."

"Cami Radich?"

Ansel seemed to take a quiet but fervent interest in that question. "Yes. Actually, that is the case. How did you know that?"

He shrugged. "He said, the deputy said, it happened six years ago. That's the only person I know who left about that time."

"Left? What do you mean?"

"You know. Went away. Wasn't around anymore. Left."

"Do you have information on her departure? Did your brother say anything to you?"

"He said he didn't do anything."

"In those words?"

Micah was getting the sense that Ansel was trying to get him to say something incriminating about Tucker, and it made him mad.

"Yeah, in those words. I asked him if he did anything, and he said he didn't."

"Why would you think he might have done something to Cami?"

"Nothing, no reason. He just left at about the same time as she did, and I wondered if maybe they left together."

"And what did he say about that?"

"Nothing. I didn't ask him about that."

"But … you just said …"

"Sergeant Ansel, I didn't come to talk about my brother. I came because I have information in another case."

"Oh? And what case might that be?"

Micah opened his mouth to speak, but he hadn't given much thought to what he would actually say.

"It's not exactly a local case, but it sort of is. It involves the death of a local guy."

Ansel's interest was perked anew. "Whose death?"

"His name was John Dallman."

"Dallman." Ansel shook his head. "I'm not familiar with that case."

"He died about a month ago."

Ansel squinted in thought. "Oh yeah. I remember him now. There's not an active investigation. That was a suicide ruling."

"Well, this is sort of … it has to do with why he did it."

Ansel's expression changed, and Micah knew he'd lost the sergeant.

"I'm sorry, Mister Dodd. I'm afraid why someone committed suicide isn't something we would be involved in. We have enough on our plate with the living. So … thanks for coming in."

"You don't understand, the reason he did it was because of something illegal."

Ansel sighed. "OK. What was illegal?"

"Well, he was blinded. John Dallman. He was injured in a logging accident. Blinded. And that's why he committed suicide."

"OK. And? Where's the crime?"

Micah was getting flustered. He hadn't thought this would be quite so difficult, and he wondered if he was making a mistake even trying to turn himself in to the county sheriff. Maybe he should just go back to the house and wait for the Mad Bull to show up.

"The accident wasn't an accident, really. Somebody spiked a tree, and John's saw hit the spike and he was blinded."

"Somebody spiked a tree. Where was this?"

"In California."

Ansel sighed again. "In California. And you're telling me this why?"

"Because I think maybe I spiked the tree."

"You think? You're not sure?" Ansel shook his head, clearly ready for this to end.

"It could have been me or somebody else. But I was the Falcon, so either way, it was my fault."

"OK, listen, I don't understand what you're talking about, but it sounds like none of this took place in this county, so if you want to turn yourself in somewhere else—"

Ansel looked up and beyond Micah. "Yes?"

Micah looked over his shoulder.

A deputy was at the door. "Need to talk to you for a second, Sarge."

"Mister Dodd, I appreciate your coming in, and good luck on that ... issue. Oh: If you hear from your brother, call us, will you?" Without waiting for an answer, Ansel walked down the hall with the deputy.

The front entrance being that way, Micah followed. He could hear the conversation.

"Looks like we got another flier at Kacheel Falls, Sarge," the deputy said.

"Christ," Ansel said. "Tell me it's not a kid. Do we have a body?"

"No, and you know how tangled up that river is, Pete. Snags everywhere. We may never find a body. Got a witness, though. And get this: R.P.'s a bounty hunter from California."

Micah's breath caught in his throat. *Bounty hunter. California.*

⋏

Amanda didn't recognize one of the two vehicles in front of Micah's mother's house when she pulled up. The second one was a patrol car.

As she hurried through the gate and across the yard, someone inside the screen door moved to the door to intercept her. It was a deputy or a police officer, something like that, and Amanda felt an immediate sense of something terrible.

Before the deputy could open the screen, step into the gap and say a word, she was opening the door and exclaiming, "What are you doing here? Where's Micah?" She could hear Gulliver barking furiously, muffled by walls and doors.

"Excuse me, miss. *Miss.* Are you a family member?"

"No," she snapped, angry and afraid. "Are you?" And she proceeded to push past him into the house, shouting Micah's name.

There were three other men in the front room, another policeman and two men in jackets she'd never seen before. Their conversation ceased when Amanda burst in.

"Who are you guys? Where's Micah?"

"Miss!" The second deputy, presumably the senior of the two, regained control of the room. "We're conducting an investigation, and you're interrupting that. Who are you and why are you here?"

"My name's Amanda Devlin and my—my boyfriend lives here," she said.

The deputy exchanged a glance with a barrel-chested man with a two-day growth of beard. Whatever the look meant, it unnerved Amanda even more.

"Ma'am," the deputy said, "what's your boyfriend's name?"

"Micah Dodd."

The deputy looked at the bigger of the two men again.

"That's the name we had, but I don't know," the big man said. "I don't know if that's who this guy was. But I know he's the guy we were looking for."

"What guy?" Amanda demanded. "What are you talking about?"

"Miss," the deputy said, "my partner and I are responding to a call made by these men having to do with … well, a man living in this house has apparently fallen over the edge at Kacheel Falls."

She felt her legs buckle.

"Or maybe jumped," the big man said.

Amanda glared at him, her eyes wild.

He shrugged. "I can't say for sure. But he definitely went over."

She felt the deputy taking her by the arm. She felt numb and didn't object as he maneuvered her next to one of the kitchen chairs. "Perhaps you should sit down," he said, and she did.

"Miss, what's your boyfriend look like?" the big man said.

The second deputy shushed him with a hand. "Give her a moment."

The deputy at the door opened it, and in walked Sergeant Ansel with yet another deputy, prompting Gulliver to renewed vigor. The sergeant looked around the room as if remembering something. "Who lives here?" he asked, looking at each of the three people in the room who were not his employees. The two men shook their heads. He looked in anticipation then to Amanda.

The second deputy shook his head to the sergeant. "Looks like the flier may be her boyfriend," he said, only mouthing *flier.*

Amanda was settling into quicksand. The presumption of death that pervaded the room made her want to scream, not knowing if they were talking about Micah. She had heard of Kacheel Falls but had never seen it.

"Is Kacheel Falls big?" she asked.

Everyone in the room knew what she was really asking.

Ansel sat on another kitchen chair, facing her. "A lot of people have fallen over the years," he said. "No one's ever survived."

Amanda tried to swallow and couldn't. Tears welled up as certainty set in.

"We don't think so, anyway," the first deputy said. Ansel shot him a *shut up* glance. "Well, some of 'em never got found," he added defensively.

"No way he survived that," the big man said.

Ansel looked at him. "Who are you?"

"This is the R.P., Sarge—"

"I'm asking him." Ansel's eyes never left the man. "You the bounty hunter?"

The big man held his gaze without a hint of apology. "This isn't a bond case, but yeah. Name's Matthew Bullard. I'm licensed to operate in this state. And I'm authorized to carry the handgun your assistant here is holding for me."

From within the walls of her numbness grew a vengeful wrath. *Bullard.*

"You killed him," she said, turning to him. "You came for the Falcon and you meant to kill him all along, you son of a bitch."

"Hey, I didn't kill anybody. He killed himself. Or fell. But oh yeah, he was definitely the Falcon."

Ansel frowned in confusion. "What or who is the Falcon?"

A car door slammed outside

"Hold on there. Who are you?" It was the deputy at the door.

"I live here," somebody said, and Amanda's heart skipped a beat.

⅄

All the way home, the siren from Sergeant Ansel's cruiser beckoning him to follow, Micah had been consumed with a wrenching fear that kept lapsing into sorrow.

As he knew it would, the siren led him to his mother's house. The momentary elation of seeing Amanda's car out front was tempered by the foreboding of all the strange and official-looking vehicles that surrounded it. Nothing in his overheard conversation at the sheriff substation said anything about the flier being a man; maybe she had tried too valiantly to protect him. Knowing the notion was irrational didn't make the fear less real.

So when he pushed past the officer, seeing Amanda had a profound effect.

The emotion enveloped them both; Amanda hurried to him, threw her arms around him and held him tightly. The urgency in that embrace told him how much air had been sucked out of the room the moment he walked in.

Over her shoulder, Micah saw Sergeant Ansel rising from the seat next to the one Amanda had vacated. He did a cursory study of the men in the room, his eyes coming to rest on a thickset man near the back door. Even without the Fu Manchu, he knew in an instant who it was.

He was about to say something to the Mad Bull when Amanda spoke first.

"Micah," she whispered in such a way as to arrest anything he might say. "I have terrible news." She pulled back from the embrace enough to hold him firmly while forcing him to look into her eyes, to catch every nuance of the message she was sending.

"These men told me a person fell over the falls," she said, gripping his waist when he felt the urge to move, to flail, to storm. "Micah, they say it was somebody called the Falcon."

He cringed and again tried to pull away—this was too much emotion to stand still, but still she held fast onto him with an unspoken yet unmistakable admonition: *Say nothing. Give nothing away.*

Micah was reeling. The Falcon was dead, what? Who? And then he knew.

"Tucker? Tucker!" he called, then lurched away from Amanda's grasp toward the hall.

"Mister Dodd!" Ansel boomed. "Your brother is not here."

Still, Micah pulled open the boys' bedroom door, then his mother's, unable to stop himself. Gulliver came charging out of the first door, yapping away, and Amanda quickly gathered him up. Seeing Tucker in neither room, and knowing what must now be inevitable, sapped Micah's emotional strength; he sagged against the hallway wall, suddenly needing its foundation to keep from collapsing. He almost couldn't find the strength to ask the question. "Will somebody please tell me where my brother is?"

"Yes, Bullard," Ansel said. "I think we'd all be interested in hearing this."

Amanda came to Micah's side at the head of the hallway and put her arm around his side. The tiny gesture felt, to Micah, like the warm glow of permanence. It gave him a lifeboat as he waded into that which threatened to suck him under.

"We came in, Cannon and me, we were talking with this guy who was here, asking him where this Micah Dodd was—" Bullard gestured to Micah. "Mistaken identity, I guess, but that's the name we had. Anyway, we tell him we're looking for this terrorist who calls himself the Falcon, and this guy said he'd take us to him."

"*Terrorist?*" Micah blurted, and felt Amanda's hand pressed into his hip.

"Yeah. Terrorist," Bullard said. "What else would you call a guy who tries to tear down an entire industry and doesn't care who he hurts doing it? Or kills."

"Who is he?" Ansel demanded. "Did you even get a name?"

"No, he wouldn't give it. But he knows you," he said, nodding toward Micah.

"Go on," Ansel said.

And Bullard went on. The walk on the trail. The fence. Sending Cannon back to the house. Taking that spine-tingling route down to that dangerous-looking little bridge to that little landing.

"He's talking about the Under Look, Pete," the second deputy said to Ansel. "He pointed it out from the top of the falls."

"I know what he's talking about," Ansel grumbled. "Go on."

"He said that's where his hiding place, this cave or whatever, was over on the far side of this Under Look place."

"There's no cave there," the second deputy said. "You can see that from the falls."

"Yeah, well, I didn't know that. I'm not from here," Bullard snapped.

"Hayden. Shut up," Ansel said to the deputy and nodded at Bullard to continue.

Micah closed his eyes and Amanda, watching him, squeezed his hand.

"So he jumps over onto this flat spot, and then I follow him, and that's when he took my gun from me. Just as I landed, he was ready."

"You had him at gunpoint?" Ansel demanded.

"What do you think, he was leading us to the Falcon because we asked nice?"

Ansel was shaking his head. "So you had a potentially dangerous man you didn't know at gunpoint, and you followed him to a place like that. Incredible."

"Damn it," Micah said. "Are we talking about my brother or not?"

"You tell me," Bullard scowled. "He came to your door when we knocked. What's your brother look like?"

With a fury that had manifested itself just once before, and only the day before, Micah stepped to Bullard in one swift step, grabbed his collar and jerked him toward the hallway. Though Bullard outweighed him by a good sixty pounds, Micah's sudden vehemence had Bullard off-balance before the nearest two deputies could step in. As they did, Bullard had regained his balance and had his hand around Micah's throat, with both deputies there to pull him off.

Micah didn't even care about the hand at his throat. He had spent a lifetime avoiding confrontation, and the first punch he had ever thrown in anger was that wild swing at Tucker the day before. Now he was ready to take on this man who may have killed his brother, and it didn't frighten him in the least.

"He looks like that, you asshole," he shouted into Bullard's face and the deputies separated them. It took Bullard a moment to realize Micah was pointing at the photograph on the wall behind him—a striking color portrait of Tucker fighting Jammin J James on pay-per-view at the big casino in Vegas. "Was that him?"

Bullard looked at the photo.

"Yeah. That's the guy," Bullard said in a tone that bordered on contempt. "That's your brother? Pro fighter, huh? Well, sorry. Pro fighter, dead terrorist."

Micah lurched at him again, but the deputies were now in physical control.

"Enough!" Ansel shouted. "Bullard, you're in my county. You will shut up and you will stand over there. You, Dodd. Over there."

Micah moved to the far side of the fireplace, Amanda by his side.

"I'm going to get to the bottom of this if I have to haul in everybody in this room," Ansel declared. "Bullard. What happened when he took away your gun?"

Bullard made a show of adjusting his jacket collar. "Not much more to tell. He took my gun and he threw it back over across the little bridge. Then he pulls this stone out of his pocket. It's got the Falcon's mark on it, in the same color green ink as he used on every note the Falcon left behind on any of their vandalism and terrorist activities."

"Including tree spiking," Ansel said meaningfully, looking at Micah.

"Yep," Bullard said. "You're Amanda, right? The mark on that rock was the mark on that card. That's the guy who spiked the tree that got your friend Dallman."

"He is *not*," Micah said, and Amanda squeezed his hand again and put the other hand on his torso to stay him.

"Dodd. Not now," Ansel directed. "Bullard. What happened?"

"Well, then he pulled up that little bridge and chucked it over the edge, with me still standing out there on that little Under Look thing. Guy's fucking nuts. Pardon my French, miss, but he was. Then he says it's time to go. I say, go where? And he says you're going over the edge with me. Says it's time for the Falcon to die for what he's done. I'm like, fine, yeah, you go right ahead, and he says, what, you're not willing to die for what you believe in? If the Falcon's willing to die, why aren't you? Guy's nuts. I'm tellin' ya."

"So where's Tucker?" Micah asked softly, knowing the answer already.

"Yeah, what happened," Ansel said.

"That's when I jumped. He was gonna take me over with him, and I jumped across where that bridge used to be, got to the other side, and I went for the gun and I got it, and when I turned around, he was gone."

"Gone," Ansel echoed. "What do you mean, gone."

"I mean gone. That pigeon flew."

Micah closed his eyes. Amanda clutched his arm with both hands.

"Did you actually see him fall?" Ansel asked.

"No. But there was nowhere else he could have been. He didn't come across with me. You say there's no cave. So unless he survived the fall, and you said there's no other way in or out of there, hey. He's dead."

Ansel looked at the second deputy. "Did you check around?"

The deputy nodded. "Couldn't find a thing."

Ansel sighed. He looked at Micah, who was finally allowing the first tears to flow. "Sorry, son," the sergeant said. "We'll get search-and-rescue on the river as soon as we can, but it's a long shot. Probably have to wait until the body turns up downriver. And that's only if it does."

Ansel turned to Bullard. "So you're saying you have no doubt it was Tucker Dodd, the man in that photograph. That's this Falcon guy you were looking for, yes? You have no doubt? That's the man who fell?"

"Or jumped," Bullard said. "Yeah. I seen him once before. At a work site."

Micah blinked behind his tears.

"I almost caught him that night, too. Got a look at him, not a good look, but I remember him," Bullard said, nodding. "And he remembered me, too."

Micah began to sob, not just because Tucker was gone, but from the knowing—what his brother had done.

What he had chosen to do.

⅄

It was late afternoon before Ansel, Bullard and the rest of them finally left. Ansel, the last to leave, stopped at the door.

"Micah," he said, leaning in. Amanda gave Micah a wan smile, unraveled herself and carried Gulliver into the kitchen. Micah was in the hangover of sudden mourning, but he stepped out into the yard with the sergeant.

In relative privacy on the lawn, Ansel put a hand on Micah's shoulder.

"Micah. You seem like a decent kid. I thought that back when your dad was missing and you were trying so hard to be the man of the house," he said. "And I also remember your brother not giving a damn. I'm not sure I understand what you were trying to do today at the station. But I'll tell you what I think. You were being a good brother. You were willing to take the fall for something your brother did. Hey, that's an admirable thing. Really. I respect that. But here's the thing: He's not worth it."

"You're talking about my brother."

"I'm talking about a guy who didn't give a damn about his own father being missing and dead. Another thing, this week we find out he saw Cami Radich die. At least, that's what he told her brother. Said he was talking to her, they argued and she took a swing at him—and then she just happened to fall into the river, just above the waterfall. Now you tell me: How does that happen? And if she just fell and wasn't pushed, how come he didn't call us and tell us what happened? Then he goes off and gets involved with a terror-ist group, hurts some people. Who else did he hurt along the way that you just don't know about?"

Ansel nodded as if he were imparting great wisdom, turned to leave and stopped for a final thought. "That," he said, "is not the kind of person you take the fall for."

Micah turned away, biting hard on his desperate wish to tell the truth. But saying aloud just what kind of person his brother was would be the same as betraying Tucker's final act. So, instead, he said nothing and went inside to Amanda, whose arms were not enough to console him.

"I have to go see for myself," he said to her.

She nodded. "I know."

They left Gulliver in the house and followed the creekside trail, crossing over on the same hopscotch trail of elliptical rocks he and his brother had traversed so many times as boys. Amanda followed him, as fearless as Micah had become. In minutes, they reached the top of the falls, the vantage point upon which Micah had so often aspired to be his brother while knowing he could never be.

Micah stepped, with Amanda a tenuous step behind, to the edge opposite the Under Look. He edged forward until he could see the violently crashing water at the bottom of the river canyon below, looking in vain for a glimpse of his brother. A hint of life in the water devil.

He looked a final time at the Under Look, the last place his brother had stood.

And he saw the crack.

He squinted. Could he be seeing what he thought he was seeing?

"Micah, let's go back," Amanda said.

"Wait a minute. Look," he said, pointing to the crack from which Deano had once liberated the falcon stone.

Amanda followed his direction. "What? What do you see?"

"I have to check something. Wait here."

"Not a chance," Amanda declared. "Wherever you're going, I'm going."

"No, that's not a good idea. It's—well, it could be dangerous."

"What are you talking about?" She gawked at the Under Look. "Going down there? What for? Are you crazy?"

"There's something I have to see for myself."

"Fine. But I'm going with you. And don't try to talk me out of it, because you can't. You might as well know that about me now."

That made him smile. So he led, and she followed. When they got to the fence, he did that which he had never done but which now seemed not so terrifying. He swung around to the other side.

Amanda gaped at the dropoff and considered the fence. "Is this thing sturdy? Will it hold?"

"It'll hold if you do," he said. "But I'd really rather you wait for me."

She took a big breath. "Back up, sonny." And she swung around to join him. "Whoa," she said as she straightened up on the downhill side. "That was a rush."

"OK, I've never been down this way, but I hear it's slick and dangerous. I'd be a lot happier if you'd wait here."

"And I'd be happier if neither of us went down there. I don't know what you have to see that's so important," she said. "But if you're going, I'm going."

And so she did.

Micah led the way down the precarious path, looking back every step or two to make sure Amanda was OK. On one of his protective peeks he lost his footing for just a second and she grabbed his arm to steady him.

"Quit worrying about me," she said. "You watch out for yourself. I'll be fine. I've worked on trails that aren't for the weak of heart."

He smiled. "You got it."

They came around the last bend. There was Kacheel Falls across the way. And there was the Under Look.

He turned to her and said, "OK, now you *will* wait here. No discussion."

She looked at the gap and nodded. "OK. But I still don't like you doing this."

"There's something I have to know." He poised himself to jump across, then stopped himself and turned back to her. This was the one thing that still scared him.

"And there's something you have to know, too. It wasn't Tucker," he said, tears welling up. "He was protecting me. He wasn't the Falcon. I was. He didn't do those things. I did."

She held his sad eyes. "I know."

"I never meant to hurt anybody. But I did."

"You can tell me about it some day. But not now, OK? Do what you have to do and let's get out of here." And she gave him a smile that filled him like nothing ever had.

He turned to the Look. Once, even the sight of that gap from above the falls would have made his knees and legs tremble. Now, Micah simply approached the bridge-less gap and leapt across to the other side, afraid but no longer frozen by the fear.

And he took the few steps to the crack.

Which was in a narrow depression in the wall, perhaps two feet wide. A vertical nook, wide enough for a person to stand in.

He stepped into the cranny and put his back to the wall. He looked to his right toward Amanda, but couldn't see her without peeking out.

Which meant she couldn't see him.

He craned his neck to his left, and there, wedged into the crack just below eye level, was the falcon stone.

Relief flooded over him. Then joy.

He pinched the falcon stone from its hiding place, clutched it in his fist and pocketed it. He stepped out of the nook, beamed at Amanda's questioning expression and jumped easily back over the gap to her.

"What was that about?" she said.

"Let's go up and I'll tell you," he said, breaking out in what must have seemed to Amanda like an incongruous smile.

"OK, then no more disappearing acts," she said.

He laughed, feeling almost weightless, liberated from fear and despair.

"So you couldn't see me! That proves it," he said, shaking his head as he figured out how Tucker must have pulled it off. He followed her up and around to the fence and beyond, laughing in relief and glee when they reached the safety of the riverside trail.

"He's alive!" he exclaimed. "Amanda, Tucker's alive!"

He reached into his pocket and pulled out the falcon stone. She looked at the stone, then at Micah, not understanding what he understood.

"He had that stone," she said. "Yesterday, when I went looking for you to warn you, and ended up talking to him. He had that."

Micah nodded. "He put it there in his old hiding place for me to find."

As Micah said that, he realized something: Tucker had known he would go onto the Under Look and find it. He had known Micah had the courage before Micah realized it himself. In that instant, Micah felt a pride he had never known.

"What do you mean? How do you know?" Amanda asked.

"Don't you see? He put it there to let me know that's where he was when Bullard thought he had jumped over the edge. He was hiding there. You couldn't see me, right? Well, Bullard couldn't see him. By the time Bullard made it back up to the falls, Tucker was already off the Under Look and on his way. He's probably halfway to Arlington by now, just taking the trails. But he left the falcon stone there so I'd find it. He left it as a sign."

"I don't know," Amanda said, her eyes full of doubt.

"He's alive, Amanda," Micah insisted. "My brother's alive."

"I don't know what to think. I just know your brother loved you. And so do I."

Micah felt no fear. "I love you," he said, and pulled her close.

She held him tightly, profoundly uncertain about what had happened on the Under Look that day, but not remotely uncertain about the man in her arms.

He held her just as tightly, feeling as if his entire world was within his grasp.

And within his right fist, just as tightly gripped, was the falcon stone.

It was a gift from his brother.

THE END

Made in the USA
Monee, IL
02 January 2023

20171065R00197